Also by Jessica Duchen

Rites of Spring

JESSICA DUCHEN

ALICIA'S GIFT

HODDER

ISBN 978 0 340 83933 1

Typeset in Plantin Light by Palimpsest Book Production Limited,
Grangemouth, Stirlingshire

Printed and bound by Clays Ltd, St Ives plc

Hodder Headline's policy is to use papers that are natural, renewable and
recyclable products and made from wood grown in sustainable forests.
The logging and manufacturing processes are expected to conform to the
environmental regulations of the country of origin.

Hodder & Stoughton Ltd
A division of Hodder Headline
338 Euston Road
London NW1 3BH

For Tom

Acknowledgements

Thanking everyone who has helped this book into existence would take up most of the next 400 pages if I gave them all the credit they deserve. I've always loved the way that composers like Mozart, Schubert or Chopin could use minimum notes to convey maximum emotion, so here are a few select thank-yous, which, though too brief, are delivered with all my heart.

First, this book would never have come into being without the encouragement of my marvellous agent, Sara Menguc, and my equally marvellous editor at Hodder & Stoughton, Carolyn Mays. Thanks to them and their devoted teams.

Next, thank you to the many teachers, friends, colleagues and musicians through whom, over many long years, I've learned the agony and ecstasy of life at the piano. You know who you are, and I love you all. But special thanks must go to the fabulous pianist Leon McCawley for his expert advice; to Steve Cass, who helped me understand a little about how motorbikes work; to Allison Sharpe and Stuart Band for insights into Chatsworth; and Herbert and Gisela Eisner, long-time Buxtonians, for double-checking the local Derbyshire detail.

Alicia's favourite French poems are 'En sourdine' by Paul Verlaine and 'Le poison' from *Les Fleurs du mal* by Charles

Baudelaire. I have deliberately left these extracts in French only, but translations may easily be found online.

Synaesthesia, a 'union of the senses', is a condition experienced by numerous musicians; further information about it can be found at the UK Synaesthesia Association's website, www.uksynaesthesia.com.

Finally, boundless thanks to Tom for introducing me to both Derbyshire and Denmark; for putting up with me so patiently; and for hiding the chocolate on top of the kitchen cupboard.

Jessica Duchen
London, 2006

Alicia used to imagine living inside a perfect raindrop. Her father would hold her up to the window and she'd watch them in the dusk, trapping white-gold lamplight in a shimmering kaleidoscope. They streamed down, merging, gathering pace towards the edge of the pane. Each was a tiny globe of possibility trembling on the glass in front of her when she raised her fingers to press against them from the safe, dry inside.

Her tears and the autumn rain distort the moorland night into a morass of water, wobbling around her like a hall of mirrors. Nothing seems firm, not the Tarmac under the wheels, or the sheep that glare towards her out of the darkness, not even her body or mind. Part of her seems detached, watching while she drives as fast as the spray on the dark road will allow, watching while she tries to catch her breath and stop crying, but fails.

An isolated structure looms ahead – the pub that tops the moor close to home. Her headlamps catch its name: the Cat and Fiddle. She wonders how she's managed to travel so far west. Mirror, signal, manoeuvre, said her driving instructor, but Alicia has neither checked nor signalled during her headlong plunge out of Yorkshire. Nor has she looked back.

A few cars and motorbikes are parked behind the pub and Alicia, numb with exhaustion, pulls in alongside them. In the neighbouring field blank-eyed sheep form a glowering, unwanted audience. She switches off the engine. Rain drums random music on the roof. The drops slide down the windows, glinting in the dim light from the pub, which feels a hundred miles away. Alicia raises a hand to the windscreen – her fingers strong and slender, nails cropped short, as a pianist's must be – and presses on the raindrops from inside.

She sees what she's looking for in the shadows near the pub's outbuildings: an incongruous hosepipe, redundant in this damp, moortop desolation. Her mobile phone churns out a Tchaikovsky melody that she's begun to loathe. Her detached self says she should silence it: either answer or turn it off, never to be switched on again. The rest of her has thrown open the car door and is running through the rain towards the hose, which beckons to her, a coiled smile that promises salvation.

I

BUXTON
IN THE PEAK DISTRICT

The green notice marks the Roman road's final approach from moor to town: Buxton, a grey stone fan spreading across the Derbyshire hills, which undulate like the phrases of an English folk song. Buxton is one of the highest towns in England, proud of its water, proud of its once-flourishing spa; sometimes it imitates Bath, complete with eighteenth-century crescent (a low-calorie version). Hikers gather at the pubs, knocking mud from their boots outside, comparing notes on the day's adventures around the Peak District's moors and villages. In the well-tended Pavilion Gardens, children feed the ducks and their mothers and grandmothers gather in the tea room to eat Bakewell tart and sip a good, warming brew to keep out the bitter north wind. By the bridge over the stream stands the Bradley family's favourite road sign: a red triangle bearing the immortal words DUCKS CROSSING. How, Alicia asks herself, are the ducks supposed to know?

One side of the Bradleys' house begins higher up than the other. It and its semi-detached partner stand well back from the road, which curls up a hill in Buxton's Park area, protected by a spruce hedge and a row of sycamores that, as Guy was quick to point out when they first saw it, is just far enough away not to threaten the foundations. Tall rather than wide, the house is Victorian, made of the goldish-grey local stone that gives so much of Buxton its reassuring solidity, as if it had grown organically out of the hillside without a vestige of human help. The slope cuts through the base of the building, which has been levelled so that the inhabitants can imagine they are living on a safe, steady surface, not perching precariously on top of a remote and soulless mound of limestone.

To visit the Bradleys, you'd turn into the gravel driveway beside the hedge and pass the small oval lawn that Guy tends on Saturday afternoons. You'd walk up three stone stairs to the blue door and press the bell, which plays an imitation of Big Ben, and you'd hear Cassie the collie barking in ecstasy at the prospect of visitors. The big front window would show you an oblique view of the lounge; you'd glimpse the shiny curve of the piano and Alicia's fair hair gleaming as she curls over the keyboard, concentrating. And you'd hear her playing, perhaps a Chopin study or a carefully extracted line of Bach. You might catch a whiff of roasting chicken from Kate's dinner preparations, or smell simply the sweet, fresh country air, the light, watery scent of moorland wind through the trees.

On the day when everything will change, though nobody knows this yet, Kate opens her eyes to find Guy leaning over her, his face full of tenderness and worry. Her pillow is damp and her pyjamas soaked with sweat. Her eyes feel sore.

'It's OK, darling,' he whispers.

'I had the dream again.' Unwept tears clog her throat.

'I know. You're fine now. It's morning.'

Kate sits up and reaches for a tissue. Downstairs the dog barks and from the second floor, where the children's rooms are, comes the sound of Adrian flushing the loo. Kate moves her feet around, looking for her slippers, while Guy kisses her cheek and vanishes into the bathroom. Her mind is still half closed in the after-effects of her dream. Somehow she pulls herself upright and makes her way down to fix breakfast for her family and the overjoyed collie, who is five months old, with flailing paws that are too big for her.

Kate switches on the radio and hears that three hundred thousand people in Strathclyde have defaulted on the poll tax; terrible clashes have taken place around elections in South Africa; and a demonstration in East Germany has been brutally dispersed. It all seems a very long way from the Peak District – except, of course, for the poll tax. Guy spends his days focusing on local news for northern England; sometimes Kate wonders whether they're in the same galaxy as the world that's portrayed on the radio and television. It's easy to forget about the Berlin Wall when the biggest event of your day tends to be your son grazing his knee or your husband losing his shoes.

'Katie,' Guy calls from upstairs, 'do you know where my brown shoes are?'

'Probably where they were yesterday and the day before.'

'They're not. I can't find them.'

'Why can't you keep them in the same place every day? Then you'd know where they are, instead of always having to ask me.' Kate pulls the coffee canister out of the freezer and thumps the door closed.

Just as exasperation is setting in, she glances round and sees Alicia's shiny pale hair and round face, her small arms encircling the puppy's neck, her cheek pressed to its brown and white hair as if both their lives depend on it. Cassie turns her long collie snout to lick the nose of the little girl who loves her. They'd stumbled on the name Cassie by accident, during a scrambled attempt not to call the puppy Lassie. Kate finds herself smiling. Ali is only three, but her love shines through the kitchen as brightly as the sun. How can a three-year-old have such an instinct for love?

Ali, says the nursery-school teacher, is a sweet, affectionate child. Kate knows she's more than that. She can see a radiance in Ali that she can't see in any of the other tinies there, let alone Adrian's primary-school classmates. Sometimes she wonders if she's kidding herself, whether she sees in her daughter what she wants to see, because she happens to be her mother. Or because she needs a daughter with such capacity for love to help blot out the memory that sparks her recurring nightmare.

Guy has wolfed down cornflakes, toast and coffee and is whirling about in his usual morning chaos, looking for things. His glasses. ("They're on your face," Kate says.) His notes for the editorial meeting, which he'd worked on the previous night. His briefcase. His diary. His wallet. His keys. And, of course, his brown shoes. How such an absent-minded, disorganised man manages to edit anything, let alone a section of a newspaper, is a perpetual mystery.

"Wear the black ones."

"I can't, not with brown trousers."

"Wear different trousers, then."

Guy whistles the tune he always whistles when he can't find things – a twiddly, satirical theme from Walton's *Façade* that Kate is extremely tired of hearing.

Ali, cuddling her dog at the end of the kitchen, begins to sing it too. While Kate juggles her morning preparations – getting Guy out of the house and Adrian into school uniform, preparing Ali for nursery and herself for work – it occurs dimly to her that three-year-old children generally can't repeat a tricky melody so well.

Guy pulls on his coat and rattles the keys that he's located, at last, in its pocket. 'I'm off,' he says. 'You OK, love?'

'Fine,' Kate says, kissing him. He squeezes her waist. They're the same height, but for half an inch in Guy's favour: he is five foot ten, she is five foot nine and a half. He's considered slightly too short; she's considered a little too tall. 'Go carefully,' she says, as she usually does. Guy has to drive for an hour and ten minutes every morning and evening, to Manchester and back.

'Will do. Love you,' he replies, as he usually does. 'Be good at school, Adie. Bye-bye, Ali, be a good girl.'

'Bye-bye, Daddy,' Ali pipes from behind the dog. Guy swoops across the room and sweeps her into his arms, where she squeals with joy. Then he ruffles Adrian's hair, grabs his briefcase, says yet again, 'I'm off,' and is gone. Kate hears the car pulling out into the road.

For a few seconds she feels alone. Then it's action stations, getting the children's shoes and coats on and loading up her briefcase with notepad, sandwiches and some chocolate. She's been fighting a half-hearted battle against chocolate addiction for years.

Ali doesn't want to wear her coat, although there's a bracing wind.

'Cassie's wearing her coat,' Kate encourages.

'Cassie's a *dog*,' the rational Ali says.

'Dogs always have their coats on. They're born with them, so they're always warm.'

'I wasn't born with my coat on. Why wasn't I, Mummy?'

'Mum, I want to get to school and play,' Adrian butts in, glaring at his little sister.

'Coat on, Ali, *now*. We're making Adie late.'

Ali begins to whine as Kate shoves her arm into the pink woollen sleeve, then holds her firmly with one hand, fastening the buttons with the other. They set off down the hill at as brisk a pace as Kate can make the children walk. Adrian loves school; he strides tall and proud for his five years, his brown head bobbing along by her waist. But when they reach the busy street that leads uphill to school, their progress slows again because everybody in Buxton simply has to stop and say hello to the puppy.

Kate tells herself three times a day how lucky she is to have her job. Her office looks out towards the green hill beneath the Palace Hotel, close to the spreading dome of the Royal Devonshire Hospital. She is a solicitor with a local law firm that deals mainly with conveyancing, divorces and small financial disputes. There's always something to do, but never too much for comfort, at least where Kate is concerned. Her boss, Mike, is happy for her to work until three every afternoon, then leave to collect the children; she's willing to take work home, but mostly she doesn't have to. Now, to cap it all, he's letting her bring her dog to the office. Cassie is already well trained enough to curl up and snooze the morning away, giving an occasional canine snore while Kate sips coffee and makes her first phone calls.

Kate has never quite stopped thinking of her job as occupational therapy. Their fresh start in Buxton was an escape from the stresses of London, which Guy partly blamed for what had happened – probably, Kate thinks, because he had to blame something. Kate, if she blamed anything, blamed herself. Guy, though, had always hoped to move out of the capital. Perhaps it was his excuse to do what he wanted; a suitable time to convince her, while she was at emotional rock bottom, that it would be good for both of them.

Guy's job had appeared at exactly the right moment. She couldn't have denied it to him: becoming an assistant editor at the *Manchester Chronicle* in his twenties was an exceptional opportunity, especially as his dream was to live in the Peak District, where his great-grandfather had been born. Family legend had it that this historical Bradley used to walk across the moor from Buxton to Macclesfield to court his sweetheart. Infused with that fairytale from childhood, Guy had always sensed his roots in the bleak, heather-strewn landscapes, nourished by mysterious waters bubbling through the caverns beneath.

More practically, he'd argued that in Buxton they could have a house three times the size of their London flat and, someday, a dog to share it with them; his parents' place in Cheshire would be only an hour and a half away; best of all, every weekend they could drive for a few minutes and find themselves bang in the middle of what he considered the best hill-walking in Britain.

Kate met Guy on a University Walkers' Club ramble in the Cheviots. She can still picture him pacing along, leading twelve bedraggled students in rain trousers and cagoules, his hair blowing around in at least three directions. Undaunted by the driving Northumbrian rain, the mud, the bitter wind, he was making a joke about needing windscreen wipers on his glasses. Kate had been wondering what could have possessed her to join this walk, other than that she could think of nothing more different from her weekend activities back in north London. Talking to Guy had warmed her, despite the chill. His broad smile, his bright eyes, his gameness for whatever the day threw at them made her trust him. He was positive, active and extremely bright. And although he was studying English and history and said he wanted to be a journalist, he was also physical, strong, oriented to the outdoors. She found the combination compelling.

Looking for him later, she found a note on his door saying that he was – to her surprise – practising. She found him in the small music room, sitting at the piano, improvising. Kate played the viola and faithfully joined every orchestra in the university, all of which clamoured for her services; good violists were few and far between. But even with her comparatively substantial musical experience, she had never before met anyone who could improvise on the piano.

He greeted her with a generous smile, and while they talked he kept playing, picking out intriguing chords, delicate patterns, startling combinations of sounds. After ten minutes they'd agreed to meet for supper in the refectory – and Kate had lost her heart to him somewhere in the airborne spaces between the notes.

They were soon inseparable. Even in the peculiar music-and-hill-walking clique that gathered around them, they were no longer two individuals, Kate Davis and Guy Bradley, but just

Kate-and-Guy. Perhaps they seemed an odd couple: he was dark and alert, active as a busy bird in spring; she was fair, big-boned, inclined to dreaminess.

Law wasn't her decision. Her parents would not allow her to study music. Guy empathised with this more than anybody she'd ever met.

'You could have been a pianist if you'd wanted,' Kate pointed out one night, while they lounged companionably together in Guy's bed, sipping cocoa. 'If I'd had your talent, maybe I'd have had more ammunition to throw at them.'

'Oh, Katie, it's not fair.' Guy was running his fingers through Kate's long hair in the same absent-minded way he'd run them over the keyboard. 'You wanted to be a musician, you play beautifully, you could have had a life in it, and your parents won't let you. My parents would have let me do anything I want, but I don't fancy being shut in a practice room for eight hours a day. I love playing, but I don't want to end up hating it because I have nothing else in my life. I like being in the middle of things.'

'What "things"?'

'Well, if Ted Heath comes to give a talk, I want to be there asking him questions, preferably doing an interview. If the president of the United States resigns, I want to find out the truth and tell people why. Katie, there are thousands of pianists who play a million times better than I do. I'd be much happier being a journalist.'

'At least you had the choice.' Kate felt a familiar surge of resentment. What she couldn't understand, couldn't begin to imagine, was how her parents could have encouraged her to practise her viola, love it and long to perfect it for so many years – yet as soon as she'd wanted to pursue it seriously, they'd snatched away her dream. They'd threatened to cut her out of their wills if she were to study music instead of something sensible with proper employment possibilities, such as law.

'I can't believe it,' Guy said. 'Katie, it's so bourgeois. It's so bloody middle-class. You push your child into learning a musical instrument, you force her to take exams, you put up her certificates, and when your friends come to dinner you make her play to show off your marvellous, talented family. But if she's really good, in kicks the old British instinct – a daughter on the stage? Heaven forfend!'

'Hmph,' Kate grumbled, into her cocoa.

'But how can they? How can they have a daughter like you and behave like that? How can they have a daughter like you *at all?*'

Moving to Buxton, of course, meant that they were a long way from Harrow. There, the Davises' house was spotless, gleaming with magnolia paint, a brass carriage clock on the mantelpiece and never a vestige of clutter, let alone anything as messy as a book or a record in the living room. Any they possessed lived in Kate's bedroom. The first time Kate brought Guy home to meet her parents, William and Margaret Davis offered him vol-au-vents and sherry and asked why he wanted to go into journalism. Wasn't it dangerous? Wasn't there a risk of injury in cars that travelled too fast, chasing a story, or being caught in the crossfire of a war zone? Guy tried to reassure them that he had no thought of becoming either a *paparazzo* photographer or a war reporter, although he wasn't averse to politics. Meanwhile, Kate had taken an instant liking to Guy's parents, Didie and George, and to the florid, open-hearted Cheshire countryside around their house. The decision to go north was much eased by their closeness.

Kate's phone rings; the dog's ears prick up. Kate answers and speaks to a client who's buying a farm outside the town.

She has not touched her viola for eight years.

At three she leaves the office, Cassie trotting at her heels, and goes to pick up Ali from nursery school. She ties the dog's leash to the railings outside and wanders in, sniffing the aroma of Plasticine and milk, biscuits and finger paints and looking at the bright pictures pinned to the wall – each page of splodges a source of immense pride to its creator's parents.

The children are clustering round a cassette player; Lucy, their teacher, is putting a tape into the slot. As Kate listens in the doorway, out comes the sound of a piano playing something strongly rhythmical. Kate recognises it: it's the 'Ritual Fire Dance' by Manuel de Falla. Lucy has given each child an instrument: one a drum, another a triangle, a third a tambourine. She encourages them to make a noise with the instruments on the beats. One small girl begins to jump up and down. A little boy puts his hands over his ears.

Ali stands slightly apart, staring at the cassette, ignoring the drum in her hand. At home, Kate and Guy keep their still-new CD-player and burgeoning CD collection on a high shelf, well out of harm's, or at least Adrian's, way. Ali is apparently hypnotised by the spinning tape. Lucy glances at her, but as Ali is listening, even if she's not participating, she doesn't interfere.

Afterwards, Ali, Kate and Cassie fetch Adrian, then head home for tea. Kate gives the children toast and Marmite. While they're eating, she hangs up a load of laundry, puts in another and runs the vacuum-cleaner across the lounge. She'd stopped to buy fresh flowers on the way back and puts them in a white vase: her favourite anemones, a vibrant mix of crimson, carmine and imperial purple, with black stamens standing to attention.

Adrian wants to play in the garden, so she goes with him, listening while he rattles on about school. Watching him and trying to calm the barking Cassie, who wants Adrian to throw his ball for her to retrieve, she's also attempting to keep an eye on Ali, who's jumping about on the patio in some unfathomable game of her own.

Kate is filled with dread if she takes her attention away from Ali for longer than four seconds. For a child of Ali's age, every household object threatens disaster. She's curious enough to pick up a bottle of detergent to see what it is, but not aware enough to know she mustn't drink it. She can open doors, go up and down stairs or in and out of the house, but Kate can't be certain that she won't run into the road. Kate panics too easily over Ali. Somehow she's never worried about Adrian in the same way. She knows her feelings are conditioned by the trauma eight years ago – but she still can't stop them taking her over, sometimes bringing on trembling, sweating and even nausea at the slightest hint of danger.

The sound of small, skipping feet has gone.

'Ali! Where are you?' she shouts, diving into the house.

She hears a note sound, then another. The piano?

Guy's old upright stands against the lounge wall. Ali has managed to lift the lid and is prodding gingerly at the keys. Kate is about to demand whether her hands are clean after the Marmite, when she notices that Ali is using more than one finger on the keyboard. As Kate watches, Ali lifts her left hand and begins to press the bass notes too.

When he has a spare moment, Guy still loves to plough through some of his favourite pieces, Beethoven sonatas or bits of Chopin. Ali often stands next to him, watching, her mouth slightly open. Kate has never thought anything of it. All children are fascinated by musical instruments and love to see the peculiar antics of adults coaxing out the noises; or, even better, to try it themselves. Ali always begs Guy to play; and she always wants to have a bash at it herself, though Kate worries about sticky paws on the keys. But now—

Ali has got her bearings. Her chin level with the keyboard, she has somehow worked out which sound comes from which note. She looks up at Kate with huge blue eyes and says, 'Mummy, I can play it.'

'What, lovie?'

'The music. On the tape.'

'Can you, darling?' Kate smiles, tolerant. But Ali is bouncing impatiently and Kate understands and winds the piano stool higher for her.

Ali beams a thank-you, gives her hair a proud shake and shunts her small behind to the dead centre of the piano stool's edge, as if to say, 'There we are, at last.' She sits up straight, lifts her right hand and begins to pick out a tune. It isn't perfect, as she hasn't found out what the black notes are for, but the complicated rhythm is unmistakable. Ali pouts. 'That's not quite right.'

'It's nearly right, though, darling,' Kate says, astounded. 'Try again.'

'I'm going to,' Ali declares, clearly outraged at the notion that she might do anything else. 'Mummy, what are these?' She points at the black notes.

'Try them and see.'

Ali's forefinger moves from F to F sharp. Her eyes widen. A few minutes later, she has learned to play what is essentially a chromatic scale.

Kate, dazed, picks up the phone. 'Any chance you could come home a little early?' she asks Guy. 'Ali has something to show you.'

Guy, delayed by antisocial newspaper hours and a long drive, usually arrives home after Ali is in bed. Her routine with Kate is always the same. There's bathtime, where Ali plays with a white plastic swan and a yellow plastic boat. Then the pantomime: 'I don't want to go to bed'; 'Oh, yes, you do'; 'Oh, no, I don't.' One way or another, Ali ends up in her pyjamas, and in her bed. Her room and Adrian's are opposite each other on the second floor; Ali's overlooks the garden. African animals parade across the curtains; the walls are primrose yellow. Kate puts on the nightlight; in its soft glow, she sits on a bean-bag by Ali's bed and plays a cassette of soothing songs. It has never occurred to her that there's anything unusual about Ali singing along, even though Adrian used to listen to the same tape and had never learned the words, let alone the notes.

Then Ali always asks the same question. 'Where's Daddy?'

'Daddy's coming back from work,' Kate whispers, reassuring. Ali's little face looks worried, her eyes entreating, her forehead creasing into a childish frown. Kate puts her arms round her baby daughter and kisses her. 'He'll be home very soon and he'll come and kiss you goodnight when you're asleep. Daddy loves you very much.' Ali is a real Daddy's girl. A child psychologist whom Kate had met at a talk in a bookshop had assured her that this was quite normal for a three-year-old, along with the requisite pink dresses, fairy wings and princess tiaras.

'I love you, Mummy.' Ali's eyes are closing and she wriggles down under her covers, putting her thumb in her mouth.

'I love you too, baby. Sweet dreams.' Kate gently extracts the thumb. Ali, asleep, doesn't stir.

Today, when Guy walks in, Ali hasn't even had her bath. She flings herself across the hall, yelling, 'Daddydaddydaddy!'

No homecoming could be happier for Guy. He's had a tough day, dealing with late copy and last-minute information, and he's had to think of a lame excuse to get away. Telling Martin, the editor, that his three-year-old daughter wants to show him something is not calculated to inspire confidence, so he'd invented a bad throat and temperature for Ali, plus difficulties looking after Adrian, then made a dash for the car. As soon as Ali appears and he gathers her up, every moment of the day becomes worthwhile.

'How's my lovely girl?' He looks at her shining face and then at Kate's. 'OK, what's happening?'

'Come on, Daddy – come *on*!' Ali, on her feet, tugs at his hand.

'It's a surprise,' Kate says.

Guy dumps his coat on the banister. Kate picks it up and hangs it on a hook.

'It's stupid,' says Adrian, stumped by his sister's absorption in the piano, though glad it kept her out of his way while he repulsed some intergalactic invaders from the back garden.

'It's not, so.' Ali sticks out her lower lip and pulls on Guy's hand.

'It's certainly not stupid, Adie.' Kate tries not to snap at her son.

Ali climbs on to the piano stool – where she's spent the better part of the last two hours – and plays the tune she's worked out, with a basic but deft accompaniment. It doesn't have the twirls, snaps and intricacy of the 'Ritual Fire Dance', but the outline is definite. Guy's mouth falls open.

'Ali, where did you learn that?'

Ali, absorbed, doesn't look round.

'Lucy played it to them,' Kate says.

'What? And she remembered it? And worked out how to play it all by herself?'

'Well, I helped her a little, but mostly she did it on her own.'

'Gordon Bennett!' Guy takes off his glasses and rubs his eyes. 'Ali, do it again.'

He stands beside her, watching her fingers on the keys. When she's finished, he dashes to a shelf and pulls out a CD of the piece, played by Arthur Rubinstein. A few seconds later the disc has told him what he wants to know.

'There we are.' Guy stops the record. 'You again, Ali.'

Now Kate understands: Ali begins the tune unerringly on the right note, the same as the recording. She is three years old and she has perfect pitch. What's more, she knows how to find the notes on the keyboard.

Kate and Guy stare at each other over Ali's head. Perhaps Guy can see, in Kate's wide blue eyes – the adult replica of their daughter's – an inkling of what lies ahead; perhaps she can glimpse in his bird-like gaze the revelation that they've given life to an energy more powerful than themselves.

Perhaps it's premonition, or merely imagination, but a ray of understanding passes between them: they, and their children, may be embarking upon a profound, irrevocable journey.

For now, only one thing is obvious: they need to find Ali a piano teacher.

2

In the first version of her dream, Kate relives everything as it was. She's gazing into an aquarium-like tank in which her daughter, weighing one and a half pounds, is a helpless minnow wired up to a Pompidou Centre of tubing, oxygen, monitors and drips. She can detect her minuscule breaths, but she can't lift and cuddle her because taking her out might kill her. In a fit of optimism, she and Guy had named her Victoria.

In the second version, Kate is at home, with Victoria strapped to her body in a baby sling. Life carries on. She can be cleaning the kitchen, hoovering the stairs, getting ready for work, but Victoria is there, silent, motionless. Probably dead, though in the dream Kate never remembers this. The baby hangs on her, growing heavier and heavier until Kate feels that the weight will break her neck, and just as it becomes too much to bear, she wakes up.

The third version shows her and Guy at the kitchen table, feeding their children. Ali is eating. Adrian is being naughty. Victoria is eight years old and is helping Kate, fetching fruit juice from the fridge, scolding her brother, laughing at her sister's crumb-coated face. It's a normal family scene, but with three children instead of two. And this is the version that leaves Kate, when she wakes, feeling that a medieval torture rack has pulled her to shreds.

Kate and Guy married young, some thought too young; they'd never had any doubt that they'd spend the rest of their lives together. First they'd sailed through three carefree student years. Guy became editor of the university newspaper and secretary of the students' union, booking cutting-edge politicians, writers and broadcasters to speak there – including Margaret Thatcher, who had just become the first woman leader of any British political party. He played his piano, attended all Kate's performances with her string quartet, and dragged her out for walks in the Cheviots. Often they'd go to concerts in the cathedral and sit deep inside its ancient darkness, drinking in the sounds they loved – Schubert, Sibelius or Guy's favourite Beethoven. Surely life would always be as beautiful as this. Strolling by the river not long before their final exams, while the leaves were young and tender on the trees, Guy said, 'Let's get married when we move to London?' Kate said, 'Yes, let's.' And that was that.

After graduating they had engineered a year together in Guildford. Kate, her engagement ring the envy of her fellow students, tackled her obligatory stint at law school and Guy took a junior editorial job on a local paper. But only when they'd found work placements in London did they take the plunge and tell Kate's parents that they'd like to get married in a register office with nobody there except family and a few close friends.

As they'd expected, William and Margaret took it as a personal affront that their daughter was refusing the big church wedding they'd saved towards for years. But Kate and Guy didn't want fuss. They were together; that was all; that was how it would stay. The best things, they insisted, were the simplest.

Margaret took Guy aside over sherry one evening and explained that, in her day, it was accepted that a church wedding blessed the couple in the sight of God; marriage without this was not a real marriage. Guy heard her out. Then, quietly, he told her that to him and Kate, their love was already so sacred that no outward demonstration could make it more so. Kate, more practically, pointed out that they'd prefer to use the money to set up home while they started their new jobs. Guy, with his impressive track record in student and local journalism, had been accepted on to a graduate-trainee scheme at a national newspaper; Kate was to do her articles with a firm of lawyers on Gray's Inn Road. A chorus of approval went up from George and Didie, who provided funds for them to have a honeymoon in Paris.

At the wedding party at a small hotel in Harrow, William and Margaret shook hands with George and Didie; and if dark, sparkling Didie in her tailored purple suit, Chinese jade necklace and high heels was remotely fazed by the hard stare of Margaret in her beige blouse, flat shoes and pearls, she did not show it once as she enfolded her son's new wife in her welcoming arms.

Kate had rarely been out of Britain. Davis family holidays had mostly consisted of annual fortnights on the Devon coast, during which she, her older brother, Anthony, and their younger sister, Joanna, had squabbled all day every day. In Paris, twenty-three and newly married, she walked on air. She filed away under 'daft' the protests of her best friend, Rebecca, the cellist in her string quartet. She and Guy were ready to tell the rest of the world to leave them alone for ever. 'If people say we're doing the wrong thing, they're obviously not our real friends,' Guy pointed out.

'But, Katie, you've never slept with anybody else,' Rebecca said, when Kate glanced round her door in college, sporting her brand new solitaire diamond. 'How will you ever know if what you've got is the right thing?'

'I do know.' Kate beamed. 'I'm happy with Guy. Why should I want anyone else?'

'But don't you want to live a little? Don't you want to explore, find out what you like, meet more people or see the world before you settle down?'

Rebecca's room was opposite Kate's in the hall of residence. Her eyes were chocolate-brown and her hair sleek and midnight-dark. She wore translucent Indian-cotton skirts over her long legs, usually with sandals. She came round to Kate's almost every day, often with stories of her latest meditation class, consciousness-raising group or all-night party. She'd been through a number of boyfriends – college rumour had it that she'd tried a girlfriend or two as well – and she was planning to travel round India for a year before looking for a job.

'Are you happier than me?' Kate challenged her.

'I hope not,' Rebecca riposted.

Kate and Rebecca had met on the landing on the first day of their first term. Kate wasn't sure quite how they'd become such good friends. She suspected that it had been Rebecca's decision and that she had found it easier to comply than reject her, especially when they started the string quartet, which was also Rebecca's idea. Rebecca's risqué private life and upmarket, progressive-boarding-school education sometimes made Kate feel strait-laced, conventional, suburban and deeply inadequate. Yet best friends they remained.

'Maybe she gives me adventure and I give her stability,' Kate told Guy, after he had met Rebecca for the first time.

'Sounds like you're married,' he teased her.

But, back in bed after a late Parisian breakfast of café au lait and croissants, Kate reluctantly agreed with Guy that she could scarcely maintain a friendship with someone who thought she knew what was good for Kate better than she did herself – and whose nose had been put ridiculously out of joint when Kate started going out with Guy. Kate remembers that only too well.

She'd come back to her room after a concert – it was the Sibelius Violin Concerto in the cathedral, it had been pouring with rain and her umbrella had flipped inside out on the front steps. After bidding a lingering goodnight to Guy, who wasn't yet staying, she'd knocked on Rebecca's door across the hall. It was unlocked, so Kate went in. Rebecca was sitting in her threadbare armchair in front of the electric bar heater, staring into space. She gazed up at Kate and said nothing. Just looked at her with those big, reproachful eyes. Kate wondered what she'd done wrong. Rebecca couldn't possibly have taken it personally that she'd gone to a concert with Guy, not her? She didn't know what to say, except 'Tea?' It wasn't a comfortable moment. Kate spent too much time silently puzzling over her friend's reaction, but never dared to raise the matter with her, or anyone else.

After graduation Rebecca took off for India – something Kate couldn't have afforded even if she'd wanted to. By the time she returned, Kate and Guy were so busy with their new jobs, not to mention gutting, rebuilding and decorating their flat in Stoke Newington, that they had neither time nor patience for travellers' tales of far-off lands. Rebecca and her cello disappeared into the past. Gradually Kate began to forget about her. Life as an articled clerk ensured that.

It didn't take her long to work out that the senior partner had employed her not because she was bright but because she was a tall, long-legged blonde. She spent her days preparing bills, photocopying and running bizarre errands for the partner including several to Marks & Spencer lingerie department. Guy bounced out every morning, eager to get to his office; by contrast, she was bound to a vile company merely because her parents wanted her to be a lawyer. On the rare days when she didn't work late, she practised her viola, trying to keep her technique up to scratch – though 'scratch' often seemed an appropriate word. She joined an amateur orchestra, which sounded appalling but was enjoyable as long as she concentrated on playing rather than listening.

'I dread every day,' Kate admitted to Didie, visiting Cheshire.

'Try not to let that beastly man demoralise you,' Didie comforted her. 'He's the problem, not you, because he has the power.'

'You're so sensible, Didie. But I don't know how I can stick it out.'

'Eventually you'll have a proper job. It's a matter of doing your time to qualify.'

'I wish I'd never got into this. I wish I could just stop and have kids.'

Didie pressed Kate's hand. 'Give yourself time, darling.'

Kate felt relieved. If she'd confided these thoughts to her own mother, Margaret would have told her to stop complaining: 'Stiff upper lip, dear.' No matter whose choice her profession really was, her feelings would have been judged entirely her own fault.

It should have been so simple. It seemed to work for everyone else. All around her, young professional women were getting married, setting up their first homes, blossoming into pregnancy. An unsettling pang would sweep through her when she passed pushchairs in the supermarket. One day an ex-colleague came into the office to show everyone her eight-month-old son. Kate picked him up and loved holding the warm, laughing child so much that she almost couldn't bear to put him down.

It was 1980. Guy's newspaper declared that half of Britain's married women were now going out to work, the highest proportion for any country in the EEC. A career was essential. Broodiness wasn't top of the agenda in women's groups, as Kate discovered when she tried one. Listening to the others' stories over tea and Bourbon creams, she wondered if she was a freak. Several women had toddlers and had come to the group to express, in a supportive environment, resentment against the ties that bound them. Others were fighting for promotion at work. One was suffering with a violent husband. Kate's husband was supremely unproblematic, beyond his preoccupation with the British Olympic Association's refusal to boycott the Moscow Olympic Games after the USSR invaded Afghanistan. Her issue was the only thing that seemed, to her, impossible to talk about: the gnawing, aching, physical longing to hold in her arms a baby of her own.

It should have been so simple. She'd stopped taking the pill when they got married. But nothing had happened.

They went for tests. Guy was fine. So was she. Nobody could say why this young, healthy, loving couple were unable to conceive a child. The doctor started Kate on a regime of hormones that soon made her fractious and sore; and she had to keep a diary of data, taking her temperature several times a day. When the correct signs were there, she was supposed to call her husband, drag him home and get him on the job immediately. This was easier said than done; but after the fifth month of hormones, thermometer, diary and shoulder-stands after sex, she missed her period and began to experience nausea in the mornings and hypersensitivity to the smell of coffee.

Their first child was due in mid-March 1981. Kate and Guy phoned every family member to break the news. Kate's colleagues gave her a bouquet; Guy's boss provided a bottle of champagne, which Kate, laughing, declared was unfair because she shouldn't drink any. They painted their second bedroom a bright, baby-friendly yellow and bought a cot and a pushchair; on the bus going to work, Kate taught herself to knit. Inside, she felt small fluttery motions; gradually they strengthened into kicks. She lay in bed at night with her hands pressed to her bump, loving the child within her.

Driving home after Christmas Day at her parents' house, Kate remarked, 'My back is really aching. I must have lifted something heavy. Maybe the turkey.' It was an innocent enough observation.

By noon on Boxing Day, her backache was worse; and discomfort between her legs signalled a discharge streaked with blood. 'Don't panic. Give it another day,' Guy said.

The next morning, while Guy was at the office, Kate went to the GP, who sent her straight to hospital.

Kate stayed there, with constant checks kept on the baby, around which there was apparently less amniotic fluid than there should have been. Everyone told her not to worry. Guy played cheerful, though she knew he wasn't: 'Don't worry, darling, I'll look after everything at home.' Her mother told her not to worry: the family history was one of strong and plentiful children. Didie sent flowers and volunteered to come down the moment they wanted her; they mustn't worry about asking. Kate's boss told her not to worry about being off work. Kate spent her days telling her concerned callers not to worry, and her evenings lying flat, trying to read, trying to knit, repeating silent prayers.

One day just into the new year, she walked to the ward door to see Guy off. As she raised her arm to wave to him, something gave way deep within her and a rush of warm liquid cascaded down her legs.

After a short, terrifying labour, Victoria appeared, only to disappear. Kate, weeping in the delivery room, her nails leaving crimson incisions in Guy's hand, thought she heard the faintest of cries as the minute baby was whisked away to the incubator. When Kate was finally allowed to see her, Victoria was swamped by tubing, wiring and monitors, her tiny face so wrinkled and skeletal that she looked a century old. It wasn't even safe for Kate to pick her up.

During the worst weeks of her life, each day lasted a year. She existed in a state of heightened awareness in which every glimpse of a doctor heading her way induced blind terror or irrational hope. She'd had no idea that so much could go wrong with a premature baby. Twice Victoria stopped breathing and turned blue, only to rally as Kate was giving way to despair. The doctors warned that some of her organs might not be properly formed. Her hearing or vision might be impaired. Her brain might be damaged. She might not survive. Equally, she might grow up well, normal and happy.

Hope, then hopelessness. One moment, certainty that Victoria would live; the next, no doubt that she would die. Panic, elation, panic again. The formerly self-assured, self-contained Kate felt that she was drowning in seas of emotion with fluxes and tides all their own.

Guy brought her some tapes, music that he thought might calm her. In a quiet room in the unit, her head on his shoulder, listening to the slow movement of Ravel's G major Piano Concerto and watching Victoria living from second to second, she reflected that she'd never known such extremes were latent inside her, never suspected how suffering can mangle time and leave it distorted and misshapen. Victoria was inches long and weighed less than a bag of sugar. Yet everything had to carry on, regardless. Guy was dealing with the inauguration of a US president called Ronald Reagan, the charging of a serial killer known as the Yorkshire Ripper and the rumoured imminent takeover of his newspaper. Whole worlds were exploding, compared to one tiny creature fighting for her life. But this helpless baby was Kate's universe.

Kate stayed in hospital with Victoria. Guy visited early each morning and late each evening. In between, he had to keep going, maintaining a semblance of normality for all their sakes. Kate could see the strain round his eyes, the shadows deepening by his nose. He seemed to have aged ten years in two weeks.

He'd sit by Victoria's incubator, holding Kate's hand, talking about goings-on at work. One editorial assistant had broken her wrist. His boss was getting married for the third time and threatening to leave if the takeover went ahead. If it did, there could be multiple redundancies. In his view, Thatcher's ruthless administration was destroying the moral fibre of—

'Guy,' Kate cut in, 'I really don't care.'

There was a short silence, but for the slow tenderness of Ravel.

'No,' Guy said. 'Neither do I.'

Guy grew quieter during his visits. They'd sit together waiting, wondering, not talking. Now and then a doctor would bring them good news. Sometimes it was less good. Then good again.

Alone in the flat, Guy sometimes let himself cry. He stayed busy, working, keeping their families informed, fielding phone calls and trying to talk himself into a positive frame of mind. But some solitary nights, he began to wonder whether this would go on for ever, whether he and Kate must spend the rest of their years waiting for Victoria to live or die. In his worst moments, to his horror, he almost wished that none of it had begun, that they had neither conceived the child, nor got married, nor even met each other. If he'd taken up the place he'd won at Oxford, not decided to rebel and study in the north, Kate would have lived in blissful ignorance of him and Victoria would never have existed. Fate, he decided, is character plus timing plus a large dose of luck, good or bad.

He detached himself by deciding to approach the incident as he would a journalistic assignment. He would experience it for the sake of documenting it. Then, perhaps, once Victoria was safely home, he could write an article, maybe a book, to help other families encountering the same trauma.

He started to keep a diary, writing down everything that had happened since Christmas. Back from the hospital around midnight, he'd sit at the kitchen table covering page after page of a spiral-bound notebook with scrawls in black biro. On the seventeenth day of Victoria's life, he drafted a pitch to show the editor of the newspaper's health section.

On the eighteenth day, he arrived at the hospital to find a doctor, grey-faced, saying, 'Guy, Victoria isn't doing quite so well today.'

Guy began to run. He came to a halt in the doorway. Kate was standing by the incubator, her gaze fixed on the tiny bundle she was cradling.

She handed him Victoria without a word. The baby's eyes were closed. Although she was warm under her white woollen blanket, he could scarcely sense her breath. Her skin had the bluish tint of a northern winter sky.

'We can hold her now. There's no hope,' Kate said, taking her back from Guy although he had barely grown used to the sensation of having his child in his arms.

They sat together all morning, holding Victoria. At two o'clock in the afternoon, she died.

In the weeks and months that followed, Kate cried every day. The office gave her compassionate leave; she stayed home and let the tears flow. She had had no idea that her mind could leach such leaden despair, or that her eyes would not become exhausted from crying but would go on until there seemed to be nothing left in the world except grief.

Guy held her, comforted her, but said little. No soft words could make her feel better – or him. Margaret suggested that Kate should stay in Harrow for a while, to escape the room that should have been Victoria's, but Kate preferred to be at home. At least the nursery meant that Victoria had once been real.

Kate's siblings rallied round as best they could. Joanna was still at university, though, and when she came to visit, Kate could see how frightened she was at the sight of her level-headed sister falling to pieces. William and Anthony, emulating him, soon found that their instinctive 'Come on, old girl, pull yourself together, things to be done, chop chop,' got them, and Kate, nowhere.

Margaret's next idea was more productive. She took Kate out to lunch in town, then steered her towards the haberdashery in John Lewis, where she bought her a present of some wool, some patterns, a range of knitting needles and a wicker basket to hold the lot, plus a book of challenging Kaffe Fassett designs. Kate, attracted by the warm, bright colours, the varying soft- nesses of mohair, lamb's wool and merino, and the patterns that showed happy families wearing fabulously patterned sweaters, accepted her mother's gift and carried the bulky pack- ages home on the seventy-three bus.

When Guy had gone to work the next morning and the tears had temporarily worn themselves out, Kate blew her nose, sat on the floor with a cup of tea and unpacked her parcels. Margaret had suggested a simple jersey to start her off. Kate knew the basic stitches; a half-finished yellow blanket, intended for the baby, had vanished when Guy decided to clear out every disposable reminder. But knitting a full-sized sweater felt way beyond her.

The thread under her fingers required control. She needed to find the correct tension and keep it constant. She had to concentrate; if unsteadiness set in, the knitting began to sag, scrunch or stretch. She made herself per- severe by leafing through the Kaffe Fassett book. Once she'd mastered the technique, then she, too, would be able to create fantastical patterns in flame-hued diagonals, blue, green and white snowflakes, or gorgeous mottled designs that looked as if they had been plucked whole from the contours of a coral reef.

Her jersey was far from perfect. It fitted Guy – she'd meas- ured it against him so many times that it could scarcely not – but in the cream-coloured fabric lurked tremulous kinks where the tension was inconsistent. It was evidently home-knitted by a beginner, but Guy insisted on wearing it to work. Kate knew that that was just to make her happy. But it did make her happy. It showed she'd produced something useful; and that Guy cared.

She seemed to need reassurance of that now. Curled in her armchair, feet tucked under her, a needle in each hand and a ball of wool in her lap, she wondered whether they had talked to each other more often, more freely, before all this had happened.

Long silences dominated their evenings. She couldn't remember those happening at university. Perhaps as you get older, as you spend more time together, there's less to say; companionable quiet becomes an end in itself. These silences, though, didn't always feel companionable. They isolated her from Guy, as if they each retreated alone to worry at their wounds without troubling the other. Victoria and the grief that went with her were being driven underground.

Kate, clicking away, felt a twinge of sympathy for Guy. It couldn't be easy, living with a woman whose heart had been ripped out. But Victoria had been his daughter as well, even if he had not carried her inside him, feeling her fluttery kicks through the days and nights. He had lost a child too, but he was trying to live. He didn't cry for hours on end. He'd try to avoid waking her and go off to work without breakfast – he'd have a croissant and coffee later in the canteen. In the evening, he'd come crashing back in, telling her about the features he was fitting to the page, the admin that drove him bananas and the office gossip that bored her rigid when he repeated it to her, but at least kept him in touch with the world outside their claustrophobic flat. While he was out during the day, she barely noticed that she didn't miss him.

Men, Didie reminded her on the phone, aren't good at expressing their feelings.

'If keeping going helps him,' Kate said, 'then he's lucky. I wish I could.'

'You will, darling. Take all the time for yourself that you need,' Didie encouraged. It was good to hear that. Kate's mother was growing restive, prodding her gently but insistently to go back to work. And of course, Guy reminded her, they could try for another baby as soon as she felt ready.

Kate returned to Gray's Inn Road after six months – not least because she couldn't stand the flat any more. Even walks to the café at Clissold Park were wearing thin, thanks to the endless stream of mothers and babies she'd see there. Besides, she didn't want to forget her training and render herself an unemployable lawyer as well as a useless mother. The office wasn't so bad – better than eyeing other people's pushchairs and imagining what Victoria would have looked like now, sitting up, smiling, laughing.

She brought her knitting with her for bus journeys and lunchtime. Her colleagues came in to admire her latest effort: a Fair Isle scarf, although it was midsummer. The first weeks dragged, leaving her exhausted, but the routine propped her up; soon she could pass whole half-days without descending into her private pit of grief. Periods of twenty-four hours could go by without her shedding a tear. Work was the best therapy.

Going home was more difficult. Every time she passed the closed door of the nursery, it seemed to accuse her of failing its intended occupant. She suggested to Guy that they should think about moving. She offered to visit an estate agent and get a valuation.

'It's a good idea,' he said at once. 'But could we hang on here for a tiny bit longer? Just a few months? Would you be OK with that?'

Kate didn't ask why. Presumably he had his reasons. Her bus ride home had taken twice as long as usual, she felt exhausted and she didn't fancy sparking another flood of Guy's newspaper gossip. It was easiest to agree.

Two weeks later, Guy whirled into the flat carrying a bottle of wine and a bunch of roses. 'Sit down, Katie,' he demanded, pushing the bouquet into her hands. 'I'll pour you a glass of this and then there's a lot to tell you and a lot to ask you.' He grabbed two wine glasses from the cupboard, opened the bottle with a flourish of corkscrew and sat down next to her. She wondered when she'd last seen him smile like that.

A job had come up at the *Manchester Chronicle*: assistant editor of the weekly news-review section. His boss had recommended him, so he'd been up for an interview—

'You went to Manchester for an interview?' Kate exclaimed. 'When?'

'Last week. I didn't want to tell anyone in case I didn't get it.'

'You went to Manchester for the day and I didn't know?'

'You weren't supposed to, love. They might have hated me, I might have hated them, it mightn't have worked out, so there'd have been no point in you worrying about it.'

Kate took a moment to digest this. Then she reached for her knitting.

The environment was a little less stressful than his present one, he went on, and the pay a little better – if modestly so, because the site was out of London – but, still, it was a dream job, an extraordinary opportunity for a journalist still in his twenties.

'It would be a fresh start,' he said, holding her wrist. 'Just stop knitting a second and tell me what you think.'

'I don't know what to think. It's wonderful for you. But I can't believe you didn't tell me sooner. I had no idea that you were up to anything – and suddenly you're talking about moving two hundred miles?'

'Darling, I thought you'd be happy. You seemed keen to move. And you're finishing your articles, so the timing is . . .'

'Yes.' Kate's needles clicked.

'Katie, put down the knitting. *Please.*' Guy put both his hands over hers to still them. 'What do you want? Tell me. I need to know.'

'I want—' Kate looked into his anxious eyes. She couldn't tell him that she wanted him not to grow more and more distant from her just when she needed him to come closer. 'I only want a home and family like everyone else. A normal home with normal, happy children,' she said eventually. Though true, it sounded lame.

'So do I,' Guy said. 'And we could enjoy having all of that near Manchester, couldn't we? There'd be so many advantages, Katie. We could live in Cheshire, or Buxton, or a village in the Peak District.'

'I'd prefer to be somewhere with trains and shops.' Kate imagined a scenario – irrational but vivid – in which every person in a small, nosy village would know that she had failed her first baby.

'Buxton, then. We could have a wonderful house there. Look at these.' Guy pounced on his desk and extracted a sheaf of folded pages from a drawer.

'You sent off for a property paper and I never noticed?'

'At the office. Look.' He pointed at a row of adverts for beautiful stone cottages in Derbyshire that cost roughly the same as their Stoke Newington flat. Startled to discover her basic indifference to her own fate, Kate looked, listened, nodded and forced a smile.

Guy's traineeship at the newspaper and Kate's articles in Gray's Inn Road came to an end at the same time. They put the flat on the market. They took to driving north late on Fridays, staying overnight with Didie and George and setting out to house-hunt in Derbyshire first thing on Saturday morning. Kate saw the world through a glass thicker and darker than the windscreen of their old Beetle. From its wrong side she watched herself going through the motions: telling estate agents what they needed and could afford, enthusing to Didie about how happy she was that they'd live closer to her, explaining to her own shell-shocked parents that this was an opportunity Guy could not possibly miss. She'd look for a job once they'd made the move.

Buxton pleased her when they wandered about, 'casing the joint', as Didie put it. The air's freshness made her feel cleansed inside (how different from Stoke Newington) and the properties they viewed were roomy and light. They investigated a detached 1920s house on a busy road, a brand new town-house on a cul-de-sac, an older, sandstone villa on a quiet side-street; but on their third visit, the agent took them up a curving hill past the house where Vera Brittain had spent part of her girlhood, as a blue plaque told them, and thence to a tall, semi-detached Victorian pile in a state of considerable disrepair. It needed total modernisation – it had no central heating in a town where it was too cold to grow apples. 'But there's your chance to make it your own,' the agent pointed out, 'and, of course, the price is much lower than you'd normally see for a house of this quality.'

'How can anyone live in a house like this and let it get into such a terrible state?' Kate wondered aloud. 'It seems so uncared-for.'

'It's too easy to stop noticing things when you've been among them for a long time,' Guy suggested. 'Katie, look at these windows. Look at all this light.'

Kate, gazing out at the back garden's neglected lawn, felt a prickle on the back of the neck: the intuition that told her she was looking at her new home.

They sloped off to a pub to confer over a ploughman's lunch. Afterwards, they strolled back to the house and stood under the sycamores, looking up at it, picturing themselves living inside. A normal home with normal, happy children. Hill-walks close by, Didie and George an easy drive away and no memories clinging to the stones around them.

Kate's sole condition was dramatic: she wanted to move Victoria's grave to Buxton. Guy balked at the idea of digging up the coffin, reburying it, going through the whole trauma again; but when Kate made it clear that if Victoria didn't go, neither would she, he nodded assent. They could manage. They'd managed worse things before.

The day before the move, while Guy was wrapping the wedding crockery in newspaper and piling it into cardboard boxes, Kate went to his desk to pack his files. She lifted too many at once and the top wallet fell, spilling its contents at her feet. She bent to gather up the papers. Words caught her eye at random. 'Statistics' . . . 'greatest pain' . . . 'Victoria' . . .

'Guy? What's this?'

Her husband looked at her and she thought for a second that he had turned pale. 'Oh, Katie,' he said, 'I've been meaning to run this by you. The thing is, I didn't want to upset you, I didn't want to bring it all flooding back.'

'You're writing about Victoria.' Kate sat down at the kitchen table, one hand pressing her forehead under her untidy, moving-house hair.

'Darling.' Guy swooped in beside her. She felt him gazing into her face, but she wouldn't look up. 'I wanted to write something that might help people going through what we went through. The health editor thought it was a marvellous idea.'

'And the health editor has let you write *twenty pages*?'

'The thing is – well, I want to do an article, but that would be a kind of pilot for this publisher I've been talking to. It'll help to prove that I can write something that will really compel people, something they identify with that mirrors how they feel . . .'

'You want to write a *book* about Victoria?' Kate seemed to be sinking into a swamp that waited below the kitchen to swallow her. 'You don't just want to write it. You're writing it already.'

'It's valuable, Katie. It means so much to me. Can't we find a way to bring some good out of what happened to us? If we can help other people, give them something to make them feel they're not so alone . . .'

'*We?* I don't recall hearing I'm part of this. You never even asked how I felt!'

'I was waiting for the right moment.'

'Christ, Guy. How could you?' Kate pulled away her hand and stood up. Guy shrank back in his chair. 'Did it occur to you to wonder how I feel? No, of course it didn't! You're only thinking of yourself, your brilliant career, your marvellous move to Manchester. You wouldn't care if I said I'd kill myself!'

'Katie! Calm down. You know that's not true.'

'From where I am, Guy Bradley, it looks true. How can you do this to me?'

'Darling, can't you see? It's not only for other people, it's for us, so we won't have suffered and Victoria won't have died in vain.'

'But it's my grief! It's private. It's not for everybody to read and pry and say, "Ooh, look at them, look how miserable they are, they couldn't keep their baby alive." What made you think that I'd ever, in a million years, consider making that public?'

'Sweetheart. Please don't cry.'

'Leave me alone. You're a bloody journalist. You don't give a damn.'

'Katie—'

'Just leave me alone.'

The van arrived at eight o'clock the next morning. Kate, standing on the front step, her hair blowing about her shoulders, let the movers in. She made them some tea and packed the valuables into the back of the Beetle. Guy, who hadn't slept all night, swallowed two cups of coffee and a caffeine pill in preparation for the long drive north. That morning when they locked the flat for the last time, climbed into the car and started the engine, they had spoken three words to each other that were not directly connected with moving house.

Through the car window on the M1, Kate watched her old life receding into the distance, imagined the new house lying ahead, needing to be rethought, remodelled, rewired, replastered and repainted, and wondered what was to become of them now.

3

'I don't really know what to do with her,' Glenda Fairburn says, after Alicia has had two piano lessons. 'I've never seen anything like it. She just – knows.'

'She does, doesn't she?' Kate says.

'She doesn't have any trouble co-ordinating. She doesn't see why she should play with one hand at a time. The most incredible thing is that she concentrates. How do you do it? Do you not let them watch TV?'

'We're a completely normal family,' Kate says, smiling. 'They're the same as any other kids.'

'Well, this one's special.' Glenda's face is full of tenderness. She's a young Scottish musician who's recently moved to Buxton with her husband, a scientist at the Safety in Mines Research Establishment. 'I'll do my best for her, Kate, but I need you to know I'm feeling my way. With most of the little ones you just do the animal songs and the first exercise books and hope they take some interest. You don't generally find a child picking out pieces by ear.'

Alicia reaches out her hands to the keys. They loom huge in front of her like a row of pale ice lollies. She touches and sounds C, then D, then E. Deep red, royal blue, lemon yellow. The piano is better than a paintbox, for colours blend, flicker and dance through her mind when she hears music and the world seems delicious for it. Each note has its own colour in her head. The colours of the white notes are easy to identify, solid and bright. The black ones are more difficult: peculiar, in-between purples, greens and pinks. Except for B flat, which mysteriously looks like chocolate.

Alicia hasn't told her parents that she sees colours in music. Once she began to explain it to Mum at bedtime, but Mum looked so indulgent and said, 'Yes, darling, go to sleep now,' so many times that Alicia knew she hadn't grasped any of it. As for her beastly brother, there's no point trying. Adie, who is enormous, a whole two years older than her, does nothing but tease her. Once he caught a frog in the garden and put it in her shoe, where she nearly trod on it; worse, when she shook it out, it started leaping around the kitchen in slimy green arcs and Mum screamed. She wonders what it would have been like not to have a brother. Or to have a sister instead, a sister who was like her, understood her and was her friend, not her enemy.

Cassie is her best friend. Alicia, looking into the big canine eyes that gaze back at her with such love, wonders what Cassie would say if she could talk. Sometimes the dog jumps on to her bed to wake her up, cold nose and rasping tongue prodding her face in the hope of games ahead. 'We shouldn't let her go on Ali's bed,' Mum protests, but Dad insists there's no problem – 'Oh, come on, love, a dog like Cassie would never hurt a child, especially not Ali.' Alicia loves Cassie so much that if she cries when Mum leaves her at nursery school it's not because she misses Mum – it's because she won't see her dog for hours.

Alicia wants to tell Dad about the colours in the music, but he's usually gone too early in the morning for her to talk to him; and by the time he gets home, she's asleep. Sometimes, when he tiptoes into the enfolding darkness of her room to kiss her goodnight, she pretends that she's sleeping even when she isn't, because Mum will be upset if she thinks he's woken her. Later she opens her eyes in the traces of downstairs lamplight and hears him playing the piano before she drifts back into her dreams. She feels she's falling asleep on a boat, floating on a lake of music.

At weekends, she asks him to play to her. She stands close, watching, transfixed by his fingers, so certain, so strong, so fast. Hers won't move like that. When she grumbles to Glenda about it in her piano lesson, Glenda, who is her favourite person apart from Grandma Didie, laughs her lovely Scottish laugh and assures her that by the time she's thirteen, her fingers will be able to do anything she wants. That makes it worse. Alicia can't believe she'll ever be as old as that.

She can never remember the name of the composer who wrote her favourite piece. A short, funny name, like Shopping. 'Please, Dad, play the riding-over-the-moors piece,' she'd beg. At first Dad didn't know what she meant. Now he knows exactly and begins it at once. He says it's called a Ballade, which means a song telling a story. Alicia has made up her own story for the music. 'Four friends are talking to each other. Then they go on horseback across the moors. There's a witch or wizard, something evil, that tries to stop them and scary things happen. But in the end they find each other again and they're so pleased that they forget all about going out riding.'

Dad is surprised and stays silent for a minute. Eventually he asks her, 'Why do you think that, Ali? Why do you think they've forgotten?'

'Because their talking tune comes back, but the riding-over-the-moors one doesn't.'

'Gordon Bennett,' Dad says. 'You're full of surprises, Ali. Shall I play it again?'

'Yes, please!' Alicia bounces. Dad's face melts into his sweetest smile and he turns back to the keyboard. Alicia sits cross-legged on the floor and lets her favourite tunes dance behind her eyes in deep golds, burnished reds and emerald green.

At the end, Dad says, 'You know, Ali, one day you'll be able to play this yourself.'

'It's too hard,' Alicia protests. 'I'm too small.'

'Darling, you'll be much bigger very soon.' Dad beams.

'Come on, give us a hug.' She jumps on to his lap and hugs him, his woolly jersey warm and scratchy against her cheek.

Adrian has been given a camera for his birthday. After Dad has left the piano to mow the front lawn, Alicia pulls at her brother's sleeve and begs him to show her how it works.

Adrian adopts his most bossy older-brother voice. 'You look through here, Ali – that's it. Don't drop it. What can you see?'

'It's all blurry.'

'You twist the lens. Like this. That's right.'

'Everything's sharp now.'

'Yes. It's called focusing. You're bringing the picture into focus. That's what Dad says.'

Alicia nods. She understands exactly what he means, because that's what music does to her world. In nursery school she sits daydreaming and never knows the answers to the questions, until Lucy puts on the music – then everything sharpens and brightens, coming into focus. Dad brings home into focus when he plays.

Sometimes, though, she thinks he focuses things just by being *there*. At weekends, when he takes his place for break-fast and tucks his napkin into his shirt to protect it from spilled marmalade or egg, the wooden table edge seems firmer to her; when the scent of fresh-cut grass drifts through the window and she sees his curving shoulders as he pushes the mower along the lawn, each leaf in the garden seems bril-liant and sure of itself; and she always wants more of Mum's sponge cake at teatime, because it tastes extra good when Dad's there. She sometimes doesn't realise how much she misses him when he's at work until he comes back, making her world clear, bringing it into focus. She thinks she'll never forget the day he came home early specially to see her play the piano.

Nobody understands her the way Dad does. At nursery school, everyone seems to think she's strange when she talks about music. She'll say, 'You know that bit in the Ballade that sounds like a witch?' and her friends, Sarah and Matthew, look at her as if there's something wrong.

'Let's play the piano,' Alicia says, at Sarah's house one Saturday.

'We don't have one,' Sarah says.

Worse, when Matthew, his brother Tim and their mother come round, Alicia pulls Matthew over to the piano and starts to play, while Tim runs off to the garden with Adrian. Matthew sits awkwardly beside Alicia and prods at the keys with one finger, too loudly and on completely the wrong notes.

'Yuck!' Alicia puts her fingers in her ears. Matthew starts to cry.

'I think we'd better go home,' Matthew's mum says, gathering up the bawling child. Alicia begins to cry too, because she likes Matthew so much and doesn't understand why he's upset. He has sweet eyes and he's quiet, not preoccupied with making noise, playing football and hitting people like most boys. The other children tease her and say she fancies Matthew, but she doesn't. She just likes him. What's wrong with that? The next day he doesn't want to talk to her. Alicia has to gather every bit of courage she can find in order to go up to him and say, 'Matthew, I'm sorry, will you be my friend again?'

Matthew looks at his feet and mumbles something that sounds like 'All right.'

'Ali,' Mum says later, giving her and Adrian their fish-fingers, 'you've got to understand that not everybody has a piano and not everybody who does have one can play it.'

'Why?' Alicia demands. 'It's so easy.'

'Darling, it's not that easy for everybody. Piano lessons cost money and not all people are as keen to learn as you are.'

Alicia says nothing. She wonders why on earth they wouldn't be. Nothing else is so much fun. It's like walking inside a map. When she's playing, she knows exactly where she is.

*   *   *

'I don't really know what to do with her,' says Jonathan Bowen, two years later.

'I'm not sure anybody does,' Kate replies.

Jonathan is Parkhill Comprehensive's head of music – or, rather, what's left of music, post-Thatcher. He's also organist at St Edmund's, the church to which Ali and Adrian's primary school is attached. Glenda, abdicating reluctantly, had told Kate he's the best piano teacher in Buxton; Ali should have the best. Glenda is afraid of not giving her the right guidance; besides which, she's expecting a baby.

'How are you getting on at school, Ali?' Jonathan asks her.

Aged five and a half, Ali is holding on to Kate's hand, swinging herself back and forth as if dancing, anchored, to some unheard melody. 'It's OK. I don't really like school, though,' she says, looking up at Jonathan with her huge blue eyes. 'I wouldn't really like any school.'

'No, Ali, I expect you wouldn't. Kate, do you play yourself? What would really benefit Ali is if you or your husband were to practise with her. Not just supervise, but work with her – show her the movements and stop her getting into bad habits. Would either of you be willing to watch her lessons and put some serious time into this? Your daughter has exceptional talent, Kate. She's not just good. She's something special.'

'I'm special,' Ali sings. Kate senses that she's singing out the words without taking in the meaning. Ali hears the musical contours of sentences more than their content.

'It's a hundred years since I last played, but as of next time, I'll join in,' Kate assents. 'OK, Ali?'

'I'm special, I'm special,' Ali sings. 'Where's Cassie?'

Kate's boss, Mike, has been to the house and watched Guy playing the Note Game with Ali. She turns her back to the piano; Guy plays a note and asks her what it is. 'F,' declares the gleeful Ali. He plays another. 'A flat.'

She's always right; that's nothing new, but Guy never fails to give her a hug and say, 'Well done, you clever old thing!'

So, when Kate asks Mike for extra time away from the office – as Jonathan points out, it makes no sense to teach a small child in the evening when she's tired and fractious – Mike suggests that she might consider a four-day week. Guy has been promoted to assistant editor of the newspaper, with an associated salary rise, so Kate's day off is financially viable; and she's relieved to have Thursdays free, with time to get to grips with everything that she and Ali have, together, to learn. She's grateful for Guy's extra income – although, as she tells her mother, she hadn't expected to spend it on high-class piano lessons and multiplying stacks of CDs. Luckily Adrian is happy with football boots.

Watching Jonathan moulding Ali's little hands to the keyboard, seeing the games he plays with her to strengthen her ear, Kate becomes absorbed in something more significant than herself. Jonathan knows how to tap into the mystery that is Ali's music, how to stimulate her mind and how, Kate thinks, to inspire her. At the end of each lesson, he plays to her for a few minutes. Sometimes he improvises – being an organist, he's good at this – but sometimes he plays a whole piece and asks her if she likes it and whether she knows the composer's name. Ali says she likes Mr Shopping best.

Free Thursdays also give Kate the chance to begin redecorating. The house is a gift for anyone with a feel for interior design, which Kate, loving wool, fabric and colour, has aplenty. Its initial decorative makeover had had to be cheap and functional – new wiring and central heating had eaten up swathes of cash. Nine years on, it's time for an upgrade.

New carpets; new paint. Paint first. What's the point of beautiful new carpet if you spill paint on it afterwards? For the lounge, a creamy, eggy yellow that makes the most of the sunshine and will keep the house looking warm during the cruel Derbyshire winters. The stairs will be two lighter shades, one below the dado rail and the other, paler, above it. The carpet will be a burnished ochre that doesn't show the dog hairs too much.

Kate decides to make the lounge curtains herself: white damask patterned with roses. She buys a sewing-machine – something for which she's hankered for years (she isn't good at buying herself presents) – and sets it up on a table in the first-floor guest room, which also serves as her space, accommodating her store of leftover wool. Guy's study, beside the children's bedrooms in what had once been a loft, is a no-go area. Even she can't enter it without knocking. She suspects that he doesn't want anyone to see what a mess it is.

Their bedroom needs decorating too.

'You choose, darling,' Guy says at breakfast, when she suggests it. 'You always choose wonderfully. Have you seen my keys anywhere?'

'Why can't you keep them in the same place every day?' As always, it's a rhetorical question.

When he's gone, she wanders up to the bedroom, imagining. Though airy and large, overlooking the front lawn, it feels neglected. The walls are a dull white and, by the windows, diagonal cracks plough through the plaster. The carpet by the bed is wearing thin. On Guy's bedside table stands a tower of books that could topple with one false move of a feather duster. A biography of Margaret Thatcher perches on top, Guy's place kept by a pencil with which he's been underscoring the passages that make him most angry. Kate's bedside table houses a volume of Kaffe Fassett patterns, a childproof bottle of painkillers and a box of wax earplugs.

The chintz has to go; better curtains will help to keep out the cold in winter and the early light in summer. She'll put in the same gold-coloured carpet and the walls will be rich cream instead of flat white. And they need a new bedspread, maybe an ethnic pattern. Indonesian batik is very *in*, according to the magazines she dips into at the doctor's surgery, to which she takes the children constantly with sore throats, stomach upsets and, alarmingly in Ali's case, earache.

Why do her kids get sick so often? Each time, worst-case scenarios shoot through her mind: a headache could be meningitis, a sore throat may be tonsillitis requiring an operation, a tummyache might signal a burst appendix. The doctor always says something soothing. 'With most of these viruses, Mrs Bradley, you really just have to keep them warm and let nature take its course. Kids haven't been around long enough to meet all the germs and build up their resistance. It's quite normal.' Kate is reassured; still, deep down, she expects the worst.

The magazines make her taste look impersonal. Liven up your bedroom, they shout, by using sensual props. Put a deep, warm colour on the walls. Put up a shelf and stand vases of contrasting flowers on it; burn incense sticks or use scented candles to create a sexy mood. Put attractive, silk-covered cushions on the bed to evoke eastern exoticism, like a harem. In Derbyshire?

Kate experiments. While the children are at school, she drives to Manchester – she has a car of her own now – and goes to her favourite department store. There she runs her fingers across rolls of watered silk and deep-piled velvet in rich blues, greens and purples, and bright cushions edged with beads. She can't picture them in her bedroom, which presumably will emerge from its refit looking as functional as it had when she began. At home, she puts on her dressing-table a vase of her favourite black-centred anemones. It doesn't help. Harem, indeed. The bedroom has become nothing more than a domestic commuter-belt, with the lounge as the capital city in which the family energy is spent and the piano the seat of government at its epicentre.

The bedroom, in short, depresses her. So she starts with the lounge – and when Ali sees the piano covered with a

dustsheet, her howl is so loud that Kate is afraid the neighbours will hear.

Coming out of the department store in Manchester on a damp
winter Thursday at lunchtime, Kate pauses, her hands full of
plastic carrier-bags. Instead of decorating equipment, she's
bought a sports shirt for Adrian, some dog treats for Cassie
and some white wool to knit a jumper for Ali. The *Manchester
Chronicle* offices are a ten-minute stroll away. Perhaps she
could drop in to see Guy. Her drive had been worse than
usual. There'd been road closures and jams; eventually she'd
parked over a mile from the centre and trudged the rest of
the way. Even then she'd been surprised to see some streets
entirely shut off, pavements included; she'd had to take a long
way round. It has left her reluctant to go back to the car too
soon.

How funny, she thinks, that she should hesitate to arrive
unannounced to see her husband. Newspaper headquarters,
though, are frenetic places.

'Is Guy Bradley available?' she asks the receptionist.

'I'll try him for you. What name shall I say?'

'I'm his wife.'

It's years since Kate last visited Guy at work. The people
he talks about are nothing to her but names; and now that
he's been promoted, he has a new office and she can't even
picture him going about his day's work.

'Darling!' Guy bursts into the lobby from a side door.

'I was passing so I thought I'd drop in,' Kate says, feeling
awkward.

'Come up. I've got a meeting in a minute, things are
completely manic today, as you can imagine, but Diane's made
some coffee . . .'

Kate hurries after him through long, modern corridors of
grey paint and greyer carpet. An air of intense concentration hangs over the open-plan offices. Through glass insets

she can spot people typing on computers and talking on phones.

'I'm in the nerve centre now,' Guy tells her, opening doors, bounding up stairs. 'Diane,' he calls to a dark-haired secretary, 'this is Kate. Any chance of a coffee?'

'Hi, Kate!' Diane jumps to attention.

A door opens and someone shouts from inside: 'Guy! Dave needs you to call him urgently about the bombing. The photographer's biked round some shots.'

'OK, Mart,' Guy shouts back.

'Mrs Powers called about the complaint she wants to make,' Diane tells him, from the percolator. 'I said you'd be in touch, but she was a bit upset, so can you call her?'

'Di, please, next time, can you ask her to write to the readers' editor?' Guy begs. 'I keep telling her. She's got to take it on board some time.' He ushers Kate into the rare private office that is his. 'Darling, I won't be a mo,' he says, and dashes away.

Kate, sniffing the synthetic scent of industrial carpet and sipping impossibly stewed coffee, watches her husband through the doorway as he darts around like a beagle responding to a hunting horn. He hurries into another, empty, room and she sees him barking into a phone. There's little to look at outside except the block opposite, where plants on the window-ledges have begun to wilt. Guy's office contains no plants. A picture of the two of them with the children sits beside his computer. His desk is invisible under piles of paper and his shelves are crammed with overflowing box files, reference books and telephone directories.

A plump, balding man in a shirt and tie half strides into the room, then pulls up short on seeing Kate. 'Where's Guy?' he demands.

'Over there.' Kate points. The door shuts as fast as it had opened. Kate feels redundant. The coffee, cooling in the chipped mug, tastes more bitter and poisonous by the moment.

'Guy,' she hears the intruder yell, 'editorial meeting, we need you *now*.'

Guy waves from the phone, finishes his conversation, scoots back to Kate like an actor on speeded-up film. 'Darling, I have to run. The bombing this morning has thrown everything completely. Don't worry, enjoy your coffee, and I'll see you tonight, OK?'

'Bombing?' Kate echoes, but he's vanished before the word is out.

She leaves the mug on the desk and makes her way downstairs. In any case, it's time to head back to collect the children.

No wonder Guy is so tired when he gets home, if he spends his days functioning at such intensity. She feels guilty – she'd intruded on him when a visitor was the last thing he needed. She decides to make amends by cooking him a special dinner.

Kate drags the kids round the supermarket, fielding their demands for crisps and chocolate. She buys chicken, fresh tarragon, a lemon and vegetables, plus a bottle of Australian wine, which the food and drink section of Guy's paper says has recently become more popular than French.

Once the children are in bed, she sets about transforming the kitchen into a more romantic environment, if not quite a Derbyshire harem. She prepares the chicken in a casserole, lights several candles, dims the overhead spotlights, tidies away the toys, then goes upstairs and digs out of a bedroom drawer a low-cut, mid-blue sweater that Guy used to say matched her eyes. She expects him home by eight.

By nine, the candles are burning low and the chicken is more than well cooked. Her stomach is rumbling. Kate opens a packet of Adrian's crisps and pours herself a glass of wine. Her mind delivers disasters. Overturned lorries on the motorway, a mudslide in the hills, a sheep in the road. Sheep are the most dangerous creatures in Derbyshire. She wishes her parents wouldn't laugh at this, because it's true. There are no fences on the moors; sheep can wander freely about. If a sheep goes into the road in the dark and you don't see it in time . . .

Her mother has been telling her about mobile telephones, brick-like gadgets prized as status symbols in London by estate agents and young stockbrokers. Damn the status symbol, Kate thinks, the wine releasing the fury she won't usually let herself feel. It shouldn't be a status symbol but a convenience tool so that people can let each other know when they're going to be late home. Cassie leans her snout on Kate's knee, gazing up at her with deep collie eyes. Kate pets the dog's ears and tries not to let a stubbornly forming tear escape on to the makeup over which she's taken so much trouble.

She drifts upstairs, past the test patches of paint on the walls, and peers into the children's rooms. Adrian is flat on his back with his mouth open, sleeping as only a tired-out small boy can sleep after an afternoon on a cold, muddy sports field. Ali is curled under her blankets clutching a toy penguin, a present from Didie. The sight of them, so small and vulnerable, deepens Kate's maudlin mood. She shouldn't have had so much wine on an empty stomach. She can't help picturing another, imaginary door off the landing; behind it, a small desk bearing a school-book covered in childish handwriting, and in the bed Victoria asleep, ten years old, with blonde hair like her little sister's.

At nine forty-five, the dinner has dried up and Guy is still not home. Kate removes her blue jersey and cleanses away her makeup. In her old towelling dressing-gown, which used to be white, she makes herself a sandwich and a mug of cocoa, then heads for bed.

She is semi-conscious when a warm presence creeps round her in the dark and kisses her forehead.

'Darling. I'm so sorry. These IRA bombs – we had to rejig the front page a hundred times, and then the reports kept coming and—'

'Where were they?'

'In Manchester! You didn't hear? Two IRA bombs went off this morning, one in Parsonage Gardens and another near the Anglican cathedral. How did you manage to be in Manchester and not hear about it?'

Kate, half asleep, can't think straight. Her head hurts – she'll have a hangover tomorrow – and her eyes are sore from crying. So that was why her journey had been difficult. Her mind had been so full of carpets, colours and Ali that she hadn't registered the closures were more than mere roadworks. In the house the radio is tuned permanently to BBC Radio 3, for Ali's sake. She hadn't bothered listening to the news. She remembered hearing someone in the office mention a bombing, but she hadn't imagined that such a thing could have happened right there.

'Darling, you've been crying.'

'I'm sorry,' says Kate. 'I had the dream again.'

4

Guy and Kate, with the children strapped into the back seat and Cassie confined to the luggage area, drive west across the windswept moor. As they descend past brown-red Victorian Macclesfield, the countryside softens. At this lower altitude, the trees seem happier to grow, crops push up green and hopeful in the spring fields and the children shout at the sight of lambs tottering about on unsteady legs.

'Mint sauce!' Guy says.

'Don't be horrid, Daddy,' Alicia chimes.

'I know these lanes so well, children, that I could do the whole drive in reverse gear,' Guy declares over his shoulder.

'You say that every time we come here,' Kate reminds him.

'Will you do it, Daddy? Just once?' Adrian begs. 'It'd be so cool.'

'I don't think Grandma would see it that way,' Kate says.

'*Please*, Dad?'

'Nearly there,' Guy announces. Alicia is singing to herself. Cassie shunts about, making the pleading noises that dogs make when they long to bound unleashed through open, green nature.

The house where Guy grew up stands in a tiny complex at the end of a tree-lined lane. He manoeuvres the car in a flamboyant semi-circle and reverses through the gate, which makes Adrian bounce with excitement. Alicia shouts, 'Grandma!'

Didie is in the drive to welcome them, wearing an apron emblazoned with a cartoon of a woman snoring happily on a sofa while a frazzled man does the washing-up. Alicia charges into her arms. 'What an affectionate child Ali is,' Didie often says. Kate reflects quietly that a child's affection doesn't always direct itself to the mother.

George is in the greenhouse, feeding his plants – he's growing tomatoes, gooseberries, raspberries and a delicate, tangled complex of sweet-peas. He loves retirement with a passion; Didie insists he's busier now than he ever was in accountancy. He wanders out, waving, then ushers them into the house for a glass of refreshing sparkling wine.

Alicia doesn't follow them. A brook crosses the end of the garden; she runs as fast as she can down the sloping lawn to watch the ducks. Grandma Didie, knowing Alicia's Cheshire routine, goes after her.

'These are mallards,' Grandma tells her, taking her hand to stop her getting too close to the water's edge. She's brought out some bread so that Alicia can feed them. 'The ducks with green heads are the males and the brown, speckled ones are the females.'

'They look like different kinds of duck,' Alicia remarks.

'Yes, but they're the same species. And they always know that they belong together.'

Alicia tosses out a handful of bread and the ducks stream towards it, ruffling the water, pecking at each other in their haste. Then her eyes widen. 'Here they come!'

With a smooth motion at the bend in the brook, a line of stately visitors glides into view. A large white swan sails ahead, leading the procession; behind it swim three fluffy, grey cygnets; another adult brings up the rear.

Alicia holds out her hands. Grandma fetches, from beside the garden wall, two plastic bowls, which she fills with loose stuff that reminds Alicia of Mum's breakfast cereal. Grandma hands one bowl to her; she places it ceremoniously, in a familiar ritual, on the grass by the stream.

One by one, the swans drift across and lumber out of the water towards the bowls, abruptly clumsy on their huge black feet. Alicia holds her breath. However often she's seen the swan family come to lunch, she can never quite believe it's real. 'Now will you do the other birds?' she asks.

Grandma winks. She takes two handfuls of seeds, goes to the middle of the lawn and whistles. A moment later the air is shivering with wings. Dark, speckled wings, rustling, swishing, diving. Alicia shrieks, then stops, trying not to scare them off: the starlings soar down from nowhere, some to peck the food from the grass, some to alight on Grandma's hand and grab a seed from her palm. A squirrel loops out of a bush; when Grandma bends and reaches out to it, it makes a lightning motion towards her, then bounces away, a hazelnut in its mouth.

'You can learn a lot from animals, Ali,' Grandma tells her softly. 'What do they say to you?'

'Dunno,' Alicia says. 'But I love them.'

'Why do you love them?'

'Because . . .' Alicia knows what she wants to say, but has trouble finding the words. Animals are easy. You know what they want; you know what they do. Sometimes, with people, you can't tell what they're going to do or say next.

'They're natural,' Grandma prompts her. 'It's lovely to be natural. Sometimes nature can be cruel, but mostly it's beautiful and good.'

Alicia drinks in the horizon of grassy hills and turquoise sky, and nods.

A volley of barks from Cassie, furious to have been shut inside while this goes on, sends the birds wheeling into the air. Alicia dances back to her dog. Adrian trails out of the house. 'Adie, we saw the swans and the ducks!' Alicia cries.

'I hate ducks,' says Adrian. 'They give me the creeps. Quack, quack, quack. They sound like Mum fussing over you.'

★   ★   ★

Didie has been busy in the kitchen, making a pot of vegetable soup, baking olive bread and setting out delicious bits and pieces from the village delicatessen. Guy and Kate prefer Didie's unpredictable feasts to the overcooked beef and soggy Yorkshire pudding that always greets them at Sunday lunches in Harrow (luckily, comparatively rare events). Didie displays roasted Italian peppers, sun-dried tomatoes and some Parma ham as if exhibiting them at the Chelsea Flower Show; in the centre a blue and white tiled platter, a souvenir from Amsterdam, is set with a selection of intriguingly patterned cheeses.

'"Cheese, please, Louise,"' Guy quotes.

'You always have to say that,' Kate growls.

'I remember,' says George. 'That advert, back in the sixties.'

'I don't remember the ad,' Guy says, 'but *you* always said, "Cheese, please, Louise", so it stuck.'

Kate finds that it's hard to laugh at a joke when you have heard it more than four thousand times.

'Then there's the baked beans one . . .' Guy begins to sing a decades-old jingle.

'Fresh out of baked beans, dears.' Didie notices Kate fidgeting. 'Adie, darling, have some more bread.'

'Don't like olive bread.'

'Where's Ali?' George asks.

'I know exactly where she is.' Didie smiles.

A thread of music reaches them from the lounge. Nobody thinks of confining Alicia to lunch when there's a piano around. She's had some food – and gone. The others fall silent, listening despite themselves.

'Did she bring her music?' George asks.

'No,' Kate says. 'She plays from memory.'

'Katie,' Didie says, 'I know I say this every time, but she's *musical*. She makes you listen to her, God knows how. She doesn't sound like a child who's only six years old. She plays like a real musician. How—?'

'Does she know?' Guy finishes the sentence. 'We don't understand either.'

'Didie . . .' Kate has been trying to pluck up the courage to face an issue that she doesn't want to face; if the answer is what she expects, her little girl is no longer a baby, but something much more complicated.

Didie's wise, dark eyes are all attention.

'Do you really think Ali has something extra? Some kind of natural gift? A vocation?'

'Anyone with half a brain can see that,' George declares. 'Katie, that granddaughter of mine is a flipping child prodigy.'

Kate looks at Didie, who nods.

There's a sound of heavy, childish footsteps and Alicia appears in the doorway. 'Come on, everyone!' she announces. 'I'm ready now.'

'She always has to do this.' Adrian kicks the table leg. 'It's boring! She always has to play. She always has to make everyone stop what they're doing and listen. I hate the piano.' He kicks harder.

'Adrian! Stop it!' Kate snaps.

'All right, Ali, let's be having you, then, lass.' George leads the way to the lounge. Cassie has already taken up her vantage-point beside the piano.

Her audience in place, Alicia goes out and conceals herself behind a wall. Then she marches in to obliging applause. She's big for her age, as Kate had been as a child; her feet and hands resemble the large paws that betray the size to which a lion cub will grow. She walks with the determination of a shot-putter and the pride of an Olympic champion, then bows as if she has never seen her family before.

She plays, in succession, all the pieces she has already run through in a rehearsal that she doesn't know is called a rehearsal. Her memory never falters. The piano hasn't been tuned for a year and some of the notes stick; Alicia pulls a face when she can't induce the exact sound she wants.

'Show-off,' Adrian grumbles.

Kate knows she isn't showing off. She is doing what an Alicia does. A swan knows that it must live upon water. Alicia, too, is a child of nature. She doesn't question why she is who she is, but she knows she must play a piano and she wants, instinctively, to play to people. There's no reason for it. It's just how Alicias are made.

Taking the baby Adrian in her arms for the first time, Kate's initial sensation was relief. The next was dismay. She'd expected something else. She wanted the feeling she'd experienced before: the sense that that helpless, microscopic creature needed her so much. The new infant was all he ought to have been. He weighed eight and a half pounds, yelled with well-formed lungs and wriggled and kicked with a vigour that told her he wanted to get away from her and head out to the football field, fast. She wasn't sure how to hold him, how to soothe him, how to breastfeed him. His greed left her nipples raw and painful. His restless nights meant that she had to walk him up and down the lounge for hours, jigging and humming, which seemed to make no difference.

She had what she'd wanted: a healthy baby. Yet now that she had one, she didn't know what to do with him.

'I can't help it,' she admitted to Guy one weekend, when Adrian was seven months old and they were all confined to the house with raging colds. 'I still keep looking at him and expecting to see Victoria.'

'Katie.' Guy's head was under a towel, where he was inhaling eucalyptus. 'Different baby. He's strong. He's normal. He laughs and cries and has a healthy appetite, and if you dropped him, he'd bounce. What more do you want?'

Kate could hardly disagree, but neither could she understand why she didn't love Adrian enough. Perhaps because he was a boy; his experience would never match hers. Or perhaps because he had committed the innocent yet cardinal sin of not being Victoria. When he eventually took the bottle instead of the breast, she felt guilty and relieved in almost equal measures – the balance favouring the relief.

Alicia arrived two years later, surrounded by magic numbers. She was Kate's third-born, thrice blessed. Her birthday was the third day of the seventh month and Kate laboured for seven hours to give birth to her. The sun was shining and Alicia's eyes were as blue as the sky when she first gazed upon it. And why Kate connected at once with this infant the way she could not with her sulky, whiny two-year-old – perhaps even more than with their sister, lying in the cemetery on the outskirts of Buxton – was something as mysterious to her as the birth of a child is in itself.

'Aren't there any of those little competitive music festivals in Derbyshire?'

Margaret, during one of the Davises' rare visits to Buxton, is pondering Alicia's future.

'She's too little.' Kate is terse, annoyed. Having her parents to stay, with their judgemental views on child-rearing, isn't her favourite way to spend a weekend.

'But these events are so good for children, dear. We put you in for your first one on that little three-quarter-sized violin when you were nine.'

'Ali is only seven. And you weren't too pleased when I started taking the viola seriously.'

'I'm not suggesting for a moment that Ali should follow this as a profession. Merely that you give her a chance to be motivated. Winning a prize . . .'

'In case you hadn't noticed, Mother, Ali *is* motivated. I can't keep her away from the thing. But she's too little to go on stage.'

'Maybe after another year, then. Depending on how she develops.'

'We'll see, Mother.'

Kate finds it difficult to keep the anger out of her voice. She's not sure which is worse: her mother advising her to follow the same course of action that had caused Kate herself so much pain, or the idea of Ali being turned into a performing monkey, to be gawped at by the good people of Derbyshire. A premonition slews through her mind: she'll have enough of this later.

From the *Buxton Advertiser*, 18 May 1995
ALICIA IN WONDERLAND

Little Alicia Bradley (left), 8, wields her trophy proudly after winning the Under-11s Piano Class in the Ashton Music Festival last week. 'I'm really happy,' the Buxton schoolgirl said. 'And my dad's pleased too.' Alicia Bradley's father, Guy, 39, is deputy editor of the *Manchester Chronicle*.

Alicia, with her long fair hair and blue dress, looked as if she had stepped from the pages of *Alice in Wonderland*. She played a movement from a Bach French Suite and the Waltz in D flat major by Chopin to gain her prize.

From the *Derbyshire Herald*, 10 July 1996
ALICIA PULLS IT OFF

Alicia Bradley (10) is the winner of this year's Under-12s piano class in the Derbyshire Festival. Alicia, described by her teacher Jonathan Bowen as 'the most talented pupil I've ever had', played alongside 15 other competitors to carry off the prize.

'I wasn't nervous,' Alicia said, backstage after performing a Mozart sonata and a Chopin mazurka, which drew gasps of delight from the audience. 'I never get nervous. I just enjoy playing. I love being on stage.'

Alicia's mother, Kate Bradley (40), says that Alicia gets up at six every morning to practise before school. 'It's part of her daily routine,' said Mrs Bradley.

What of Alicia's future? Could this Derbyshire lass one day

grace the platforms of the country's finest concert halls? 'Alicia has the natural gift to go anywhere she wants,' said Mr Bowen. 'But becoming a professional pianist takes a great deal of hard work and nothing in the musical world is ever certain, even for those who have such talent. I hope she has the chance to fulfil her potential in every way.'

From the *Sheffield Gazette*, 12 September 1998
PEAK DISTRICT PRODIGY

The North of England Festival yesterday made an unprecedented award to a 12-year-old girl from Buxton, Derbyshire. Instead of entering the Under-13s piano class, Alicia Bradley followed the suggestion of her Manchester-based teacher, the eminent professor Deirdre Butterworth, and performed in the Under-16s section. She faced stiff competition from students several years her senior.

Young Alicia wore a plain blue dress and flat shoes. She played a movement from Beethoven's 'Pathétique' Sonata, Mendelssohn's 'Spring Song' and a challenging piece by Debussy entitled 'Gardens in the Rain'. 'I live in Buxton, so I know a bit about rain,' Alicia joked afterwards, preparing to pin up her certificate on a bedroom wall that, according to her mother, Kate Bradley, is crowded with similar success stories.

Mrs Bradley, 42, has recently resigned from her job as a solicitor in Buxton to concentrate on taking care of her exceptional daughter. 'Alicia's talent demands complete commitment from us as her parents,' she explains. She ferries Alicia weekly to Manchester for lessons with Mrs Butterworth, who was recommended to the family by Alicia's former teacher, Jonathan Bowen, until last term head of music at Parkhill School where Alicia is now a pupil. This month he takes up a post as head of music at Elthingbourne College, Dorset.

'We couldn't be happier,' said her proud mother. 'I can imagine no better vocation than giving Alicia the attention, help and support that she needs.'

'Are you sure?' says Guy.

'One good reason why not?' asks Kate.

'You're good at your job. Your clients like you. Mike values you.'

'What you mean is, because you're at work the whole time, I should be as well. Because otherwise I'll just be at home wondering where you are.'

'Katie, for heaven's sake—'

'Well? Isn't that so?'

'I worry that you're going to be lonely.'

'I want to be there for Ali. If I can help her with her practising and drive her to her lessons and yell at the school when they try to make her play dangerous ball games, then my time will be well spent.' She doesn't meet his gaze.

Every Wednesday Kate bundles Alicia into the car with her books of music, which now include the second volume of Beethoven's piano sonatas, as well as Chopin's Études and Rachmaninov's Preludes. Alicia finishes school early on Wednesdays. The other kids have sport, drama and occasional outings to local stately homes or walks on the moors; Alicia goes to her piano lesson in Manchester.

Mrs Butterworth teaches at her home, a double-fronted Edwardian house in Withington, its front garden florid with lilacs. She lives alone; Mr Butterworth, an architect, has been dead for years. Kate's tentative enquiries about what had happened to him produce a stony response.

Jonathan's recommendation hadn't been without sub-clauses and small print: 'She's tough but very effective, and she'll equip Ali with a sound technique for life,' he'd said. 'She's controversial in some circles, she's not for everyone, but I have great respect for her. Why not just see how you get along?'

'When I met my husband in 1965 and set up my teaching practice,' Mrs Butterworth tells Kate, at Alicia's initial consultation, 'I had to contend with the fact that there is no *system* in this country. Children do well at school, they go to good universities, they do sport, sport and more sport. But music? Forget it. There's no system.'

'What about the Associated Board exams?' Kate asks.

'Oh, yes. Music exams.' Mrs Butterworth stifles a yawn.

Kate stares at Mrs Butterworth's hair, mid-brown and bundled into a chignon above the tiny, light-boned figure that she makes up for with force of presence. She wonders whether the chignon is a wig.

'Everything here,' the sharp-eyed teacher carries on, 'is built around helping amateur children to impress amateur parents. They play nicely to the dinner guests and sometimes they play for school assembly and everybody claps. They're nice, middle-class children showing off, by implication, what nice, middle-class parents they have. Isn't that *nice*? That, Mrs Bradley, Alicia, is not what my teaching is about.'

Kate nods. She's starting, unaccountably, to like Mrs Butterworth. She may seem a tad scary, with her uncompromising manner and fierce gaze, but she knows all about the social scene that had damaged Kate so much.

'No!' Mrs Butterworth slaps a hand against the arm of her chair. Kate jumps. 'The British view music as a diversion, an amusement, something that it's not quite cricket to be too good at. If you're talented, people think you must be a snobby little élitist. But in Paris, where I studied first, young pianists were properly equipped with technique from the start, both pianistic and musical. They learned *solfège*. They could play anything in any key. And in Russia, where I studied for years, great art was almost a matter of life and death. I have a talented student. He's twenty-one, he's going to play in America for the first time. And his visa says 'Entertainer'. At the Moscow Conservatoire we were taught to be *artists*. Not clowns. Not acrobats. Not fire-eaters. Those are entertainers. We have something profound to say about life, why we're alive, what it means to be human. We don't jump through hoops to show our parents' friends how talented our parents' offspring are. Now, *do you understand?*'

Kate flinches, but declares, with feeling, 'I certainly do.'

'And you?' Mrs Butterworth's piercing gaze falls on Alicia, who has been sitting, silent, in the corner of a large leather sofa, one hand on Cassie's head (fortunately Mrs Butterworth likes dogs). 'Are you ready? Because this isn't going to be fun and games. This is not an afternoon out, enjoying yourself. You've been playing at playing. You have talent, young lady, but you've barely scratched the surface of the technique you need if you're going to make music your life. If you come to me, Alicia, you will be working harder than you've ever imagined. But remember this: what you sow, you reap. And when you come out, you won't be an English amateur. You'll be ready to become an artist. Is that what you want?'

Kate watches Alicia raise her chin, look Mrs Butterworth in the eye, and say, 'Yes.'

The reality is less easy to accept.

Mrs Butterworth sets her three times as much work as Jonathan had. The studies by Pischna and Moszkowski are supposed to stretch her – but it takes three hours at the piano every day to get through them and all the new pieces, without the frequent playing-through that is, naturally, what Alicia likes best. That's forbidden, and would be even if she could already play, fluently, every note on the pages. As for the scales—

'I can't,' says Alicia, at six thirty one freezing January morning.

'You can. You always have,' Kate reminds her.

'Not Russian scales. Not now.'

Russian scales involve processes that Kate suspects Jonathan Bowen has never heard of. Alicia starts at the bottom of the keyboard and goes up the scale for two octaves. Then her right hand continues up for another two octaves while her left hand goes back down in 'contrary motion'. Both hands return to where they left off; in 'similar motion' they continue up another two octaves then down the same two octaves; then part company for two octaves, back and forth, in contrary motion; finally they run back to the starting point at the bottom. She has to play this pattern fluently and fast in every key. Next she has to do the same, but with her hands a third apart and then a sixth apart; with different kinds of touch – legato, non-legato, staccato; and in rhythms that Kate hadn't realised scales could have.

As for the technical studies, each has to be played accurately in its original key – then transposed into any key that Mrs Butterworth happens to name. A piece in E major must suddenly be played in B flat major. Alicia's unerring ear is an advantage. But for every triumph, there is a stiff price (apart from Mrs Butterworth's fee, which, compared to Jonathan's, is from another planet). One task successfully accomplished means another for next week commensurately more demanding – set not with praise for Alicia's achievement but with a brusque, wordless nod. It reminds Kate, applying ash-blonde colourant in the bathroom, of the rumour that if you pull out one grey hair, two, twice as strong, will grow in its place.

'I can't,' says Alicia.

'You must,' says Kate.

'I can't,' Alicia says, in the car, a year later, outside Mrs Butterworth's house in Withington. 'I can't go in.'

'Ali, we've been here for fifteen minutes and it's not going to get any easier. The longer you leave it, the harder it will be. So go in. *Now.*'

Alicia gets out and walks slowly up to Mrs Butterworth's house. There she slumps on to the step with her back to the door, head in her hands. Cassie, confined to the car, watches, whines and barks.

Kate follows Alicia and sits down next to her. A film of sweat laces Alicia's forehead, and she is breathing too hard.

'Ali, are you all right?'

'No! I'm bloody petrified!'

'Language. Please. Darling.'

'You try, then! You don't know what it's like because she won't let you in the room while it's going on!'

'Ali. Sssh. It's going to be fine. You've made so much progress—'

'I can't go in.'

Kate puts an arm round her shoulders and holds her. 'Got the envelope?' she asks. Mrs Butterworth likes to be paid her substantial fee in cash, in a white envelope that must be handed over upon the student's arrival. Her eyes gleam when her fingers close round it, Alicia reports. Kate, listening to her description, tries not to imagine an iguana curling its tongue over a fly. 'In you go. OK?'

Alicia rises on shaky feet and presses the bell.

The latest festival, delivering Alicia's biggest trophy to date, declared her its most gifted winner ever. Alicia had accepted with the requisite modesty. It's not really *done* to admit the hours of slog involved – somehow the public expects music to be as natural as breathing – so Alicia says little about how hard she works. Kate says nothing to her interested neighbours or her book club (discussing *Captain Corelli's Mandolin* over coffee at the Pavilion Gardens) of the way she too gets up at six and stands directing Alicia like a conductor. 'Again! And again! Once more for luck . . . Now try it in D minor . . . and F minor . . .' She doesn't even tell Glenda, whom she sees frequently and who always wants to hear about Alicia's progress. Some instinct tells her that Glenda might respond in the wrong way.

'Katie,' Guy says wearily, searching for his keys one morning, 'Ali's only thirteen. This is ridiculous.'

'I didn't ask her to be talented,' Kate retorts. 'I didn't ask her to want to be a pianist. But she can't have it both ways. She can't expect to be what she wants to be without hard work.'

'On Sunday afternoon, why don't we go out, like a normal family? We'll go for a walk at Dovedale, or we could take the kids to Alton Towers . . .'

'Ali can't go to Alton Towers. The rides are too dangerous.'

'No, they're not. Thousands of kids do those rides every day.'

'Thousands of kids don't depend on their hands for their career.'

'Oh, it's a career now, is it?'

'To me, this hardly looks like a hobby.'

'I've got to go. I'll be late for the editorial meeting. Have you seen my keys?'

'Just keep track of your own damn keys for once!' Kate slams the lounge door.

'Oh, Mum,' comes Alicia's muffled, tearful voice from the direction of the piano, 'please don't yell at Dad. It's not his fault.'

5

They go to Dovedale, not Alton, for a January Sunday of fresh air, exercise and countryside. In summer, they avoid this walk – it's one of the Peak District's top tourist favourites, thanks to its deep-sliced, relatively sheltered valley and a set of wide stepping-stones upon which everyone loves to leap across the fast-flowing River Dove. But today only hardened locals are about, greeting each other when they pass on the pathway; the sole tourists are a distressed-looking Spanish couple who aren't used to the cold.

Walking is good for us, Kate reminds herself, tucking her scarf into her padded jacket. Walking is when talking can take place, assuming it ever will.

It's freezing, but unusually bright; the air feels as if it's been poured out of a mountain glacier; the river, swollen with winter rain and melted ice, dances along its pebble-strewn bed more excitably than usual. Alicia, high on freedom, taps her brother's shoulder. 'Race you!' she shouts – and they're off, running, yelling and pushing each other like any teenage brother and sister in the sunlight. Cassie bounds along beside them. Guy and Kate, watching, join hands.

'Let's stop at the Hartington cheese shop on the way back and get some Stilton,' Kate suggests.

'"Cheese, please, Louise."' Guy looks at her from the corner of his eye. 'We could try their Wensleydale with cranberries for a change.'

Kate smiles. She's enjoying this. It's a long time since the Bradleys last had an afternoon out. With the demands of Guy's office, never mind the Derbyshire weather, they're lucky if they have even one Sunday each month on which they could, potentially, go for a walk. But Guy is still a hiker, the way Ali is a pianist, a swan is a waterbird and Adrian is – whatever Adrian really is, which so far hasn't become apparent.

They cross the arching wooden footbridge and Guy sets a brisk pace along the riverside path, his boots laced up to his ankles, a stick in one hand and one of Kate's home-knitted scarves round his neck.

'Adie, don't!' Kate hears Alicia say.

There's a plop and an angry rustle of wings and webbed feet on water: Adrian is throwing stones at ducks from the riverbank.

'Adrian! Stop it!' Kate runs towards him. 'What do you think you're doing?'

'I hate ducks. They're disgusting. I hate the noise they make.'

Kate senses the eyes of at least five other huddles of walkers burning into her and her peculiar son. The poor ducks: helpless scapegoats for a lot else that Adrian hates. 'I don't care whether you like them or not,' she snaps. 'You're not going to throw stones at them.'

'You're talking to me like I'm a kid.'

Adrian's dark eyes are so resentful that an image of a changeling with horns skids across Kate's retinas.

'If you behave like one, what do you expect?'

Guy is keeping a safe distance; she wonders vaguely why he doesn't come to help her with a little discipline. He looks oddly distant; as if only half of him is standing in Dovedale waiting for his family to get its act together. Exasperated, Kate turns her attention back to her teenagers. Someone has to.

Alicia and Adrian barely seem like siblings, though physically they are almost replicas of their parents. Adrian could have been made to a template of Guy aged fifteen and Alicia to one of Kate at thirteen – but for the addition, in Adrian's case, of rapidly increasing height, complicated by a taut, sizzling frustration that resembles a furious wasp; and, in Alicia's case, an inbuilt candle flame that reignites no matter how hard anyone tries to extinguish it. Ali, Kate fancies, represents day and Adrian night. She and Guy are the opposite. Guy is the warm, active sun and she – even if she wasn't always – has become the moon, filled with inexpressible shadows in shades of deepening grey.

'What do you think?' Guy is asking her.

'Sorry, I missed that. I was miles away.'

'About Adrian and school. Mr Browning didn't mince his words.'

The parents' evening two days earlier hadn't been the best of occasions. First, the PE teacher had had views on Alicia's music. 'Such a pity she can't enjoy the piano as part of a broad spectrum of interests,' she'd remarked. 'It seems rather sad and a little precious that she must miss out on hockey to protect her hands. It's not like she's going to be Daniel Barenboim.' Kate, furious, had demanded, 'Have you *heard* her play?' and the woman had admitted she hadn't. As for Adrian's Mr Browning—

'He doesn't mix easily with the others, though, goodness knows, fifteen is a tricky age,' he'd remarked. 'He's a good lad, though. He's good at French.'

'French? Adrian?' Kate was incredulous.

'And art. He's a creative boy, but complicated. Angry, I'd say.'

'I'd had the impression he wasn't much good at anything,' Kate admitted. 'Getting him to do his homework is a daily battle. He only wants to watch television.'

'Like every other lad his age. Perhaps a little more encouragement?'

'It's not like we don't try.'

'He's capable of doing well. He's bright,' Mr Browning

affirmed, shaking their hands. Just as they began to move away, he cleared his throat. 'Um, Mrs Bradley. Are you aware that Adrian didn't come in on Wednesday?'

'Wednesday? This last Wednesday?' A brake screeched in Kate's brain. 'I was out all day after twelve – it's Ali's piano lesson on Wednesday – but as far as I know Adrian went to school in the morning.'

'I'd like you to keep half an eye on him. Make sure he's where he should be when he should be. All right?'

Now, in the ravine beneath the steep hills and bare trees, Kate looks at Adrian's back a little way ahead: dark hair, fleecy jacket, a determined walk, as if he's been watching gangster movies and is bent on emulating them. He's growing fast; perhaps his build is following her father's. William had been a keen rugby player and still looked the part, tall, broad and hulking. He'd been a Boy Scout and a prefect at public school; he'd done a stint in the army. He and Margaret go to church every Sunday. He'd had a calling, Kate thinks, to be *good*. Adrian, though, moves between shadows and light without noticing the difference.

Kate can hear a thread of music through the soft rush of the river. Alicia is singing to herself.

'I guess it's not easy to be her brother,' Guy remarks quietly.

'Do you think it's true about him not going to school last Wednesday?'

'Wednesday?' Guy echoes.

Suddenly he isn't with her any more. He's – somewhere else. What had happened on Wednesday? Kate remembers the day she'd failed to hear about the IRA bombings and wonders what she's missed this time.

They turn back after an hour, the children and dog well exercised, Kate chilly, tired and aware of something uncomfortable in her husband's state of being. All of them are looking forward to a good hot drink from the wooden coffee and ice-cream stall beside the car park. On the final stretch, Kate and

Alicia hurry ahead for the loos; Guy goes to buy some tea. Adrian waits with Cassie on the riverside path, upstream from the weir.

When Kate and Alicia return, the spot that had held boy and dog is empty.

'Adrian!' shouts Kate.

Guy comes up the path, two cups of tea and two of hot chocolate balanced between his hands.

'Where's Adrian? Where's the dog?' Kate demands.

'Probably throwing stones at ducks again,' Alicia grumbles. As she speaks, there's a splash and a shout, and before she knows what she's doing, Kate is running, terror-stricken, across the muddy stretch of grass and bracken towards the riverbank, her walking-boots too heavy on her feet.

'Adrian!'

The boy, who'd been hidden by a clump of bushes, comes out into the open and Kate gasps with relief – until she sees that his eyes are fixed on the water, a pair of pointed ears and a set of frantic, scrabbling paws. Cassie loves to splash about in shallow rivers, but she's not used to this powerful winter current. Somehow she's paddled further in than she should have and the water has grabbed her, threatening to sweep her away towards the narrow yet treacherous stone weir.

'Cassie!' yells Alicia. Before Kate can grab hold of her, she's off.

Everything happens so fast that Kate barely has time to take it in. Yet those twenty seconds also move in slow motion, opaque beads of spray springing around Alicia as she charges into the water. Kate hears herself scream, 'Ali, *no*!'

'Ali, come back!' Guy rushes after her.

A crowd of fellow walkers assembles to try to help. 'Call the warden!' someone shouts. 'The poor things, they'll freeze!'

Alicia is reaching towards the struggling Cassie, wading forward through the surging current. Guy stumbles towards her and grabs her waist. Alicia gives a shout of protest, turns and, as Kate watches, misses her footing, felling them both. Alicia is briefly submerged; Guy, picking himself up and trying to pull her out, twists, then yelps as if in pain. At the same moment, someone bumps into Kate and the jolt sets off tears of fright that she doesn't want to shed in front of her son. Why can't she turn the clock back just ten minutes? How could she have been stupid enough to leave Adrian to his own devices? This is his fault, which means it's hers.

'There, there, love, they'll be all right.' A stranger's arm is round her shoulders. 'The river's not deep. Don't you worry, we'll have them out in no time.'

'My little girl,' Kate chokes out. She feels faint; black dots fizz behind her eyes. It's the shock, the anger and, of course, the alarm that assails her as it always has when Alicia is in danger.

A big, sopping, brown and white shape is loping towards her; stopping nearby, it shakes a fountain of river water out of its long-haired coat before leaping up to lick her face. Cassie is fine. Just a dog going for a swim, her big, innocent eyes tell Kate. Dogs like swimming. What's wrong with that?

Kate rubs tears and wet dog out of her face and sees Guy and Alicia, supporting each other, hobbling along the riverbank. Guy releases his drenched daughter, then flops on to the grass, clutching his foot.

'Mum, is Cassie OK?' pleads the saturated Alicia. Water is streaming from her clothes and hair.

'You *stupid* girl! What the hell did you think you were doing?' Kate explodes.

'Katie.' Guy, on the ground, is ashen. 'I think I've broken something. I bashed my ankle and it's bloody excruciating.'

Alicia, hugging her sodden dog, is shivering.

'Guy, we've got to get Ali home, she'll catch her death. Can you walk to the car?'

Guy, who's shivering too, tries to stand up, but can't.

'Ali, are your hands OK?' Kate demands.

Alicia nods, big-eyed and shame-faced.

Adrian is hanging his head in a way that Kate recognises. 'Adrian, why did you let Cassie go into the water?'

'But, Mum, she just, like, went off and—'

'And what were *you* doing? Can't I trust you to be on your own without causing trouble for even two minutes?'

Guy has been helped up and is now supported by the girl from the coffee stall on one side and Alicia on the other. Together they manage to manoeuvre him across the last hundred yards to the car. Kate takes the driving seat and rifles through the road atlas to locate the nearest hospital with an A and E department. Guy, beside her, props up his injured foot on his backpack; he breathes deeply, trying to bear the pain. Kate pulls off her own jersey and insists Alicia wears it instead of her wet clothes. Alicia huddles in the back seat, sipping hot chocolate. Cassie, in the rear, and Adrian, beside Alicia, are in disgrace.

Kate stews together relief, fury and a perplexed sensation that she can't identify. *What kind of a child rushes into a winter river to save her dog?* It's unthinking instinct. The urge to rescue something she loves.

Alicia grins at her mother in the mirror. 'Dad saved me,' she declares.

'Just don't ever make me do it again,' Guy groans.

Guy is trying to hide extra distress that he's afraid Kate will notice: there's more on his mind than a broken ankle.

'Bosnia?' said Martin.

'Sarajevo,' said Emily Andersen.

Guy and Martin, as deputy editor and editor, were spending Wednesday afternoon interviewing candidates for the post of staff reporter.

'This is what I wrote. And here are the photos.' Emily handed

Martin a plastic folder. Guy took in the headline, the pock-marked walls, the dark-eyed children.

'It was an incredible project.' Emily's voice cracked a little as the memory moved her. 'The way music helped those children was one of the most extraordinary things I've ever seen. It taps into emotions they can't express any other way.'

Guy glanced at Martin's notepad, where the editor had written:

BAGS OF INITIATIVE
BAGS OF COMMITMENT
NICE TITS

'I know certain parts of the north-west can resemble a war zone at times,' Martin was saying, 'but your work here would be a little more mundane. You'd be reporting on issues like cleanliness in hospitals, talking to people having difficulty paying their council tax or, if you're lucky, rooting out corruption in the running of a posh golf club. How are you going to feel about that after your freelance adventures?'

'Fine,' Emily said. 'That's what I need at the moment.'

'So, basically, you'd like a salary because you want to settle down?'

'I want a place of my own, I want to live near my mother, because she's alone now, and I'd like a little more security in my life.'

Emily looked each of them in the eye. She had a strong, direct gaze, neither aggressive nor defensive. Her eyes were a peculiar silvery grey. Her father, who had died a year ago, had been Danish and she'd spent her early years in Aarhus. Her hair was brown, but shone gold when sunlight struck it. Her skin was fair, her mouth wide and full-lipped. She had shortish legs, a deeply curved lower back and a generous, spreading behind. Her CV told Guy that she was thirty.

'Any special enthusiasms – other than war zones – that you'd like to be writing about?' Martin asked her.

'I love walking, which is another reason I want to live here. I love music, and I'd like to write about that more than I do. But I like talking to people about what's important to them. I like being in the middle of things.'

'Pressure? Deadlines?'

'No problem. I work well under pressure.'

'Which are your favourite walks?' Guy asked her. He didn't know why. The words slipped out before he could stop them.

'The Peak District,' Emily replied, unhesitating. 'I love it. One day I'd like to live in one of those wonderful villages in Derbyshire, like Castleton.'

'Castleton!' Guy echoed. 'I go there whenever I can! And do you know the cheese factory at Hartington?'

'Best Stilton in the country!' Emily's face lit up.

Perhaps at this moment, or perhaps earlier – he would never be certain of anything except that it had happened – a synapse in Guy's mind flipped silently inside out. 'Did you ever try their Wensleydale with cranberries?' he was saying, semi-conscious yet super-conscious.

Martin cleared his throat softly, with a pointed glance at the office clock.

'Anything else we can tell you about, Emily?' he said. 'Apart from Wensleydale with cranberries?'

Guy sat alone in his office with his face in his hands. He pressed his eyelids with his fingers until he saw rippling patterns in red and orange rolling from left to right.

This, he reminded himself, is one of the greatest mysteries known to mankind. One moment you're having a normal day; the next, you look into a stranger's face and recognise it, as if you and she have known one another for longer than both of you have been alive. You love your job. You meet fascinating situations, interesting people and beautiful women all the time. But this experience is beyond you. There's no obvious reason for it. Of course there's beauty in the soul of someone who's moved by music therapy for children in Sarajevo and who's brave enough to go there to write about it; and there's beauty in grey eyes and soft, shining hair. But why she should give him the jolt of recognition that changes the structure of the world in one stroke – that nobody can explain; and nothing can change it now that it's happened.

He wasn't sure which would be worse: Emily getting the job, or Emily not getting the job. If she did, he'd have to see her around the office, make chit-chat with her in the canteen, sit across the table from her at meetings, have her presence constantly, excruciatingly close. A small, quiet pressure, like water-torture. Perhaps he should insist that they don't accept her; he should say she was too ambitious and internationally minded for a provincial paper. She'd use them as a stepping-stone and move on.

The alternative, though, was never to see her again. And that he couldn't stand. His world was half the world it had been two hours earlier.

'So, Guy, what do you make of our candidates?' Martin wandered into Guy's office and sat down.

'Thinking it over. What about you?'

'Emily Andersen is head and shoulders above the others.'

Guy thought of the scribbled notes on Martin's pad. Emily did have nice tits, it was undeniable, but that, oddly, didn't matter to him. It wasn't what he saw when he looked at her. *O she doth teach the torches to burn bright.* Nice tits you can deal with. Shakespearean *coups-de-foudre* you can't. 'I wonder whether she'll stay, given that she's so talented,' he said. Perhaps it would be better to prise her out of the picture before she'd entered it.

'Yes, she may not be a staff reporter for long,' Martin assents. 'But there's plenty of room for someone so bright to climb the ladder. I think we should grab her. I'll draft the letter right away. OK?'

So Emily Andersen is about to join the *Manchester Chronicle* and not only Guy's ankle, but also his mind is in splinters.

Guy makes his way to his desk under the eaves; the sound of Alicia's piano drifts from the lounge. Going upstairs takes a long time with his injury. Now that he's there, he may as well stay. He pushes aside a pile of papers on the floor, unlocks the desk's bottom drawer and takes out a yellow notebook he hasn't looked at for years. This was the book in which he used to attempt to write poetry. It's been a decade or more since he last tried, but he still keeps it near him, just in case. He leafs through the pages, noticing the long-term evolution of his own handwriting. These days, it's no longer the impulsive scrawl of an ambitious youngster; it's smaller, marginally neater, but the pressure is stronger, the lines fuller and more sensual.

He reads words he barely remembers writing, phrases about the mystery of balance between life and death, as fine as a skein of silk; about painful inability to get through to the person you love, however much you adore them; about the way a landscape can be part of you and you a part of it, as if you are made of earth, stone and water. Some of the poems, he acknowledges, are appalling. Others aren't as bad as he'd expected. He opens a fresh page and makes a mark on it with a ballpoint pen. The words won't come. He may be a writer, but even he can't find the language to express the cataclysmic shock of looking into Emily Andersen's face.

There's a knock on the door. Guy shoves the notebook under a heap of paid bills awaiting filing (as they have been for several months).

Kate looks round the door, her gaze taking in Guy Bradley in his natural habitat: papery chaos. 'Coffee?' she says.

'Darling, you're a mind-reader.' Guy pushes his chair back

and pats his knee. Kate comes over, casting around for spare desk space on which to balance the coffee cup. She perches briefly on his lap and kisses his nose.

'It's wonderful being home,' Guy says. 'Can't we go to bed while the kids are at school?'

'It's Wednesday,' Kate points out. 'It's Ali's lesson.'

'Tomorrow, then.'

'What about your foot?'

'I don't need my foot in bed.' Wednesday again, thinks Guy. It's a whole week ago; yet only a week. He's acting out the self he had been then. He's speaking on automatic pilot words he'd have spoken genuinely just eight days ago.

'When did you last tidy up in here?' his wife asks.

'I can't find anything if I tidy up.'

'But all these filing cabinets—'

'When I file things, I can't remember what I filed them under. This way I know where things are. There's method to my madness, Katie.'

'Glad to hear it.' Kate makes for the door. 'I have to get Ali ready to go.'

Kate. The same Kate he'd always loved, but remoulded by life like a pebble watered and whittled under the stream. The same, yet not the same. In the woman he can still see the girl, the golden-haired student with her extraordinary smile in the Cheviot rain, but he can never grasp the essence of what makes her herself. How can he imagine that he understands Emily Andersen, after a single meeting, as securely as if she were his twin? Is he going crazy?

With a pounding noise on the stairs, Alicia is there, a bolt of electricity bowling towards him. Her arms fly round his neck and her warm cheek presses against his.

'Darling,' he says. 'Have a good lesson.'

'Dad, I wish you were home all the time!' She kisses him noisily beside one ear. 'Gotta run, see you later.' And she's gone.

Stranded at home, he's been listening to her practising, with incomprehension, delight and deep-seated fear. Hearing her soar through Beethoven's 'Les Adieux' Sonata, he can't help wondering what her gift means for her future; all their futures. 'A good servant but a bad master,' was how Margaret had once described Kate's passion for the viola. The piano was neither servant nor master to Alicia: she simply couldn't do without it. He thought of her running through Dovedale, her fair hair flying, before she went charging into the river after her dog. One moment she was a normal child. The next, she was not.

Now, from the low-set loft window, Guy can see her climbing into the car beside Kate, cradling a bulging music case. Guy has never met Mrs Butterworth. He doesn't like the sound of her and he doesn't like the way she makes Alicia spend her time. When he hears the finger exercises, the studies, the transpositions, the Russian scales, he can't help wishing that his daughter had been good at netball or gymnastics instead.

He rubs his eyes. He's not sleeping. He's told Kate it's because of the pain in his ankle. When he goes back to work, Emily Andersen will be at her new desk, waiting to greet him with her eyes like pewter planets and her wide smile and her skin that he wants to touch so badly that he doesn't know how he can look at her again without doing so. He'd forgotten what it's like to want anything so much.

And what would happen? Supposing his feelings aren't one-sided? There'd be no stopping it. If he had an affair with one of his journalists and the company found out, he'd have to resign. If Kate found out, he'd have to leave home. How would he feel now, if the door were to open – a different door in a different home – and his wife said, 'Coffee, darling?' yet the wife was not Kate, but Emily?

And Alicia wouldn't dash in and embrace him; he would no longer hear her practising; he wouldn't be there to give her the support she needed as she followed her gift. How could he bear that? His mind is running away with him. He knows he's thinking nonsense, but he thinks it all the same.

His foot aches in its plaster cast, helpless, hurting and immobilised.

6

Mrs Butterworth sends Alicia into her studio and gives Kate a conspiratorial wink. The sound of warm-up exercises reaches the front room. Kate smiles automatically. She has a wary respect for her daughter's teacher and her perfectly placed wig (it has *got* to be a wig).

'Katherine, I would like a quick word if you have time,' Mrs Butterworth says. She is the only person who insists on calling Kate Katherine. It's disconcerting, especially as Kate dares not call Mrs Butterworth by her first name, Deirdre. Mrs Butterworth pats a cushion on the sofa and Kate sits down, obedient as any pupil.

'Your daughter,' Mrs Butterworth begins, 'is a talented girl. Are you serious about her career?'

'Do you think she can have a career?'

'Katherine, I believe that Alicia is not only a good pianist but potentially a great one. She has something exceptional. She has charisma.'

'I always feel there's something radiant in her,' Kate says, nodding. 'But it's difficult for me to judge.'

'Of course. I know how this feels.' Mrs Butterworth's eyes seem to cloud for a moment.

Kate glances round the room for signs of grown-up children – postcards, photographs, mementoes. There are none. 'So you think . . .' she prompts.

'Yes. But there is something she needs. I know it's asking a lot. Grand pianos are not cheap, but without one she's handicapped. Working on an upright is fine for most schoolgirls.

But to develop as an artist, to form a sense of colour, nuance, a full range of dynamics, Alicia must have a grand piano, and a good one. Otherwise when she gives a concert, she will play a grand piano and not know how to handle it.'

Kate moistens her lips and her fingers twitch a little. She wishes she had her knitting. 'How much *do* grand pianos cost, Mrs Butterworth?'

Kate drives into the centre of Manchester and makes for the city's largest music shop. The ground floor is occupied by racks of sheet music and CDs. There Kate notices a section marked SOLO PIANO and browses through the discs. Each bears a picture of a beaming or brooding virtuoso, or a painting to match the character of the music. The pianists, scores of them, some alive, some long dead, are in alphabetical order from Martha Argerich to Krystian Zimerman. Only a few are women; very few are British. Alicia is up against long odds.

A CD under NEW RELEASES catches her eye: the Chopin Études. Alicia struggles daily with these. The pianist is French. Kate doesn't recognise his name, Lucien Delamain. The front cover shows a personable man, about her own age: dark, smiling, clad in polo-necked jersey and tweed jacket, against a blurry background of winter trees and pale sky. On the back, press quotes declare Delamain 'inspired', 'exciting' and 'a poet of the piano'. That sounds good, so Kate buys the disc. Then she goes down to the basement, which houses the piano department.

Kate had never realised how many different permutations of wood, strings, felt, imitation ivory and gleaming pedals pass by the name of PIANO. To one side masses an array of electronic instruments, from basic keyboards played through earphones – like heads that have lost their bodies – to sophisticated creations that appear to be normal pianos, but can be transformed into electronic ones at the flick of a switch. Next, she spots a group of new, clean, unbattered uprights, which show how well-worn their own has become. And at the far end, the grands stretch out like a pride of lions, black and white teeth bared, proud of their glowing cases. Some are french-polished in matt black, others coated with veneers of mahogany, rosewood or richly gnarled walnut.

Among them stands a black, nine-foot concert grand, its lid raised, its trademark in gold letters reading STEINWAY. Kate runs her fingers softly over the keyboard and the piano purrs in fine, sensual response. How extraordinary that human beings could invent such a bizarre contraption to make music; how strange that a child could be born with a natural affinity for something so contrived.

Then she sees the price tag.

Outside, Kate turns away and plods through the dank afternoon. There's a possible alternative, though she doesn't much like it. At Alicia's music festivals, talking to other competitors' parents, she's been garnering information about different options for educating musical children. In an ancient building, one of Manchester's oldest – complete with baronial hall and historic library – there is a specialist music school. Its gifted pupils study music alongside normal lessons. Most of them are boarders.

Before long Kate finds it. It's built of dark brick, encompassing gloomy archways and a Gothic courtyard; only a modern wing beyond the entrance gate betrays the fact that it's a functioning, contemporary school. From the windows drift the clank of pianos, a glimmer of a flute, the deep song of a cello. If Ali were to join this school, she'd be among children and teachers who understood her. Kate can't deny that Ali's school, so far, has been remarkably accommodating to her needs and proud of her achievements. But the thinning-out of birthday-party invitations from classmates, a running battle with one PE teacher and two exam papers – physics and chemistry – that had appeared almost unmarkable are proof that normal school and Ali aren't particularly compatible.

But Ali would have to go, physically *go*, to Manchester. The whole family could move there, of course, but that would also mean uprooting the already troublesome Adrian and sending him to an inner-city comprehensive, which Kate doesn't fancy. Assuming that isn't an option, Ali would have to board or, alternatively, commute. Theoretically she could travel with Guy; but then she'd spend more than two hours a day in a car, time in which she could neither practise nor do homework; and there'd be late evenings, because Guy often works until eight and sometimes ten. Ali would be sitting in school, practising there, waiting – then she'd come home, exhausted. But if she were to board, she wouldn't be home at all.

Without Ali, Kate would be alone. Guy's working hours are utterly antisocial. Adrian isn't interested in keeping his mother company; he's either out with his friends, mooching about the Pavilion Gardens, or in his room watching TV (she hadn't wanted him to have a TV, but since Ali practises ever longer in the lounge, it seemed only fair). And though Kate goes to her book club and meets fellow reading enthusiasts, neighbours or mothers for occasional lunches, there's nobody in Buxton to whom she feels genuinely close. Glenda Fairburn is the only other music-oriented woman she knows there, and Glenda has her hands full these days with her own children.

Kate can hardly remember what it's like to have a close friend. She'd lost touch with her old university companions after Victoria – how unfair it would be, she'd felt, to unload her grief upon them. With the move to Buxton, the uprooting had been complete. She, or maybe Guy, had imagined that a good-sized guest room would be ample temptation for visitors; but those visitors tend to be William and Margaret, who leave Guy fuming, or, rarely, Joanna, or Anthony and his family, who are worse.

Joanna, still single, works for a merchant bank and enjoys a lavish lifestyle with frequent postings abroad – most recently to San Francisco, where she hopes to stay. Anthony, who'd set up home in Harrow near their parents, has a wife named Fiona whom Kate and Guy describe to each other as '*so* nice, *but* –'; and their three children don't make life easy for Alicia and Adrian when they visit. They shiver in the icy Buxton wind, grumble when it rains – as it frequently does – and want to know where the *real* shops are. In the last year or two, the three 'Horribles' (as, to Kate's chagrin, her son and daughter call them in private) have become wary of their country cousins. They court Alicia at her piano as if trying to tempt a beautiful Persian cat into a garden – she seems exotic to them, which is fair enough since none of the three, at ten, eight and six, appears to have a morsel of talent for anything. And they shrink from Adrian, who at fifteen seems immeasurably old, has an aura of faint, threatening remoteness and hates them coming into his room to watch TV.

Kate's days pass: collecting Alicia from school, taking her to her piano lessons, trying to keep a futile eye on Adrian and making small-talk with women among whom she still feels an outsider because of her stubborn home-counties accent and her talented child. When they ask about Alicia's progress, she tells them of the latest festival or a photo in a newspaper – then feels embarrassed when they return quietly to discussing the merits of removing tonsils or what to do about appalling school dinners.

When Alicia comes home, Kate's life begins. She'll have tea and cake ready to boost her energy, and she'll often try to find some novelty to interest her: a tape of a concert from the radio, a book about a composer from the library, or a CD – like Lucien Delamain's Chopin disc. She will give Adrian tea and cake too, then persuade him to do his homework. Soon she'll be ensconced with Alicia at the piano, ready to spur her on if she feels disheartened, or to point out when she's straying from Mrs Butterworth's copious demands ('Darling, you're strumming now, do that page again, slowly . . .'). If there are tears, she'll be there to dry them. Alicia feels her music very deeply and any hint of failure can send her spinning into excessive emotion, which the onset of puberty doesn't help.

Supposing Alicia went to boarding-school? How would she manage? She's so young, so raw, so instinctive. She hasn't learned to hide behind the masks that her schoolmates are already forging for themselves. What Alicia feels, she shows. What she wants, she declares; what she doesn't want, she will never accept. If she loves someone, she hugs them. If she hates someone, she ignores them. If she respects someone, she obeys them, and if she doesn't respect them – well, the PE teacher was a case in point.

Most young girls love to wear makeup, but Alicia has never experimented beyond a smudge or two for the stage. Most other teenagers want to be cool, but she appears not to care about the style of her clothes, though she likes blue, which suits her, and is unaccountably fussy about the colours she wears for performing. Adrian, in a rare bout of Making an Effort with Little Sister, gave her a khaki T-shirt that he'd outgrown, emblazoned with the logo of a chart-topping band; Alicia thanked him, but hasn't worn it once. And this is a girl with a capacity for devotion that can induce her to plunge into a winter river after her dog. How would such a self-willed, innocent child survive in a boarding-school? It's unthinkable. So, if Alicia is not going to the music school, she must stay where she is and practise at home. That means she must have a grand piano.

'Well, why do you think we never had one?' Guy is lying on his back, staring at the bedroom ceiling, which still needs replastering. His foot, he's been joking, should change places with it.

'But it's madness. How can we spend eighty thousand pounds on a piano?'

'We can get a good one second-hand for a lot less, you know. It's a question of finding one she likes.'

'Are they really that different?'

'You bet. I'll keep a look-out in the small ads.'

It's half past eleven at night. Guy reaches towards his bedside drawer.

'What's that?'

'Sleeping pills. The foot's been hurting.'

During his first days back at work, Guy has been keeping the lowest profile that a deputy editor reasonably can. The sandwich man appears with a tray at lunchtime, so he can avoid the canteen; Diane brings him as many cups of coffee as he can drink; and if Martin needs him, he knows where he is. At editorial meetings, Guy makes sure he's half concealed by a door or a potted plant.

It is therefore from behind the conference room's *Ficus benjamina* that Guy catches his next glimpse of Emily Andersen's left profile: the concave tilt of her nose, the breadth of her forehead, the slant of the grey eyes that have been haunting him. She's wearing jeans, a black sweater and the merest touch of makeup. Her pen and notebook are poised, ready to snap into action. She's still the new girl, but looks as if she's worked at the *Chronicle* for ever. He watches her; she hasn't noticed him. She's talking to her colleagues, joking around as if they're old friends. He keeps watching, but soon stops observing: all he can think is: 'God, she's lovely.'

Emily turns her head. Her gaze lands on him and he feels the jolt of contact: recognition, a question-mark, pleasure. She raises a hand and waves.

After the meeting, he doesn't go to her; instead, she comes to him. Around them the others disperse to their desks.

'Guy, how are you? How's the foot?'

'It's seen better days, but it's mending, thanks.'

'I'd been looking forward to talking to you about all those local walks,' Emily sparkles, 'but on my first day they said you'd jumped into a river to save your dog!'

'Actually, it was my daughter. She thought *she* was saving the dog.'

'But she's OK?'

'Very much so. Thanks.'

They hover outside Guy's office. He wonders whether he'd seen a flicker of doubt in Emily's bright smile when he said 'my daughter'.

'What are you doing for lunch?' she asks.

Guy tries to say that he's busy, but instead says that he's free.

Alicia isn't afraid to go out alone with Cassie, and Mum isn't afraid to let her, especially when Mrs Butterworth has wound her into a state of tension that can't be soothed by a cup of hot chocolate. Mum imposes a half-hour time-limit, but it's long enough for Alicia to centre herself as well as walking – or, rather, running – the dog. Alicia can't see why she has to have a time limit while Adrian doesn't; but she makes the most of her brief freedom.

She grabs Cassie's leash and they head for the fresh air and wide, peaceful space of the golf course down the road. They're allowed to run there as long as they don't bother any golfers. Alicia keeps half an eye on Cassie to make certain she doesn't go after the balls, but Mum has trained her to leave them alone. Dad – whose attempts at exercise are sparse but enthusiastic – has advised Alicia that real jogging is slow, steady and sensible. But she prefers to sprint as hard and fast as she can, with Cassie galloping alongside, all four paws outstretched in the welcome air.

Here, you can see for miles, up into the empty moors. She feels she could run for ever; that if she could reach the grey horizon at the top of the farthest hill, she could puncture it where the earth and sky meet, and break through it, like a silk screen, to the other side. There she'd find rainbows and shooting stars; she and Cassie could fly out, defying gravity, with no need for wings to rise and soar.

Alicia feels as if she's a piece of jewellery that her mother keeps in a box, wrapped in cotton wool. Mum takes her out and polishes her, then wears her round her neck like a pendant of Blue John, Derbyshire's answer to amethyst, which glistens raw in the caverns under the hills. Even if Alicia's arms are aching, her shoulders are stiff, her fingertips are sore and her head is humming, she mustn't stop practising. Mum will say, 'Have a little break and a Panadol, darling, and then get back to it, because if you don't you won't be able to play for that music club,' or 'We'll have to cancel your Buxton Festival recital because you won't be ready,' or simply 'Mrs Butterworth will be able to tell straight away.'

She barely stops practising even at school. Lessons in maths, IT, physics and biology flow past without touching her; her fingers tap on her legs under the desk while her mind plays her the notes. Sometimes the teachers scold her, though that's becoming half-hearted.

The other kids taunt her. 'Freak,' spits Kelly, who chews gum with her mouth open. 'Icky-sicky classical music! Ali pally, silly cow! Ali pally, silly cow!' Alicia's latest newspaper report from a competition in Sheffield has been pinned to the school noticeboard, beside clippings about pupils' successes in the pony club, and the football team's triumph against a snotty private school in Yorkshire. But Kelly, or somebody like her, has defaced Alicia's picture by drawing a moustache and beard on it.

Adrian swoops to her defence from two classes higher. Finding his sister crying at lunch break, he pulls down the paper and says, 'When I catch them, I'll break their legs.' Silently Alicia hopes he doesn't catch them, because she fears he really might do it – Adrian is huge these days. It was nice, though, to feel he'd protect her.

Alicia does have a friend. A new friend whom she can't see easily because she lives in Birmingham and goes to school in Surrey. At the competition in Sheffield she had wandered over and started talking to Alicia: an Indian girl named Anjali Sharma, a year older than herself, shepherded by a tall, fierce-looking father who never took his eyes off her. While Mum talked to Dr Sharma, who seemed keen to tell her about his daughter's concerts and competitive successes, Alicia and Anjali shyly exchanged stories. Anjali attends a specialist music boarding-school for exceptionally talented children.

'It's very small and everyone is really into music,' Anjali said. She had a wonderful accent that combined a twang of Birmingham, a twist of Indian subcontinent – her family came originally from Madras – and a slight resonance of posh Surrey exclusivity. Alicia listened to the intriguing sound of her voice almost more than to the words she spoke. 'You'd get in easily, I'm sure,' said Anjali, whose fine-featured, modest face could break abruptly into the loveliest of smiles.

The school's pupils are supported by scholarships, Dr Sharma told Mum, so paying fees isn't an issue. The real trouble is that Surrey is at the other end of the country.

When Alicia hints at home that she likes the sound of a school where everyone is musical, Mum and Dad look so upset that she's filled with appalling guilt. She acknowledges that she'd have to board, like Anjali.

'But, darling, I hate the idea of you not being at home, having a normal family life,' Mum explains. 'Those schools are such hot-houses. I can't imagine you being happy in a place like that.' Alicia doesn't know what she means, but suspects that Buxton would be too cold to possess a hot-house of its own.

Alicia had given Anjali her address and it's not long before a parcel with a Surrey postmark arrives, containing a glossy prospectus. In the privacy of her bedroom, Alicia turns the pages: extensive green lawns, a long programme of school concerts, a piano on every page. She shows it to Adrian, who thinks it looks brilliant. 'There's a school a bit like that in Manchester,' he tells her, 'but I guess you'd have to be a boarder there too.'

'Why?'

'Because Mum would say you're wasting two hours a day travelling when you could be practising.'

Adrian is right: as soon as Alicia raises the possibility, Mum homes in on exactly that. 'A normal family life is so important,' she adds.

'Bollocks,' Adrian interjects.

'What do you mean, Adrian?' Mum says, icy.

'We don't have a normal family life, do we? Call this *normal?*'

'Oh, and isn't that your doing? You never want to join in anything we do any more.'

'I never *did* want to. This family gives me an effing headache. Can't you see Ali doesn't have any friends?'

'But she's got her family round her. That's much more important.'

Alicia looks on, mute. It's not only that Mum isn't listening to Adrian; it's as if she can't even hear him. Alicia doesn't bother trying to get a word in edgeways. She wonders silently whether she'll ever have any say in her own life.

Admittedly, if she went to music school as a boarder, she'd have to leave Cassie at home and she'd hardly ever see Grandma Didie. Also, the teachers might be less good than Mrs Butterworth. Alicia loathes Mrs Butterworth, but she can't deny that she gets results: Alicia's technique is racing ahead and she can't remember the last time she'd failed to win a competition. Mum says that the reason Mrs Butterworth doesn't teach at any of the music schools or colleges is that she's too good for them, too demanding, too individual. She must be fantastic, because she charges a vast sum for Alicia's lessons.

The information has finally reached them on the grapevine – Glenda, via the friend of a friend – that Mrs Butterworth had had a daughter who died when she was twenty, from a rare form of bone cancer. She had been a very promising pianist; and although it had happened decades ago, Mrs Butterworth has never got over it. Alicia feels sorry for her. But when she goes out running with Cassie, for that half-hour she can let herself think things that she's not allowed to think inside the house – and then, occasionally, she wonders what it would have been like to be Mrs Butterworth's daughter. And she feels almost more sorry for the girl before she became ill.

Kate looks up from a recipe book when a rush of chilly air, a slam and a volley of barks signal that Alicia and Cassie are back. The kitchen clock shows that they've been out for precisely thirty minutes.

'Hi, Mum.' Alicia bounds over and gives her a big, damp hug. Her clothes are coated with gossamer drizzle: for some perverse reason, she hates umbrellas. She dashes upstairs to change into something dry.

'An hour till supper,' Kate says, when she returns in clean jeans and sheepskin slippers. 'Are you going to practise?'

'Can't I help you cook?' Alicia adores food in all its forms, and Kate worries that what is currently puppy fat may grow worse if she carries on.

She lets Alicia off the hour's practice: she has already survived Mrs Butterworth's onslaught today. Mother and daughter stand side by side at the worktop; Alicia puts leaves, olives and cherry tomatoes into a salad bowl and Kate chops onions and cucumber. They switch on Radio 4 and listen to a comedy programme that soon has both of them in stitches. Adrian is out with his mates. Guy has phoned to say he has to work late and won't be home for another two hours.

'I thought it went really well today,' Alicia remarks, once the broadcast is over. 'Mrs Butterworth actually said, "Good."'

'Would you like to ask her,' Kate says carefully, 'what she thinks about the idea of you going in for the BBC Young Musician of the Year competition?'

Alicia freezes, tomato in hand. 'Do you think I could?'

'Of course you could. But you'd need your teacher's consent.'

'Oh, she'll be fine. If you want Mrs Butterworth to be happy, enter me for a competition!' Alicia rolls her eyes heavenwards. She catches Kate's eye; they laugh. They both know what makes Mrs Butterworth tick. 'I think Anjali's entering it,' Alicia adds. 'I might ask her how it works.'

After supper, while Alicia is in the bath, Kate tiptoes into her room. The yellow paint and African animals are long gone; now it's lavender and white, a calm, pretty space to soothe a busy young girl to rest. Guy sometimes remarks that it looks more like a unit in a bed-and-breakfast than a child's room. On the bookshelves stand competition trophies: silver cups bearing inscribed plaques that could have been for tennis or swimming, but happen to be for playing the piano. Framed certificates garnish the wall, prizes from the competitions that don't give trophies.

Alicia has a desk at which she's supposed to do her homework. Not much of it gets done, but Kate is impressed by how tidy the surface is. Alicia is chaotic in certain ways: no worldly ploys or manipulative tricks, no sense of 'cool'. But she's punctual, polite and – at the piano, where she always seems older and more sophisticated than she is – extremely confident. Strange girl. Strange and marvellous, Kate smiles to herself.

She spots on the desk, the latest letter from Anjali, whom Kate thinks Ali is in love with, in the way that young girls sometimes are with slightly older girls.

Last weekend Lucien Delamain came and did masterclasses with some of the sixth-formers. He was AMAZING. He showed us all kinds of things about the way the melodies relate to each other. I came away feeling like I'd heard the pieces for the first time, although I thought I knew them very well. Ali, I wish you'd persuade your parents to let you audition. You'd love it here. It would be so great to have you.

From the bathroom comes the sound of water gurgling down the plughole. Kate puts the letter back in exactly the position she'd found it and makes her way downstairs, troubled. When Guy comes home, she'll discuss with him the issues of boarding-school, the competition and excessive affection for other girls. But he's working late.

Guy, as it happens, is not working late. He's in the pub with Emily Andersen. The paper's local is typical – he would have written – of gloomy, industrial Manchester's transformation into a modern metropolis, full of go-ahead people and newly fashioned media companies. Once a cavernous Victorian monstrosity, its interior has been remodelled with chandeliers of opaque glass globes casting luminous reflections into big mirrors. Moreover, Guy tells Emily, it offers one of the best selections of draught beer in the city.

'You should come to Denmark one day,' she says, with a smile, leaning on the counter while he waves a ten-pound note towards the barman. 'We have great beer.'

Guy orders two pints, two packets of crisps and a platter of cheese and biscuits. Emily tries to pay for her share, but he refuses. 'My treat.'

They settle at the quietest table they can find.

'So, tell me about Denmark,' Guy says. 'I've never been.'

Emily, hands cupped round her glass, begins to describe her home town, Aarhus. There, they had lived on a long hill overlooking the harbour; on Saturdays her mother would nip down to the fish market and bring back a bucket of fresh prawns for lunch. Nearby, the old town's low, historic buildings, pink, yellow and white, would be abuzz with cafés, bars and students on bicycles. It was easy to get out into the countryside, which looks, she says, a little like Suffolk, only prettier. Lots of sky;

lots of sea; forests of beech trees that burst into leaf over a few days in early May.

Guy, listening, pictures Emily walking through a Danish beech forest. 'So why did you move to England?'

'My mum never quite got the hang of the language, so Dad finally caved in and looked for a teaching post here instead. I don't think Danish is so hard, really. It's like Geordie English, only a thousand years out of date.'

'I bet that helped,' Guy teases her. 'Give us a demo?'

'*Rød grød med fløde.*'

'What?'

'That's what we teach foreigners to say first, because they usually can't! It means stewed red berries with cream.'

'I can't hear any consonants.'

'Oh, there are consonants. It's just that we don't pronounce them.'

'I feel for your mother,' Guy says. 'So you're bilingual?'

'Kind of.'

'Homesick?'

'Sometimes. I like it here, though. How's life in Buxton?'

'Much as ever. You must come over one day and we'll go for a good walk.'

'Are you from Derbyshire?'

'I grew up in Cheshire, but Buxton's home. My great-grand-father lived there. He used to walk all the way to Macclesfield across the moor to court my great-grandmother.'

'Wow, that's romantic!'

'What's a few hours on a moor to true love?' Guy says – then wishes, peculiarly, that he hadn't. To distract her, he leans back and puts on his best Derbyshire voice: 'Ye knaw what they say, eh, lass? "Derbyshire born and Derbyshire bred, strong in arm but weak in 'ead!"'

Emily laughs. Her face lights up as it had during her inter-view. Arrows pierce Guy's brain. He beams back at her. 'Derbyshire equivalent of your red berries,' he remarks.

'Try some of this. It's good.' Emily motions to the cheese platter.

'"Cheese, please, Louise."'

'Sorry?'

'TV ad from the sixties. I always find myself saying that. It drives my family bananas.'

'Oh, but it's *cute*! Anyway, I don't remember TV ads from the sixties. I wasn't conscious until about 1975.'

Guy takes a long swig of beer. Emily is more than a decade younger than him. She is gorgeous, fun and straightforward, he's completely in love with her, and he is middle-aged and married and has to see her every day at the office. What is he doing?

But sitting in the pub with her, laughing, listening and talking as if he's known her all his life, he knows exactly what he's doing: he's flying.

7

Things happen, life-changing things, with the simplest of signals: the ring of a telephone or the plop of a letter on to the doormat. The latest plop involves a large brown envelope, which heaves in one morning to Cassie's noisy welcome. Kate slices it open. Inside is the information pack she'd requested from the BBC.

Kate fills in the application form and buys a large Jiffy-bag. Into it, with the form, go a CV as long as the dog's tail, a reference from Mrs Butterworth that would make Apollo himself blush, a copy of Alicia's birth certificate, a photo, an audiotape and a video-cassette. She seals it with packing tape and strolls down to the post office. Some weeks later, there comes the inevitable news that Alicia has been accepted.

The wheels grind into action. The competition is spread out over more than a year from application to final. First there are regional heats – for Alicia, in Manchester. She's pleased to find she has to play for only fifteen minutes. Mrs Butterworth plans her programme: a Chopin study, a short but deliciously showy Mozart Gigue, and Ravel's *Jeux d'eau*. Pianos, Alicia tells the BBC people afterwards, are good at evoking water. The chains of notes are like rivers, rain and fountains because they're both fluid and defined, or should be.

'It's your fourteenth birthday tomorrow?' asks the regional administrator, double-checking her form. 'Do you know what presents you're getting?'

'Probably some books of Chopin that I don't have already,' Alicia says eagerly.

'What about going out to celebrate? A movie? A party?'

'The thing is, there's no cinema where we live and my friends are – well, music's what I love best.'

The administrator and her assistant exchange a glance.

Three months later the regional finals take place: back to Manchester, fifteen more minutes of music and, this time, TV cameras. Everyone's performances are recorded now, just in case.

> *Dear Alicia,*
>
> *I heard you got to the quarter-finals – so did I! I'm so glad you'll be there too. Which concerto are you learning? I wanted to do Saint-Saëns Two, but Dad says I should do something with a little more 'depth'. He only likes German music. So I'll probably learn some Mozart, not that I'll be performing it in any case. We must get together in Birmingham and go out somewhere afterwards. Here's a picture of school. See you in December!*
>
> *Love,*
> *Anjali*
>
> *Dearest Anjali,*
>
> *Thanks for your postcard!!! Yes I'm in the quarter-finals and it will be great to see you again. I'm learning the Ravel G major Concerto, I know it isn't 'deep', but its SO beautiful and Mrs Butterworth says I should go for it cos I love it. I hope I'll have a chance to play it, but who knows. Mum is coming with me to Birmingam and we'll all go out definatly afterwards. Do people keep asking you if you're nervous? I'm not and everyone keeps saying 'she's not nervous, why isn't she nervous?' which nearly makes me scared, only not quite. See you very soon!!!!!*
>
> *Luv,*
> *Alicia*

While the cogs turn and Alicia plugs away at her next programme, the phone rings. Guy's voice says, from the office, 'Katie, I've got an idea. Why don't we have a dinner party for some of my colleagues?'

Dinner parties at the Bradleys' are rare events. Most guests have been family, Kate's former employers, or neighbours who chat about the weather while Kate fusses over chicken and salad. At least the newspaper people, if they can be persuaded to make the journey over the moor, should bring with them some livelier conversation. Guy wants to invite the editor, Martin, with his wife, Liz, and two of the best young journalists: a girl named Emily Andersen and a boy named Robert Wilder. Emily, he says, reports on the arts, education and community issues, and Rob specialises in politics. Kate agrees, but stresses that they must avoid Tuesdays and Wednesdays because of Alicia's piano lesson.

Kate's latest acquisition for the house is a larger dining-table, made of reclaimed oak floorboards; it sits at the garden end of their sizeable kitchen-diner and opens up to seat ten. It strikes Kate that since the children won't be taking part and the evening risks being dominated by newspaper talk, perhaps they could ask someone else as well.

Mrs Butterworth has never been to Buxton.

'That,' Guy says, 'would be extremely interesting!'

Sometimes you don't know a life-changing moment – that ring of the phone, rustle of paper or, in this case, chime of the bell – until years afterwards. When the doorbell sounds Big Ben at seven thirty on the last Saturday of October, nobody suspects that it will presage anything but an informal meal with friends.

Alicia and Adrian are deemed, respectively, too young and too unsuitable for a dinner party. Adrian has gone to see his friend Sam. Alicia, having feasted on breadcrumbed fish and oven chips, is using the last of the visitor-free early evening to practise. The window is slightly open; Ravel, all glitter and poise, floats into the drive and greets the guests as they gaze up at the house on the slope. They arrive together. Martin and Liz, who live near Withington, have agreed to bring and return Mrs Butterworth; and Rob Wilder has brought Emily Andersen.

Emily pauses at the bottom of the steps and takes in the wide bay window, the sound of music through the chestnut-dark autumn evening and the gleaming hair of the girl at the piano, whose face is hidden.

'All right, Em?' asks Rob, who fancies her.

'Sure. Just got to fix my shoe,' she says, bending so that he can't see her eyes.

Mrs Butterworth looks in at the upright piano – no second-hand grand in good enough condition has yet presented itself – and shakes her hand.

Kate has spent the afternoon preparing her house and herself. The ground floor, the bathroom and the stairs have been scrubbed and vacuumed within a millimetre of their lives. The books are ranged in ruler-straight rows on the shelves; Alicia's music, normally piled beside the piano, has been concealed in the cupboard where it ought to live, and even the kitchen shows little sign of the frantic chopping, stirring, roasting and garnishing that has been taking place. The wine glasses gleam on the table, each with an expertly folded red napkin tucked into its bowl; a vase of lilies adorns the side-board; and at perfect intervals along the table stand three slender red candles. Kate's hair is freshly coloured, a slightly more golden shade than usual, and she's wearing a long, sleek, flowered skirt and a loose, oatmeal-coloured jacket. Round her neck is a string of chunky mock-ivory beads. The aroma of rosemary, garlic and lamb melds into the scent of fallen leaves and the sound of Ravel.

Alicia's choice of the Ravel G major Concerto is

unfortunate. Kate can't hear the slow movement without thinking of the dying Victoria; they'd listened to it constantly in the hospital. But it's Alicia's favourite and unless Kate is willing to explain why – which she isn't – she's in no position to convince her to choose something else. Gradually, painfully, she's getting used to it.

She steps forward to welcome her guests. 'Martin! Liz! How wonderful to see you, it's been far too long. Do come in . . . And Mrs Butterworth!'

'Deirdre. Please, Katherine. Tonight I am Deirdre.' The matchstick figure of Alicia's piano teacher glides into the house, incongruous out of her normal context.

'Deirdre's been telling us all about her studies in Soviet Russia. It's quite hair-raising. I think we should do a feature,' Martin tells Kate, giving her a kiss.

'Darling,' Guy says, 'I'd like you to meet our two bright young things. This is Rob. And this is Emily.'

'Welcome to Buxton.' Kate smiles, shaking their hands. She's struck by the openness of Emily's face, the clarity of her complexion and the unusual hue of her eyes. Unaccountably, this girl makes her feel her age more than she normally does.

Rob is much taller than Kate, and as fresh-faced in his own way as Emily, who, Kate thinks, inspecting the vibes, may be his girlfriend; or perhaps he merely wants her to be. His features are even, his curly brown hair plentiful (unlike that of the older men) and his smile is wide and friendly. Mrs Butterworth gazes up at him, pressing his hand as warmly as if she herself were the hostess.

The front-room door opens. Alicia looks out, her face tired and hopeful. She's wearing faded jeans and a Minnie Mouse T-shirt. Emily swings round from talking to Guy and meets the young girl's gaze. For a moment their eyes lock. Then Alicia's swerve to her teacher. 'Hello, Mrs Butterworth,' she says quietly.

'Hello, Alicia dear.' Mrs Butterworth sounds unusually benevolent.

'Ali,' Kate exclaims, 'you don't need to stop. Go and finish the last movement.'

'Oh, Mum.' Alicia looks at the guests.

'Everyone knows you're in the competition and we all love to hear you playing, so it's no problem. Go and finish your practising.'

'Yes, Mum.' Alicia slides back behind the door. A moment later there comes the clack of a metronome and the careful rattling of Ravel passagework at half speed.

Emily and Rob exchange a glance. Emily does not look at Guy.

'Let's sit in the kitchen,' Kate suggests – Alicia occupies what used to be the lounge. Guy makes for the fridge where two bottles of champagne lie chilling.

Soon the glassy edges of formality have dissolved amid the bubbles. Alicia is finally permitted to stop her metronome and go to her room; for background music, Kate puts on an Ella Fitzgerald album. Guy taps his fingers in time and Emily's feet dance under the table despite themselves. Kate brings out the starter – smoked salmon and cucumber mousse with dill sauce and triangles of crustless toast. Guy refills the glasses. In the golden light from the red candles, Mrs Butterworth bats her eyelids at Rob, who appears transfixed by her stream of horrific stories from the world of international piano competitions.

'. . . And then you know what the competition director, this great, legendary pianist, says? He declares, "Well, I'm deaf. Let's give the prize to the prettiest girl!"'

Emily, Rob, Martin, Liz and Guy laugh. Kate doesn't. Convinced that Mrs Butterworth isn't making this up, she's wondering how often such incidents affect the fortunes of young women in supposedly musical contests.

'But surely they're looking for the best pianists?' Emily protests.

'Darling, if only that were true. But I've seen decisions taken in competitions that would make your hair stand on end, if not fall out altogether!' Mrs Butterworth, beaming, reaches out a hand and ruffles Rob's light brown curls.

Kate, fork poised half-way to her mouth, can't believe her eyes. Especially when Rob – who has plenty of hair-raising stories of his own, when he's allowed to get a word in – doesn't object, but laughs. 'Deirdre, one word from you and all those corrupt jurors would run for their lives!' he declares.

'Deirdre', who eats so slowly that she finishes her mousse ten minutes after everyone else, is the only person who accepts more. Kate goes to the oven to remove the lamb, which would otherwise turn from suitable, moist French pink to very unsuitable, dry school-dinner brown. Mrs Butterworth, despite her delicate build, is evidently fond of her food, and her drink too. Kate wonders how she manages to stay so thin; she must burn up all her energy in teaching.

After another fifteen minutes, during which Mrs Butterworth works her way morsel by morsel through her second helping, Kate, her head spinning from slightly too much champagne, asks Guy to carve the lamb.

'This is such a lovely house,' Liz enthuses to her, while Guy turns his attention to the meat. 'Guy tells us you've designed everything yourself, Kate. You've got the most wonderful eye.'

'I'm glad you like it,' Kate says, 'but it's very simple . . .'

There's a clonk and an expletive. Guy's hand has slipped. 'Damn it!' He dashes to the sink to run the cut under the cold tap.

'Oh, God, are you all right?' Emily gasps.

Rob glances at her, surprised.

'You must never let Alicia handle a kitchen knife,' Mrs Butterworth advises Kate. 'Far too dangerous.'

'I know. It's a shame, because she loves cooking,' Kate says.

'Sacrifices must be made for such a talent.'

'You didn't go on holiday this year, did you?' Liz says.

'No – with Ali being in the quarter-finals, we didn't want to take her away from her piano for two weeks. It wouldn't have been fair. We can have wonderful days out locally in any case.' Not that they often do. Kate pushes, impatient, past her injured husband and takes over the carving.

'Wouldn't it do her good to have a break? To be a little refreshed?' Emily is watching Guy at the sink; he's wrapped his bleeding finger in kitchen towel and is rummaging in a drawer for a plaster.

'It's really up to her,' Kate explains, cutting lamb in neat slices beside Guy's irregular chunks. 'She's very happy this way.'

'I hope you don't mind me asking,' says Liz, fidgeting with a curl of her hair, 'but isn't she missing out on things that most children do? Going to the seaside, seeing her friends . . . ?'

'Alicia is not "most children".' Mrs Butterworth answers before Kate can. 'Alicia is unique. In all my years of teaching, I have never found a talent like hers. And here, in a little English town known only for its mineral water! It's quite incredible.'

'She does miss out,' Guy growls. 'Of course she does.'

'She doesn't have many close friends she wants to go out with,' Kate says. 'It's difficult, being the only exceptionally talented child in her school.'

'Katherine,' says Mrs Butterworth, 'she does still need a grand piano.'

'Fourteen is such a difficult age,' Liz says. 'Our Harry was in all kinds of trouble when he was fourteen.'

'Emily, I hope you're hungry?' Kate piles meat, gravy, potatoes and vegetables on to a plate. Emily's expression, sombre in the candlelight, suggests she's miles away. She starts visibly at the sound of her name, but gives Kate a quick smile and says, 'Yes, thank you.' Kate notices later, though, that Emily is eating almost, if not quite, as slowly as 'Deirdre'.

'Sorry about that.' Guy is back at his place. Emily asks him quietly if he's in pain. 'Just being stupid. Not concentrating,' he tells her. Kate plonks a plate in front of him.

'. . . So then he says, "And what might *your* business be?"' Rob is talking to Mrs Butterworth, imitating a broad Scottish accent. 'So I explain I'm a journalist out for a holiday ramble, and he says, "Not here, you're not. Not on *my* land. How'd you like it if fifty thousand people came *rambling* across your office in their mucky boots?" And I pointed out that my boots were quite clean, as boots go, to which he says, "Aye, there's muck and there's muck . . ." And this was a public right of way! But you can't tell a nutcase like that where to go, in case he's got a gun in the van . . .'

'How's your son doing?' Liz asks Kate.

'He's fine, thanks. He's at a friend's place tonight.' Kate hates to think of what Adrian and Sam might get up to together, but this is no place to say so.

Guy, at the head of the table with Emily at right angles on his left, reaches downwards, apparently looking for something. Emily pulls her chair closer in.

When the plates are (mostly) empty, the wine bottles depleted and the faces flushed and happy, Martin taps his glass for attention. His face is red and content and his eyes full of beneficence as he lumbers to his feet.

'Friends, Buxtonians, countrymen,' he begins. 'I want to say two things. First, a huge thank-you to Guy and especially to his wonderful wife, Kate, for this fabulous gourmet cuisine!' He waits for the noises of approval to die down. 'Next, I've got some news. I've decided, after much soul-searching, that it's time to cash in my chips. The newspaper needs a new look, a new approach. Not tired old me, ploughing on through the production line after twenty years.

So I'm going to take early retirement, join the golf club, if they'll have me, and see something more of my home and my long-suffering family.'

Kate takes a breath, guessing what comes next. Guy is serene, smiling up at Martin, showing no surprise – or, indeed, anything else. Fury flashes through her: has he known about this all along, without telling her? Was this the reason for his hare-brained dinner-party idea?

'The *Manchester Chronicle* has a distinguished background,' Martin goes on. 'It was founded, as you know, over a hundred and fifty years ago and has been through a chequered history, every time rising from the ashes like a phoenix – because the *Chronicle* needs Manchester and Manchester needs the *Chronicle*. Together they've gone from strength to strength, enriching each other like an old married couple. I'd like the finest possible person to carry on our tradition of fairness, justice and quality writing. Therefore I've recommended the perfect candidate to the top dogs on the top floor. Who better than my noble deputy – our host – the one and only Guy Bradley of Buxton?'

Emily, Rob, Liz and Mrs Butterworth cheer.

'Oh, my God,' says Kate.

Guy takes a deep breath and stands up. 'Martin, I can't thank you enough for your faith in me,' he says. 'It's not only a wonderful job. It's a huge responsibility, an honour and a privilege. And – if Kate and our kids will forgive me – nothing could make me happier than to accept.'

The scene swims in front of Kate's eyes and there's a peculiar buzz in her ears. Perhaps she shouldn't be surprised that she hadn't seen the news coming before; or that Guy has kept it a secret – he'd have had the best of intentions, as usual, wanting to surprise her; or that once again, he's made a decision that affects all of them without consulting her. On the other hand, he's acting to salve her anxieties: replacing the income that she hasn't earned since quitting her job and affording the expensive support – lessons, concert dresses, transport and the rest – that Ali needs, not to mention a new piano. Her husband is about to take the best editorial post in the north of England. She mustn't complain, even if she knows it means he will now never, ever be at home.

'Darling,' she announces, forcing herself to stand beside him, 'I couldn't be happier.' Guy turns and embraces her. Their guests give another cheer.

In the deep-blue darkness of her bedroom, Alicia lies still, eyes closed, listening. Her brain latches on to sound; her hearing dwarfs her other senses. Music echoes, magnified, inside her brain cells; it won't leave her alone. She follows every note of the Ella Fitzgerald CD being played downstairs. Cassie, in her basket by the foot of the bed, slumbers on regardless.

Alicia hears the faint thread of voices making speeches – the fat man, Dad's boss; then Dad; then, briefly, Mum. Cheering. Then Mrs Butterworth, rattling on and on, probably making everyone feel that everything she says is of the utmost importance.

Someone is coming upstairs: a light female step she doesn't know. It's certainly not her mother's brisk footfall and it's unlikely to be Mrs Butterworth, who'd be wearing fancier shoes with sharper heels. The guest – either Mrs Boss or Miss Journalist – goes into the bathroom. There's the sound of the loo flushing and the gurgle of water in the pipes. Whoever it is comes out on to the landing and pauses. Cassie shifts and gives a grunt. Alicia keeps quiet. The steps move closer. Instead of returning to the kitchen, they're continuing up the stairs towards the second floor.

Dad's study is directly beside her room. It's firmly out of bounds to her and Adrian; if Dad is in there, they have to knock, in case he's working. When he's out, he doesn't lock the door: he's always said that he trusts them not to go in, and

they don't. Yet now the strange steps are creaking on the floorboards next to Alicia's wall. She pictures the guest – probably
the pretty young journalist, who doesn't know any better –
standing in Dad's office, gazing aghast at the mess.

She's not sure how much time has passed when she hears
another footstep, this time bounding and vigorous, unmistakably Dad's. He, too, pauses on the first floor landing; instead
of making for the bathroom, he continues up, more quietly,
past her room and into his study. She hears two voices, low,
indistinct. She tries to make out their words, but she can't;
she's too tired. Her arms are aching, there's a painful point
between her shoulder blades and sleep is just too tempting for
her to stay awake another moment.

'Sorry about the mess,' Guy says.

Emily is standing in the middle of the study under the eaves,
looking at the stacks of paper that half bury his computer on
the unvarnished wooden desk. 'The shelving's marvellous,' she
says. 'Did you build all this?'

'With Ikea's help.'

'It's nice to be able to picture you here, writing. Will you
still write when you take over as Big Boss?' Emily teases.

'God knows. God alone knows what's going to happen.'

Emily walks up to him. They stand face to face.

'Your wife is very striking,' Emily says. 'She's nothing like
I'd expected.'

'What were you expecting? A dragon?'

'Not exactly . . . Just someone a little more – this sounds
awful, but I thought she'd be more housewifey. More mumsy.
She seems like a London businesswoman who's been trans-
planted to Buxton.'

'Kate used to be a solicitor. Now I'm afraid her business is
Ali.'

'Ali's lovely.'

'Yes. Ali is lovely.'

'And how does she – er – get along with Deirdre Butterworth?'

'I do worry.' Guy sits down on his office chair. Emily presses his shoulder briefly. 'I worry,' he goes on, 'that everything we do for Ali might be wrong. There's an equal possibility, of course, that everything we do for her is right. It's so hard to know.'

'I can imagine. I love music, but I wouldn't know what to do with a talented kid.'

'It's so silly, Em. Every parent dreams about having a gifted child. But it's actually a big headache, because whatever you do is going to feel wrong in some way.'

'Is there anything I can do to help?'

'You do. You help just by being you.'

'I'm not always too happy being me. Not at the moment.'

'What is it, Em?' asks Guy, before he understands.

Emily moves away and stares into a bookshelf. Her back is to him. 'You know Hans Christian Andersen?' she says. 'My compatriot? My "distant relative possibly"? You know *The Little Mermaid*?'

'Sort of.'

'The Little Mermaid goes to the Sea Witch to have her tail turned into legs so that she can go on shore to win the man she loves. But when she has her feet, every step feels as if she's walking on knives.'

There's a short and dreadful silence.

'I don't know how I can go on like this,' Guy says at last.

'Guy, are you fighting what I'm fighting?'

'Oh, God. Em, if only you knew . . .'

She goes to him, takes his hand. 'Really?' she asks. Her eyes are bright with tears as their palms touch.

'I don't know what to do.' He can barely meet her gaze. 'Em, I want you, I want to sleep with you, I can't bear it. I think I'm falling in love with you. Do you mind me saying this?'

She looks away. 'You know . . . sometimes I wake up in the morning – and I wonder why you're not there with me.'

Guy stands and lifts Emily's chin towards him. As he bends his head to kiss her for the first time, his mind glazes over with the sweetness of red berries and cream.

Downstairs, Kate has opened another bottle of wine. Rob, clearly annoyed at being abandoned by Emily, who hasn't come back from the bathroom yet, has one arm round Mrs Butterworth and the other round Kate.

'I never thought I was going to be surrounded by so many lovely lasses on the same evening!' he declares.

'Tell us about you, Rob,' Kate says, moving closer. She's tipsy enough to find that the sensation of this much-younger man's arm across her shoulders makes her want to purr like a cat. 'Where do you come from? Where do you want to go?'

'I come from Worcester and I want to go everywhere,' Rob says, his hand moving up and down Kate's back. 'I want to see Machu Picchu. I'd like to cross America on a motorbike. I want to go across Asia overland.'

'Wouldn't you be worried?' Liz asks. 'About the wars? Bandits? Dysentery?'

'Oh, a nice strong boy like you,' says Mrs Butterworth, who's still working her way through the final quarter of her lamb, 'you wouldn't need to worry.'

'Martin wants to write his memoirs once he retires,' Liz says. 'He's seen a thing or two in the north of England that could make your blood curdle!'

Martin has quietly nodded off, his head bobbing down towards his substantial paunch.

Kate has been smiling at Rob and feeling her face flush. If Mrs Butterworth, who must be seventy if she's a day, can flirt so shamelessly, then so can she. She's glad to find she's not entirely forgotten how to feel the buzz in the blood that comes from an approving male eye trained on certain parts of her anatomy. Recently she's been too busy taking care of Ali to think about whether she's losing her looks or settling into middle-aged spread. Not that she'd dream of getting close to any man other than Guy. But since he's been so busy at work, and their sex life has dwindled to once every three weeks (maybe once a month – she dares not count), perhaps a little harmless flirtation after copious champagne isn't so dreadful.

'Where's Guy?' Liz asks.

Just as Kate is about to wonder that herself, the telephone rings. She extricates herself from Rob's arm, leaving him to the tender mercies of Mrs Butterworth, and picks up the receiver.

'Mrs Bradley?' The voice is unfamiliar; local and male.

'Speaking?'

'I'm calling about your son.'

'Sorry?' Kate puts a hand over her other ear. 'Did you say my *son*?'

'Adrian Bradley is your son, I believe?'

'Yes, he is.'

'I'm calling from Buxton police station. My name is Sergeant Walker. Adrian is with us. We'd like someone to come and get him.'

'What's he doing there?' Kate feels abruptly sober.

'He's been in some trouble. Suspected arson, since you ask. Now, if you or your husband could oblige us . . .'

'We'll be right there,' Kate says. She rings off and wonders, in a blinding, horrible second, how she will explain this to her guests.

Guy appears on the stairs. One look tells him what's wrong.

'I've had too much to drink,' Kate says. 'I can't drive.'

'Me too. We'll have to ask Liz. Or Rob.'

'We can't tell them what's happened. Your promotion—'

'What's he done?'

'Arson. They think.'

'Shit.'

'We'll have to go and get him.'

'I'll go. You stay and look after everyone. Don't let them know. I'll drive very slowly. It's not far.'

'Be careful.'

'Don't worry.'

Guy takes a long drink of water – which he needs badly – then makes his way to the door alone. Starting the car, he sees in the mirror a smudge of pale pink on the side of his face. Kate, thank heavens, had been too preoccupied to notice it.

The sight that greets him in the police station is not pleasant. Under the glaring fluorescent light three drunken louts are spitting abuse at an officer. A distraught woman with a black and purple bruise across one cheek is being led into a side room by a WPC. And, on a bench in the corner, two teenaged boys slouch together over the baseball caps in their hands. Adrian looks up and his brown eyes burn reproach into Guy before anyone has said a word.

Guy can imagine that he looks reproachable. There he is in dinner-party garb, the worse for a few glasses of wine, and though he's done his best to wipe away the traces of Emily's lipstick, some may have lingered.

'What on earth—?' he says.

'So, now you're interested, are you?' his son grunts.

'Adrian, there's no need for that. What's going on?'

'You're this young man's father, are you?' Sergeant Walker is beside them, surveying Guy in a way he doesn't like.

He looks him in the eye and says, 'I am.'

'Found these two legging it from the allotments. Good blaze they'd got going in that shed. Nice surprise for the geezer who grows them tomatoes.'

'Weren't us,' mumbles Sam – who, since Guy last saw him, has shaved his head and acquired a ripe crop of zits.

'"Weren't us",' the sergeant whines in imitation. 'Course not. Never is, is it? Little shits, both of you. If I had my way, you'd be locked up. Better still, deported to Australia.'

'Yes, please,' Adrian ripostes.

'How old would they be, sir?'

Guy has never heard such a sarcastic 'sir'. Restraining himself from slugging Sergeant Walker for calling his son a little shit, he gives him the details he needs. How fortunate for the Bradley family's reputation, he reflects, that a gutted shed is not earth-shattering news in the north-west, in parts of which people shoot each other comparatively often. Besides, the law, not tallying remotely with the teenage brain, stipulates that Adrian is too young to be publicly named. Even if he has to appear in court, nobody need know that the son of the editor-designate is, in present-day terminology, a yob.

'Ought to breathalyse you while I'm about it,' Sergeant Walker mutters after Guy. 'Try teaching your kid some respect for authority, rather than sitting about sipping your bloody champagne.'

'Authority?' Adrian snipes. 'What's that?'

'Shut it, Adrian. *Now.*' Guy marches him out.

Guy and Adrian drive home in silence. When they reach the house it's one a.m. and the guests' cars have gone. Guy's heart, which he'd assumed couldn't sink any lower, falls an extra metre through the Derbyshire limestone.

He switches off the engine and sits beside his son in the dark. 'Did you do it?' he asks.

'Do you care? No, you effing don't.'

'I effing do. Because you should know better.'

'Why should I? I can do what I like. Cos you're not going to stop me, and nor's Mum and nor's school and nor's anybody. Not that shitty policeman either.'

'I am going to stop you,' Guy says. 'Adrian, you're grounded.

From now on your mother is going to walk you to the school gate and collect you in the afternoon—'

'I'm not a kid!'

'You are a kid. You're a stupid, irresponsible, idiot kid and you're not going out on your own again until you learn to grow up.'

'So I have to sit in the effing house and listen to my sister play her effing piano all day? You've got to be fucking joking.'

'In Victorian times, if children used language like that, their parents would wash their mouths out with soap.'

'You can't,' Adrian snarls. 'You'd get done for cruelty.'

'You just *won't be told*, will you? Listen, you're grounded and that's that. Curfew is end of school day. Every evening I'm going to look at your homework, and if it's not done you shall stay up and work until it's finished. OK. In we go.'

Adrian half opens his door, then turns back, staring at Guy under his cap. 'What would they say,' he grunts, 'if they knew I have to set fire to some sad bastard's garden shed before you know I exist?'

One week later, Guy and Emily slope out of the office in succession and go, separately, to Emily's flat nearby in central Manchester. After two hours Guy, shattered, exhilarated and almost tearful with the relief of opening the floodgates, leaves to drive home, wondering how he can tell Kate that he is in love with another woman and wants to live with her.

When he pulls into his drive, he sees that something in the house has changed. The shape in the front window is not squat, but long, black and elegant. Alicia is sitting by it, darting about its keyboard, conjuring a shining, magical sound out of its sensuous belly that in no way resembles the clattery noises that used to emanate from the upright piano.

'She has to have the best,' says Kate, standing in the lounge doorway, watching her.

The bill and the paperwork are on the kitchen table. Guy picks them up and discovers that his mortgage has increased by £80,000. And Alicia has the face of a brand new angel freshly initiated into heaven.

8

In May, a week before Alicia is to play in the BBC competition final, Kate goes to Manchester on Saturday afternoon to buy herself a new suit for the occasion. Guy is at the office. Adrian is out with Sam. His grounding had lasted barely two weeks: Kate had been too busy with Alicia to walk him home from school every day and, as Guy always said, he 'would not be told'.

Alicia is alone, sitting at her beautiful grand piano, working on the Ravel Concerto. She knows it backwards. She could play it in all twelve major keys if she needed to. But although she's given recitals all over Derbyshire, Yorkshire and Staffordshire, as well as the Buxton Festival, she's never played a concerto with an orchestra before. At the semi-finals she'd found the TV cameras alarming while they swooped about her like small prehistoric carnivores. It wouldn't be so bad if they'd keep still. On the day, she knows, she'll be surrounded by distracting things in motion: the musicians playing, the conductor waving his arms, the cameras curious and prying, and she'll have to fight to keep her concentration. If her fingers know the notes so thoroughly that they'll play accurately even when her brain is in meltdown, all will be well.

'Ali,' Mum said, driving home from Withington a few days earlier, when Alicia had voiced one frustration too many, 'do you realise what a responsibility you have? A lot of people have invested a great deal in you. Think of your father. He nearly collapsed when he saw the cost of your piano. Think of Mrs Butterworth. She says you're the most talented pupil she's ever had. I gave up my job so that I could help you. When you win this competition, we'll all win with you. We'll be there with you, going through every moment of it. You won't be on your own.'

Alicia almost said, 'And if I don't win?' but decided against it. Reading between the lines, she deduced that if she didn't win, she'd be letting them all down.

How can they place such a load on her? Why can't Mrs Butterworth give her own concerts instead of obsessing about her pupils? Why can't her mother go to work, like normal mothers? Why does she *have* to win this competition or face hellfire and damnation?

It hadn't felt so bad up to the quarter-finals. That was easy. Fifteen minutes of music (again), this time in Birmingham, with Anjali backstage in her gorgeous orange Indian trouser suit waiting, laughing and joking with her, until Mum sent her off to warm up. Which was sensible. She'd needed to warm up, but she'd enjoyed being with Anjali so much that she'd forgotten to give herself enough time. Alicia has to admit that sometimes she needs Mum to help her keep her head.

Afterwards they went out with Anjali, her parents and her little sister to an Indian vegetarian restaurant, where Alicia munched through a massive rolled-up pancake called a dhosa, unlike anything she'd eaten before. Dr Sharma told her about the medicinal properties of cardamom and ginger, new to her since her mother never cooks with them. Later, the girls were still so excited that, instead of going straight home, the Bradleys went back to the Sharmas' house, a little way out of Birmingham city centre.

Here, while their parents talked about Having Talented Children, Anjali spirited Alicia upstairs and helped her try on a sari (it belonged to her mother) made of glorious, deep blue silk. Anjali wound the material round and round Alicia's torso, tucking and pinning; eventually, staring into the mirror, Alicia thought she looked like a fairytale princess. She'd never seen a blue to match this, and the draped silk struck her as infinitely more beautiful than the frilly, little-girl dresses that her mother bought her for her concerts. She's always disliked frills. She gazed at the kaleidoscope of colours in the cupboard – Anjali's mum had quite a range – and each sang a different key, a distinct and seductive sound to her. Anjali put one on too, in emerald green. They couldn't have looked more different – Alicia tall and fair, Anjali tiny and dark with enormous eyes, like a night creature from a tropical forest; but wearing similar clothes, Alicia declared, they could pretend to be sisters. 'You're like the sister I never had,' she told her friend.

Later, on the way home, Alicia suggested that she'd like a sari as a concert dress.

'Darling,' said Mum, 'it's totally inappropriate.'

'Anji sometimes wears them.'

'Anji's Indian.'

'So what?' Alicia protested. 'She wears Western concert dresses too, so why shouldn't I wear Indian ones?'

'Don't be silly, darling,' said Mum, who evidently didn't know how to answer this.

After that, the competition's pressures had started to mount. Next came the semi-finals, which involved a twenty-five minute recital, plus an interview with a BBC presenter and a camera crew filming her at home. They nosed round the piano room looking for good angles and remarking on how pretty Buxton was – and she'd been wearing the wrong colour for the piece they wanted her to play and had had to persuade Mum to distract them while she ran to her room to change. Playing wasn't a problem; and of course she's used to being watched. Now, though, she senses invisible eyes all around, thousands of them, trained on her every move.

Since she's won the entire piano section, Alicia will play her Ravel Concerto, pitted against the winners of the strings, percussion, brass and woodwind sections, live on national TV. She feels as if she's in a tunnel, pulled from one end and pushed from the other; she's trapped with nowhere to go except forward, hurled inexorably on with no power to turn back or stop time in its tracks.

'Ali?'

Alicia pauses in mid-melody. Dad is in the room, smiling at her.

'When did you last go for a walk?' he asks.

'A *walk*?'

'Come on, love. It'll do you more good than hammering away all afternoon. It's not like you're unprepared.'

'Mum'll kill me.'

'No, she won't. She needn't even know we've been out. And if she gets wind of it, I'll take the flak. Promise.'

'Can we go to Mam Tor?'

'We'll go wherever you like.'

Alicia dashes upstairs. Guy watches her: away from the piano, she's a normal girl again, a blonde teenager bounding around like any other – as she ought, perhaps, to be.

She comes down in a blue and white Kate sweater; it's May now, but although London is reportedly enjoying twenty degrees, in Buxton the temperature has only reached twelve. Driving away, they feel like a pair of children playing truant.

About twenty minutes outside Buxton, in the Peak District National Park, Mam Tor rises out of the landscape like a capsized ship buried under the rocks since time began. It's an Iron Age fort and the beginning of the Pennine Way, where the earth presents two hundred and seventy hilly miles that you can, if you wish, walk in their entirety. This, Guy has often told Alicia, is the backbone of England.

At the top, a look-out point with a telescope gives Alicia a full circle of wonder. On every side, the view offers her colours as elusive and mutable as those she pictures in her music. In late summer the moors are flecked with purple heather and the ground hums with the bumbling of a million bees. In January the world transmutes into black and white; and when the frost strikes, the rugged, hilly outlines are rapt with shades of silver. April brings emerald edges to the valleys and October and November turn them to bronze; July is dusty, warm and peculiarly artificial, for this almost treeless landscape is most natural in winter, sluiced with slanting rain, low clouds impaled on outcrops of rock, the wind tearing at Alicia as if determined to lift her off her feet and over the edge. That's when she loves it most. She can stand with an ecstasy of rain drenching her, letting the elements pour out the feelings she can't pour out herself except in music.

Today, though, it's spring. It's remarkably quiet for a Saturday; the Easter tourists have gone home, the summer ones haven't arrived and day-trippers, fearing showers, have stayed away. A few hang-gliders haven't been deterred: they sail in soundless flight over the wide, wild space, tiny amid its treachery. Alicia and her father watch white puffballs of mist swirling in the valleys. The only interruptions to the silence are the whispering wind and the high chatter of a skylark.

'You might see into the future on a day like this,' Alicia says, her gaze scanning the horizon.

'You spend a lot of time thinking about the future, don't you?'

'I guess I haven't much choice.'

'Ali, you're fourteen. Try living in the present a bit. It's good, sometimes, the present. Practising isn't everything. You need to do some living too.'

'That might be easier after next week.'

'It might. But what worries me is that it might not.'

Alicia turns. 'What do you mean?'

'You're thinking of the concerto final as the end. But it might be the beginning. It doesn't matter whether you win or not because everyone will see you on TV and if people like your playing, they'll want you to give concerts. There might be agents watching. Anything's possible.'

'Dad, do you *want* me to win?'

'Oh, Ali, of course I do! I just want you to know that it's not the most important thing on earth.'

Alicia leans against the telescope and looks at her feet. She's growing, fast; each weekend, when Guy has a moment to catch his breath between crises of one kind or another, he notices a change in her. Soon her height will match Kate's; she's already among the tallest in her class at school. The puppy fat is giving way to long, lean legs and a healthy, developing figure.

'What do *you* want, Ali?'

Her back is to him, her golden hair hanging in loose trails. She says nothing.

She wants to say too much, but she doesn't know how. She can't find a way to tell him that she wants him to be proud of her; that one word of approval from him would be worth ten of Mum's and twenty of Mrs Butterworth's; that it's his approval she craves because it's the rarest. Without it, she's just a lump of growing cells and young, hopeful energy that has landed in the middle of Derbyshire and learned how to play the piano. An image lingers from her childhood, of her father lifting her to the window to watch the raindrops slide down the panes; and of how, when there was music, he would come into focus. Perhaps the music was conjuring him for her, like magic.

Even before the final begins, Kate, sitting beside Guy in Symphony Hall, Birmingham, seems to be looking back on this day from a moment far in the future.

The competition buzz is centred on Alicia. She's the youngest of the five finalists. She's up against a violinist two years older than herself, a clarinettist who is nearly eighteen, and two contestants who, in Kate's opinion, are a waste of space: a trumpeter and a percussionist.

'What's the use of making brass and percussion players do concertos?' she remarks. 'They'll only end up in orchestras, wondering why they're not famous soloists.'

'Most pianists end up bashing out exercises for ballet classes,' Guy reminds her.

'Not Ali.'

'I didn't mean Ali.'

'Steady on, you two,' says George, a couple of seats away on the other side of Adrian. 'No fights, please. This is Ali's big night.'

A bright, dark figure turns round from the row in front and waves to Kate.

'Hello, Anjali,' Kate says. 'How lovely that you could come.'

'How's she feeling?' Anjali asks. Kate assesses her deep eyes, sleek hair, slender, self-possessed face. There's not an ounce of malice in her. Just as well, since Ali has beaten her.

'She's fine. A little nervous, perhaps, but very excited.'

'She's got to win. Everyone's saying they've never seen anything like her. My piano teacher watched the semi-finals and went into ecstasies. I'm so happy for her.'

Kate is surprised at Anjali's lack of competitiveness. Watching her and Ali taking their turns in the quarter-finals, Kate had been so impressed with Anjali's playing that she'd found herself half hoping that some disaster would befall either the piano (a broken string, an insecure lid, a sticky key) or maybe Anjali herself (a gently sprained finger or brief dose of flu). Such emotions weren't pleasant; but on the other hand, this was Ali's big chance and it was essential that nothing should get in her way. What's the point of devoting such swathes of time and energy to music if somebody else does better?

'Anji,' Kate says, 'this is Adrian. You haven't met before, have you?'

'Hi, Anji,' Adrian mutters. He's not generally shy around girls, Kate has noticed, unless he likes them.

'Lovely to meet you.' Anjali, her head turned over one

graceful shoulder, smiles at him. He smiles back for a split second, then stares down at his hands. Anjali's father, beside her, gives her a brief, sharp glance.

Backstage, Alicia had locked herself inside her dressing room, telling Kate that she wasn't nervous, but wanted to be alone. Kate had trusted her and left. She's so nervous that she couldn't feel worse if she had to play the concerto herself. Her stomach ties itself into reef-knots, her palms are sweaty and freezing – she's dreading having to shake anybody's hand – and there's a humming in her ears, maybe the hall's air-conditioning, maybe a creation of her stressed-out mind. How does anybody achieve the remotest degree of accuracy on a musical instrument if this is what nerves do to their bodies?

Mrs Butterworth, her small, bony figure encased in dappled blue and violet silk, turns from three rows in front to nod to them. Kate nods back, noticing with satisfaction that some of the people around them comment quietly to one another, 'That's Alicia Bradley's mother; that's her teacher, Deirdre Butterworth . . .' Her stomach jolts again.

The clarinettist plays first. She's a large, smily girl who gives what the television commentators will describe as an incredibly musical performance of the Mozart Clarinet Concerto. Alicia is to play last. They wait amid the audience on red seats, surrounded by pale wood and brilliant TV lights, through the percussion concerto, the violin concerto and the interval; then they'll have to endure the trumpet concerto before Alicia's turn.

'And here we have Alicia Bradley's family.'

Kate glances round, startled; she had barely glimpsed the television presenter, a cheerful young woman named Isabel, heading their way with a cameraman in tow. The lights make her blink as Isabel bounces up to them, microphone at the ready. 'Mrs Bradley, how are all of you feeling tonight?'

'It's very exciting for everyone, but especially Alicia.' Kate gives her widest smile.

'Of course the competition's very stiff and she's the youngest by several years. How does she feel about that?'

'Absolutely fine,' Kate says. 'She's here to make music. We're all here to celebrate music-making, first and foremost. And whoever wins the prize, I'm sure he or she will be a very deserving performer.'

'Well, best of luck to Alicia Bradley, who's been the hot favourite in a very special year for this competition,' Isabel says, into the camera. 'The stage has been rearranged, the piano is in place and in a moment Alicia Bradley will be coming on to play Ravel's glorious Piano Concerto in G major.'

Kate's whole body is trembling as applause blazes round the hall – and Alicia is there, sailing across the platform in her turquoise dress (she'd insisted that was the only colour she could wear to play this concerto). She strides to the piano as confidently as a woman of thirty. Rustles, whispers and thrills go through the audience. Kate reaches for Guy's hand, almost as clammy as her own.

Alicia, her back tree-trunk straight, her hands poised to begin, fixes her gaze on the conductor. He smiles at her – a famous maestro with a rack of awards and titles, grinning at Kate's fourteen-year-old daughter as if she's a colleague, an equal. He raises his arms. A snap like a whipcrack, the first note of Ravel's score, and they're off, Alicia's fingers glittering, flickering, coaxing, the orchestra sitting forward to listen during her solos.

It's not Kate's intense slow-motion experience; it's not her imagination; it's not just because Alicia is her daughter. Something extraordinary is happening. An enchantment is settling over the hall that defies breath. The audience is motionless. Nobody coughs. Nobody wriggles, not even Adrian. The sounds reaching their ears are not like the sound of Alicia practising. The figure on stage is not that of a schoolgirl ploughing through her first concerto.

Alicia is making the piano sing in a way that pianos usually don't. She turns Ravel's jazzy phrases almost like Edith Piaf or Ella Fitzgerald. The glint in her eye as she toys with the music, the glances she exchanges with the orchestra members who duet with her, the shared confidences with the conductor, the sophistication in the sounds – none of these match the unsophistication of the Alicia who bounds about at home and goes running in the rain with no umbrella, her dog trotting beside her. She is the music and the music is her. The piano is an extension of her. As she plays the sustained, unaccompanied start of the slow movement, the mesmerised atmosphere deepens. Silent ecstasy emanates from a thousand people towards the Birmingham night sky. Kate's cheeks are wet with tears; she has no idea how they've got there, whether they're for Ali or for the ghost of Victoria, haunting the music to which she had so briefly lived, then died.

At the end, the hall explodes. Kate's head spins. Anjali and her family leap to their feet. Didie on the other side of George is wiping her eyes, Adrian is whooping and whistling and the cheers and stamps around them won't stop. The place is in a frenzy, shouting for Alicia Bradley.

Alicia has retreated off the platform with the conductor, but he sends her back alone and she's greeted by a roar like a storm at sea. Tall and radiant in her turquoise silk dress, she extends both arms in a gesture of thanks, as graceful as a ballerina, to Kate's astonishment – she thinks of her daughter as gawky. What seems too loud and too large close to is transformed, on stage, into a personality that projects to perfection.

Guy is motionless beside Kate. 'So it's true, then,' he says. 'This isn't the end. It's only the beginning.'

With Mrs Butterworth strutting behind them like a small hawk that's fallen into a pot of purple paint, and Anjali alongside laughing with joy, Guy, Kate and Adrian struggle upstream to get backstage. Kate can see Alicia's bright hair and blue dress; she's surrounded by well-wishers, the BBC team, members of the orchestra, some contestants who've been eliminated, people in suits or expensive dresses who have a vague air of importance . . .

Then Alicia spots them. Kate holds out her arms.

'Dad!' Alicia cries, flinging herself on to Guy's neck.

Kate is poised between breaths, lowering her hands, wondering how to laugh this off, when someone brushes her elbow.

Life-changing events can be crowned with TV cameras; they can start with the ring of a bell on door or phone; and, sometimes, they're heralded by the soft touch of a finger upon an arm.

'Kate?'

The voice is oddly familiar. Kate turns and looks into the face of a slender, sinewy woman with short-cropped hair and deep brown eyes, wearing an elegant linen trouser suit and an exotically fashioned gold necklace.

'You don't remember me, do you?'

Kate's brain dredges images long forgotten, traumatised by time. She knows these eyes. *'Heavens!'*

'Rebecca – Rebecca Young, from university. And quartet. Don't say you've forgotten me, Kate?'

'Oh, my God,' Kate says.

'You must be a very proud mum.' Rebecca presses her arm harder.

'Yes! My God – Rebecca . . . Just a moment – *Ali*!'

'Mum!' Alicia reaches out and hugs her. Kate can feel her exhaustion – the dress is soaked with sweat and the muscles are trembling slightly – but her face is alight with triumph.

'Ali, this is Rebecca. I haven't seen her since university,' Kate says.

'Congratulations, Alicia,' Rebecca says. 'You were outstanding.'

'I haven't won yet,' Alicia reminds her. The jury is absent, considering its verdict.

'I'll be amazed if you haven't,' Rebecca declares. 'They're mad if they don't give you the prize. Kate, it's so fantastic to be here and to see you and meet your family. We must get together and talk properly. But I can tell tonight's going to be difficult.'

'It's fantastic to see you too. Call me?' Kate grabs a pen from her handbag and writes the phone number on the front of Rebecca's programme.

'Here's my card.' Rebecca presses a small red rectangle into Kate's hand. It reads:

EDEN CLASSICS
Rebecca Harris
Director, A&R

Before she can ask what A&R means, or why Rebecca was backstage trying to meet Alicia, there's a peal of electronic bells and a flurry of anticipation as the jury troops by, heading for the stage.

'See you later, darling. Fingers crossed,' Kate whispers to Alicia.

Adrian hasn't had a chance to talk to his sister, beyond a peck on the cheek; neither has Anjali; but, Kate notes, they seem quite happy talking to each other.

Ten minutes later, Alicia Bradley has been named BBC Young Musician of the Year. Some while after that – nobody is counting now – Guy and Adrian hoist her on to their shoulders and carry her out of the hall into the crowd that has amassed outside the stage door to cheer her. The next morning, the front page of *The Times* displays a huge photograph of Alicia aloft, smiling and shining across a forest of wild, clapping hands.

Two days later, they're at home, trying to rekindle normality. Kate, shadows under her eyes, sips a third, much-needed cup of morning coffee, wondering whether she was dreaming and what her next step should be, assuming she wasn't. As if in response, the telephone rings.

'Is that Kate?'

'Speaking.'

'Kate. It's Rebecca.'

9

Alicia wakes late, when Cassie jumps on to the bed and licks her face. She's sweating. She hadn't been able to sleep for hours, feeling too churned up; she'd finally drifted off at four o'clock, when dawn was breaking. The dog has woken her from a nightmare.

It was about Cassie – Alicia's worst nightmares always are, usually about the day she was nearly swept away in the River Dove. This time Cassie was in the water, trying to paddle upstream, but great lumps of ice were cascading from the hills, intent on carrying her with them. Alicia leaped in after her, only to find herself submerged beneath an ice floe.

She'll never forget how the water felt. She'd only been in it for a few moments, but the cold had been more bitter than she could imagine, and the current stronger. The fright of falling and feeling it had nearly winded her. The most terrifying thing, she thinks, is the power of natural elements – water and earth, fire and air – because each is filled with energy greater than that of anything alive. That energy can crush a human being whenever it likes.

As the dream went on, she and Cassie were trapped by a freezing, solid mass that scarcely let them breathe, and Alicia was more worried about Cassie than about herself, yet at the same time confused over which of them was which. She couldn't move her legs; she tried to scream, but no sound came out. Mercifully, at that point the real Cassie arrived and woke her. Alicia found that her legs were entangled in the duvet, which was why she couldn't move them. Now it's nearly half past eleven, but luckily this is half-term and she doesn't have to go to school for a week.

The competition is over; she's won it; the future stretches ahead, paved with teeth. What will happen to her now? The final had had a momentum of its own. They had stayed in a wonderful modern hotel; she had spent the next day giving interviews, and in the evening the Sharmas met them and took them to their favourite Indian restaurant. They drove home so late that Cassie barely looked up when they arrived. Alicia is grateful that their neighbours don't mind looking after the dog now and then; otherwise she'd have spent the whole time wondering whether Cassie was all right without her.

She couldn't stop remembering, though, that she had 'beaten' Anjali, among all the others. There should be nothing to 'beat'. They'd played different pieces of music in their own ways. Who was to say that hers was better? Maybe she'd played faster, maybe she's a little more confident, but that's no reason for her to become famous overnight while Anjali goes straight back to being a schoolgirl.

Anjali's father, who'd showered Alicia with praise and insisted on paying for dinner for everyone, had taken some photos of them in the restaurant, promising to send them to her. He kept telling Anjali that she must try to work as hard as Alicia does; advice that made Alicia uncomfortable. Dr Sharma is a GP and Anjali says that his patients adore him. Alicia admires him too, because he's so interested, so proud of Anjali, so much there for her – unlike Alicia's dad. But Anjali looks positively scared of him.

It's time for her to face her own family. Dressed, she takes a deep breath and opens her bedroom door to go downstairs and see what's waiting for her there today.

The phone calls and letters haven't stopped. Mum puts on the answering-machine, then shows the letters to Alicia: from agents, record companies, PR companies, fans ('Dear Alicia, I am six years old and I loved seeing you play on the TV, now I am going to have piano lessons too . . .'), music festivals, music clubs, concert promoters, dress designers and charities ('Of course we can't pay you, but we hope that you will find the concert a worthwhile experience . . .'). The BBC has an association with a young musicians' advisory scheme, which offers guidance to all the finalists for the two years until the next competition; even so, Alicia wonders how she's supposed to make head or tail of her new situation.

'What are we going to do?' she asks, eating Weetabix. She's itching to learn some new pieces. Mrs Butterworth has told her to choose anything she likes and she's picked the most difficult things she can find: a Prokofiev sonata, more Ravel, lots of Chopin and the famous Piano Concerto No. 1 by Tchaikovsky.

'I had a call from a very old friend,' Mum says. 'You met her backstage – her name is Rebecca Harris. She works for a record company and she thinks she can help us, so I've suggested she comes to stay for a weekend and we can talk it through. She knows the music business. Of course, the advisory scheme will be useful, but it might be nice to have another viewpoint as well. Don't you think it's a good idea?'

There's a clomp on the stairs and Adrian, his face pale and his eyes full of sleep, peers round the kitchen door. 'Is there coffee?'

'"Good morning, Mum, good morning, Ali, is there any coffee?"' Mum prompts.

Adrian grunts, 'Whatever,' and pads across to the percolator. 'Hey, Ali,' he says, without looking at her. 'I'm proud of you.'

'Really?'

'Sure. You were *cool*. All those cameras and crowds and you just went on and did it. The lads said they saw you on TV and they were dead impressed.'

Alicia jumps up and hugs her brother.

'OK, OK, cool it,' he says, turning red. A moment later he's vanished, taking the rest of the coffee with him.

Kate surveys the empty pot with some anger, wondering why such small matters annoy her so intensely. After she's loaded the percolator with more ground coffee and water, she succumbs to something she's desperate to do. She's been keeping one eye on the clock, waiting until a suitable hour, not wanting to appear too eager. It isn't her normal attitude towards making phone calls. Her pulse, irrationally, seems to have increased. She dials the number on Rebecca's card.

'How about this weekend?' Kate suggests.

'I shall drop everything and run,' declares Rebecca.

By the end of the afternoon, juggling practice, phone calls and discussions with Mum, Alicia feels that her head will burst like a balloon if she doesn't get some air. The weather is clear, the clouds puffy and sparse. She pleads, 'Half an hour, Mum?'

'OK, half an hour. Mind how you go darling.'

Running down the hill towards the golf course, Alicia looks at Cassie and wonders why, in her dreams, she muddles herself up with her dog. Perhaps it's because they need the same things: fresh air, exercise and, now and then, the blessed freedom of being let off the leash.

It's an amazing time of year: everything is bright and sprouting. The posters for the Buxton Festival in July are in place outside the little opera house and the flowerbeds in the Pavilion Gardens have become rich blocks of colour that dazzle Alicia like the sun. Cygnets swim on the pond and the hills are teeming with lambs – lovely as long as you don't think too hard about what will happen to them later.

Alicia and Cassie haven't been out for five minutes when a bicycle whirs down the hill towards them, wobbles, then stops. Someone calls her name. Alicia, Mum says, must get used to people recognising her in the street (something Mum seems to like more than she does herself). But this is only Matthew Littlemore, who's in her class at school and had been at her nursery school too. Alicia has known him all her life, though never sees him much beyond the school gates.

'Hey, Ali, I saw you on TV,' Matthew says. His eyes are sweet. They always were.

'Yeah?' Alicia beams. 'Thanks.'

'Me and my brother Tim, we're having a party tomorrow. Want to come?'

'A party? I'd love to. But I don't know if Mum'll let me. It's my piano lesson the next day and I've got all this new stuff to learn.'

Matthew's face falls. Probably his mum lets him do whatever he likes, as most mums seem to, other than hers.

'It'd be so cool,' he urges. 'There'd be all uz crowd and then in walks the Young Musician of the Year. You'd be guest of honour. Please come, Ali. Have you got our address?'

'Write it down?'

Matthew has a pen, but there's nothing to write on except the back of Alicia's hand. When he touches it, he does so as carefully as if it were made of icing sugar. People are funny about Alicia's hands. She nearly tells Matthew that just because they play the piano it doesn't mean they don't do normal things too, like scrunching the loo roll. But her half-hour is running by.

'I'll try to get there,' she says. 'See you later.'

'See you, Ali.' Matthew swings one long leg back over the bike and sails away downhill. Cassie is jumping and whimpering, impatient to get moving, so they spend the rest of their time sprinting for all they're worth.

They arrive home sweaty (Alicia) and panting (both of them). Mum looks surprised. 'What's that on your hand?' she asks.

'Oh, that. It's Matthew Littlemore's address. He asked me to a party tomorrow. I can go, can't I, Mum?'

'Oh, Ali. It's the night before your lesson.'

'So?' Alicia gives her best Adrian-like pout, but Mum isn't amused.

'So, you have to prioritise. What's more important? Piano lessons or parties?'

'I have a piano lesson every week. I hardly ever go to a party.' Alicia feels tight anger pressing out from her solar plexus – why does she has to fight for every little thing she wants to do away from the piano? 'I don't see why everything has to revolve around Mrs bloody Butterworth!'

'Ali, don't use language like that about your teacher.' Mum, of course, overreacts. She reminds Alicia of Grandma Margaret. 'She's just helped you win the biggest prize in the country. Ali, don't you see? You've got to put your playing first, because now there will be concerts for you to do in some very, very important places and . . .'

'Does that mean I can't go to one party at the house of a friend I've known my whole life, who lives round the corner?'

'Yes, Ali, that is precisely what it means. Now, feed that poor dog, will you? And then go and practise.'

'But, Mum—'

'*Now*, Ali.'

Cassie is whining for her food; probably whining because Alicia is unhappy, too. At least, Alicia thinks, somebody is on her side. She gives Cassie a bowl of her favourite meat; after gobbling it down, the dog follows her to the piano. Some dogs howl when musical instruments are being played, but luckily Cassie can't be bothered. Instead, she lies under the Steinway and goes to sleep.

On the piano sits the plump volume that is Tchaikovsky's Piano Concerto No. 1, waiting for Alicia to learn it. It's extremely difficult, but working out how to get round that is half the fun. After two and a half hours, Alicia feels as if she's only been there for ten minutes, making the music that she adores come alive in her hands, discovering how to shape it as she wants to. It will be hers and she will belong to it. There's no feeling in the world as astonishing as this.

Eventually Mum calls her for supper. Alicia washes her hands and Matthew Littlemore's address rubs off in the soap, but it doesn't seem to matter any more.

Adrian, though, has other ideas. He knows all about the Littlemores' party through Matthew's brother, Tim. 'You've got to go, Ali,' he says later on.

'How can I?' Alicia is lying on her bed, reading. 'Mum's right. It's Mrs B the next day.'

'Mummy doesn't always know best.' Adrian slinks in and closes the door. His eyes are permanently angry these days – maybe because he has GCSE exams soon. But sometimes she thinks he's cleverer than the rest of them put together. Adrian sees things as they are, more clearly than she does; his head isn't filled with Tchaikovsky and Ravel.

'You're nearly fifteen, but Mum's treating you like you're nine,' he insists. 'You've got a life of your own and you look fit – all my friends think so. You should have more fun. You can't play music well if you don't have fun.'

'How do you mean?'

'Music says something, right? It's not just a load of notes designed to keep you plugging away until you can play them?'

'Yes. No. I mean, yes, it means something, and no, it's not just there to keep you working.'

'So if you never do any living, how are you ever going to feel anything that you can put into the music?'

'But—?'

'I like that thing you were playing earlier. What is it?'

'The Tchaikovsky Concerto.'

'It's – what? Half an hour long, or more? And it's full of all kinds of different feelings. So if you never have a chance to feel those feelings for yourself . . .'

'It's not that I don't feel them. I do. I just haven't done anything about them.'

Adrian obviously hasn't thought of this any more than Alicia has until now. 'Well,' he says eventually, 'if you want to go to that party, you tell me and I'll help you.'

'Aren't you coming too? Mum wouldn't say no if she knew you'd be looking after me.'

'The whole point is you don't get looked after, for once. Anyway, that wouldn't make a blind bit of difference with Mum. She doesn't trust me, she never has. And she doesn't *mother* you, she *smothers* you. She's like a mother elephant that goes completely fucking nuts if anything threatening goes near her baby, and when the stampede happens, I don't want to be in the way.'

At the thought of Mum as a stampeding elephant, trumpeting and charging in Alicia's defence, Alicia and Adrian both crack up laughing so hard that Alicia falls right off the bed.

If Mum is an elephant, Alicia is a baby elephant and Adrian is a lion cub – a wicked one, but a lion cub all the same – she wonders where that leaves Dad in their Buxtonian family jungle. She pictures him as a marmoset, shimmying to safety up a tree where he can swing from branch to branch and watch everything beneath, without getting too involved.

'I love you,' says Guy.

Emily is lying in his arms, her hair soft against his chest. He's moving his hands against the nubbly curve of her spine, the shadowed hollows of her neck, the fine, sweet skin on her inner thigh. He can't stop touching her, now that he's started. She turns her face to him and, in the glow from a single lamp on the floor, he sees tears in her eyes. He kisses them away, tasting salt.

'I love you too,' she says. 'Stay with me.'

'I have to go. It's half past nine.'

In the street a siren wails. Blue lights shimmer against the curtains.

'Don't worry,' she jokes, 'they're not after you.'

'Perhaps they ought to be.'

'Nonsense. I'm guilty too. I don't have to do this, you know. You're here because I want you to be. I know you have to go home, even if I wish you didn't.'

'I worry about you living here. It's not the safest area.' Every time Guy is round, a hundred police cars and fire engines seem to career past the block.

'I'm a big girl. I can look after myself.'

'You should have someone to look after you.'

'I don't want anyone to look after me but you, and you can't. That's nobody's fault.' Emily pushes back the covers and crosses to the window to peer out, concealing her nakedness with the long curtains.

'God, you're beautiful.' They've made love twice in two hours, but Guy, looking at her, is still faint with longing. He reaches out his arms and she comes back to him and wraps the essence of all that she is, her musky skin, her clear grey-eyed gaze, her open soul, round his aching body. In a few minutes he'll have to leave her bed, shower away every trace of her and drive out of Manchester across the moor to Buxton, which to him is no longer one of the highest, coldest towns in England for no reason.

'Couldn't you stay?' Emily coaxes. 'Can't you tell her something came up, you're too tired to drive and you're going to stay in a hotel?'

It sounds so easy that Guy hesitates before shaking his head. If he does it once, he'll do it again. Before he knows what's happened, he'll be spending several nights a week in a fictional hotel and then Kate will find out.

'She's already angry because I refused to put Ali's picture on the front page,' he says.

His own staff had been surprised. Local girl wins national

competition? Of course she should be on the front page. But she happened to be the editor's daughter. He would, he'd explained to one perplexed young journalist, be in deep ethical shit if he put a picture of Alicia on the front of his newspaper. It wasn't a sackable offence, but he'd lose his credibility at the office.

Instead, he'd lost his credibility at home. Kate couldn't understand it. The point was Ali, not him. What was the use of his powerful position if he couldn't help his daughter? Guy was so startled by her attitude that he fell over his words trying to explain simultaneously that that wasn't why he'd taken the job, that that kind of action was precisely what it was his duty to avoid and that in any case it wouldn't make the slightest difference since Ali had already snaffled the prize live on TV and had had her picture on the front of *The Times*, compared to which the *Manchester Chronicle* was small fry. Kate hadn't seen it that way. She couldn't see it any way but her own – just as her parents couldn't see any possibility for Sunday lunch other than overcooked roast beef.

'You did the right thing,' Emily says, 'and you know it.'

'Thanks, love. Glad someone believes in me.'

'Guy, come to Denmark with me?'

'*What?*'

'Please. I'm dying to take you there. There's so much I want to show you.'

'Sweetheart, there's nothing I'd like better, but how am I supposed to get away? What am I supposed to tell them?'

'Tell them – as so many men do when they're having affairs – that you're away at a conference. Just be consistent. Yes, I know, I'm shameless. But I want to take you to Denmark and I know that other people do this kind of thing, and if they can, then we can too.'

'Em, I'm not proud of this, you know. I don't *want* to have "an affair". I don't *want* to cheat on my wife.'

'But you are. So either do it, or don't do it. But for heaven's sake, *don't* lie in my bed and make love to me saying you don't want to!'

Guy closes his eyes in despair.

'Hey.' Emily taps his chest with one finger. Through half-raised eyelids he sees her face close to his, shining with helpless affection. 'You're not the first man to have an affair and you won't be the last,' she says. 'Other people manage to go away on trips with their "mistresses". So you can manage to go away with me if you want to. You just have to decide whether you want to. If you do, we'll find a way. I never set out to do this either. I don't want to have an affair with a married man. But I can't pretend I don't love you. I can't go against the feelings we have for each other. If this is the only way we can have them, then this is how it has to be.'

'It's not who we are, but it's what we're becoming. Is that dreadful?'

'Of course. And of course not. Come on, darling, it's nearly ten. You'd better get going.'

Guy takes the dreaded shower, then puts on his suit and prepares to leave. His feet feel like lead as he laces up his shoes.

'Briefcase,' says Emily, handing it to him. 'Glasses.' She retrieves them from the kitchen table, where they're lying beside her pasta bowl, which contains the tomatoey leftovers of their supper. 'Keys.' She fetches them from the floor where, earlier, they'd fallen out of Guy's pocket as he pulled off his jacket in a hurry.

'You're an angel,' Guy says. 'We'll find a way. I promise. See you tomorrow.'

Emily waves to him from her door as he dashes away down the stairs.

Alicia, preparing for bed, hears something light strike her window. At first she thinks it's rain. A louder tap convinces her that it isn't. She pulls back the curtain. Adrian is standing in the garden, throwing pebbles. 'Adrian, what the—'

'Come on, Ali!'

'Mum'll hear.'

'Just do it! Cos if you don't, you'll be sorry. Hurry up, and say goodnight to Mum first. She's doing letters, she won't even look up.'

'Where's the dog? She'll bark!'

'She won't. I gave her some extra grub and she's fast asleep in the kitchen. Useless watchdog, anyway.'

Alicia doesn't like the idea of her dog being manipulated, but she can't help smiling. Cassie would probably bound up to a burglar and lick his face. She goes to her door and calls, 'Night night, Mum.' A faint call comes back from the spare room, which is slowly being transformed into a study: the sewing-machine, knitting basket and guest bed now cohabit with a desk, two filing cabinets and a computer.

She picks up her trainers and inches on tiptoe towards the stairs. She can hear the faint patter of Mum typing. In the kitchen, the over-fed Cassie is sleeping off her feast, nose on paws. At last Alicia manages to edge through the front door and, to her astonishment, she and her brother are soon making their silent way up the hill towards Tim and Matthew Littlemore's home.

The Littlemores live on a cul-de-sac in a small, semi-detached brick house that matches all its neighbours. As Alicia and Adrian approach, they can hear a thumping beat and whoops from inside. Shadows dance on the curtains, silhouettes jumping around and drinking from plastic cups. Alicia stops. 'I can't go in there.'

'Yes, you can. Don't be silly.'

'Please stay. Don't just leave me there. Please, Adrian? Otherwise I'm going straight home and I'll tell Mum.'

'You little blackmailer! I'll stay but, remember, it was for your own good that I didn't want to. Now, ring that bell.'

Alicia steps forward and presses. The door swings open and Matthew is in the doorway, his face registering first surprise, then delight. 'Ali! You made it!'

Tim – a taller, even lankier edition of Matthew – waves a greeting to Adrian, who wanders past his sister into the kitchen.

'It's so great you could come,' Matthew enthuses, ushering in the hesitant Alicia. 'Let me get you a drink.'

'Orange juice, please.'

'Oh, come on, have something stronger. Your mum's not here. What do you like?'

'I don't know,' Alicia admits. 'I've never tried.'

In the hall, Tim is saying to Adrian, 'Your sister's cute, but she doesn't have a clue, does she?'

'Yuck.' Alicia, in the kitchen, is sampling a lurid alcopop.

'I'll have that,' says Kelly from school, whom Alicia hates. Her clothes tonight are so skimpy that Alicia – in a home-knitted yellow jersey and jeans – wonders why she bothers to wear any at all. Her face is caked with makeup. Alicia puts on a little basic makeup for concerts, but hates it: it makes people look like clowns. She hands Kelly the drink, wishing it were even nastier than it is.

'Try this one instead.' Matthew pours a mix from two different bottles, tops it with orange juice and gives it a stir. Alicia sips. Kelly and her group smirk, then snort with laughter as Alicia pulls a face. She decides to stick with the drink to spite them. So much for being Matthew's 'guest of honour': she's up against the resident nasties here too. Being Young Musician of the Year doesn't change that. Matthew's the only person who thinks it matters; as for the others, not only will her prize fail to stop the taunting, it may make things worse.

Tim, Adrian and Sam have sloped away to Tim's bedroom, from which sweetish smoke is now drifting down to the hall. When Alicia breathes it in, it makes her dizzy.

'Want to dance?' Matthew asks her, ignoring Kelly and her crowd.

'Will you teach me how? I never tried dancing before.'

Matthew looks confused, but nods. 'This is the Young Musician of the Year!' he announces, to his friends in the front room, but the music is so loud that nobody hears him. Alicia is glad.

She stands opposite Matthew and jigs around. It seems a slightly pointless exercise. The drink has left a vile taste in her mouth and she can't hear what anybody is saying through the noise. 'Don't the neighbours mind?' she shouts at Matthew.

'So what?' he shouts back.

Behind them, a group of lads from school – the ones who get up to no good in the Pavilion Gardens – are slumped on the sofa and armchairs, drinking beer from tins and pretending they're gangsta rappers.

'Yo, bitch,' says one of them – Alicia recognises him as the biggest troublemaker in Adrian's year, always being hauled to the headmaster for truancy, fighting and, once, carrying a knife. She hesitates. She can't always tell what's real and what's being put on to tease her. The troublemaker's name, she vaguely remembers – she never concentrates on who's who at school – is Garth.

'You's the cool bitch what won a TV prize,' says a boy with pop eyes like a fish, who comes from a farm at the edge of the moor and speaks, at school, with a plain Derbyshire accent. He's trying to be the coolest thing since ice-cubes, but this time Alicia isn't taken in: he sounds like a total plonker.

'You know Alicia,' Matthew says to them, an arm round her. 'She's famous now, but she's still one of us.'

'Hi,' she says. She's sweating desperately in her jersey.

'So where's your mum?' Garth asks Matthew. The Littlemores' father had left them years ago.

'Seeing my auntie in Wolverhampton for a few days. "Be good now, boys. Bed by half past ten."'

Alicia is beginning to wonder what time she's going to get home from this weird experience. Mum was right: she has her lesson tomorrow. Everyone else is on half-term, and although some of them should be revising for GCSEs, they obviously aren't. The clock on the mantelpiece – it reminds her incongruously of her grandparents in Harrow – tells her that it's nearly eleven thirty. In fifteen hours, she has to play her Tchaikovsky to Mrs Butterworth for the first time.

'Playing the piano?' says the fish-eyed boy in his normal voice. 'Why d'you do *that*?'

'Dunno, really,' Alicia says. 'I just do.'

'Is it hard?'

'Yeah, but it's fun.'

'Ali's dad is editor of a newspaper,' Matthew says, stroking her arm. Alicia wishes he wouldn't. The lads swig beer and look at her legs in their tight jeans. They don't care about what her dad does, what she does or, she thinks, anything much else.

'Where does your mum work?' she asks Matthew.

'She's a secretary at the quarry. It's OK. She's cool.'

'Won't she mind this when she comes back?'

'She won't know. We'll clear up. We always do.'

At the end of the room, Kelly is snogging her boyfriend. Garth, who gains street cred for always skipping school the day after he's sent to the headmaster, extends a lordly hand towards the thinnest, blondest girl from Kelly's group. She teeters towards him in her high heels and half collapses into his lap. Alicia feels as if the music's beat is hitting her repeatedly on the back of the head. The room spins round her. This is meant to be *fun*?

'Have another drink,' says Matthew. Alicia tries to refuse, but he gets her one anyway.

A muscular boy who plays in the school football team has wandered in and is watching the thin blonde girl kissing Garth, outraged.

'That's Flaps's boyfriend,' Kelly tells Alicia. 'Even he doesn't dare hit Garth!'

'I thought her name was Flora,' Alicia says.

'It is. We call her Flaps because – well, work it out.'

'Ali.' Garth, disgorging the leggy blonde from his lap, waves a regal summons to her. She walks towards him, but keeps a safe distance. 'Flora wants to make her boyfriend jealous,' he explains, 'so she kisses me, to make him keener. Who do you like, Ali?'

'Nobody, really,' says Alicia, glancing about to see if Matthew's listening.

'No boyfriend? Why not? You're fit, you know. You should come to Manchester with me. Come out shopping. We'll get you some proper gear.'

'I like what I'm wearing. I have to dress up for my concerts so I prefer not to the rest of the time.'

Garth recoils. Then – apparently remembering he's supposed to be cool – he gives a slow smile instead. 'So what you got under this?' he says, plucking at her knitted yellow sleeve. 'Hot in here, isn't it?'

'Yeah, a bit.'

She doesn't know how it's happened, but a minute later she's no longer wearing her jumper. Under it is a white camisole with a low, round neck. She knows it shows her bra a little, but it can't be helped. The gazes of the boys on the sofa seem to carry barbs as they turn towards her. Feeling self-conscious, she heads for the kitchen, where Matthew gives her another drink and strokes her arm again, this time on her skin.

'What're you doing Saturday?' he asks her. 'Fancy coming to Stockport with me and your brother and Tim and Tim's girlfriend? We're going to the Leonardo DiCaprio movie.'

Alicia has never been to the cinema with a group of friends. She has no group of friends; and the nearest cinema is in the next town.

'I'd love to,' she says, 'but Mum's got this friend coming to stay who has something to do with the competition and I think they're expecting me to be there.'

'It's all your family and your music and your career with you, isn't it?' Matthew looks not only sorry, but annoyed too. 'Why aren't you allowed to let your hair down?'

'That's what Adrian said. They don't bother keeping *him* in the house.'

'He wouldn't let them if they tried. You got to assert yourself, Ali. You're not there just to please them.'

Alicia, through the spinning room, the thumping beat and the smoke from the older boys' spliffs, dimly registers that the clock is showing midnight. She wonders where the time has gone. She's trying to find words to explain why she does what she does. Instead, she realises there's a tear on her cheek.

'Ali. Don't cry,' Matthew says softly. Before she can stop him, he has kissed her where the tear had been and his hands are stroking her long hair. Muddled, she hesitates a moment too long and then his mouth is on hers, pushing her lips apart, his tongue prodding at her teeth. Her nostrils are full of his scent – beer, crisps and something very boylike, plus some aftershave – and she finds that her left arm is round his neck. Waves of sensation wash through her stomach and weaken her legs, her neck is tingling and her skin, under his hand, feels warm and alive.

'Ali,' he whispers. 'Mmm.'

'Mmm,' she echoes. She feels so muzzy-headed and wobbly that she lets him manoeuvre her into another room, she's not sure what it is, but there's nobody else there and it's dark. He kisses her harder and his hands move under her camisole and over her breasts and it feels absolutely wonderful.

'I thought you'd be scared,' he says.

'No,' says Alicia, whose heart is pounding, but not from fear.

'You haven't done this before, have you?'

'No.' Alicia giggles. 'Have you?'

'Once or twice. I prefer doing it with you, though.'

Alicia leans her back against the wall while Matthew leans

his front against her and snogs her. Her lips feel swollen and sensitive and her joints are hot. He's breathing fast and pressing her rhythmically with something hard inside his trousers.

'What's *that*?' she asks.

The door bursts open and a hand grabs her elbow. 'What the hell's going on?' Adrian, in his best big-brother mode, has inadvertently saved Alicia from more embarrassment than she had imagined possible. 'Get off my sister!' he barks at Matthew. 'She's only young. Ali, you're drunk and really stupid and I'm taking you home.'

'You stink,' Alicia says. He reeks of smoke, herbs and beer.

'Where's your jumper?'

'In the lounge. You sound like Mum.' She realises her words are slurring into each other and, after her protracted snogging session, she's having trouble standing up straight.

'Yo, Al.' Garth tosses her jumper towards her when she wobbles back, looking for it. 'Don't forget, you're coming shopping with me in Manchester.'

'Can't take you anywhere,' Adrian mutters, half shoving her out of the front door. She's giggling – somehow she can't stop – and, as the night air hits her, she finds she has hiccups as well. It's a difficult mixture to cope with and suddenly she discovers she's going to be sick.

Adrian stands by, hands in pockets and back turned, while she doubles up over a patch of wallflowers in a front garden. 'Good to get that out of the way,' he remarks.

'Oh, God.' Alicia is praying that she will never see an alcopop again. 'What's Dad going to say?'

'Dad mightn't even be in. Anyway, it's the mother elephant you've got to worry about.'

'She thinks I'm asleep.'

'Let's keep it that way. Think you can make it back?'

'I don't know. Oh, God . . .' and she doubles over the wallflowers again while her insides turn outside.

'Try to walk,' says Adrian. 'You're going to be fine. Drink

pints of water when we get in, and I mean *pints*, and you'll feel OK in the morning.'

Adrian marches and Alicia staggers, supported by him, down the road and into their street. The house is dark and silent: Mum and Dad have evidently gone to sleep unaware that their kids have so much as ventured outside. Adrian unlocks the door.

'Just go slowly,' he whispers.

The journey to the second floor seems insurmountable. She won't make it; she'll slip, fall down and break her hand or arm or finger. Or her back. Or she'll throw up again, on Mum's beautiful golden carpet.

What's Mum going to say? Even if she doesn't fall, tomorrow could be nastier than she can bear to think about right now. Sometimes she wishes she could be normal, like Kelly and the others. She inches upwards.

'Al, *hurry.* They'll wake up.'

Adrian and Alicia don't know that their mother can hear nothing, wearing earplugs against Guy's snoring; nor that their father is dead to the world, worn out by too much work, too much driving and too much sex with someone he's not meant to be having sex with. It's only when Cassie gives a quiet, relatively useless yap from her basket near Alicia's empty bed that the prospect of real danger makes Alicia accelerate. At last she finds herself, with immeasurable relief, inside her room.

She manages to calm Cassie, pull off her clothes and slide under her duvet. Before she's had time to wonder how she'll explain herself in the morning, she's sunk into irresistible sleep.

10

Rebecca arrives on Saturday afternoon, her black Golf GTi crunching into the drive while the Bradleys are finishing lunch. She steps out of the car, cool and relaxed: a helicopter might have transported her to Buxton in twenty minutes. Her hair glistens with highlights and her jeans, under a Burberry summer raincoat, look more expensive than a fur wrap. Gone are her Indian skirts, open sandals and flowery necklaces of the seventies. Rebecca's eyes, though, have not changed, despite the crow's feet at their corners. Kate, through the window, glimpses the chocolate brown she used to know so well and finds she's running down the front steps towards her.

'Katie!' Rebecca cries. Nobody but Guy and Didie has called Kate 'Katie' for twenty-five years.

'You're really here!' Kate hugs her. 'Come in. Let me take your bag.'

'It's fine, don't worry.' Rebecca picks up her Louis Vuitton case and follows Kate inside; her gaze rests briefly on the curve of the piano in the window.

'This,' says Guy in the hall, 'is incredible.'

Rebecca – who'd been no great fan of Guy's at university – kisses him on both cheeks. Adrian steps forward, slightly pink round the ears, and shakes her hand brusquely before sloping away, claiming revision. Alicia hovers nearby and allows herself to be embraced and congratulated. The Bradley family is presenting a united front. There's no point in discussing with a newcomer, who is there to help them, the ongoing nuclear fallout from the Littlemores' party.

The years concertina upon Kate. But for the competition final, she hasn't seen Rebecca since before Buxton, before Stoke Newington, before Victoria – yet those long years of despair and relocation and the discovery of Ali's talent have compressed to the size of a pinhead. 'Milk and two sugars?' she says in the kitchen, making coffee.

'Black, please,' Rebecca says. 'And I gave up sugar. It's extraordinary, isn't it? At eighteen you can have as much sugar as you like, but after forty, one spoon and you're up a size.'

'Oh, come on, Becs, you haven't changed a bit.'

'Older. Much older. And, hopefully, wiser.'

The piano starts up in the front room: Alicia is practising Tchaikovsky. Rebecca blinks.

'Five days,' Kate says. 'She's only been playing it for five days, and listen.'

'You're joking.'

'I wish I was. Becs, my daughter is a prodigy and I don't know what to do!'

'That, darling, is why I'm here.' Rebecca reaches over and presses her wrist.

'I thought,' Kate says, a lump in her throat, 'that this afternoon I could show you Buxton, and tonight I'll cook dinner at home. And tomorrow we could go to Chatsworth House, if you like.'

'You're so lucky, living in the middle of this marvellous countryside.'

'And you're so lucky living in the middle of all that marvellous culture. I worry about Ali not having access to it. There's plenty going on here, but not often on the level she needs now. The best we can do is a touring opera or two per year at Buxton Opera House and sometimes a concert in Manchester.'

'You must bring her to stay with us whenever you like. My two boys are in their teens, I'm sure they'd get along.'

'Becs, you have to tell me *everything*. I didn't even know you had two boys.'

Rebecca laughs into Kate's smile, though her eyes look oddly moist. She sips her coffee and begins to talk. After university, she'd spent a year in India and Nepal, where she'd experienced spiritual revelations, Himalayan trekking, an encounter with a black rhino and amoebic dysentery. Eventually she'd come home – to find that her friends had moved away, she had no job and nowhere to live and her cello technique had sunk to an all-time low. She'd started temping and ended up working for a record company, where she'd answered phones and done the boss's typing before becoming an assistant press officer. The company was taken over; she'd been made redundant, moved on to another record company; and so it continued, a slow but steady climb until the news reached her that the A&R director of Eden Classics was emigrating to Australia. By then, she knew the classical CD market inside out; and A&R – Artists and Repertoire – was the field she loved. It involved selecting musicians and helping to choose what they should record. She'd applied, and here she is. Kate, listening, feels the hair prickle on her neck.

'Darling?' Guy looks in. 'I've got to go to the office for a few hours.'

'Must you? Will you be home for supper?'

'Yes. Absolutely. Home by seven.' He vanishes.

Rebecca looks at the empty doorway, then at Kate's expressionless face.

'It's the job. I shouldn't complain,' Kate declares. 'He loves the work and, goodness knows, we need the money, with that piano to pay off.'

'Ali will be paying off her own piano very soon. You'll see.'

'You think?'

'Come on, Kate. She's Young Musician of the Year. The whole country knows her. Even people who think they don't know anything about classical music know her. All we have to do is to make sure she's got the right support.'

Cassie trots up to Rebecca, wagging her substantial tail and sniffing at the visitor with her new scents (which, Kate notices, include more than a whiff of St Laurent's Paris). 'What a *wonderful* dog. *Aren't* you?' Rebecca rubs Cassie's back. The collie lowers her snout and lets her.

'How about a walk?' Kate suggests.

Leaving Alicia at the piano and Adrian 'revising' upstairs, Kate and Rebecca set off down the hill, falling naturally into step as they used to at university. Kate had forgotten this; it happens of its own accord. She points out the wide dome of what used to be the Royal Devonshire Hospital and is now being transformed into a new section of Derby University. Nearby lurks the ageing splendour of the Palace Hotel in its grounds, while round the corner, in the Pavilion Gardens, a craft fair is in full swing. Rebecca exclaims on the prettiness of the flowerbeds, the freshness of the air, the cuteness of the little Victorian opera house, which is advertising a show for children starring a former TV presenter. At the spring-water fountain on the Crescent, she insists on stopping to sip some from her cupped hands. Kate leads her up to the market square and down again past an olde-worlde pharmacy, an antiques arcade and, in due course, DUCKS CROSSING, which makes Rebecca crease up with laughter.

'Do you have many friends here?' Rebecca asks, as they amble along.

'Not that many,' Kate admits.

'No string quartet? No local orchestra?'

'I haven't played my viola since 1981.'

'Oh.' Kate registers that her friend has recognised problem territory. Rebecca changes tack: 'Don't you meet people through the children?'

'I know a lot of nice people. Ali's first teacher, Glenda, is a friend, and I used to go to a book club, but I'm afraid I've let that slip – I'm too busy with Ali. You know, having a musical child changes your life. People can find it intimidating, even

Glenda. I don't mean her to, or anyone else. We haven't changed. We're exactly the same. It's just that people expect us to be different, so they treat us differently.'

'You must be lonely, with Guy working so hard, Ali practising, Adrian busy being a teenager.'

'How do you *manage*, having two teenage boys?'

'We're lucky. They get along, they're at a good school and they're sporty. Their dad got them both season tickets to Arsenal. That keeps them happy.'

Rebecca's husband – ex-husband, rather – is finance director of a large electronics firm. The boys attend one of north London's most expensive private schools.

'I don't know what to do with Adrian,' Kate confesses. 'You wouldn't believe what happened the other day. He smuggled Ali out of the house . . .' The full story comes out: Alicia's first hangover had not been a pretty tale. Rebecca laughs, though, and Kate finds herself smiling, despite insisting that it wasn't funny at the time. That was a massive understatement – she'd been so alarmed that she'd not slept for two nights – but she doesn't tell Rebecca that.

'You know, it might be good to get Ali out a little more, have her meet boys who are more suitable,' Rebecca suggests. 'Just because she plays the piano, it doesn't mean she's not a normal teenager. Come to London. We'll go to a concert and she can meet James and Oscar. Who are her favourite musicians?'

'She's been smitten with that French pianist, Lucien Delamain, since his Chopin disc came out,' Kate tells her. 'I've bought her all his recordings and she adores them.'

'Lucien? Interesting. He's unusual. And very attractive. That curly hair. Those *eyes*.'

'Evidently.'

'But what I like is that he's such an individual. He's one of the few pianists you can recognise right away by his sound. You can switch on the radio and know it's him in a few seconds . . .'

By the time they're back at the house, it has been agreed

that when Lucien Delamain plays in London in July, Kate will bring Alicia to hear him, and they'll stay at Rebecca's place in Hampstead Garden Suburb. Perhaps Alicia will find a new interest there when she meets Rebecca's sons.

Meanwhile, Kate has learned a great deal about the music industry. Having explained which artists' management firms have contacted her via the BBC, she now knows which Rebecca thinks are a waste of time and which she likes – 'It's so important to have the right manager,' says Rebecca – and she has gathered that engaging a PR company might be no bad thing to manage all the press interest.

In Kate's study, where Rebecca will be sleeping, they sit on the floor together, sift through the letters and divide them into piles marked Good, OK and Fuck Off.

'Can't Guy help you organise this?' Rebecca asks, surveying the sea of paper.

'If you think this is bad, try *his* study.'

Rebecca encourages Kate to make a list of Alicia's repertoire – setting out, under Solo Works and Concertos, which pieces she can be engaged to play. She'll need a file of reviews, easily reproducible via computer – until now, Kate admits, colouring, she's been pasting them into a scrapbook – and some good photos. 'With professional hair and makeup,' Rebecca adds. 'Now, where do you buy her concert dresses?'

By six o'clock, Kate's study has morphed into a managerial office: everything has been reorganised, from filing system to letterhead, from calendar with sticky labels to positioning of desk (away from the window, to discourage daydreaming). The sewing-machine and knitting basket have been stowed away under the bed.

At ten past six, while Kate is pouring gin and tonic, the doorbell sounds Big Ben and Cassie barks. Adrian crashes down the stairs. On the doorstep are the two gangly Littlemore boys and a girl of about sixteen in a very short skirt.

'Is she coming?' Matthew says to Adrian.

The piano music breaks off and Alicia bursts into the hall, pushing her hair out of her eyes. 'Oh, please,' she says to her mother. 'We were going to go to Stockport to see the new Leonardo DiCaprio movie! Adrian, I can be ready in five minutes.'

'Ali, Rebecca's come all the way from London to talk to you,' Kate reminds her. 'It's really not a good day to go to swanning off to the cinema.'

'Mum, *please*! I never, ever go to the cinema!'

'Please, Mrs Bradley?' Matthew echoes. 'We'll take good care of her.' His eyes are caressing Alicia's soft, bare arms.

'I'm afraid it's out of the question today,' Kate says, more firmly. 'It's a very important time for Ali and we need her here. Don't be back too late, Adrian.'

'Ali!' calls Matthew.

'I'm sorry.' Alicia reaches out a hand. 'I'd really like to go. See you at school.'

'*Al—*'

The door closes once again between Alicia and the rest of the universe.

Alicia deflates. She crouches to hug the dog, hiding her face in Cassie's coat.

Rebecca looks on. 'I'm sorry, Ali. I know you wanted to go out with your friends,' she says gently. 'But you'll be glad this time that you stayed with us. I promise.'

'That's kind of you. Thank you.' Alicia, head against Cassie's neck, doesn't turn round.

'Gin?' Kate says to Rebecca. They troop back to the kitchen, leaving the girl and the dog at the foot of the stairs. They're half afraid to look back.

Guy comes home an hour later, when Kate is basting the chicken. There are dark circles under his eyes and his step seems heavy and tired, but there's extra warmth in the way he embraces Alicia, who needs hugs tonight. Kate divines that he must be glad to get back; the office and the drive on a busy Saturday exhaust him excessively.

'Having fun, girls?' he says to Kate and Rebecca – and disappears into the bathroom without waiting for their gin-relaxed answer.

Alicia sits at her place at the dinner table. Mum has made roast chicken – as usual, slightly overcooked – and Dad has opened a good bottle of wine for Rebecca's benefit. Alicia chews a drumstick while the conversation jets over her head. Rebecca and Mum talk about artists' management firms, occasionally turning to her and saying, 'Don't you think so, Ali?' or 'You'd be so much better off with someone like that, wouldn't you?'

Alicia says, 'Yes,' because she doesn't know what else to say. From the way Rebecca is talking, you'd think that music was a business, not an art. Even Mum looks slightly shell-shocked.

Alicia imagines Matthew, Adrian, Tim and Tim's girlfriend in the cinema, eating popcorn and watching the lovely Leo. Why did Mum think she needed to be home for this conversation? She could have gone to Stockport, then come back and been told everything and it wouldn't have made any difference. Above all, it strikes her as peculiar that although Rebecca works for a record company she hasn't suggested that Alicia should make a CD. Why not? Alicia doesn't like to ask. Maybe Rebecca had hated her playing, but is embarrassed to say so. She half closes her eyes and imagines Matthew kissing her in the cinema.

This week seems to have lasted two years. During the day, she's been playing at being Young Musician of the Year, which involves hours on the phone talking to the BBC people, the conductor (he wants her to play with his orchestra as soon as possible), and journalists who want to interview her – why do they all ask the same questions and why are they fixated on whether she has a boyfriend? Any calls about potential management or concert bookings she delegates to Mum. The rest of the time, she's either dreaming about Matthew snogging her or remembering performing her Ravel concerto, when she'd reached the point where earth and sky touch and sailed through to the other side. Soaring. Adrian has told her he smokes weed because it makes him high, but she can't imagine feeling higher than she did that night.

And so she stays at the dinner table. She listens, she's polite, she takes notice as the adults talk about what she should wear, which pieces she should learn, where she should play. Because perhaps, if she does what they say, she can keep playing like that for ever.

'But it's *Derby*shire.' Rebecca is gazing up at the intricate bronze-brown turrets of Chatsworth House, serene in its parkland under a grey, blowsy sky.

'There's a legend that the king made a mistake,' Kate explains. 'The first thing I heard was that James I said "Devonshire" instead of "Derbyshire" by accident when he was bestowing the title and it was never put right. But that turned out to be complete nonsense. Actually, William Cavendish purchased his barony and the Devonshire title happened to be available. There never was a Derbyshire dukedom.'

'It's amazing how these legends go on and on. I once heard that "Thames" ought to be pronounced "Thaymes", but instead we all have to imitate George I's German accent!' Rebecca remarks. 'That's probably rubbish too. Honestly, the things people say. Rumours. And soon everyone thinks they're true.' She wraps her coat round her. '*God*, it's cold here. It's meant to be summer. How do you survive?'

'We're used to it. Or, rather, Guy is,' Kate says pointedly. Guy doesn't feel the cold. But he, of course, isn't out in it today. He's at work – as is usual, now, on a Sunday afternoon. 'Are you warm enough, Ali?' she asks.

'Fine, thanks.' Alicia doesn't feel the cold either. She's striding ahead, enjoying the wind in her hair. She gives herself to the breeze, lifting her chin, radiating Aliciariness.

'People notice her,' Rebecca remarks quietly, watching as passers-by glance at her despite themselves. 'Even if they've no idea who she is, they spot her and look twice. She's got charisma.'

'One review compared her to Jacqueline du Pré,' Kate says. 'It said she's the most important British talent since du Pré and that she has a similar quality, that incredible, natural, joyous gift for communicating, reaching people just by being there – but I don't want to sound conceited.'

'I saw that one. I think it should be the lead paragraph in her biography. It's about personal radiance. Jackie du Pré had it. So does Ali. I mean, look at her. She's amazing.'

'Becs, I so want to get this right for her.'

'We'll get it right together.'

They stroll through Chatsworth's Capability Brown gardens, past an elegant rectangular pond where a fountain blows rainbows of glittering drops into the breeze. Heading uphill, they skirt hedges of box and bay, explore concealed pathways and discover protected enclaves that entice the weary-footed with white wooden benches. They climb along leaf-shaded tracks and gaze down at the house in its splendour amid the greenery, shielded from the outside world and its dangers. Here there is nothing but elegance and peace, despite the number of noisy day-trippers.

'"*Luxe, calme et volupté*,"' quotes Rebecca. 'Take away all those people and Baudelaire could have been writing about this place. It creates an atmosphere of its own, just because of the way it's designed. Nobody could build it now.'

'You're into French poetry?' Kate says.

'Ah, I picked that up from someone who is. Someone I'd like Ali to meet. An agent.'

Alicia, strolling apart with Cassie on her leash, isn't listening. She's humming Chopin and moving her fingers.

While Alicia is out of earshot, Rebecca quietly changes the subject.

'Katie,' she says, 'can I ask you something? There's one thing I don't understand. Why did you leave your job and London? It seems so – *cataclysmic*. One minute you were setting up that flat in Stoke Newington, you worked for a good firm, Guy was on a national paper. The next minute you shift to Buxton. It doesn't add up. And you said you haven't played your viola for years. You know,' she adds, when Kate doesn't respond, 'when I was thirty, my mother and father died within eighteen months of each other. I haven't touched the cello since. It's as if something went out of me.'

'I'm sorry, Becs. That's awful.'

'I hope you don't mind me asking – but did something happen to you?'

Kate hesitates for a good ten seconds. She fights herself. She's not sure why she wants to confide in Rebecca, having confided in no one for so many years. Yet now she longs to let go, give herself up, tell her everything. Ali knows nothing of the history and this is not the time to reveal it; but as she's a safe distance away, Kate breathes in and turns to Rebecca. She won't indulge in an outpouring. She'll only give her the facts.

'Yes,' she says. 'Something did happen. We had our first baby. She was premature and she didn't survive.'

'Oh, my God. I'm so sorry. I had no idea.'

'No reason you should have. It's a long time ago. But—' Kate doesn't want to cry in front of someone she hasn't seen for decades. 'It was very difficult to get over it,' she says. 'We needed a change of scene and Guy's job came up.'

'So you left your whole world behind. Friends, family, job, all your support systems. You didn't even call me to let me know.'

'Becs, how could I? It had been such ages.' Kate blows her nose. 'I couldn't ring up out of the blue and say, "Oh, this awful thing happened . . ." Sorry . . . I'm not normally a running tap. But I haven't told anybody for years.'

Rebecca presses her arm. 'It's OK, Katie. You can tell me

anything. You always could. Your family's stiff upper lip can be destructive. It's good to let it out sometimes.'

'Oh, Becs. You don't know how much I missed you.'

'Probably not as much as I missed you,' Rebecca says quietly, putting an arm round Kate's shoulders. 'Do Ali and Adrian know what happened?'

'We never talk about it.'

'I guess you wouldn't.' Rebecca looks at the ground. 'What about Guy? Can you talk to him?'

'That,' says Kate, lips tightening, 'is a story all its own.'

'I see.' Rebecca reflects for a minute, in silence, watching Alicia running along the path with Cassie. 'Now, can I cheer you up?' she says, suddenly brisk. 'Might Ali like to make a CD?'

Kate brightens at once. She's been waiting for this for twenty-five hours.

'Ali,' she calls, 'come here a minute, darling.'

Alicia, the dog at her heels, bounds up to them, her hair blowing across her eyes and her flushed cheeks. Apart from that unthinking charisma, Kate reflects, Ali is becoming beautiful. No wonder Matthew Littlemore wanted her to go to the cinema. What appalling timing it would be if Ali started having boyfriends now.

'We were wondering, Ali,' Rebecca says, looking her straight in the eye, 'whether you'd be interested in making a recording for my company. It would be your debut disc, a musical portrait of you, with your picture on the front. You could play a selection of your favourite pieces. What do you think?'

Alicia clasps her hands together and stares at Rebecca, mute.

'I mean it. We all love your playing and we'd like you to have that opportunity, if you want it,' Rebecca encourages.

Alicia bursts out laughing, dives forward and hugs the astonished Rebecca.

'I think that's a yes,' says Kate.

★   ★   ★

They adjourn to the tea room to talk things over. By the time they've munched their way through chocolate cake, Bakewell tart (Kate insists that Rebecca tries the local speciality) and, for Alicia, a home-made scone laden with fresh cream and strawberry jam as white and pink as her skin, it's virtually settled. They'll start as soon as she's ready – the sooner the better, Rebecca adds, so that the competition is still fresh in the public's mind. Alicia can come to London and make the recording in the finest studio available – this CD will *sell*. After that, they can discuss what she should do next.

'Beethoven,' Alicia says, eyes shining. 'And lots of Chopin.'

'Concertos,' Kate prompts. 'How about the Tchaikovsky? With a good orchestra and a big-name conductor.'

'Expensive, but not out of the question.' Rebecca's smile gives nothing away. Kate remembers, from the distant past, that it never had. Rebecca had always been good at smiling her way through any public expression of opinion, then revealing later, in private, that her own views were a little different. For her, timing was everything.

'We must also talk about Mrs Butterworth at some point,' Rebecca says, through her smile. Alicia glances quizzically at her.

Guy, back from work at eight that evening, takes off his glasses and keeps quiet while Kate tells him the day's events. The monologue takes ten minutes.

'Well?' Kate finishes.

'Well, what?'

Kate thinks that while she's been talking, Guy seems to have aged several years. 'Isn't it fantastic?' she prods. 'Ali is going to be plastered all over every record shop in the country.'

'Katie,' Guy says, 'Ali isn't fifteen yet. Why so much, so fast?'

'What exactly is your objection?'

'She's a little girl! What are you trying to do to her?'

'She's not such a little girl any more.' An image flashes through Kate's mind of Ali standing in the wind at Chatsworth. 'Rebecca's right – one has to strike while the iron's hot. There's no point in Ali being Young Musician of the Year unless she uses it to her advantage. It's obvious she's never going to do anything except play the piano, and you have to seize the opportunities while they're there.'

Guy takes an open bottle of white wine out of the fridge and pours himself a large glass. 'Just because Rebecca, of all people, pitches up on our doorstep and starts taking over your life – which is what she always wanted to do – that doesn't mean she's right. It doesn't mean Ali shouldn't study longer, grow up a bit, save the recording for a couple of years' time when she'll be more developed as a musician and as a person. And it doesn't mean she shouldn't have the chance to live a normal life rather than being chained to that three-legged monstrosity!'

'I see,' Kate says, trying to replicate the inscrutability she has been learning from Rebecca. 'I didn't think you'd feel this way.'

'I object to you making decisions about Ali's future without running them by me.'

'You're never there to have anything run by you.'

'For Christ's sake, she's my daughter too.'

'Perhaps you should spend more time being a father to her, then.'

'So, Ali is going to have her childhood amputated by greedy music-business moguls, with your full co-operation, and it's all my fault for going to work.'

'Nobody is trying to amputate Ali's childhood.' Kate breathes deeply, keeps her hands folded, controls her need to move her fingers. 'I want her to make the most of her opportunities. She *wants* to be a pianist. She *wants* to be successful. She's never going to want to do anything else.'

'Has she been asked?'

'Of course. Rebecca asked her at Chatsworth.'

'But does she know what she's letting herself in for?'

'I want her to have the chances she deserves. Because I know what it's like to want those chances and to have them taken away from you. There's nothing crueller. I don't want Ali to have the experience I had.'

'Katie, it's not remotely comparable.'

'Well, how do you think she's going to feel if you suddenly tell her she can't do it because you don't want her to, now that she's got this far? If you stand in her way, Guy, do you think she will *ever* forgive you?'

Guy says nothing. He looks desperately tired. Kate watches him leave the kitchen. When he's gone, she reaches for her knitting.

Guy trudges up the stairs. On the landing, he pauses. A chink of light under Ali's door shows she's still awake. 'Ali?'

'Hi, Dad.'

Guy opens the door. Alicia is sitting up in bed, reading a book about Chopin. Cassie, in faithful attendance, is asleep in her basket, paws twitching as she dreams of long, cool walks through landscaped gardens.

'You OK, Dad?' Ali puts her head on one side and gazes at him with such affection that a lump rises to his throat.

'Yes, love. What about you? What's all this about making a CD?'

'It's funny, Dad – I know this'll sound weird, but something in me feels like I've done it all before.'

'What?'

'It just feels kind of familiar. Maybe I did it in a previous life. Anjali was talking about India the other day and she was saying how they believe that we don't just live once but we come back again and again and relive certain things until we work them out of our spirits. It's called *karma*. And I thought, Oh, that explains everything.'

'Gordon Bennett, Ali, you're full of surprises. Listen. Do you *want* to do this?'

'Sure.' She yawns, stretching her arms up towards the ceiling.

Guy looks at her hands and wrists. 'How would you feel,' he says carefully, 'if you didn't?'

'Dunno. Daft, I guess.'

'Ali, it's got to be your decision. You know that, don't you? And you know that whatever you decide, I'll stand by you?'

'Oh, Dad. I must go to sleep, we've got double chemistry first thing tomorrow.'

Guy closes the door quietly. Behind him, the light goes out.

Rebecca stays in Buxton an extra night so that she can be with Kate when the offices open. On Monday morning at nine thirty, she picks up the phone. By noon, Alicia's life has been reorganised as thoroughly as her mother's study.

She has an introduction to an upmarket artist's manager named Phyllida Brown, who works for a big firm in west London – the agent, Rebecca adds, who likes French poetry. A PR company is waiting in the wings ('Expensive but extremely effective,' Rebecca assures Kate, who gasps with shock at the fee). A recording studio in London has been booked for early September, so that Alicia can have the summer to practise, without missing school. Rebecca also has a long, flirtatious conversation with a gay photographer, whom she persuades to clear his diary the day after the final recording session. 'We'll find you a selection of wonderful dresses for the shoot,' Rebecca muses, looking Alicia up and down.

'Must I?' Alicia protests. 'I just want to be me.'

'That,' says Rebecca, 'is exactly the point. Being you is one thing; projecting that "you-ness" to the audience is quite another.'

When Rebecca arrived in Buxton on Saturday afternoon, Alicia was a talented teenager. By the time Rebecca leaves, Alicia is a concert pianist.

★　★　★

Kate calls the young musicians' advisory scheme to tell them what's happening. The director likes Phyllida Brown. She's not so sure about the CD. 'Are you quite certain Alicia feels ready?' she asks.

'Absolutely,' says Kate.

'Mrs Bradley, I know it's exciting, but do be careful. Try not to rush into the first opportunity that presents itself.'

'I'm not worried.' Kate scarcely takes the director's tone of voice on board. 'I've known Rebecca Harris for more than twenty years. She won't let us down.'

'Us?' says the director.

11

When Alicia steps off the train at Euston, the air assails her with unaccustomed warmth. It smells smoky and semi-chemical, with none of the fresh edginess she's used to in Derbyshire. Clutching her bag and staying close to her mother in the crowd surging down towards the Underground, she feels as if she's arrived in another country.

The tube, rattling up towards north London, is hot and fascinating. To one side, a couple talk in an extraordinary African language; opposite sit some young people not much older than herself, who Mum says are Polish. Mum, though, is thinking about other things.

'Shoes,' she says, somewhere near Camden Town.

'What shoes?'

'Did you bring any?'

'I'm wearing some.'

'No, something smart. We're meeting Phyllida Brown tonight, so you should try to look respectable.'

'These are fine.' Alicia's shoes are her favourites: pink, trainer-like walking-shoes that keep her as comfortable as the day is long.

Mum shuffles, tense, glancing at her watch. Alicia absorbs the adverts and the tube map above them, the grimy windows, the exotic array of fellow travellers, like a child at a theme park. She hasn't been on the tube for two years, not since they last stayed with Uncle Anthony, Auntie Fiona and the Horribles, and they'd dragged her round the London Dungeon.

The journey lasts twenty minutes. Outside East Finchley station a familiar black Golf is waiting. Mum's face lights up when Rebecca waves.

James and Oscar thunder into the kitchen while Rebecca is preparing much-needed mugs of tea for Alicia and her mother, who are perching on bar stools. The boys are rugby players by build, heavy-set for their age, and speak with posh public school voices. Alicia says, 'Hiya,' and they look at her as if she comes from Mars. James is seventeen and Oscar fourteen, so one, she decides, is too old for her and the other is too young. That's fine. She doesn't feel much like talking anyway because she's getting her period and her brain feels wrung out along with her body.

Mum and Rebecca are discussing business and university friends and recipes in an extraordinary muddled rush of enthusiasm, washing in waves over Alicia. 'Do you like Oasis?' James asks her and she replies, 'Not really.' Then Oscar wants to know which her favourite pop group is and she admits she doesn't have one. That stumps them – despite the expensive school, they're no different from the kids in her class in Buxton, who don't know anything about anything except pop music. Alicia asks Mum if she can go upstairs and take a pill for her stomach-ache.

She beats a retreat to the bathroom, which is white and modern with gilt-edged accessories, loo brush included. Beside the basin stand no fewer than three electric toothbrushes. Alicia pushes a button on one and watches it spin. She's never seen an electric toothbrush before and, meanwhile, she's almost afraid to tread on the bathroom floor for fear of contaminating it.

The minute she's back downstairs, Rebecca accosts her. 'Ali, darling, won't you play something for us? James and Oscar would love to hear you.'

Like hell they would, thinks Alicia, glancing at their impassive faces – Rebecca must have put them under orders. The piano is a small but pleasing upright; when Alicia tries it, the touch is even and the sound warm, so she pulls up the piano stool and begins the Ravel Sonatine. She can feel the boys' eyes on her back. What a country bumpkin they must think her. Just like the Horribles, who are sure they're *it* just because they live in London. In the slow movement she thinks she can hear them making bored noises, whispering. Probably poking fun at her accent. She'd like to see them last two minutes in her school with their voices. But their mother is effectively her employer now, so she has to be on best behaviour, even if they don't. It's not fair. She plays the last movement extra fast to make up for it. That impresses even them. Her playing is its own best defence.

The spare room is in the converted loft of Rebecca's small but perfect house, overlooking its cottage garden where white and pink roses are in bloom. Alicia and Mum will sleep on two futons, which feel like no bed Alicia has tried before. She wants to escape upstairs after she's finished playing, but Mum comes after her and begins to talk about something she thinks Alicia could play better in the Sonatine. Alicia is feeling so upset and shaky that she starts to cry. Mum looks awkward for a minute, but eventually obliges her with a reasonably comforting hug.

Then they have to shower, change and go out to dinner; there's no more time for crying. Part of performing successfully, Mum explains, is being able to do it at any time, no matter how awful you're feeling – and having dinner with a prospective agent is almost as much a matter of performing as playing the piano is.

Rebecca has booked a table in a smart restaurant near Notting Hill Gate, where they will meet Phyllida Brown. Alicia puts on a clean blue t-shirt, jeans and her pink shoes. Rebecca looks her up and down. 'What else did you bring, Ali?'

'Not a lot,' Alicia says.

Rebecca nods, inscrutable. 'Tomorrow we'll go shopping

before Lucien's concert, if you like,' she suggests. 'We could go round Covent Garden, or Selfridges, whatever you fancy.'

Alicia can feel her face flushing – not at the prospect of a London shopping trip, but at the way Rebecca had casually called Lucien Delamain by his first name.

Alicia hasn't told anybody how much she loves Lucien Delamain. She wants to marry him. She's taken the booklets out of all his CDs and pinned them up on her noticeboard – Mum won't let her put them on the wall because the sticky stuff would damage the paint. Lucien Delamain has the darkest of dark eyes, curly black hair and a snowy-toothed smile; when he plays, it sounds as if he's improvising poetry. His biography says he comes from Provence, which she imagines as a warm, sunny, French version of the Peak District, sprouting lavender instead of heather. And now she's not only going to see him play, but perhaps even meet him. She closes her eyes, feels that she's found a magical place where glimmering stars can spin and dance inside her.

Once they subside a little, though, she finds she's worried about how she looks. She doesn't care a jot what James and Oscar think of her, but Lucien Delamain is another matter. Alicia has never been into what she thinks of as 'girly stuff'. She doesn't want to be like Kelly and her crowd, who wear micro-skirts and push-up bras that show everything. Adrian calls them 'slappers'; they look as if they'd go with any boy in Derbyshire. She loathes the way the boys watch them – Adrian included, and Tim and even Matthew – like builders eyeing a breakfast fry-up. Alicia would love to have a boyfriend, but not one who looks at girls like that. She wants a kindred spirit. Someone who loves everything she loves: music, the country-side, dogs, not necessarily in that order. If Lucien were to be a kindred spirit . . .

While Alicia is in the shower, Oscar and James galumph out of the house – they're meeting friends in a local café, then going on to a party. Obviously they won't invite her. They live in a different world. Or she does. She has to spend her evening in a posh restaurant. She sits still and lets Mum put powder and blusher on her face, while Rebecca offers to lend her a necklace, a plain gold chain. Finally, Mum suggests she puts on some pink lipstick. Both women look at her shoes and sigh. Alicia decides she does look better wearing lipstick. Certainly a little older.

She sits in the back of the car on the way to Notting Hill, watching forests of unfamiliar streets go by. She imagines that she is as old as she's trying to look – perhaps twenty-one – and that she is a professional pianist and lives here on her own. She'd need to find her way round these convoluted one-way systems, deal with the noise, the traffic, the people . . . The thought is so alarming that she imagines, instead, staying in Buxton and marrying Matthew Littlemore. That doesn't appeal either.

Rebecca leads the way into the restaurant on Kensington Church Street. Alicia gazes. She's seen big, trendy places like this in Manchester, but the family never eats there. Mum has suggested once or twice that after Alicia's piano lesson they could meet Dad in town and have dinner – but Dad is either busy getting the paper 'to bed' or, Alicia senses, finds some excuse to say no. Strange. Normally he's keener than Mum on going out and having fun.

The ceiling's gaping height makes Alicia feel extremely small. The walls are black, the tables silver and the lights are tiny halogen bulbs suspended on fine wires. On each table stands a white vase containing one orange flower. A fair-haired woman in a dark suit catches Rebecca's eye from a round table by the window and raises a hand. This is Alicia's first sight of Phyllida Brown.

She'd imagined an 'artist's manager' as a larger-than-life individual – perhaps flamboyant, perhaps too thin or too fat.

Phyllida, however, is so normal that she could almost have been Alicia's aunt. Alicia decides at once that she prefers Phyllida to her aunts – she never sees Auntie Jo, who lives in San Francisco, and she can't stand Auntie Fiona. Phyllida, she reckons,. must be about the same age as Mum, maybe a little younger. She wears slender rectangular glasses across her sharpish features. Her nose is long and fine, reminding Alicia of a rodent in a riverbank. Her eyes are close-set, perhaps a little too close, though they're a fascinating, unusual turquoise colour; and as she looks at Alicia, their edges soften. When they've shaken hands and ordered some drinks, she begins to talk to Alicia at once.

Phyllida tells her that she lives in south London, has no children and had trained as a pianist. In no time, they're chattering about the pieces Alicia is learning, some of which Phyllida has played too; they talk so much that Alicia forgets about her period pains and the waiter has to come back three times before they're ready to order their food.

Alicia samples the white wine – it tastes of vanilla and even the few sips she's allowed make the lights seem brighter and the voices louder. She chomps her way happily through a Caesar salad, then seared tuna with a pepper crust and sweet-potato mash – she's never met a sweet potato before – and rounds off with chocolate mousse flavoured with coffee and almond liqueur. If this is life as a concert pianist, she likes it.

Mum and Rebecca make good headway with the wine; especially Mum, since Rebecca is driving. Alicia has never seen her mother's cheeks so pink; talking about their days at university, she and Rebecca giggle as if they're younger than Alicia. Odd to think they've known each other longer than she's been alive.

She'd expected Phyllida to be serious and work-focused, wanting to discuss conductors and the concertos Alicia can play. But Phyllida is more interested in getting to know her. What's her teacher like? What does she do in her spare time?

Is her brother musical? Does she have a boyfriend? She side-steps the last question and tells Phyllida about Cassie. Phyllida says she adores dogs, but can't have one because she works such long hours. She's out at her artists' concerts almost every night. 'You're coming to hear Lucien tomorrow, aren't you?' she says. 'He's one of mine.'

Alicia gasps: she's going to have the same manager as Lucien Delamain. 'He's so incredible!'

If Phyllida notices her extra enthusiasm, she's tactful and says only 'He's wonderful, isn't he? You must come backstage and meet him. I'll introduce you.'

Alicia fumbles for words to tell her how thrilled she is, but she can't find them. Instead she reaches out and hugs Phyllida, who looks surprised but not displeased.

Mum and Rebecca, sitting next to each other across the table, have been so absorbed in their own conversation that Mum's salmon fillet is growing cold on her plate. Alicia, Lucien-powered stars circling in her brain, barely notices until the unfamiliar sound of her mother's voice singing reaches her ears. Mum and Rebecca are, unbelievably, singing together. Softly and in harmony. Two different lines of the same tune. Phyllida pulls up in the middle of a sentence. 'Schubert?' she asks, looking at the two women.

'We used to play it in our quartet,' Mum explains. 'A very long time ago.'

'Too long,' Rebecca adds, refilling Mum's glass.

Mum looks nothing like her normal self tonight: she's relaxed, glowing, *happy*. She has an amazing smile: it's rare, but when she uses it, it's brighter than any halogen bulb. Rebecca seems unable to stop watching her.

'Do you still play?' Phyllida asks.

'Sadly, no,' Mum and Rebecca reply in unison.

Alicia seems to be surrounded by women who used to play musical instruments, but no longer do. It's an alarming obser-vation. However much Mrs Butterworth scares her, however

upset she is by Mum breathing down her neck about practising, life without the piano would not be life. It's her real
world, the world she steps into when she's on stage or alone
in the house, free of people telling her what to do. That's where
she feels truly alive. She gathers some courage, turns to Phyllida
and tells her. She's never put it like that to anybody before.

'I understand perfectly,' Phyllida says. Alicia had known she
would. Still, she says nothing about the colours. Nobody knows
about Alicia's colours.

When coffee arrives, Phyllida begins to explain the business
arrangement, should they decide to go ahead. The company's
commission will be twenty per cent of Alicia's concert fees,
which sounds steep but is apparently standard.

'Phyllida knows everyone who is anyone,' Rebecca points
out, when Kate looks as if she's about to protest. 'Even the
Young Musician of the Year needs the right manager with
the right contacts, and the advisory scheme director will
agree.'

All Alicia knows is that if Phyllida manages Lucien, she'd
trust her with her life.

It is past eleven o'clock when they leave. Alicia is so tired
that her body is awake, walking about and talking, but her
brain has shut down, leaving her functioning on borrowed
time. All she can take in is the black night, the silvery street
lamps, the cloakroom attendant handing her back the Mum
jersey she'd brought but hadn't needed. Her eyes are dry and
sore, while her hands feel under-exercised. Then she hears
something that doesn't make perfect sense but alarms her all
the same.

'I think you should know,' Rebecca is saying to Mum and
Phyllida, 'that since Alicia won her prize, Deirdre Butterworth
has doubled her fees for her other students.'

Mum breathes in. Phyllida's eyebrows twitch upwards. Alicia
had told her everything she really feels about Mrs Butterworth
– once she'd started, she couldn't stop. Maybe that hadn't been

sensible, but it was a relief to find someone who understood and let her get it off her chest.

'We need to discuss Mrs Butterworth some time,' Rebecca says to Mum, as she had at Chatsworth. Nobody says anything to Alicia.

Although she's exhausted, Alicia can't sleep. She lies on her futon, listening to Mum snoring, new impressions shuttling through her brain and the prospect of meeting Lucien Delamain beckoning out of the night as if nothing could induce time to move fast enough to make it happen.

Outside Selfridges, an ornate clock guards heavy revolving doors; inside, Alicia gazes around at the shining railings, pale lights, elegant accessories and counters for more brands of makeup than she'd known existed. She's so boggled that she doesn't know where to start.

Rebecca takes charge, marching them to her own favourite and persuading the cheerful salesgirl to give Alicia a makeover. 'You've got to learn to do this properly,' Rebecca tells Alicia. She sits on a stool, a towel round her neck, and keeps her eyes closed until it's over.

Mum looks on. 'She's only fifteen, you know,' she says, when layers of dark mascara are being applied to Alicia's sandy lashes.

'It's a lovely age,' the girl replies, either missing or ignoring Mum's censorious tone. 'I've been wearing all this since I was thirteen. There you go, love, all done. How do you like it?'

Alicia, staring into the mirror, says, 'That's grand. Thank you.' She doesn't like to say that she'd much rather be out in the open countryside, mascaraless, walking her dog.

Mum decides which makeup Alicia should have and Alicia lets her. Next they go upstairs to look at concert dresses: Alicia picks the colours, but lets Mum choose the style. They buy two: one mid-blue, the other sophisticated, versatile black. Rebecca looks from her to Mum and back again, without commenting. Rebecca's silences, Alicia thinks, speak louder than her words.

The teenage section is more fun. Alicia bounces happily through the railings, emerging with a good selection of upmarket-fifteen-year-old gear. Later in Rebecca's house, after sleeping for half the afternoon, she puts on an entire new outfit to go to Lucien's concert. Rebecca looks efficient and expensive in a trouser suit, Mum wears her long linen jacket, beads and a frazzled expression, but Alicia glows in fresh eyeshadow, lip gloss and trousers in a shiny, greenish-beige fabric, with a light top that shows off her cleavage and, finally, deep-brown court shoes. James and Oscar, slumped in front of the TV, stare at her for the first time as if she is a girl, not a Martian.

'I think it's wonderful,' Alicia breathes, on the terrace outside the Royal Festival Hall, soaking in the atmosphere. The trees along the South Bank are rustling in the breeze, the Thames twinkles under the early-evening sun, and close to Hungerford Bridge someone is clinking out a Hebrew folk song on Jamaican steel drums.

'You're going to play here, you'll see,' Rebecca declares. Alicia looks up at the concrete and glass façade of the hall and its curving, copper-green roof. She says nothing; she simply radiates.

Phyllida is coming towards them, walking with a distinctive, brisk springiness and apologising for being slightly late. She's been backstage with Lucien and has told him all about them: he knows they'll be at the recital and is eager to meet Alicia.

'How old is Lucien?' Alicia asks.

'He's in his forties, though he doesn't look it,' Phyllida remarks. 'There's something youthful about him. He's still like a little boy in some ways.'

'That twinkle in the eye? That Gallic charm?' Rebecca's

tone is gently barbed. Phyllida's cheekbones and long nose redden.

'He's into French poetry, I take it?' Mum says, mysteriously.

Alicia, musing, follows them into the Queen Elizabeth Hall foyer, next door to the Royal Festival Hall. If Lucien were forty-five, like Mum, he would be exactly thirty years older than she is. The thought unsettles her. At fifteen, she may not feel like a little girl any more, but a man of forty-five would think her exactly that. She excuses herself, goes to the loo, then stands at the mirror to apply another layer of mascara and more of her new lip gloss.

It's soon obvious that in this piano-literate audience Alicia is being recognised. Walking towards the coffee bar, she spots several people following her with their eyes, others noticing her and whispering with their companions. Soon a smiling mother and a child of about ten come up and tell her how much they enjoyed watching her on TV. The child gazes up at her with huge, admiring eyes.

'What's your name?' Alicia asks her, bending. 'Do you play the piano?'

The girl lisps a reply and nods. She wants Alicia's autograph. Alicia signs her own name on Lucien's concert programme – it doesn't feel entirely right, but she does it anyway and gives her a kiss on the cheek. The child, pink and pleased, clutches her mother's hand as she walks away. Alicia watches them go, smiling, feeling warmed. She's surprised that Rebecca and Mum seem unmoved by the incident, though Phyllida says, 'That was nice, Ali.'

As they head into the auditorium, Alicia realises that her entourage of three adults has effectively formed a protective phalanx around her, ready to ward off intruders.

The hall is packed; the lights dim; and on to the platform strides Lucien Delamain, as dark and bright and shining as in the photographs on Alicia's noticeboard. There's a propulsive energy in his step when he comes forward to bow. Then he goes to the piano, and a second later the gloomy, concrete space is ablaze with Beethoven. Alicia notices the way he choreographs the music not only with his arms, shoulders and hands, but with his whole body. Soon she's lost in listening.

'What do you think?' Phyllida asks her, during the interval, while Rebecca and Mum go to the bar. Alicia has played both the Beethoven sonatas Lucien has just performed, knows their dangers from the inside and can dissect almost everything he had done with them. But while she's talking, people keep coming up to them and interrupting. Phyllida introduces her time and again. Alicia smiles and plays her new celebrity role as best she can; she can't remember all the names and the company titles mean nothing to her. She only wants to think about Lucien. She sips orange juice and gazes at the grey evening beyond the tall windows. Nothing has been the same since Matthew Littlemore snogged her. It's not that she'd like to kiss *him* again – rather the reverse – but the kiss itself was another matter. She wonders what it would be like to kiss Lucien.

The daydream stays with her through the second half. Lucien plays French music: Fauré, Debussy and Alicia's favourite Ravel. He plays 'Ondine' from the set *Gaspard de la nuit* more slowly than she does, and with a more beautiful tone, letting its pace ebb and flow as if he's telling a story. Mrs Butterworth has made Alicia concentrate more on the clarity of the notes than on telling stories. That kind of thing can come later, Mrs Butterworth says – for now, the stronger Alicia's grasp of the mechanism, the better. In general, Alicia has applied herself to exercises and études, learning to be as at home on the instrument as a dolphin in the sea. Magic, Lucien-magic, hasn't come into it much, except when she's on stage, free to play as she wishes, without interference.

'I'd like to play it like that,' she whispers to her mother, when the Ravel has drawn to its close. She's beginning to feel that she's been missing something.

The crowds backstage remind her of the competition; but now she's just a groupie. She feels very young, too young, and her new shoes pinch her toes. Her lip gloss helps her confidence, though; so does her height. She's beginning to enjoy being tall for her age.

Phyllida pays no attention to the green-room crush and the long line of people waiting to talk to Lucien. 'Come on, Ali,' she whispers, propelling her forward. For a moment there's annoyance at their queue-jumping; then, as Alicia is recognised, the crowds part like the Red Sea to make way for her. A second later she is face to face with Lucien. His eyes, alert and interested, sparkling despite post-concert tiredness, gaze straight into her own.

Phyllida kisses his cheek. He puts a hand briefly on her waist and says, 'Phyllie, *ça va?*'

'*Ça va.*' Phyllida looks at him, then away. She takes a breath. 'Lucien, this is Alicia Bradley, the young pianist I was telling you about.'

'Ah, the Young Musician of the Year! *Enchanté*, Alicia.'

To her astonishment, Lucien, who pronounces her name 'Alici-*a*', doesn't only shake her hand but lifts it to his lips. She flushes and tries not to laugh. 'I love your work,' she manages to say, trying to sound grown-up.

'And I am hearing great things about yours. It's true that you have learned all the Chopin études and all the Bach preludes and fugues?'

'Yes – yes, it is.'

'Amazing! And who are you studying with?'

'Deirdre Butterworth in Manchester.'

Lucien's smile doesn't change, but something in his face seems to freeze for a second, like a paralysed frame of film.

'We must talk some time,' he says, looking intently into her face. 'I would love to hear you, if you would like to play to me one day soon?'

Alicia, not having anticipated this, wonders what Mrs Butterworth would say if she were to consult another professional who might give her different advice. She finds a useful way out by grabbing her mother's arm. 'This is my mum, Kate Bradley.'

Lucien repeats the hand-kissing routine. Alicia notices that her mother is as fazed by it as she'd been.

'Alicia is a tremendous fan of yours,' Mum tells Lucien, after taking a fraction of a second to recover, the sort of fraction that only Alicia would have noticed. 'Whenever she stops practising, the house is full of the sound of your CDs. It feels like you're one of the family.'

'You have such a talented daughter!' Lucien is beaming at Mum. 'So young, such a gift!'

'She's just had her fifteenth birthday.'

'And she could not have a better manager than my lovely Phyllie.'

'Oh, honestly, Lucien,' Phyllida exclaims, glancing around. There are beads of sweat on her forehead.

'Phyllida will give you all my contact details,' Lucien assures Alicia. 'I hope to see you soon. Come and play for me, Alicia, any time. Promise?'

'Promise!' Alicia takes her last chance to experiment: she widens her smile to its most radiant, gazes at her hero and flutters her mascara-curled eyelashes. To her astonishment, Lucien's smile widens in return, his eyes gleam and his expression deepens for a second into something glowing; potentially, she senses, a little intimate. She's not sure which is more startling: the fact that he responds at all, or the understanding that she can make it happen so easily.

The trip back to Macclesfield, where Kate has left the car, feels very different from the journey to London.

'I can't believe we've only been away for two days,' Alicia remarks, sipping tea from a plastic mug as the train sails past Milton Keynes. In the luggage rack, their suitcase bulges with new acquisitions: not only Alicia's spoils from Selfridges, but also Lucien's latest CD, given to her by Phyllida, the concert programme which he'd signed ('*Pour Alicia, avec toutes mes félicitations, Lucien xx*'); and, most important of all, an official letter of agreement from Phyllida's firm. Mum has promised to look after the legal details of the recording contract when it arrives, and between them, the three women have assured Alicia that she need worry about nothing. All she has to do is play the piano.

Mum is quiet, watching the passing fields and towns, her fingers twisting her wool. Alicia closes her eyes and lets the train's motion and the click of Mum's knitting needles rock her to sleep.

12

Adrian, left in charge of Cassie, takes her for a walk out of Buxton towards the Cat and Fiddle. She pads to heel, head up, sniffing the air; the moor spreads, vast and empty, around them. He can't decide whether he loves the countryside or loathes it. Untamed, craggy, austere, it's definitely in tune, as Ali might put it, with something in himself. Even so, he wishes there were more interesting things to do here than walk and go to the pub. Ali loves the moors, but she, no doubt, will be moving to London before you can say Deirdre Butterworth. 'And I,' he mumbles to Cassie (he doesn't like to admit that he, too, talks to the dog), 'will be stuck in bloody Buxton. Might as well never have been born.'

He lets Cassie off her leash. He's not supposed to – the sheep farmers hate dogs with a virulence that has earned them the right to shoot a loose one on sight – but Guy had belted Cassie as a puppy the first time she tried to chase a sheep and she's never done it again. 'You're the best dog in Derbyshire,' Adrian tells her, because it's true.

A sound in the distance catches his attention and makes Cassie look round, ears twitching: a soft roar in the hills, increasing in volume at a tremendous rate. Round the bends of the road career seven or eight dark shapes on wheels. A group of bikers, leather-clad, immensely padded, assembles here, centring on the Cat and Fiddle. The road they love is the most dangerous in the country; they ride it for speed alone, without observing natural beauty, inclement weather or the speed limit.

Adrian stops walking, shielding his eyes from the sun. He's seen the bikers often enough. Now, though, he feels an unfamiliar pang of desire, recognition, something he could almost call destiny. He wants to be one of them. He wants to feel the road tearing away under him, to vanquish mankind and nature with the force of an engine, to be untouchable through speed to law and family alike.

He's been high many times – the novelty has, oddly, worn off. Dope makes him drowsy, which is nice but limiting, and an experiment with something stronger had upset him to the point that he didn't want to do it again – not that he'd tell Tim or Sam that. He reads Dad's newspaper enough to be aware of the dangers of getting hooked. Tim and Sam never read anything and never watch the news on TV, so they don't know and they don't care.

But riding through the Peak District at what looks like two hundred miles per hour would be a conscious high of a different kind: real, not chemically induced. That's what he wants: total aliveness. The same sensation, perhaps, that Ali sometimes tells him about after she's given a concert. He knows the bikers go to the Cat and Fiddle – he's seen them there, their motorbikes stationed in the car park. Somehow he must get to talk to them.

'It's booked,' says Emily. She's standing in Guy's office, her back against the door, silvery eyes shining.

'I only hope that the recording happens when it's supposed to,' Guy says. 'If it doesn't, I can't go.'

'You'd still have a conference to attend.' Emily seems unperturbed. 'It's not like you're saying to Kate, "I can only go away when you do because I'm off to Denmark with my mistress."'

'Em.' Guy takes off his glasses. 'I've got to tell her. I can't go on like this.'

'Don't do anything too fast.' Emily walks towards him with some caution; there are glass panels by the door and anyone astute, passing, could easily spot them.

'Fast? It's been over a year! I'm being torn in half.'

'All I ask is that you don't dump me.'

'How could I dump you? It'd be like cutting off my arm. But I can't go on putting all my energy into hiding my feelings. I'm going through the motions of being the person I used to be. It's not who I am any more.'

'Are you saying you want to leave your family and be with me? Don't say that unless you mean it.' Emily crouches beside him behind the desk, concealed from the door. She takes both his hands, then lifts one to her cheek. Guy's fingers grasp and twine in her hair. 'There's nothing I want more than that,' she says, 'but you've got to be five hundred per cent certain. We've never spent any length of time together. That's one reason I want to take you to Denmark. We'll see how we really get along.'

'I don't need to go to Denmark to know I get along with you.'

'But I do.'

Guy is constantly astonished by Emily: her self-knowledge, her self-sufficiency, her inner fibre. Most women in Emily's position would be the ones in tears. Not the men – thank goodness most of his staff don't know what a soppy old softie he is. Other women would be begging the indecisive bloke to leave home and move in with her. They would be desperate for attention too rationed from a heart too divided. Instead he's reached the point where he feels half dead from hiding the truth, but she is telling him to do nothing until she's certain she can stand spending several days on end in his company.

'The fourth of September,' she is saying. 'We'll fly to Copenhagen and take the train to Skagen. We'll stay in the hotel where everyone stayed in the nineteenth century, including Hans Christian Andersen. You'll love it – it's extraordinary.'

'Any place would be extraordinary if you and I get to spend three whole nights together in it.'

'You old cry-baby.' Emily squeezes his hand. 'I'm counting the days.'

'Me too.'

'And please don't do anything rash until we come back.'

'If that's what you really want,' Guy says, 'then I won't.'

'A portrait of me.' Alicia is lying on her bed, daydreaming. Her fingers feel warm and strong – she's had a good afternoon at the piano, playing her favourite pieces, trying to pick out the ones she wants to record. If the CD is to be a portrait of her, it needs music of the outdoors, the shifting subtle colours of the hills and sky. Beethoven, then – which Dad would love. She imagines the cover: herself in her jeans, windswept and happy, her dog at her side. The Beethoven D minor Sonata called 'The Tempest'; Chopin – the Third Ballade, which reminds her of riding over the moors; Ravel – the Sonatine that sparkles like the sea; and Debussy, so steeped in nature that once you walk into his landscape you'll never come out again.

The next morning she phones Rebecca to give her the programme.

'Oh, sweetheart,' says Rebecca. 'It's beautiful. I love it. Don't you think, though, that it might be a good idea to have something a little better-known, more obviously popular and virtuoso, just to start you off? We want people to know how amazing your fingers are.'

Alicia is taken aback. 'But there's nothing there I could play if my fingers weren't good,' she points out.

'Yes, of course. *We* know that. But do the punters, darling? How about some Chopin waltzes?'

'I've never learned them,' Alicia admits, biting her lip.

'I'm sure you could learn one or two very easily. How about the "Minute" Waltz? And what about some Rachmaninov? The C sharp minor Prelude – that's very popular. Or that incredible piece by Balakirev, "Islamey", so exotic and colourful. And if you want to do Debussy, why not "Clair de lune"?'

By the end of the conversation, Alicia feels wobbly. She goes to the kitchen and raids the chocolate that Mum keeps on top of the highest cupboard to stop herself eating it. Alicia stands on a chair.

The chocolate eases the physical wobble, but not the mental one. She's certain Rebecca had said she could choose her own programme. Yet Rebecca's ideas are so different from hers that there seems to be nothing of herself left.

'Mum?' she calls.

'Come up, darling.'

Mum is at her computer, typing. A huge calendar pinned to the noticeboard bears Alicia's concert schedule in coloured letters: red for solo recitals, orange for concerto performances with orchestras. The advisory service has instructed her not to do too many concerts, at least for now, because of school and, most of all, because she is only fifteen and needs to keep studying. But her earning power has shot up since she won her prize; now everybody wants her, and Phyllida, Rebecca and Mum don't always agree on how much work she should take on. Alicia finds it odd that Phyllida, whose company benefits financially from her work, wants her performances to be rationed to one per month, while Rebecca, whose company has no share in the proceeds, encourages her to do as many as she can handle because it's valuable experience. Mum, trapped in the middle, looks exhausted.

'Mum – this recording.'

'Mm-hm?' Mum keeps typing.

'I thought *I* was supposed to choose the pieces.'

'Of course, darling. But isn't it a good idea to take Rebecca's advice? She'll know much better than we do about what sells.'

'Has the repertoire got to "sell"? Even if people know who I am already?'

Mum pauses, apparently considering her words. 'I think it would be a good idea if it could. Then there's more chance that they'll follow it up with something even better. A concerto, perhaps, with a big orchestra and conductor. Think of it as an investment.'

'But, Mum, I'm not sure I want to play all these pieces.' Alicia tells Mum the details of her talk with Rebecca.

'I'm sure just one waltz would do,' Mum responds. 'And "Clair de lune" is beautiful. Then, if you play "Islamey", everyone will know that you can play absolutely anything.'

'But I don't know it!' Alicia wails.

'Just have a look at it, love. Take it slowly and see how you feel. It's a marvellous piece – I was listening to it yesterday.'

'Yesterday? Mum, was this your idea?'

'No, sweetheart, it was Rebecca's. I'm learning as we go along, as much as you are.'

Alicia is silent. It's obvious, from Mum's words, that she's already discussed everything with Rebecca, without Alicia's knowledge.

'Now, darling,' Mum says, 'why don't you go and practise and we can talk about the CD with Dad later? He might even be home for supper.'

Alicia wanders down to her piano. Dad will understand. He'll be her supporter; he'll help to talk them round. If he can't, then nobody can.

But seven o'clock arrives, then seven thirty, then eight. Adrian decamps to meet his friends. Alicia's stomach rumbles and the chicken begins to overcook. Eventually Mum looks at the clock, gives a sigh and says, 'OK, Ali, let's eat. I bet that once we've begun, he'll walk in.' This trick has worked before, though it's not infallible.

Mum seems, in a perverse way, to have given up on Dad. If he's there, he's there. If not, she doesn't seem bothered. She's occupied with writing letters, planning Alicia's schedule with Phyllida, and engaging in marathon phone conversations with Rebecca. Alicia doesn't want to seem ungrateful, because she knows that the detail would be beyond her. This way, she's free to practise and do what schoolwork she can be bothered with. Mum's trying her best for her, Alicia knows – even if sometimes it hurts. She should do her best in return.

They eat in the kitchen with the clock ticking above them. Dad doesn't arrive. With every mouthful Alicia feels her spirits sinking lower. Mum has another card up her sleeve: 'I spoke to Mrs Butterworth,' she says, 'and she thinks Rebecca's idea for the programme is absolutely perfect for you.'

It's nine o'clock. Alicia clears away the dinner plates and says, 'Mum, can I take Cassie out?'

'Not now, love. It's getting late.'

Alicia goes to her room, wonders whether to write to Anjali, then picks up a book instead. At ten fifteen, she hears the front door opening as Dad arrives.

She jumps off the bed and bounds down. Dad hugs her. He smells of sandalwood soap, which they don't use at home. She's noticed that before. Perhaps he's joined a gym and has a shower there. He's certainly lost weight.

'Dad, you know this CD?' Alicia bursts out. 'Mum and Rebecca and Mrs Butterworth want me to play totally different stuff from what I want to play!'

'Darling, I'm sure they don't,' says Dad, whose eyes suggest he's still not home although his body is standing in the entrance hall. 'Let's talk about it tomorrow, OK? It's late and you should be getting your beauty sleep.'

Adrian, Tim and Sam are in the pub, drinking lager. Nobody has asked them how old they are, luckily – sometimes they are interrogated, then banned. When the bikers come in, the boys look on, half admiring, half afraid.

These are serious blokes, Adrian thinks, watching them grouping round the bar. They're big men, even when the helmets and jackets come off; a good bit older than him, some in their twenties, others even older. They mean business.

'How old d'you have to be to ride a motorbike?' Sam asks.

'Seventeen, I think. We could do it,' Tim says, keeping his voice down. 'You have to take a test and get a licence.'

'Nah, you don't,' Adrian says.

'Course you do, and it costs money. And them bikes cost a fucking fortune.'

'Depends how you do it,' Adrian insists. 'I mean, nobody ever looks at licences, do they? Nobody can make you do anything you don't want to do if you don't let them.'

Sam and Tim stare at him. Sam has knuckled under and started to work harder at school, thanks to his father's horror stories of his likely future if he leaves with no qualifications. His dad's a farmer and times are hard, especially since the onset of the Foot and Mouth disaster. Tim, for his part, feels guilty and responsible for his mum, who's on her own; he has to be the man of the household, which means he needs to pass some A levels and not spend too much time messing about. Adrian knows they look up to him. He's the only one who's still a real rebel and he knows, though he'd never let anyone say so, that he's brighter than both of them put together. 'If I wanted to be a biker,' he declares, 'nobody could stop me. And I wouldn't do a stupid licence and I wouldn't buy a bike new.'

'What would you do, then?' Sam demands.

'Hang out with the right people,' Adrian says pointedly (Sam and Tim will know that they're not the right people). 'Go out, learn the tricks. I'd get a bike sooner or later. I'd save up and find someone who'd sell me one cheap.'

Coming in around midnight, Adrian creaks up the stairs. The house is dark and quiet. Mum has placed a mug and a tea-bag beside the kettle as a goodnight gesture to him. He leaves them untouched. He pauses outside his door. From Alicia's room, he can hear a noise. He goes closer. Her light is off.

'Ali? You awake?'

'Mmm.'

Adrian peers in. Alicia has pulled her pillow over her head to muffle the sound as she howls into her mattress.

'Hey,' Adrian says softly, uncomfortable in his big-brother shoes, switching on the lamp. 'What's going on?'

'The CD,' says Alicia, face down under the pillow. 'Nobody wants to listen to me!'

'Cos you're fifteen.'

'But it's *my* CD! What am I going to do? Even Dad won't listen. They all keep saying the record company knows best. But they *don't*. Rebecca talks to Mum all the time, but she doesn't know anything about me!'

'They can't force you, Ali. Don't let them. If you put your foot down strongly enough, nobody can force you to do anything. You remember that.'

'Do you think?'

'However much pressure anyone puts on you, it's still down to you to agree to be pressurised or not. If you say no, you say no. You have to keep on saying no, if that's what you believe. It's about willpower.'

Alicia casts around for a tissue. Adrian finds a box on her dressing-table and tosses it over. She catches it and flashes him a sudden smile, despite eyes that are so red and puffy that he realises she must have been crying for ages.

'Actually,' she says, 'I think I know what I'm going to do. And I'll do it in the morning.'

'Good,' says Adrian. 'You do that. Don't let them force you into anything. Promise?'

'Promise! Night-night, Adie.'

'Night, Ali.' Adrian gives Cassie a quick back-rub on his way out.

In the morning, as soon as Mum has gone to the supermarket, Alicia leaps up from the piano and grabs the phone. She dials Phyllida's mobile.

'Lucien's number?' Phyllida sounds caught off-guard. Her

voice alters when she talks about Lucien – it becomes strained, flattened out. She collects herself and says, 'OK, Ali, have you got a pen?'

'Ready.' Alicia listens and scribbles down two long French phone numbers and an email address. When she's rung off, she examines them. One chain of digits, after the French '33', begins with a seven; that must be the mobile. She presses its numbers.

'Alicia! *Chérie!* How lovely to hear your voice!' says Lucien Delamain.

Alicia sits down on the stairs, astonished at the simplicity of her success. 'Lucien, can you talk? Are you terribly busy?' she asks him politely.

'Darling, I am all yours. What is new?'

Alicia begins to tell Lucien everything that's been going on. He's a pianist. He understands. If she thinks about it logically, there's nobody else she could tell who *would* understand. People at school are either impressed or envious, but most of them have never heard of Chopin, let alone Balakirev. Adrian's done all he can, Dad's too stressed out, and Mum, Rebecca and Phyllida are stacked against her. Nor can she tell Anjali, because Anjali is a thousand miles away from any chance of a recording contract and it wouldn't be fair. As for the advisory scheme, if Mum doesn't like what the director says, she ignores it.

'Darling, what I would like is for you to play it all to me and together we choose the best,' Lucien says. 'Can you come to Paris?'

'I don't know,' Alicia says, 'but I'll try.'

'Have you been to Paris?'

'Never! I'd so love to.'

'We see what we can do. I will talk to Phyllie. She will help if I ask her, I promise.'

Alicia wonders what her agent would say if *she* tried to call her 'Phyllie'. 'Thank you, Lucien! Thank you so much!'

'We talk soon, OK?'

'Wonderful! I can't wait!'

'Me too. *Ciaociao*.'

Ciaociao? Alicia says it back – some kind of sophisticated Continental farewell? – and rings off. Feeling calmer than she's felt for days, she returns to Balakirev's 'Islamey', which is so ridiculously difficult that she's rather enjoying it.

If her teacher and her father are on the wrong side, she thinks, the fingers of her right hand picking out in slow motion a decorative flourish note by note, then maybe, just maybe, what she needs is an alternative teacher – and maybe an alternative kind of father. Not a fairy godmother, but a wizard godfather. A Lucien.

'You want to go to Paris to play to Lucien?' exclaims Kate, when her daughter, with eyes like stars, announces her plan.

'I want his advice about the recording. He said if I played him everything, then he'd help me decide.'

'But, darling, there isn't time for that!' Kate closes her eyes. She hasn't visited Paris in over twenty years. Images rattle through her brain of cramped hotel rooms, lack of pianos, Ali wanting to sightsee and go shopping. Worse, though, would be Rebecca's reaction: she has intimated gently but unmistakably that the company has to be happy with the promotability of Ali's repertoire. It has to be popular, accessible, virtuoso music, she says, otherwise it won't sell in the quantities they require.

Seeing Lucien Delamain would, of course, be exciting. Kate, who bolsters herself against the chilly temperature of her marriage with work for Ali, housekeeping and knitting, can't help responding to Lucien's testosterone-fuelled aura. But as for Paris . . . Could she handle the associations? Supposing she couldn't? She might find herself dropping apart, brain cell by brain cell, confronting the scene of so much happiness. If she fell to pieces, what would happen to Ali?

'Basically, darling,' she says, brisk, 'it's important that Eden should be happy, because this is going to launch you in the CD market. They know what they're doing. Maybe you can play to Lucien another time, but I don't think that going to him now would help as much as you think.'

'But, *Mum*—' Alicia's blue eyes fill with tears.

Kate looks away – she can't bear it when Ali cries. It makes her want to cry too. But the girl can't be permitted to scupper her own best chances.

Alicia walks quietly upstairs after dinner and a moment later calls down: 'Mum, can I send an email from your computer, please?'

'Of course, love.'

A long period of silence follows until there's another, rather small-voiced call – 'Mu-u-um . . .'

Kate finds Alicia fighting with Outlook Express. 'All you need to do,' she shows her, 'is click there to put in the address; then *there* to put in the subject; then write your message *there*. Easy.'

'Machines,' Alicia grumbles. She's trying to write to Lucien. 'I can't face phoning him to say I'm not going.'

Later, Adrian finds Alicia in her room, staring at a book without seeing it. Through the house, the air is frosty and miserable.

'Trouble?' he asks.

'A little.' She looks up. 'But it's OK.'

'Don't tell me. Mama knows best.'

Adrian notices his sister's shoulders – tense, too hunched for a girl of her age. That's what comes of hours and hours at the piano. And more hours. And then letting off steam in the only way you're permitted to: walking the dog.

'Don't let them push you around,' he says.

Everything in Skagen is golden. The houses along the old village's main street are painted a glowing shade of sandy ochre, contrasting with chunky dark beams and window-frames. The Nordic sky, pale, clear and brilliant, turns topaz at dawn, when Guy and Emily wake in each other's arms, and at dusk, when they relax over beer and crisps in the garden of a small bar.

They are staying in the hotel where Hans Christian Andersen had once stayed – wooden, rickety, lovingly restored – and nearby they find the museum that preserves the house where the artists Michael and Anna Ancher had lived, as well as the gallery that displays their works and those of their friends in the Skagen Group. Guy thinks they're the Danish equivalent of Renoir and his circle. There is art in the air here. He imagines that the painters only needed to reach out a metaphorical hand and allow a picture to drop into it, fully formed, out of the translucent heavens.

In the gallery, Guy and Emily immerse themselves in the soft colours, the generous outlines, the big, beautiful canvases – the scenes simple and everyday yet their poetry absolute. Two women walking by the sea with a dog can become an étude in sapphire, a plain yet perfect moment frozen under an ultramarine spell. Guy, arm round Emily, wishes that they, too, could preserve their moment of poetic everydayness. Normally they can't walk hand in hand for fear of being recognised. But in Skagen, they're anonymous and undisturbed: just an ordinary British couple on holiday.

'My father used to paint sometimes,' Emily tells him. 'He loved this place – we came here quite often when I was little.'

'You still are little,' Guy teases her. He's not had much chance, being married to a woman his own height, to feel big, strong and protective as he does now.

They walk the length of a straight, sandy, sea-bordered road to the far northern tip of Denmark, to see the point where the Skagerrak and the Kattegat meet. Emily smiles up at him. She's pale – perhaps because of the strain they're both under, beneath the surface of this brief, gold-frosted happiness – and he remembers that she hadn't eaten much lunch. He's concerned, but doesn't want to wreck the mood by needling her about whether she feels OK.

They drift along in silence. Finally they reach the end of the land. Before them, the blue-grey seas are leaping under the arching sky. To their left, the sun sinks towards the waves.

'There,' Emily says. 'Can you see it?'

Guy can make out a watery conflict in the distance. The two seas do not merge in a seamless, peaceful unity. Perhaps something invisible to the naked eye separates them – submerged sand, or rock – but it seems to him that each sea has its own habits of motion, which aren't necessarily compatible. Where they touch, there's a faintly discernible collision: a little extra foam, a dividing line that doesn't quite divide. Or is he imagining it?

'Amazing,' he says.

'Guy,' says Emily, 'I've got something to tell you.' Her hair is bright in the low sun, her eyes trained on the horizon. 'I'm pregnant.'

Guy tries to speak. Nothing comes out.

'I'm so happy,' Emily adds. 'I know I shouldn't be, but I can't help it. I want you to know that I'm not trying to trap you, but I so want to have this baby. I couldn't bear not to because it's yours. It's due in April.'

His eyes begin to water. He puts out an arm and draws her to him. She hides her face and he can feel, from the tremor in her shoulders, what courage she has needed to break this apocalyptic news. 'We'll work something out, Em,' he promises.

'I know,' Emily says. 'I trust you. More than I trust myself.'

There's little to say while they walk back. The seas have swallowed the sun, and in the deepening twilight Guy imagines that they are wandering into a Michael Ancher painting, that they could step through the canvas into another reality, lose themselves and never return. I'm forty-six years old, he reflects, I'm the editor of a newspaper and the father of two

– potentially three – children. How can it be that deep down I'm still a kid who wants to go through the looking-glass?

Four days after Guy comes home from his 'conference', a group of terrorists fly two planes into the World Trade Center in New York. Watching on TV, transfixed with horror as the flaming towers plunge to the ground, Guy senses the beginning of the end: their world, his world, a whole era crashing to smithereens in a smoking inferno.

13

The red light glares down at Alicia. She begins her Chopin Ballade for the fifth time. She's been allowed to keep it, and has learned some waltzes to follow. Then she'll play some popular Liszt, Rachmaninov and that crazy Balakirev (at least nobody can call that a soundbite). No Beethoven and no Ravel. The only Debussy is 'Clair de lune'.

She has been in the studio all day. She's recorded half the music for the CD, most of it at least ten times. In the listening breaks, she's been summoned to the control room where electronic numbers and level indicators flash, yellow, green and red, on equipment lathered with knobs and dials. She's impressed with the way her producer, Andy, has covered his copy of the music with red pencil, the way he can pinpoint every wrong note or distant passing aeroplane; they've even had disruption from two pigeons noisily trying to mate on the windowsill. But Andy's sharp ear means she has to play everything again and again and she's convinced that even if there are fewer mistakes, she's not playing the music, as music, as well as she had first thing in the morning. Andy's lovely, though, and they'd had a good laugh together, mainly because she'd told him how much she appreciated his efforts.

Amazing, she reflects, her fingers working almost of their own accord, what a difference it makes if you tell someone that you like what he does, and mean it. Most people don't bother.

On the other hand, when a project is supposed to be about

you, presenting you to the world, yet nobody wants to do it
your way – what then?

Alicia's initial plan had been to invite the photographer to
Buxton. They could go to Mam Tor, photograph her in walking-
boots with her beloved view in the background, and Cassie
could be in it. 'Don't be silly, darling,' Mum said. 'She's a
collie. It'd look like a soundtrack for *Lassie Come Home!*'

The next best thing would have been Alicia with view, minus
dog, but it transpired that the photographer, who is awfully
expensive, would charge for spending two days away – he'd
need two days, he insists, because it's such a long way to
Buxton. The record company doesn't want to pay the extra,
and as Alicia is in London to make the recording, she may as
well stay longer and go to his studio – which had been Rebecca's
initial plan.

Rebecca books a hair and makeup artist. Alicia's hair is long
– she hasn't had time to have it cut – but after the girl has
worked on it for two hours it's obedient, sleek and gorgeous.
The makeup feels excessive, but the photographer, who's
wearing black and has spiky, blond-dyed hair, assures her that
it's necessary under his lights, otherwise she'll look like a ghost.
Alicia is wearing jeans, but the photographer and Rebecca
open an elaborate suitcase and suggest that she changes into
one of the three concert gowns inside it. She chooses a dress
that's blue and sparkly and matches her eyes. It shows rather
too much cleavage, but she loves the blue – to her, the colour
of A major. They drape her, in the dress, over a white sofa,
surround her with huge vases of white and pink flowers and
put up white umbrellas to control the light. Then the clicking
begins.

'Oh, God,' Alicia says, when the contact sheets are spread
out on the kitchen table in Buxton a couple of weeks later. 'I
look like – like – I don't know what I look like. But it doesn't
look like me.' She hates the picture: it's all hair, flowers and flesh.

But Rebecca says the CD, when it comes out, will be played on Classic FM five times a day. Mum insists it's a beautiful picture and is, in any case, just a means to an end. Dad looks at it with exhausted eyes, tells Alicia she's an angel and that it will probably be OK, then vanishes into his study.

Kate has been talking to her mother on the phone. Margaret has been encouraging her, not for the first time, to start going to church. 'Mother,' Kate protested, 'I'm not going to spend Sunday mornings doing something I don't even begin to believe in.'

'Contrary to popular opinion, it might earth you,' Margaret said. 'It gives you a structure, a system, something solid behind you. We all need solidity and consolation in these terrible times.'

'Well, church never felt solid to me.'

'It sounds, dear, as if you need something spiritual in your life. You don't seem happy.'

'I'm perfectly happy. Now that Ali's career is getting off the ground—'

'Kate, I'm not thinking about the children. I'm thinking of *you.*'

'Mother, *I'm fine.* I have to go, there's something in the oven . . .'

October leaves blow about the garden in whirlpools. Kate dishes out pasta at the table. Her kitchen is immaculate, its beechwood golden under the ceiling spotlights; her pasta sauce is home-made, a blend of tomatoes, garlic and marinated chicken; and her husband is, for once, home for dinner. The dog sits in attendance beside Alicia, gaze fixed hopefully upon her plate. Alicia slips Cassie bits of chicken when she thinks Kate's looking the other way.

There's nothing tangible about the tension tonight. You can't see it, touch it or knit with it, let alone keep it steady. Kate has no idea where it originates, no notion of how to wind it up and confine it to a safe wicker basket. It's run away with her and her family, like a ball of wool batted downstairs by a kitten.

Guy and the children are physically present, but mentally each is somewhere else. Alicia, her fingers tapping on the edge of the table, is still practising. Adrian is munching with his usual vigour and staying silent with his usual uncommunicativeness. And Guy—

Guy has dark shadows under his eyes and the grey hairs at his temples seem recently to have doubled in number. Kate can see that he is not just worried, but fearful. He has intimated that there are problems at the office – financial concerns to do with investment, advertising and ownership, far beyond the editorial issues he controls. Kate doesn't want to raise the possibility in front of the kids that the *Manchester Chronicle* could be in choppy waters. But trying to make lively conversation about school doesn't seem helpful either.

Alicia's career, amid this swamp of adolescent hormones and adult anxieties, is a beacon of light. Kate hands round the salad (Adrian takes a single leaf) and mentions that Rebecca is planning to book the same studio for the next recording, a Chopin album.

'Damn it!' Guy expostulates. 'How is she supposed to make another CD for these bloody cowboys when she's got wall-to-wall exams?'

Alicia looks up, distressed.

Kate glares. 'Cowboys? Eden is an excellent company and Rebecca's an experienced professional.'

'Rebecca is a menace second only to that wretched Butterfingers woman.'

In over twenty years, Kate has never seen Guy so angry.

'Dad,' Alicia pleads, 'don't.'

'Don't *what*, Ali? Don't sit by and watch a bunch of hysterical, frustrated women wreck your life?'

'Nice one, Dad,' Adrian grunts.

'Shut up, Adrian. Guy, how can you say that?' Kate protests, airbrushing herself out of the 'bunch'. 'Mrs Butterworth was recommended as the best teacher in Manchester. Rebecca has worked in the record industry for nearly twenty-five years. Phyllida—'

'Phyllida's a time-bomb on legs. Silly Phyllie, Posh Becs and Mrs Butterfingers! And you're putting Ali's future in *their* hands?'

'Just because they're single, older women, you're determined to pour scorn on them. All any of them has done is work for Ali's best interests.'

'If making Ali do another CD like that last one is in her best interests, then I'm the Dalai Lama. No good will come of that disc, you'll see. The "Minute" Waltz and "Clair de lune"? You think anyone's going to take her seriously if she records easy-listening favourite classical hits? Why don't you listen to the advisory service?'

'Why didn't you say any of this before?' Kate demands.

'Because, sometimes, I'm as much of an idiot as anyone.' Guy pushes back his chair with a dreadful scraping noise and thuds away up the stairs. Tears well out of Alicia's eyes. Adrian glowers at his mother. 'Now look what you've done. The first time Dad's been home for supper all week and you have to wreck it.'

'I'm not the one who started swearing at Ali's managers.' Kate's hands are shaking and when she realises she can sit down it comes as a relief. 'Ali,' she says, 'don't cry, darling.'

Alicia snuffles, hands moving through Cassie's long hair; the dog always seems to know when she's upset and comes to comfort her with the pressure of her warm snout on her knee. 'I feel so lost,' she mumbles. 'I don't know who to trust. And I thought Dad was pleased, and suddenly he isn't. I don't know what to do.'

And Kate, though she has no intention of going to church, whispers inside her own head, 'God help me.'

★ ★ ★

In his study, Guy shuts first the door, then his eyes, then his brain. What an idiot, he thinks. How could I be such an oaf? But that's how things happen: it's all in the timing.

He's been trying to decide how to tell Kate that he has a lover, a pregnant lover, and that he wants to move out and live with her. But here is Kate, wittering on about recording studios and the marvellous Rebecca – not even *noticing* that Rebecca is a dyke – while Ali sits in tears over her dinner. Kate has absconded from the family planet and is chasing some elusive star that has nothing to do with him and, possibly, not much to do with Ali.

How can he abandon Ali? Emily may be having his child, but Ali *is* his child, with all her talent and radiance, a precious gem that has plummeted into his hands for safekeeping until the world is ready to hold her – and she's surrounded by people who say that they know what's best for her although they only care about their own interests.

In this catalogue of incompetence, perhaps he's the worst. What could be more incompetent than committing adultery and fathering a child? Emily, at least, is blameless. He trusts Emily as he has never trusted anybody else. Well, perhaps he'd once trusted Kate that way – twenty-five years ago.

He won't be able to tell his wife about his mistress tonight, though it was with this intention that he'd come home early. It will have to wait, if not for the right moment – for there will never be a right moment – then at least for one that's slightly better.

A CD's gestation period turns out to be longer than Alicia had expected: months rather than weeks. When hers is finally released in April – spring, according to Rebecca, being an excellent time for launching new efforts, giving breath to new life – Eden Classics's PR department pulls out all its stops. A beautiful teenager, famous nationwide, reputedly more gifted than any British girl musician since Jacqueline du Pré, playing popular pieces that show off her wonderful abilities. Twenty CDs are stacked up at the end of the kitchen table, ready for Kate to use as promotion.

'Sex,' Adrian says.

'What?' Alicia nearly chokes on her Weetabix.

'Look at it. What they're saying, underneath the crap, is "This kid is sexy." That's why people will buy it.'

'That's horrible.'

'Why do you think they made you put on a dress that showed your tits like that? Why do you think you had to lie down on that sofa?'

'All I wanted on the front was a picture of me in my normal clothes with Cassie!'

'Yeah. The girl-next-door look. That would have been great.'

'So why doesn't Mum see that? Why doesn't Rebecca?'

'Because you're fit.'

'I'm not! I just want to play the piano and walk my dog.'

'You look sexy, though. Of course, you're still too young, but you won't be for long. Ali, don't go all shocked. Sex sells. The company's not interested in *you*, only in making money out of you.' He dumps his bowl in the sink. 'I'll take Cassie out later,' he says, going upstairs.

Alicia sits at the table staring helplessly at the pile of CDs from which her own manufactured image in its loathsome setting stares back twenty times over.

Guy has been dealing with the shock waves at work caused by Emily's maternity leave. Everyone is gossiping about who the father can be – Emily is known to live by herself. He's had to send off tomorrow's edition listening to his secretary rattling on about whether it could be Rob Wilder, the office stud, whether Emily will leave, how she'll make ends meet, how she'd always seemed such an open person yet must be awfully secretive . . .

Privately he has to deal with far worse than that. Emily went into labour at five o'clock one afternoon while he was at the office. He wanted to drop everything and go to her; between contractions, she'd mustered the self-possession to order him by text message to do no such thing. Someone would find out; there'd be a scandal; he'd lose his job and so might she. She was alone in the hospital for the birth, with no partner to stand by her and let her grip his hand when the pain became unbearable, or look on in terror and wonder as the baby slithered out into the world and was placed in her arms, or share the immortal moment when her moist silvery eyes filled with love at their first glimpse of the new little face.

He'd gone to her on her first day home and she'd filled him in on every detail. He'd imagined the scenes as she talked, a furious, pistol-whip resentment building in his chest, causing constriction in his breathing and a pain down his left arm. He should have been with her, but he had not dared break the rules. He should have broken them earlier. He should have told Kate when he'd meant to. But even if he had, how could he leave Ali? Holding his newborn daughter, whom Emily wants to name Ingrid after her Danish grandmother, he's so flummoxed by the quantity of different loves within him that he can't speak for nearly ten minutes.

The air on the moor is filled with the scents of spring: new grass, recent rain. Unleashed, Cassie trots beside Adrian, performing the nearest thing she can to a frolic. Though she's a dignified lady of advancing years, she's still charmed by April sunshine.

Adrian feels like whistling himself. He's thinking about a girl. Not something he'd like to reveal, or a situation that makes sense. He knows her only from one encounter in Birmingham, her photo on Alicia's desk and her voice on the phone. It's a quiet, modest voice, oddly blending the accents of Birmingham, Surrey and India. All he's heard it say recently is 'Hello, this is Anjali speaking. Is Alicia there, please?' Why that should seem so appealing is anybody's guess. Her image lingers in his mind, surrounded by the golden wood of Symphony Hall: a small, slender girl with huge eyes and an intelligent, serious face. Adrian can't imagine anybody more different from the slappers at school. There's no point in aspiring to an angel, of course, not for him, but his feelings aren't his choice. She's been in the back of his mind, lurking, for months on end. He's wondering, when the Land Rover approaches, whether he can persuade Alicia to invite her to Buxton.

The Land Rover slows as it comes up the hill behind him. Mud and sheep-shit congeal on its bumper; behind its wheel sits a red-faced farmer in a tweed jacket and cap, glaring at Adrian and Cassie as if they are emissaries of the devil.

'What do you think you're doing?' the farmer shouts through the window.

'Going for a walk,' Adrian says. Cassie sits obediently to his right, waiting.

'That dog's going to get shot.'

'My dog's none of your business.'

'How stupid are you, you bloody yob?' Adrian judges, from the hue of his nose, that the farmer has probably had a drink or two today and that he's most likely on his way to the Cat and Fiddle for another. 'I'll thank you to keep that dog on a leash around them sheep. Don't you know it's lambing season?'

'My dog doesn't chase sheep.'

'If I see her once more up here without a leash, I won't warn you again, I shall shoot her. Got my rifle in the back here, mind.'

'Fuck off,' Adrian says. But he fastens Cassie's leash – he believes the words about the gun. Belligerent farmers aren't his favourite people, any more than he and his friends are theirs. The Land Rover revs into indecent acceleration.

'Evenly balanced bloke,' Adrian mutters to Cassie, as they resume their walk, leash-bound. 'Chips on both shoulders.'

The encounter has left a nasty taste in his mouth, and by

the time they reach the Cat and Fiddle, he fancies a drink. Cassie is panting too, so he takes her into the car park where a stone trough is filled with water for thirsty animals. There, a sight meets him that restores his spirits on the spot.

The car park is full because the bikers are there. They've parked in spaces meant for cars and the latest arrival to find nowhere to stop on this sunny spring Sunday is the farmer in the Land Rover. He's leaning out of his window, screaming fit to bust at the biker who's grabbed the last place. 'I'll have you up in front of the magistrate by this time next week, see if I don't! Screeching over the moors and scaring my sheep in the lambing season. No respect, that's your trouble, no respect for decent, law-abiding citizens.'

'Wanker!' Adrian shouts, sticking a finger up at the farmer. 'Why don't you bugger off and mind your own business? He's got as much right to park there as you have. He got there first and there's nowt you can do about it.'

The biker, who's removed his helmet, turns and meets Adrian's gaze, looking surprised, even impressed. He has bright, piercing blue eyes and big shoulders. He's bigger, tougher and older (if not much) than Adrian and looks like the kind of bloke who wouldn't expect anyone to come to his defence.

'You again?' the farmer snarls at Adrian. 'I'll shoot that dog, see if I don't.'

'Piss off,' says the biker. 'You've no business shooting dogs when you can't even feed your livestock without making them into cannibals and spreading diseases they'd never have got otherwise. Your sort thinks the world owes you a living! Anyhow, I got that space first.'

'Move that bike. *Now.*'

'Bye-bye. Have a beautiful day.' The biker strides towards the pub; then turns and motions Adrian to follow him. Adrian, a spring in his step, needs no second bidding.

'Thanks, mate,' says the biker. 'The name's Josh. Pleased to meet you. What'll it be? Pint?'

'Yeah, thanks. I'm Adrian.'

'Great dog, that one. Pedigree rough collie, is she?'

'I think so.' Adrian watches Cassie jump up towards the biker's chest and try to lick his nose. Josh, to her delight and Adrian's, gives her a good back-rub.

'I had a dog. She was wonderful. Old English sheepdog, the kind that can't see out. Lovely creature. I miss her.'

'What happened to her?'

'She's with my family in Manchester. I don't go home much. Anyway, who do these blokes think they are, driving their fucking Land Rovers?'

In the pub, Josh leads Adrian and Cassie towards his fellow bikers. Adrian fidgets with Cassie's leash.

He once saw a documentary on TV about a pack of wolves. When a young male wolf from another valley wanted to join them, he had to approach the potentially hostile animals and let them surround him. While they growled, threatened and lunged, he had to stand firm and fearless, wagging his tail. Right now, Adrian feels that standing firm and wagging your tail takes more courage than fighting off a bunch of armed attackers single-handed.

'This is Adrian,' Josh says to the others. 'You into bikes, Adrian?'

'Well,' Adrian begins, 'funny you should say that . . .'

14

In her office – its wall laden with prints from Alicia's photo-shoot – Kate sifts through the sheaf of CD reviews, looking for quotable quotes. During the summer, quite a few have emerged; but however hard she stares at them, she can't make them any better. One praises Alicia's tone quality, fast fingers and range of colour, but disparages the presentation and populist programming. Another deems her too young and shallow. A third condemns the disc as a miserable attempt to exploit a young girl: this CD, the critic carps, is not a good idea. The advisory scheme, with a strongly worded letter, warns Kate of the same thing.

Yet when Rebecca calls her with the sales figures, the public seems to have thought the CD was a very good idea indeed.

'Becs, I don't know who to believe.'

'People are buying it, aren't they?' her friend replies. 'Critics hate anything that's popular and sells well. They always have. Just ignore them.'

'And her new album next spring? The Chopin? What will they say about that?'

'Katie, stop worrying! It'll sell. People love her.'

Kate hangs up and stares out of her window at the leaves turning from green to brown in the garden. Rebecca knows what she's doing. She must. She has to. And it's true: people are buying the CD, mean critics or no. All she can do is wait and see what next year holds.

Alicia makes a mistake at school. She lets Kelly know that she's going to London to be interviewed by national newspapers about her piano-playing. Preparing to go home at the end of a chilly afternoon, she reaches into her school bag for her gloves and feels something sharp on her skin. When she pulls out her right hand, it's streaked with red globules of blood.

Guy returns from a long, difficult day to find Alicia in tears, Kate pale and tight-lipped and Adrian in his room, pumping out the kind of music that doesn't do a stressed-out family any good.

'Adrian, turn that down!' he yells from the hall. His son can't hear him. 'Ali, what's going on?'

She doesn't reply. Instead she holds out her right hand. It's bandaged.

'Some of the kids at school thought it'd be fun to put a piece of broken bottle in Ali's bag,' Kate tells him. 'I've rung the headmaster.'

'I'm not going back,' Alicia says.

'Ali, you've got GCSEs . . .'

'I don't care.'

'It's lucky that she didn't actually take hold of it,' Kate adds. 'The cuts are nasty, but there's no damage to her tendons.'

'I'll go and see the headmaster,' Guy says. 'And I'm going to put something in the paper.'

'Thank you,' says Kate, icy. 'About time. Sad that it takes such an incident to get your daughter's name into your newspaper.'

A howl from Alicia brings them to their senses. Guy sits down on the stairs. He wants a drink, badly.

'Perhaps it's time for Ali to move on,' he says. 'How about calling the music school?'

A short conversation with the headmistress of the music school produces rapid results. The head of piano, who would be in charge of Alicia's studies, asks Kate to come and see him right away. He's younger than she is, a tall Scot with a youthful face, bright smile and a tweed jacket; his handshake is warm and firm. On his desk is a photo of his slender blonde wife and no fewer than five children. He couldn't be a greater contrast with Mrs Butterworth. He asks her to call him Ian.

'We've been following Alicia's progress with a great deal of interest,' he tells her. 'Now, tell me what happened.'

Kate explains. 'She says she won't go back to school. And when Alicia makes up her mind, she's very stubborn.'

'Was she stubborn over her CD?'

Kate tries, tactfully, to outline the difference between Alicia's hopes and the result.

'Did anyone notice that she might be right?' Ian says.

'Well . . .'

'Now, Kate, here's my view. Alicia has an extraordinary talent. But that talent has to be properly nurtured. She's been bounced, for lack of a better word, out of her depth. Everyone wants a piece of her, don't they? Her teacher. Her record company. Her agent.'

'She couldn't wish for nicer people around her than Rebecca Harris and Phyllida Brown.'

'I know Phyllida. She's great,' Ian agrees. 'It's a good agency. But they've got big plans, haven't they?'

'They're talking about a tour of Germany, and several European festivals want to book her.'

'Listen, Kate. I feel this very strongly: this isn't right. If Alicia is going to join us here, I have some very specific conditions that I need you to agree to. First, no more recordings until she's ready. And then only when she has total control of what goes on to the CD and its cover.'

'Rebecca thinks she *is* ready.'

'Rebecca would.' Ian fixes Kate with his straight, no-nonsense gaze. Kate puts a hand against the side of her neck.

'I've heard the recording,' Ian goes on. 'Yes, she's a lovely girl and her playing is often mature beyond her years. But in the bigger picture, that CD, even if it sells well, is not going to do her many favours. It's made the critics cynical about her, although they were on her side after the competition. The general consensus is that she's too young: she needs time to study and grow, but she's being coerced – by whoever – into doing too much work and the wrong kind. She's being launched on the wrong foot.'

Kate squeezes the edge of her chair.

'So: no tours of Germany – or anywhere else – until *we*'re convinced she's ready. Touring can be hell. It's tiring; it's tedious. Believe me, I've done it myself. Why put a kid through that at sixteen? These are years that Alicia needs, Kate, to consolidate her talent, to give herself something to build on for the future. It's as if you're asking her to spend her capital before it's had a fair chance to accrue.'

'I see.'

'If she's coming to us, the recording contract goes, ninety per cent of the concerts go and Deirdre Butterworth goes too.'

'Really?'

'It's nothing personal. I hardly know her, but I do know the playing of some of her pupils. Personally, I treat her teaching with caution. She has her admirers. She's good at drilling the fingers and developing technique. But a young musician needs to have her soul built too. Deirdre's methods can be effective, but her attitudes are extremely old-fashioned and a number of pianists feel they've had quite a destructive effect, long-term.'

'But the concerts . . . Alicia would have to let down halls, clubs and orchestras that have booked her to play. She'd have to break her contract with Eden.'

'Then so be it. If she has to let people down, that's a pity. But it's better than everyone else letting *her* down.'

'If we agree to all this, you'll take her?'

'We'll need to talk to her ourselves, of course, but I think there's a good chance.'

'And if not—'

'Then I'm afraid it's no.'

'I'll have to talk to my husband. And we'll both have to talk to Alicia.'

Later, Kate replays Ian's words in her mind. She'd tried to call Guy as soon as she came out of the school, but he was having a newspaper crisis; the aftermath of the events in New York on 11 September a year earlier is still sending extended jitters through every business in the country. Life is so short. Why waste the opportunities that come your way?

Her own life, as she sees it, is hopeless in all respects but one: Ali. Otherwise, what has she done that's been worth doing? She has three children; one dead, one uncontrollable and the last a child prodigy. Any one of them would have been enough to put her marriage under strain.

You have to make the most of every minute. She remembers the images of the twin towers collapsing. Who knows what will happen now? Perhaps Al Qaeda terrorists intend to bring not only America but Europe, too, tumbling into war, chaos and destruction. And they're supposed to worry about schooling, drop most of the concerts and all the recording plans, throw away every chance that Ali has now, in case something better lies in wait a few years down the line? By then none of them may be here.

Kate puts the matter to one side while they go to London; she says nothing to Alicia yet, because the girl must concentrate on her round of interviews, set up by a public-relations firm at a cost of several thousand pounds per month's work. Alicia charms all the journalists and claims that her hand is bandaged because she'd had a little accident in the kitchen. The PR company has rapidly muzzled Guy's plans to tell the truth in his newspaper. Rebecca embraces Kate and has the empathy to ask whether *she* is feeling all right.

Phyllida cooks dinner for them and Rebecca at her top-floor flat in Tulse Hill, an Italian meal that wouldn't look out of place in Rome. First, fresh mozzarella, tomato and basil, Italian cold meats and home-baked ciabatta; then pasta with pesto, and a main course of baked sea bass with fennel, lemon, capers and vegetables; and the most incredible tiramisu for dessert.

'Maybe it's because I don't have kids,' Phyllida declares, pouring prosecco, 'but I always end up mothering my clients.'

The light, bubbly wine makes them feel light and bubbly too.

'Phyllida,' Alicia asks, after her miniature ration, when her cheeks are flushed and her courage increased, 'why don't you have kids?'

'I keep falling in love with the wrong men,' Phyllida tells her.

'French pianists,' Rebecca needles.

'Not Lucien?' Alicia is horrified.

'But you still work for him,' Kate says.

'How could I not?' Phyllida's eyes, behind her small rectangular spectacles, turn towards the window and gaze over the rooftops of hilly south London as if seeking out any traces of the vanished presence for which she cared too much.

Alicia, exhausted after a long day, falls asleep in the car on the way back to Hampstead Garden Suburb. Kate and Rebecca talk quietly about Phyllida and Lucien. 'He trampled all over her,' Rebecca says. 'But she won't give him up as a client and she won't give up hope. If he had any sense of honour, he'd leave the agency – but he knows she'll do anything for him, so he stays and takes advantage of it.'

'She's crazy,' Kate says.

'Crazy about him. She says she'd rather have him somewhere in her life than nowhere, and that this way at least she can do something for him. She's still hoping she'll get him back if he thinks she's indispensable. She can't move on.'

'Does he have someone else?'

'Plenty of someone elses, besides the official one. He's living with a very beautiful girl in Paris – half Algerian, I believe. She designs jewellery. He's been with her for two years. I think she's the one he left Phyllida for, but it may have been another . . . He's got quite a network around the world.'

'Doesn't Phyllida *know*?'

'Of course she knows. But what can you do? He's a good-looking guy. He's charming, talented, charismatic, famous, and he has the cutest accent on earth. Women never could resist him. And there are always women who think it's noble to forgive.'

'You've resisted him,' Kate points out.

'That's different. I'm sorted. Since I broke up with David, I've found myself.'

'And where were you hiding all the time?' Kate teases her.

'Aha. Somewhere else.' Kate waits, but Rebecca smiles and says no more.

Kate privately adopts Guy's nickname for Phyllida: 'Silly Phyllie'. Poor girl – woman (she's forty) – slogging her guts out for a man who's ridden roughshod over her. At least if you devote yourself to working for your daughter, she's your own flesh and blood. Phyllida may never be Lucien's lover again. Kate will always be Ali's mum.

Back in Buxton, they find a letter from school on the doormat, declaring that the children responsible for putting glass in Alicia's bag have been caught and may be excluded. Alicia hovers, clutching her bandaged hand. Kate sits her down and gives her a somewhat postponed and selectively edited account of her conversation with Ian at the music school.

'What do you think?' she says at the end. 'Are you prepared to do what they want?'

'I don't think I want to keep going to any school anyway,' Alicia says. 'Maybe I could grit my teeth, go back to Parkhill and do the exams – and then just leave. I guess I can stand it for a while if they've got rid of . . . them. I don't need A levels to play the piano, do I?'

'We'll have to talk to your father,' Kate says, reeling.

But of course Alicia's father is home so late that Alicia is asleep and Kate is tired and fed up. Bundling laundry into the washing-machine the next morning, she's puzzled to spot what looks like a milk stain on the shoulder of the shirt he'd been wearing, and wonders why he sometimes comes home smelling of sandalwood soap.

'Alicia! *Bonjour, chérie, ça va?*'

'Oh, Lucien,' Alicia exclaims into the phone, 'I'm not very *bien* at all.'

She'd cried into her pillow half the night, not for the first time. Mum has often told her that everything feels worse at three o'clock in the morning, but this was the worst yet. With the bitter flavour of her home, with Mum and Dad fighting – it's grown unaccountably more extreme this year – and school, where she has to take horrible exams and has no friends, things couldn't seem much more miserable.

Mum and Dad's latest row is over school and her fervent desire not to be there any more. Mum is broadly in favour of her leaving to concentrate on music, but Dad is livid. She's caught, like Dorothy in *The Wizard of Oz*, in a tornado that's transforming people she'd loved and trusted into witches, scarecrows and Munchkins. Like Dorothy – her favourite movie character, because of the dog – she's miles from where she wants to be and she needs a wizard to help her.

Lucien the wizard listens to everything. Then he says, 'Darling, when do you next have a school holiday? Can you come to Zürich? I have started to teach at the Zürich Academy, and I will be there for two weeks. We could work together and talk this through.'

'Can I?' Alicia pleads. 'I'd so love to. I've got half-term soon.'

'Your mother didn't want you to come last time,' he reminds her. 'You must be strong, you must insist.'

'I'll try.' Alicia wants to tell Lucien about Dad's peculiar behaviour, his outbursts, his silences, his absences, but she doesn't know how to; and she doesn't know what she wants him to say anyway.

She's attempted time and again to persuade Mum that they should go to see Lucien in Paris, but so far to no avail. There's always a reason not to. Looming concerts, mainly; Alicia sometimes feels she's so busy performing that she doesn't have time to learn in any depth about the music she plays. She senses, too, that Mum and Paris are like oil and water, goodness knows why, though when she tries to bargain – couldn't Dad go with her, or Phyllida? Couldn't she go alone? – it only seems to make matters worse.

Today, when she tackles Mum in her office, gathering all her courage and saying 'Lucien' and 'Zürich' – not Paris – the response is different. Mum, at her computer, is pallid and tired. There's a deflated, defeated look about her. Alicia imagines their house rising up in the tornado, with all of them clinging on, whirling sleepless into the sky.

'If that's what you want to do, love,' Mum says, barely looking at her, 'then we'll do it.'

'Mum,' Alicia pushes, 'why do you hate Paris?'

'I don't,' says Mum.

Alicia gazes at Zürich and can hardly breathe for its beauty. When she and Mum have checked in to their guesthouse and set out to explore, she finds they're on the shore of a vast lake; across the water, dusky, smoky mountains are shrouded in a soft autumn haze. It's so lovely that it hurts. Everything is blue, bronze and purple. It's like walking through a Chopin nocturne in D flat major.

Alicia hasn't been abroad often. Lucien looks shocked when she explains her holiday routine. The family does take a break for a couple of weeks in summer – at least, they used to, before the competition – but it usually means going with Margaret and William to Sidmouth, Torbay, or sometimes Scotland, which is even colder than Buxton, but which Alicia loves for the scenery. A few times, when she was much smaller, they went to seriously hot places where Mum and Dad had crashed out on the beach – Mum still had her job in those days – and she and Adrian would mess around in the sea. But now, wherever they go, Alicia spends the first day hunting for a piano on which she can practise, and the rest of the holiday practising on it. 'Alicia,' says Lucien, 'you have to learn one thing: there's life away from the piano.'

Not that Lucien has much of a life. He travels all the time. After two weeks in Zürich, he'll be off for a recital tour in Germany and Holland, back to Zürich for more teaching, and eventually to America for three weeks. If he's lucky, he might be home for Christmas. He doesn't go home for more than a few days every month or two. He's constantly on his mobile phone – if he wants it to stop ringing, he has to switch it off – and he's the fastest texter Alicia has ever seen. It seems that he has a beautiful half-Algerian girlfriend waiting for him in Paris. She must miss him.

When Mum insists on sitting in on Alicia's lesson at the academy, Lucien tries a few charming discouragements, none of which work. Especially not when Mum turns on her own charm – something she does infrequently, but to startling effect. For Mum, to smile is to deploy a secret weapon that makes people do what she wants because they simply can't stop themselves. Lucien is no exception: when Mum beams at him, he dissolves into a hopeless grin and declares, 'You should be sisters, not mother and daughter!' Alicia wriggles inwardly: she tries, sometimes, to get him to look at her like that. Occasionally he obliges, but mostly he doesn't.

What does his girlfriend think when he looks at other women? Maybe she doesn't know that he does. Or maybe she doesn't mind. She must mind – but maybe she forgives him. Alicia hates being sixteen. There's too much that she doesn't under-stand and she's scared to ask because she's terrified of looking stupid.

In the studio, with Mum in the corner, notebook at the ready, and Lucien beside her at the piano, Alicia starts to play Chopin. Almost before she knows what's happened, two hours have passed. Mrs Butterfingers – as Alicia secretly calls Mrs Butterworth – usually scrawls instructions across her music with red pencil; when there's so much red that you can't read more, she switches to blue. She writes in the fingering for each note and tells Alicia exactly how to practise every passage: which to slow down in different rhythms, which to build up note by note, which metronome marks to use. Lucien does none of this. He asks Alicia what she thinks. What the music makes her feel. What she wants it to say. After they've worked through the Chopin, she plays some Schumann. It makes him think of another Schumann piece, he remarks, a song called 'Mondnacht'. He plays her the song, which she's never heard before; it's so magical that she nearly bursts into tears.

She doesn't know the other pieces he mentions – symphonies, a violin concerto, chamber music. She has no time to listen to recordings of pieces she's not learning to play, and she can't go to proper concerts unless she's in London or Manchester with no school the next day. Lucien turns to Mum and protests: 'A young musician has to have the background, the breadth of knowledge, the experience . . .'

Alicia knows that she's ignorant; filling in the gaps is a daunting task. It certainly isn't going to happen at school. Lucien, to her delight, agrees: Alicia won't glean the excep-tional, specialised knowledge she needs from any A-level syllabus. At least this might help to sway Dad. Lucien says nothing on the subject that Alicia couldn't have said herself; the difference is that her parents will listen to him. Alicia decides that there's only one place to begin her real education: with

Lucien. She's a sponge and he's a great fountain, as full as the violet lake, with an endless pool of wisdom in which she can soak.

They go to Lucien's studio three times that week, once he's finished with his official students for the day. In between, he's arranged for Alicia to practise at the academy. After her lessons, the three of them go to a café for supper and Lucien talks for hours. He tells them about his studies at the Paris Conservatoire – he'd started there when he was only twelve; and about his year in Moscow (how funny, Alicia thinks, that he studied in the same places as Mrs Butterfingers, yet the two of them are light years apart). In the Russian winter, he says, he got frostbite. His ears swelled and turned purple. He'd looked like a donkey. Mum laughs, relaxed, enchanted.

Alicia is so busy watching Lucien's eyes that sometimes she doesn't hear what he's saying. Every shade of emotion shows in them: they are gleaming one moment, soulful the next, switching in a flash from inscrutable to teasing to tender. Mum is silent when he speaks; Alicia thinks her pupils become three times their usual size. She wonders whether she'll look like her mother when she's her age. She hopes so, though she'd dress differently. Mum prefers somewhat formal clothes, usually with a jacket and jewellery. She never wears jeans. Alicia likes to look natural.

After their last meal together, Lucien walks them back along the lake front to their guesthouse. The lights reflect in the water, silver on indigo, and the surface ripples in the breeze that drifts from the mountains. It's warm for October; people are out enjoying the evening air. 'You couldn't do this at home,' Alicia says. 'You'd freeze.' Here, colours seem brighter – there's something grey about England, as if the light has been rolled in dust. Mum tells her it's because she finds it exciting to be somewhere new, but Alicia is certain that there's more to it. She doesn't want to leave Switzerland.

Saying goodbye, Lucien kisses Mum three times and she

turns coy like a schoolgirl. Alicia hugs him and wants never to let go. The next morning, on the plane, she closes her eyes and daydreams about him. If only Phyllida wasn't his ex-girlfriend. She tries not to imagine them together; it makes her feel like a limp brown balloon that's been left outside for too long.

Lucien has told her that she must come to his masterclasses next year at the Moorside Summer School. It will be a popular event, so Mum will send in their booking form at once and Alicia plans to exhort Anjali to join them. In the meantime, she has to go back to Deirdre Butterworth who, she now understands, may have been teaching her how to play, but not why.

'It's great.' Emily is inspecting the new white paint, the stripped wooden floor and the relatively spacious second bedroom at the back. The flat is near Victoria Park on the ground level of a converted terraced house. It's less convenient for work than Emily's current home, but the area is quieter, more family-oriented, with a child-minder in the next street and a doctor's surgery less than five minutes' walk away. Emily's apartment in the centre of town has only one bedroom and is on the fourth floor, which is hopeless with a baby buggy.

While he holds Ingrid, Guy's mind flickers images at him of his other children. Adrian. Alicia. Victoria. Pain cuts through his chest, half real, half imagined, whether physical or emotional he couldn't say: the two are inseparable.

'One day,' Emily says, 'maybe we'll be looking at a cottage in a village.'

'There are some great places,' Guy says. 'Castleton. Or Hartington.'

'A little house with a garden and a local school and a real sense of community. We miss that here. In Denmark it's much stronger.'

'Maybe we should move to Denmark.'

There's a long silence then, because they know they're

fantasising. They keep doing it: building castles in the air, only to watch, helpless, as the walls disintegrate. Guy notices Emily turn away so that he can't see her face. The baby in his arms wriggles and whimpers. He gives her back to her mother, who caresses her back with one hand, infinitely gentle.

Guy has been to see the bank manager. He refuses to shirk his responsibilities: this child is his and he is determined to support her and Emily. The question is how to do so without Kate finding out. He has set up a direct debit to an account that will be Emily's but that will bear a different title. He hates to use Alicia as a pretext, but calling it Music Fund seems sensible: Kate, if she finds it, will assume he's started another savings account towards Alicia's studies. As he signs the form, he loathes himself for it – but whatever he does, caught in this impossible web, will be wrong.

It's not that he hasn't intended to tell Kate the truth – but Kate is so *busy*. Her existence centres on Alicia; if she's not occupied with trips to London to visit Phyllida and Rebecca or, now, to Switzerland to see Lucien (which has given him the leisure to house-hunt with Emily), then it's concert planning, letters, phone calls and, of course, escorting Alicia to her concerts, which can be anywhere in the country. Every time Guy steels himself, gearing up to an explanation with rehearsed speech and sinking stomach, she'll be so busy yakking with Rebecca that he can't get her attention; or Alicia needs ferrying to a far-flung venue, or there's hassle with Adrian – there's more and more hassle, these days, with Adrian, who seems never to go to school and vanishes like clockwork every weekend. So nothing happens and time runs on.

Guy's back has been hurting, he has a permanent headache and he's afraid he's getting a stomach ulcer.

Adrian takes a bus to Macclesfield one Saturday afternoon and wanders towards a shop that his new friend Josh has told him about. He wants to earn some money.

Standing outside it, he feels like a nineteenth-century orphan pressing his nose against a bakery window. Inside are ranged the most enticing objects he's ever seen. They vary in size from largish to humungous. Their bodies are shiny – black, silver, purple, ivory or red – and their wheels sleek, made for racing. Most of the labels bear prices in four figures. Adrian has a savings account into which his parents and grandparents pay regularly, building funds to support him when he goes to university (as they assume he will). He knows he'll be slaughtered if he raids it. He also knows he's supposed to have a licence if he wants to drive a motorbike. On the other hand, he'd have to ride around with an L-plate, as well as undergoing time-consuming remedial instruction that he doesn't need, maybe for six months; the shame would be more than he could take.

During heady summer weekends on the moors, he's learned everything he needs to learn from Josh and the others. Josh lets him ride pillion, but has made it clear that he can't do this for ever. If he wants to join them properly, he has to have his own bike. He's going to have to pay the deposit and then monthly instalments, which means he needs an income and therefore a job, which has to be evenings, weekends or both, but not more, because of effing school.

It's all right for Ali: she's *talented*. Adrian sometimes wonders why one of them should have been born with a talent while the other wasn't, and why that other should have had to be him. Why couldn't he be on TV, have a posh London agent, charge through the nose for his services? Adrian vacillates between being proud and protective of his little sister, and half wanting to strangle her. He doesn't feel that way often: just often enough for it to hurt. He could murder the idiots at school who'd thought it funny to put glass in her bag; but, staring past his reflection at the array of bikes with names like Panorama, Seductor and Freedom, he admits reluctantly that he can understand why someone might. Poor Ali. It's not her fault. She hadn't asked for this any more than he had.

The shop door is open. Adrian draws himself up. Josh has given him the manager's name and tipped him off that they need Saturday help. He tries to broaden his shoulders and walks up to the counter, hoping he looks cool.

15

On Christmas Eve, while Guy is overseeing the last of the seasonal rush at the office, Kate drives Alicia back through a damp, dreary night from a recital in a music club in the West Midlands, where she has played for an audience of twenty-nine over-seventies. At home, at half past eleven, Alicia has a cup of hot chocolate and a bath, while Kate wanders into her study and switches on the computer. As the screen brightens, she finds herself face to face with a picture of a bomb.

Her hard drive has crashed. Just in time for Christmas. Luckily she's backed everything up – she's scrupulous about this, thanks to Rebecca's urgings – but it's too late at night to phone Rebecca for advice or ransack the *Yellow Pages* for a man who can help. None will be available now, she suspects, until the new year. There's no point in stewing over it; she has other things to worry about, notably cooking Christmas lunch the next day. But tonight she does need to send one short yet vital email.

She rings Guy's mobile, but it's off. He can't possibly mind, can he, if this once she goes into his study and uses his computer? She checks that Alicia is all right, then makes her way to the top of the house.

Guy's study is in its usual chaos. Kate shakes her head as she steps across the clutter to the desk and computer. She presses a switch and, as she waits for the computer to buzz into action, she glances through a sheaf of papers beside it.

Credit-card statements; drafts for leaders, which he some-times writes himself; letters, including something from the bank about a largish direct debit to an account called Music Fund, which she doesn't recognise. Odd. Why would Guy create another Ali account without telling her? Of course, he's so absent-minded that he probably forgot.

Kate logs on to the email, guessing the password success-fully (Cassie) and types out her message to the music-club director, thanking her for a wonderful evening (it's impor-tant that Ali should at least have the chance to be reinvited). When she's finished, Guy's inbox appears in front of her. She sees:

<u>emily.andersen</u>

<u>emily.andersen</u>

<u>emily.andersen</u>

<u>emily.andersen</u>

<u>emily.andersen</u>

The messages from emily.andersen, dated across the past few days, have no subject heading. Kate stares, disbelieving, hand poised over the mouse. She moves it gingerly and the cursor glides towards the first one. She can't bring herself to click.

This is crazy. She trusts Guy. He's too busy, too preoccu-pied, too hopeless to *do* anything with anybody, let alone a lovely young thing who could have had Rob Wilder with one click of her fingers. Whatever would a girl like Emily Andersen see in a scatterbrained workaholic like Guy Bradley?

With a momentum that doesn't seem to be hers, Kate's hand reaches for the pile of papers and extracts several credit-card statements. September's is among them, marked 'PAID' in Guy's messy blue capitals. On it is a list of transactions: Ikea (where they haven't shopped in years), Tesco (there's no Tesco in Buxton) and, most peculiar of all, Mothercare.

Three facts collide in Kate's fast-moving mind. Emily Andersen is half Danish. Guy once went to a conference in Denmark. Why Denmark, for God's sake? And these places and payments remind her, peculiarly, of those on her credit-card statements when they were kitting out their home after the birth of Adrian.

Kate clicks.

Darling – everything's OK, health visitor says just wrap her up warm and keep an eye on the cough. So don't worry, we're fine. Exxxx

She reads the message five times. The words don't want to penetrate her skull. This can't be real. It makes no sense. 'Darling'? A health visitor? 'We' are fine?

She clicks again.

Darling – don't apologise. You know I love you. I know you love me. That's all that matters. Exxxxx

'Mum,' Alicia calls, 'I'm turning in, OK?'

'OK, love. Sleep tight,' Kate calls back brightly. She sits in Guy's chair and breathes, counting to five between in-breath and out-breath and in-breath. Keeping it steady. Keeping the tension regular. Once Alicia's door has closed, she goes down to the bathroom and throws up.

Knowledge is power – as Kate reminds herself later, lying alone in bed, fighting bile in her throat, cramps in her stomach and the gates of hell splitting open in her brain. She hears Guy's car in the drive. The front door opens and closes. He takes off his shoes in the hall. There's the hiss of the kettle, his steps padding about as he makes tea. Now she understands: late nights, long absences, too many showers, stress symptoms that leave him constantly medicated for a stomach ulcer and a suspected slipped disc. And, of course, sandalwood soap. How has she managed not to spot what these add up to? How could she be so blind, so naïve, so trusting?

She's not as young as she once was. Her hair, if she didn't keep it artificially golden and glossy, would be turning grey; her skin is losing its elasticity, despite expensive face creams;

and the weight doesn't stay off as easily as it used to, though this is perhaps also attributable to eating out more when she's away with Ali. She hasn't yet struck the menopause, but it can't be many years off. Emily Andersen is in her early thirties; she has lovely skin, beautiful grey eyes, a shapely figure and, it seems, a fertile womb. Why such a girl should pick Kate's hopeless husband to fall in love with is rather beyond Kate. But that isn't the point.

The pillow is darkening with tears. She turns it over before Guy can come up.

Knowledge is power. She may be in pieces, but she has the upper hand. She only has to decide how best to use it. Agony and despair, knitted together, produce fury and a sickening desire for revenge. What can she do? There is, she decides, gathering her long-forgotten resources, plenty she can do.

When Guy opens the door, she lies with her back to him, letting him think she's asleep. Downstairs in the piano room, the Christmas-tree lights are dark.

During the night, while Kate and Guy lie awake, each feigning sleep for the other's benefit, the clouds drift lower and spew a malicious mix of rain and snow over the sloping streets. Then they tumble away towards the moors, and under the stars the frost sidles across to seal wetness into the town's bones. In its wake, a high covering of grey cloud sucks the colour from land and air. By the time Kate hears Alicia clumping downstairs with Cassie, the pavement outside is a sheet of mean, treacherous ice. In the distance there's a squeal of car brakes and a crunch of impacting metal.

Alicia presses a switch: the tree beside the piano flares into brilliance. 'I love Christmas!' she cries, to nobody in particular. Cassie, happy after her breakfast, lets out a volley of barks.

'Cut the racket, Al,' Adrian says, wandering by in his dressing-gown, his face stubbly and his eyes bleary.

'Merry Christmas to you too,' Guy remarks, in the kitchen.

Adrian doesn't answer. He pours himself a bowl of Shredded Wheat and abducts it.

'Adrian, it's Christmas Day,' Kate calls after him. 'I think we should all be together.'

'Later,' Adrian grunts, half-way up the stairs. 'Ali, you look like a sheep.' Alicia is wearing a thick white jumper over her jeans.

'Don't be horrible to your sister,' Kate snaps.

'It's going to be one of those days, is it?'

Kate can't say, 'You don't know the half of it,' so she keeps quiet as her son disappears to his room and her daughter through the front door with the dog, who needs walking, ice or no ice. 'Ali, mind how you go. Don't slip,' she calls after her. Then she has to start preparing Christmas lunch. There's no more time to think.

Today, of all days, both sets of parents are coming to them. Anthony, Fiona and the Horribles have gone to San Francisco to visit Joanna (something Kate and Guy have been saying for years that they really should do, too). Because of this, William and Margaret had expected Kate and her family in Harrow; but George and Didie had been intending for months that they'd go to Cheshire. It had seemed easiest to base the entire caboodle in Buxton, rather than zoom round the country trying to please everyone but themselves.

'Guy,' Kate says, chopping onion, which makes her eyes water, 'my computer crashed last night.'

'What's up with it?'

'Bomb icon. The hard drive's dead. Know anyone who can fix it?' It was a bomb icon for the entire household, but she won't inform him of this until later. She feels his gaze on her back. All he says is 'I'll ask the IT department to suggest someone.'

The turkey waits in its roasting pan, big and fat and stupid. She puts on the oven to heat. Alicia and Cassie blow in with a tidal wave of icy air from the front door; Alicia stamps her feet to warm them. She begs Kate to let her help with lunch, but Kate urges her to do some practising first.

'It's Christmas!' Alicia protests. 'And I had a concert last night. I'm not going to practise this morning.'

'You can if you want to,' Kate reassures her.

'She *doesn't* want to,' Guy points out, in front of the small, recently acquired kitchen TV where he's eating toast and staring at an inordinately jolly news programme. The presenters are wearing tinsel round their necks.

Kate rubs butter on to the turkey's skin and puts foil over its breast. Outside, snow is trying, half-heartedly, to fall. From the TV, Bing Crosby's voice intones nauseating lyrics about what Christmas ought to be like.

When the potatoes are parboiling, the Brussels sprouts have been stripped of their outer leaves and the chestnut stuffing has been thoroughly whizzed in the food-processor, Alicia wanders up to her brother's room. He's got his TV on, loud.

'Adrian,' she says, 'something weird's going on.'

'Come on, Ali, surprise me.'

'I mean, like, *really* weird. Worse than usual. They haven't said a single word to each other for an hour.' She sits down next to him. The TV patters out a tinkly carol between programmes, over a sequence showing happy children opening brightly coloured presents.

'I hate Christmas,' Adrian says.

'I *thought* I loved it,' Alicia says miserably.

'Everyone would hate Christmas, if they thought about it.'

'That's not true. It's wonderful! Everyone can stop working and be together.'

'Yeah. Look where that gets them.'

'Do you have to be so grumpy?'

'Pissed off that I can't go to work for two weeks. I'm saving up.'

'What for?'

'If you must know, one of the beauts in our shop.'

'Seriously? They must cost a fortune.'

'Worth it, though, if I can find a way. There's nothing like it, Ali.'

'How does it feel?'

'Wicked.' Adrian gives a deep sigh – the nearest thing Alicia has ever heard him express to longing. 'It's the best feeling in the whole world. I just want to get on and go.'

'Go where?'

'Anywhere. Just – away. Away from here.'

While Kate is fussing over salad, Guy creeps into the piano room, deserted but for the decked yet lonely tree, and sends Emily a text. She's going to her mother's for the day. Guy, pressing out the words 'Merry Xmas, I love you', remembers that his child by Emily has a grandmother whom he's never met – and who would probably kill him if he did. His parents have rung in cheery mode to say they're on their way. They have a granddaughter whom they'll never know; how they'd have loved Ingrid. Perhaps he's imagining it, but did Kate glare at him when she mentioned her crashed computer? There was no possibility that, in the middle of the night on Christmas Eve, she'd have been so desperate to get on to her email or the Internet that she'd have used his and seen the wrong thing – was there? His ulcer stabs like a nail in his chest.

The grandparents arrive at the same time from opposite directions, bearing gifts and having traversed afar, over motorway and moor. William and Margaret shiver on the front step; George and Didie shake their hands and smile fixedly. Alicia charges down the stairs and flings her arms round Didie; Adrian gives each grandparent a diffident peck. The presents are piled under the tree and Kate puts on a CD of a choirboy warbling, 'Peace on earth, goodwill to men . . .'

William and Margaret are staying the night, sleeping in Kate's study, and William goes upstairs slowly; he needs a hip replacement and is in constant pain, but the waiting list is eight months long. Margaret stares with disapproval at Alicia's clothes and asks Kate whether her daughter always wears jeans for Christmas. Kate says that she probably does. Guy offers them sherry or gin and tonic in the piano room to warm them up; the Harrow team chooses sherry, Didie the gin and George a strong coffee. The aroma of roasting poultry drifts into their nostrils as they sip.

'I hate turkey,' Adrian mutters to Alicia. 'It's disgusting.'

'Not the way Mum cooks it.'

'Mama knows best,' he taunts.

'So, Adrian, I hear you're going out to work,' Margaret prods, legs crossed, hands folded on her lap.

'Yeah, I got a weekend job in Macclesfield,' he mumbles.

'Speak up, lad!' William prompts, jovial.

'I'm working for this firm that sells motorbikes. It pays OK.'

'Good fellow,' says William. 'So you're saving up for your studies.'

'I don't want to go to university.'

'Don't be silly, Adrian, of course you do,' Kate says, dashing between piano room and kitchen, basting and tasting.

'What for?'

'Don't be rude to your grandparents.'

'I don't want to study nowt.'

'And, for God's sake, talk properly!'

'Leave me alone, Mum.' Adrian takes charge by changing the subject. 'You have to hear Ali play. She's got a new teacher. Everyone says he's ace.'

'Trouble is, he's in Switzerland!' Alicia laughs. She's wondering, behind her bright smile, whether she does look like a sheep in her favourite jumper. 'After my exams in summer I'm going to apply for a scholarship to study with him. He's wonderful! He's helped me so much with—'

'Just a moment, Alicia,' William interrupts. 'Do you mean you're planning to leave school without doing A levels?'

'I only want to play the piano.' Alicia shrugs.

'Honestly, Kate!' Margaret expostulates. 'We worked so hard to make sure the three of you were well educated. How can you let your children throw themselves away without decent qualifications? The piano is very nice, dear, but . . .'

Alicia is starting to lose her appetite. 'Shall I play you my Chopin?' she says, casting about for an easy escape route.

'After lunch, Ali,' Kate instructs. 'There's plenty of time.'

Kate lays the table as slowly and neatly as she can: red table-cloth, best crockery, gold napkins and a cracker at each place. Her hands are shaking.

'Hark the herald angels sing, glory to the newborn king,' sings the choir of King's College, Cambridge, on the piano room stereo. Guy winces and moves a hand involuntarily towards his stomach.

'Are you all right?' Didie exclaims.

'You know, this isn't my favourite record. Let's put on something else.'

'If we can break a rule,' says Didie, whose eyes sparkle after her gin and tonic, 'why don't you go ahead and open a present I brought for you?'

William and Margaret look briefly outraged, but Didie and Alicia egg Guy on and the CD, retrieved from under the tree, emerges from its silver wrapping. It's of Argentinian tangos. Guy puts it on and the draughty room, safe from the concrete sky, icy pavements and north wind, blazes with South American heat and light.

'I used to be a tango champion.' Didie twinkles. 'My fiancé before George was the most fantastic dancer.' Didie's first fiancé had been an RAF pilot, killed on the Battle of Britain's final day. It had been some years before she met George; Guy had arrived when she was in her late thirties. 'I used to go and see him every weekend at the air-force base,' she goes on, 'and there'd often be dances. When we did the tango, everyone else used to stand aside and watch us!' Her feet are tapping. 'Guy, how about a go?'

'I haven't done this for years,' Guy protests, but a moment later he and his mother are striding together across the floor. Alicia claps her hands in joy; George winks at her. Adrian watches in disbelief and William and Margaret in stupefaction.

'Come on! You're the man, you're supposed to lead,' Didie prompts her son. 'That's how tango works. *You* make the decisions. Put your hand on my back – that's it – and use it to show me what you want to do next.'

'You mean I'm in the driving seat for once?' Guy grins, gliding in step with her, their opposite legs moving together. Didie, for an octogenarian, is sprightly as can be.

Kate, in her apron, appears in the doorway; Alicia just has time to notice an expression of extraordinary pain flash across her face before she vanishes.

The tango has thawed the atmosphere a little; now the turkey is ready and the table is groaning with food. Alicia is the first to pick up her cracker. There's a series of small explosions; soon everyone is wearing paper crowns. With another explosion, Guy opens champagne and Kate is troubled by a memory of another dinner round this table, corks popping, laughter, flirtation, a light footstep going up the stairs. She swigs back the golden liquid in her glass. Mercifully, everyone is too busy enjoying their food and drink to raise any of the difficult subjects they'd been treading in all morning. The only disruption comes when Alicia excuses herself briefly: she tells Kate that she has to text happy Christmas to Lucien. While she's gone, Kate takes another bottle of champagne out of the fridge. She needs all the Dutch courage she can get.

Later they watch the Queen's speech (William and Margaret insist) and afterwards, with tea on the table and a Christmas cake complete with marzipan and royal icing for those who have room, they open the presents. Alicia has a necklace and earrings from George and Didie – silver with blue topaz the colour of her eyes; and from William and Margaret a new leather music case. From Adrian there's a sweatshirt emblazoned with a motorbike, which makes Alicia laugh – she's sure he must have filched it from the shop – and from Mum and Dad, the present she'd wanted most: a mobile phone. Mum has also knitted her a new blue jersey, which she puts on at once.

'Do I still look like a sheep?' she hisses at Adrian.

'Yeah. A blue sheep.'

Guy has bought Kate a gold necklace a little like Rebecca's. Kate forces herself to thank him. It's the kind of expensive gift that a husband would buy his wife when he's feeling bloody guilty. She bides her time.

The early midwinter dusk has darkened the windows. Alicia pulls a book of Christmas carols out of her music cabinet and the family gathers around the lamplit piano to sing. Alicia plays perfectly at sight. They start with 'Away in a Manger', Margaret, Didie and Kate raising their voices confidently, while the men grunt along in a trio of reluctant baritones (Adrian refuses to join in). Then they do 'O Little Town of Bethlehem', which prompts comments from the newspaper editor that there is nothing still or dreamless about Bethlehem these days; and next 'O Come All Ye Faithful' at the end of which Kate breaks into a peculiar fit of laughter.

'Mum?' Alicia says.

'Nothing, darling. The champagne was nice, wasn't it?' She longs to call Rebecca, who would appreciate the coming, in other ways, of the unfaithful.

Alicia turns the page to 'O Tannenbaum, O Tannenbaum'. Guy jokes that it's the same tune as 'The Red Flag'. Alicia says she likes the rhythms and begins to play.

'O Christmas tree, O Christmas tree,' sing Guy, George, Didie, Margaret and William.

'Hypocrisy, hypocrisy,' sings Kate. Nobody notices. When the carol is finished, she cuts the cake, pours the tea and offers a shot of whisky to anyone who wants it, including herself.

By the end of the afternoon, when George and Didie declare it's time to go home and hug them all, Kate's mind is a slurry of emotions, ranging from despair to an odd, alcohol-induced elation. Something in her consciousness has expanded, letting her step back and watch, seeing the bigger picture, sensing that probably in every household across the country pretending to love family Christmases there lurk tensions, lies, deceptions. It's taboo to hate Christmas, of course. It's inadmissible. To some, it's sacrilege. What total shit, Kate thinks.

Ali's view is the ideal: a chance for everyone to relax together. But does any family get along well enough to enjoy such an obligation? Nobody, after all, has a choice: Christmas is Christmas, whether you like it or not. The population of the UK is around sixty million, so that probably means, at a rough guess, about twenty-five million families – and that's in Britain alone – all undergoing trial by convention on the selfsame day, overspending, overeating and driving one another to distraction, year upon year.

She feels reckless, strong, amused, because if she didn't, she might throw herself out of the nearest window, which, with her children in their teens and Ali needing her help with her career, wouldn't be a good idea.

'Mother,' she says, 'why don't you and Father go and have a little rest? And later we could watch a film and have a late supper.'

'I won't need to eat again for a week,' Margaret assures her, kissing her cheek. 'Come along, William.'

'Yes, dear,' says Kate's father, following her with some difficulty up the stairs.

Kate watches them go. Alicia whistles to Cassie to come for her evening walk and Adrian volunteers to join them. Kate watches them go too, then begins clearing up. She blows out candles and sweeps up debris from wrapping-paper, crackers and napkins. An unnatural stillness frosts the house.

'Let me do that,' Guy says.

Kate straightens up from the table, plates in hand. 'Thank you,' she says.

'Kate? What—'

'We have to talk.' Kate stacks the plates by the sink, ready for the dishwasher, alongside several large kitchen knives. 'While my parents are resting and the children are out.'

'What's going on?'

'I could ask you the same thing. Why is Emily Andersen calling you "darling"?'

'Katie, listen. I can explain everything.'

'I'm sure you can. For instance, what is she doing with a health visitor? Who has got a cough?'

'You read my emails?'

'Yes, I read your emails. I had to send an urgent message last night when my computer crashed, and I thought it couldn't do any harm to use yours just this once. And, faced with a list of Emily dot Andersens as long as my arm, I couldn't help being a trifle curious.'

Guy sits down at the table and takes off his glasses.

'The ulcer. The backache. The headaches. The late evenings. The "conference" in bloody Denmark.'

'Katie—'

Guy's dark eyes turn to her and she sees pain and defeat in them and remembers how they used to twinkle at her, just like his mother's, during those walks in the Cheviots. She fights back an unexpected tear – sentimentality is the downside of Dutch courage – and steadies herself. 'What are you going to do?' she demands. She keeps her gaze on his face in the appalling silence that follows.

'I don't know,' Guy says at last.

It's his confession. At least she's wrong-footed him. At least she's in control. 'She's a lovely young thing and there's a baby. Isn't there? So I'd imagine you're going to say you want to move out and live with her.'

'I haven't made up my mind what's best. But, yes, she's had a baby and it's mine. It's a girl. Her name is Ingrid.'

'My God,' says Kate, without meaning to. It's not as if she hadn't guessed – but the confirmation still knocks her like a demolition ball. Battling waves of nausea, she forces herself to continue on her mentally mapped path. 'So you're weighing up the demands of one child against two others.'

'Katie, I do love you, I do, and I love Adrian and Ali and I don't want to lose any of you . . .'

'*But*. Don't tell me. It just happened. Didn't it? A pretty girl walked into your office and you couldn't keep your hands off her. You just couldn't help it.'

'It wasn't like that. It isn't. It's more.'

'You're in love with her.'

'I never intended it. It wasn't meant to happen. But, yes, I am in love with Emily.'

Kate snorts, trying to conceal from him that this is far worse than she'd expected. She consults her map for the next step. 'Maybe you can't help what you feel, but you can bloody well help what you *do*,' she says. 'You should be remembering your responsibilities and putting them first.'

'I tried. I tried for a long time. You've no idea how long.'

That was true. She had no idea. 'So it's all *her* fault?'

'No, Katie. It's mine. I don't deny it's my fault.'

'And our marriage, you'll say, is dead.'

'We both know it could be in better shape.'

'So? What are you going to do? I need to know, Guy. Ali is at a crucial stage of her career and her life. If you leave, you're going to ruin everything for her. She'll be knocked very hard – possibly for ever.'

'You're using Ali to blackmail me.'

'I'm telling you to remember that you have a special responsibility towards her because of who she is, what she does and what she's going to do with her life.'

'And if I go?'

'If you leave,' Kate says, cool and firm as she has planned, 'you will damage Ali so much that it will mean the end of her career.'

The front door bursts open and there's a rush of damp dog, blue wool and golden hair as Alicia strides in and hangs up her coat and Cassie's leash, Adrian trailing in her wake. Alicia is singing to herself and Cassie makes hopeful noises at the dog-food cupboard. Kate grabs Cassie's dish and piles into it the accumulated leftovers of lunch.

'You lucky, lucky girl!' Alicia cries, as Cassie plunges her enthusiastic snout into the turkey scraps. 'You never get Christmas dinner normally, do you?'

Guy presses Alicia's shoulder, then walks up the stairs towards his study.

It's not as bad as Victoria. Nothing, Kate tells herself, driving to the cemetery at a speed well above thirty miles an hour, will ever be as bad as Victoria. She hates herself for feeling any other pain, for nothing can match the loss of her baby, even if it was twenty years ago. Victoria might have been at university now. Kate parks and tramps the grassy, sodden paths to the once-white stone that marks Victoria's grave.

Although the grave was the product of considerable effort, heartache and trauma when she insisted on relocating it from north London, nowadays she doesn't visit it often enough. That's because of Ali and Adrian. They don't know about Victoria and she doesn't want to burden them with the tale. At the graveside, she throws some dead flowers out of the small vase she keeps there and replaces them with clean water and some bright pink and red anemones that have been in a vase in her bedroom for two days but can do their job better here. Then she scrubs down the stone, dark with accumulated lichen. VICTORIA BRADLEY: the lettering emerges from the greenish murk as she scours it. Her handiwork complete, Kate sits back on her heels and lets the tears come.

16

On a misty morning in late August, Kate and Alicia leave Buxton at six a.m. and drive south. They pick up the M5 outside Birmingham and travel through busy traffic past Cheltenham and Bristol; then south-west to Exeter and beyond, towards the sea. Alicia sits beside her mother, watching the landscape grow greener, the hills lusher, the sky brighter. At last the sun emerges, filtering shards of gold through the trees that overhang the country lanes, an enchantment left behind from pagan times.

Funny, thinks Alicia, to go all the way to Devon and find a summer school beside a moor. She's spent her whole life beside a moor.

She hopes her mother won't insist on showing everyone they meet the reviews of her new Chopin disc. Mum has brought a file of photocopies of the best ones: they declare Alicia a natural Chopin player, wittering on about her spontaneity and communicative immediacy. Yadda yadda yadda. Other reviews had continued the malicious carping – as Mum calls it – that had greeted her début disc, full of words like 'immature', 'oversell', 'burnout' and 'misguided'. At least this time she'd got the picture she wanted on the cover: herself (without Cassie) on top of Mam Tor – of course, one critic wanted to know what the Pennine landscape had to do with Chopin. But Lucien had made encouraging comments when she sent it to him: that was what counted.

Despite some disagreement among the judges on the panel – some appear to have thought Alicia too downmarket for them – she had won herself a good-sized grant from a famous musical trust, a pointer to which had been the parting shot of the advisory scheme, now transferring its attentions to a new set of BBC winners and, Alicia suspects, relieved to bid farewell to her mother. The grant, along with seven GCSE passes, two failures and some tears and tantrums that she was obliged to stage for his benefit, has convinced her father to agree that she can leave school; and it provides the funds for her to travel to Switzerland with her mother for lessons with Lucien every six weeks, having gently but firmly severed herself from the furious Mrs Butterworth.

'You are only what I have made you. Without me you'll be nothing. This Frenchman with his fine words . . .' Mrs Butterworth hissed, when Alicia went to see her to break the news of Lucien and the grant. How ironic, Alicia thought, that for years Mrs Butterworth had been extolling the wonders of French musical training, yet suddenly she was using the nationality as a term of abuse.

In between her Lucien trips, she practises alone at home. It's not ideal, but she feels as if she's found her way onto a mountain track that she'd been seeking for years. Now that she's free of school, she can devote her time to her real work, not be forced to write essays about the industrial revolution or explain the structure of the periodic table. She lives for her Swiss days, when Lucien spends hours with her delving into inner workings of music that she hadn't realised were there. Thinking it through later on her own helps her to grasp the aural colours that plough rainbow furrows in her mind, helps her understand why they move as they do. Key relationships, recurring motifs, sonata form, enharmonic changes. This last, clever invention she adores, for a single note can pivot you into a totally unexpected colour by simply changing its name. Beyond the piano, Lucien makes her read things she'd never heard of at school. She's recently disgraced herself by pronouncing a German poet 'Go-ee-thy'.

Goethe is fabulous, but she loves Lucien's favourite French nineteenth- and early twentieth-century poets even more. Dad had been impressed one day when he'd found her with her nose in an anthology of French love poetry. Verlaine, Baudelaire, Rimbaud. She's been learning pieces by Fauré and Debussy, and Lucien says she can't possibly understand them without reading the Symbolists. Alicia had never heard of Symbolism before, but now, at last, she has time to explore, lying on her bed with the poems, a French dictionary and a book called *501 French Verbs*.

> *Calmes dans le demi-jour*
> *Que les branches hautes font;*
> *Pénétrons bien notre amour*
> *De ce silence profond . . .*

Verlaine speaks of passion, ecstasy, veiled sensuality. For others, sensuality sometimes isn't so veiled. Baudelaire opens a trapdoor on to a universe of unsuspected dangers.

> *Tout cela ne vaut pas le poison qui découle*
> *De tes yeux, de tes yeux verts,*
> *Lacs où mon âme tremble et se voit à l'envers . . .*

Alicia finds it difficult to eat when Lucien is around. Everything he says means so much to her that she tries to absorb it ten times over. He gives her lists of pieces she must hear and learn about: at home she spends long evenings in her room, listening to countless CDs, following symphonies with printed scores from the library in Manchester. She reads avidly too: biographies of Beethoven, Ravel, Tchaikovsky and Bartók, or novels from Russia, France and America that her school curriculum had never even mentioned. Adrian teases her: 'You *eat* books,' he exclaims.

She's allowed, at last, to take a train to London alone from time to time. There she stays with Rebecca or Phyllida and spends a day or two away from the piano, going to exhibitions recommended by Lucien or to permanent collections that she's never seen. The Turners in the Tate blew her mind and now she's covered her lavender walls with prints of them: the gold, cream and slate-grey swirling clouds, which remind her of Debussy's subtle translucence; the ships' masts emerging from the mist; the storms and snowscapes, and an angel suspended, sword aloft, in the heart of a sunburst.

At Easter, Phyllida had booked some time off and Alicia had spent nearly three days with her. Freed from her office persona, Phyllida reminded Alicia of Cassie let off the leash, full of sparkle and fun, and the pair of them went out on the town.

They had facials at the beauty salon in Selfridges. They went round the National Gallery to view Rubens and Rembrandt and the Van Gogh sunflowers; they ate Turkish food, which Alicia hadn't tried before; and finally they went to see the Cirque du Soleil at the Royal Albert Hall, where, Phyllida told Alicia, the Proms might soon engage her to play a concerto. Afterwards, Alicia's head was so full of astounding things, shining gold and white and pouring like Alpine waterfalls into her imagination, that back at Phyllida's flat she'd burst into tears and found it difficult to explain that she was weeping for happiness – and for the frustration of knowing that she'd waited nearly seventeen years to discover that such wonders existed. The more she learns, the more she understands how much there is to learn.

Since her lessons with Lucien, a skin has split away from her and a new one, a fresh colour, an intriguing texture, is forming in its place. She dreams as she plays, her soul filling with fantasy. She can tell that her audiences have noticed a change in her; she senses the extra stillness in the atmosphere. One local critic said that there was an incipient volcano inside her, which pleased her tremendously – but he went on to say that she had to find another way of expressing it, rather than playing too fast and too loud, as so many of Mrs Butterworth's students tended to. Alicia fumes at the idea that her name is being linked, yet again, with Mrs Butterfingers, but deep down she doesn't care. She is Lucien's disciple now and she can recapture something at the core of her music that had gone missing. She thinks it's called joy.

Kate glances at the mirror and moves into the fast lane of the M5 at ninety miles an hour. Nothing delights her more than getting away from home, these days, and the faster she goes, the better.

'You're punishing yourself as well as me,' Guy accused her on Alicia's birthday, after the party was over and reality slapped them in the face. 'Why do you want to suffer?'

'I don't,' she said. 'But I won't let Ali be damaged. If we break up, it'll wreck her life and her career. I won't let that happen.'

'What makes you so certain?' he demanded. 'She's seventeen. She's a young woman, not a baby. Other kids cope with far worse situations.'

'Other kids are not child prodigies.'

'I'm dying in this marriage.'

Yet Guy stays. Whenever he threatens to move out, Kate always says the same thing: 'It's a straightforward choice, Emily or Ali. It's up to you.' He gives in. He stays. What else can he do? If Kate had said nothing, would he have been able to leave Alicia if he tried to? He can't find the answer, and Kate knows he can't.

Hypocrisy? Perhaps. He has a second life with Emily – it's not as if Kate doesn't know. The crucial thing, for her, is that Alicia mustn't. Her fragile adolescent imagination, drenched with Lucien-inspired cultural cramming, wouldn't stand the shock, let alone the double standards.

When Kate sees the pain in Guy's face, the agony in his chest that makes him swallow ulcer pills, the pain in his back from the burden of too much baggage, she gloats quietly. It no longer occurs to her that she shouldn't.

She hates sharing her bed with him now, but does so to keep up appearances for Alicia, her parents, Guy's parents, the neighbours and, she supposes, Adrian. Guy lies, rigid and awkward, as far from her as he can. They talk when they must, in the bedroom, like work colleagues confined within a too-small open-plan office. She suggests they buy a larger bed, two mattresses that can be zipped together. They stay unzipped. The nights are brittle around them and Guy adds stronger sleeping pills to his list of medication.

Kate, meanwhile, is worried about her hormones. She visits the GP to let off steam. The GP doesn't suggest HRT – tests reveal that it is much too early for this – but recommends anti-depressants. Kate refuses them.

Going away is such a blessed relief that Kate feels twenty years younger.

'Let's open the sun-roof,' she says. Alicia winds open the panel and the light floods in; then she twiddles the radio knob until she finds some jazz. They turn up the volume and speed wildly to the strains of Louis Armstrong crooning about how wonderful the world is. Mother and daughter feel the sun on their faces and start to sing along together.

After winding for a while through the close-set hills, Kate spots a wooden signpost to Moorside College, half concealed amid deep green leaves. They drive up a gentle slope lined with fields of golden wheat and huge, ancient oak trees and turn into the estate. Kate sniffs the humid air and Alicia gazes, starry-eyed, at the young people they pass, walking in small groups, many carrying musical instruments in cases.

Alicia can't wait to find Lucien and Anjali – her two favourite people in the world – and once they've parked, registered and found their rooms, adjacent cubicles in one of the college's modern dormitory blocks, Kate and Alicia make their way towards the archway that leads to the summer school's heart: a fourteenth-century Great Hall. Other paths radiate into the rest of the complex: landscaped gardens, studio blocks, tennis court and swimming-pool. Kate notices people glancing at Alicia, recognising her.

'Wow!' Beyond the arch, Alicia stops in her tracks at the sight ahead. The Great Hall presides over a courtyard, its lawn dotted with generous trees. Around it lingers a bubble of stillness, despite the stream of arriving students, a haphazard group of people lounging on the grass outside the bar, the distant shouts of those who've found their way to the pool. Moorside Hall is a legend in its own right, Lucien has told them. It's supposed to have a unique atmosphere: a sacred space built on the mystical convergence, so the story goes, of ley lines, accumulating centuries of mystery. Alicia and Kate, absorbing the picture, both sense at once that it might be true.

'Imagine,' Kate says, 'everything these stones must have seen in their time.'

She watches Alicia gazing up at the Gothic, arched windows and doorway. The intuition that sometimes quivers on her neck is quivering now. She doesn't know why, but wonders whether, when they leave this place, they will be quite the same people they were when they arrived. The thought is nonsensical and she banishes it at once.

A couple of hours after Kate and Alicia's departure, Guy jumps into his car and drives off to Victoria Park, leaving Adrian asleep and Cassie dozing in her basket by Alicia's empty bed.

He lets himself into Emily's flat. A heady mixture of smells greets him: fresh coffee, heating croissants, sour milk, clean laundry. There's a wail from the back room and Emily's voice calls, 'We're in here!'

In the doorway, he surveys the scene. Emily, her hair in need of washing, her face tired, strained but calm, paces slowly up and down, jigging the restive Ingrid against her shoulder. 'Why don't you have a go at calming down your daughter?' she says, handing him the angry, pink-clad one-year-old.

Guy takes Ingrid and kisses her. A rush of anxiety and adoration springs into him, as always, when he feels the warmth of her little body. He's lucky if he sees her twice a week; he doesn't understand how she can possibly recognise him. But after he's been holding her for less than half a minute, she quietens, holding on to his shoulder and staring around the room with her wide eyes, silver-grey like her mother's.

'I knew it.' Emily laughs. 'She's a real Daddy's girl. Coffee, love?'

They sit at the pine table in the compact white kitchen, with Ingrid in her high chair bashing her beaker against her plastic tray and squealing for fun. This is how they should be: Daddy Bear, Mummy Bear, Baby Bear. Goldilocks would have some trouble working out how things function in this home, though.

'Penny for them?' Emily says.

'The usual.'

There's a limit, he thinks, to the number of times he can prostrate himself with regret. He's been a coward. He's feared so much: their job security; Kate's fury; above all, the effects of the revelation upon Alicia, absorbed in her own world, suspecting nothing. He loathes concealment. It can't be healthy for anyone to live in a house where the air is filled with icicles.

It's his own fault, too, for not taking the initiative. If he'd revealed the truth before Kate stumbled upon it, he'd have held the balance of power. He could have called the shots. But because it was underhand, because Kate's discovery was accidental, because he was – at least, from Kate's perspective – in the wrong, she had been the one to make the rules. Being Kate, she put Alicia first. In her place, he might well have done the same.

So he's a coward for not risking his job, not finding the right moment to confess, not standing up to his wife. He is, basically, pathetic. How is it possible, he wonders, that such a pathetic man can edit a newspaper? How is it possible that he's won the love of a beautiful, giving young woman – and become the father of this miracle child, who would grow up into the image of her mother mingled with himself? And she, a blameless, laughing baby, would probably have to be the one who paid the price, psychologically, for his failure.

'Raspberry jam with your croissant?' Emily says.

Guy sits Ingrid on his lap while Emily bustles round the oven and the fridge.

'Don't say it.' Her back is to him as she reaches for the jam. She can sense without looking when his apologies are coming.

'You're so strong.'

'I'm not.' Emily slices the croissants in half. 'But I haven't much choice, have I?'

'It's incredible that you even talk to me, let alone feed me croissants on Saturday morning.'

Emily puts a plate in front of him. She brushes Ingrid's head softly with one finger. 'Do you seriously think that I'd be without *her* for one moment? No, Guy. I wouldn't change places with anybody in this world.'

They spend a quiet morning talking about nothing much and playing 'Incy-Wincy Spider' and 'This Little Piggy' with Ingrid; then Guy goes to the supermarket and does a week's shopping for his Manchester family. He nips into the office a little later, makes sure everything is running smoothly, and comes back by teatime.

Ingrid is sleeping, so they go to bed. First they crash – Emily exhausted by baby-filled nights and Guy by anxiety over Emily's baby-filled nights. Later, they make love, Guy hoisting Emily upright over him, seeking, deep inside her, the annihilation of his hopeless self. 'I love you,' he whispers, as she curves downwards to kiss him. 'I love you so much.'

Afterwards, he phones Adrian at work on his mobile. 'You in this evening?'

'No.'

'Can you walk the dog?'

'Oh, bloody hell, Dad. I'm in the shop, then I'm going down the Cat and Fiddle.'

'Look, I can't come back till late. Just take her out for ten minutes, OK? I'll take her again when I get in.'

'Families,' Emily says from bed, winking at him. 'Who'd have them?'

A clang from his mobile makes him start with alarm, but the text is from Alicia, not Kate. 'Having gr8 time,' it says. 'Beautiful place. Lucien 1derful. Wish u here2. xa'

Guy lies down beside the dozing Emily and breathes deeply. His chest hurts. He's not sure whether it's his ulcer or something worse. He's too young to have heart trouble. It must be the ulcer. Or stress, which can cause pains like these. One day, when he has time, he must have a check-up.

At nine thirty on Sunday morning, auditions are held for Lucien's masterclass in Moorside's largest studio. Kate and Alicia take their places side by side, close to the table from which Lucien is to officiate. It's soon evident that Kate is the only chaperoning mother; the other students are on their own.

Lucien paces in, as relaxed as if he were on holiday, wearing an orange linen shirt and barley-coloured trousers, dark hair shining in the sunlight, and his neck giving off a whiff of lemony aftershave, which, Kate decides, is rather more classy than she'd given it credit for. She thinks of Guy at home, his exhausted eyes, his bottles of medication: ulcer pills, sleeping pills, painkillers – not the kind that exacerbate ulcers – for his back. Perhaps the strain of screwing his employee is too much for him, she'd suggested. The acid of this remark was probably enough to increase the dose of ulcer medicine overnight. And there's Lucien, casually in charge, smiling, joking, basking in the adoration that wafts towards him from the would-be students and curious onlookers assembling in the studio. As Kate stares, he turns and winks at her. The floor dips under her feet.

After Lucien's recital in the Great Hall the night before,

they'd gone backstage to find him. Alicia cast herself, as she tends to, into his arms; Lucien embraced them both and said, 'You are not really mother and daughter, you are sisters!' and he held Kate as long as Alicia, long enough for her to feel the energy in his arms and his breath against her hair. Lucien is taller than Guy and this, to Kate, was a new sensation. She'd had trouble getting to sleep later. Away from home and routine, with the summer night pressing on the thin windows, she'd dreamed, only half dozing, of certain things, missing from her life, that she won't normally let herself remember.

She glances round the studio, forcing her attention back to the present and her daughter. Some of the onlookers are glancing at her and Alicia, talking under their breath. The former Young Musician of the Year and Her Mother. Yes, Ali will be stiff competition for everybody else; her audition, since she's Lucien's permanent student, is only a formality.

Alicia, who's wearing white, lifts a hand and gestures at a petite, dark figure slipping through the studio door: Anjali, who's wearing black. Anjali waves, her face lighting up. The girls embrace, the bright and the dark together. There's been no sign of Anjali until now; she hadn't appeared in the canteen for supper or at Lucien's recital, and Alicia, unable to get through to her mobile, had been anxious.

'Where were you, Anji?' she asks now, pressing her friend's arm.

'Oh,' says Anjali, 'I was tired. I went to sleep.'

Anjali is no longer a schoolgirl, but a young woman. She's eighteen, about to go to music college, and her face is thinner, her eyes more serious and her figure skinnier than Kate remembers. She hasn't seen Anjali for some time; Alicia's schedule hasn't left much room for asking friends to stay.

'Hello, Kate. Lovely to see you.' Anjali gives her a kiss and sits down beside Alicia, a book of Schubert sonatas in her lap. She holds the edges so tightly that Alicia, noticing, glances at her in concern.

'Don't worry, Anji, you'll be fine,' she says.

'I keep having memory lapses,' Anjali tells her. 'I don't know what's going on. I never had this sort of trouble before, but since I started doing competitions . . .'

'Are you the Bradleys?' someone asks Kate: a petite, auburn-haired woman around her own age with a bright, interested face and a strong Liverpool accent. 'I loved your CD, Alicia. I've just ordered the new one, too.'

'Thanks! I'm so glad.' Alicia replies. The woman smiles and Kate notices, pleased, that she looks genuinely moved.

'So talented and so young,' she remarks. 'It's wonderful. How old are you, d'you mind me asking?'

'She's just had her seventeenth birthday,' Kate says.

'I'm looking forward to hearing you play, Alicia. My name's Mary. I don't play anything, but I listen, and I sing in the choir. I'm a Moorside addict – I come here to recharge my batteries every year. There are lots of us. Glad you're on board!' She shakes Kate's hand, and Alicia's; Kate introduces Anjali. At summer school, she's starting to understand, it's mysteriously easy to make friends.

More students are gathering on the other side of the room; several are Japanese, one is German. Another sounds American: a dark, thick-set lad of about twenty, Kate thinks, wearing a navy blue T-shirt emblazoned with the words UNIVERSITY OF INDIANA. Across the studio, his brown eyes meet Alicia's blue ones. Unlike the others, he doesn't recognise her. Unlike the others, he doesn't look away. Alicia beams, radiant, towards him. For a second he's motionless, as if entranced; then he sits down and gazes at her, firm and definite. His eyes say: *You are the most beautiful girl in the world.*

Life-changing moments aren't always heralded by a doorbell, a ringing phone or even a touch on the arm. Sometimes they just happen.

'Somebody likes you.' Anjali nudges Alicia – smiling properly for the first time.

'But he's lovely!' Alicia breathes. Subterfuge, Kate understands, isn't her daughter's style any more than it's the American youth's.

'OK, everyone.' Lucien stands up and claps his hands. 'Let's begin. Who's going first?'

A Japanese girl volunteers; she tinkles through a Mozart sonata movement. Lucien catches Kate's eye. Kate feels sweat on her shoulders.

'All right,' he says, after he's stopped the girl at an appropriate chord. 'Alicia, let's have your Chopin.'

Alicia strides to the piano and begins the B minor Sonata. A shock wave wobbles through the room as the piano rings out, abruptly massive-toned. The American boy sits forward, chin on hands, watching her every move. Beside Kate, Anjali stirs. Kate glances round – does Anjali have hiccups?

'This is Alicia Bradley,' Lucien says to the room at large, stopping her at the end of the exposition. 'I'm sure you know her already. Now, who's brought some Schubert?'

Anjali puts up a hand. The American boy raises his hand too; it is to him that Lucien beckons.

'Dan *what*?' Lucien exclaims, when the boy gives his name.

'Rubinstein,' Dan says. 'No relation!'

'You're a brave man. So, Mr Rubinstein, you've brought the big C minor Sonata. *Voilà, c'est à vous . . .*'

When Dan begins, it's Alicia's turn to sit forward. 'I like this,' she whispers to her mother, who agrees: Dan Rubinstein (poor bloke, sharing a surname with one of the greatest dead pianists on the CD rack) is extremely good. Kate notices that his phrasing sings naturally and the sound is full and round, not too hard and loud, unlike – well, Ali does sometimes *bash*. Lucien is combating this, but it's a bad habit she'd developed with Mrs Butterworth and it's proving difficult to eradicate. But Dan Rubinstein plays with the assurance and poetry of one who can see the beauty that eats at the core of pain, and the pain that eats at the core of beauty – just as Schubert could. He might be only nineteen or twenty, but he plays like a man, not a boy.

Anjali's body contracts and she doubles over, pressing her hands to her mouth. Alicia grabs her arm. 'Come and get some air,' she says.

'I'll be fine.' But a second later the spasm seizes her again and she leaps to her feet and dashes for the door. Kate tries to keep her daughter where she is, but Alicia shakes her off and runs after her friend.

Alicia waits by the basins while Anjali flings herself into a cubicle and is violently sick.

'Shall I get you some water?' Alicia asks.

'I'll be fine,' Anjali insists fruitlessly.

'Are you feeling better? Shall we go for a walk?'

Anjali emerges, her shoulders drooping, her face agonised. This isn't the Anjali Alicia remembers from the BBC competition days, positive, healthy and generous-spirited, helping her wind the luxuriant silk sari round her in front of her mother's mirror. This Anjali has been laid waste by nerves. Something everyone expects Alicia to have, but she doesn't. Alicia holds out her arms and gives Anjali a hug. Anjali's breath is sour and she's battling tears.

'I have to go back in and do my audition,' she says. 'Otherwise I'll have to tell my father and he'll be livid. He has to know every detail of absolutely everything . . .'

'You'll feel better if you get it over and done with.'

'I can't. I'll screw up.'

'You won't.'

'I will. I know I will. Because I always do.'

'Come on. Let's walk in the garden, it'll do you good. We can go back later – there are loads of people waiting to play.'

The two girls set out into the grounds, Anjali doing her best to keep up with Alicia's powerful stride. They walk past a thatched gazebo, a landscaped lawn framed with trimmed evergreen

bushes, and a herb garden heady with lavender, sage and rosemary. Further away, up the hill, some long, mysterious flights
of stone stairs lead into the shade of the biggest and most beautiful trees Alicia has ever seen. 'This is amazing,' she remarks.
'It's magic! Let's go up.'

They climb the stairs in silence. The sun through the leaves
dapples their skin with brightness and shadow. The hills gleam
in the distance, the view broadening and deepening every few
steps.

'I wish I could enjoy it,' Anjali says.

'Anji, what's going on? What *happened*?'

'I don't know. If I knew that, there wouldn't be a problem,
would there?'

'But you were so confident.'

'And now I have memory lapses.'

'You only have them because you think you're going to.'

'That's what a lot of people say. But if you know you're
going to, how can you not?'

'Isn't there anything you can do? Deep breathing or something?'

'Tried that. Tried everything. Except pills. I haven't tried
pills.'

'What pills?'

'Beta-blockers. They're heart pills. They stop your heart
running away with you. They stop you producing too much
adrenaline, so you don't get the physical symptoms of being
nervous.'

'I've never heard of that.'

Anjali stares sideways at Alicia. 'Lucky you,' she says, a
sarcastic edge to her voice which makes Alicia jump.

'Would they help?' Alicia prods, trying to ignore it. 'Why
don't you give them a go?'

'Because my dad says that if I start taking them I'll never
feel able to go on stage without them again. And he's right –
I know I won't.'

'But just to get you through this patch—'

'Oh, what would *you* know?' Anjali snaps. 'You've never had a day's nerves in your life.'

Alicia flinches.

'You can do anything. You swan off to Switzerland to play for Lucien, your Mum takes care of everything for you, Daddy bought you a Steinway and you were Young Musician of the Year. You've got two CDs out. And you've never even *heard* of beta-blockers!'

'Oh, Anji,' Alicia says, crumpling, 'I never asked for any of it to happen, you know. I hate seeing you like this. I'd change places with you if only I could.'

'Sorry, Ali. Really. I am sorry, I didn't mean it. I'm just – I'm in such a mess.'

'It's OK.'

'Don't cry.'

'Nor you. Look, you've got to come and stay with us. We never see you enough. Will you come? One weekend?'

'I'd love to, if you'll still have me after what I just said. It's coffee time – shall we go back?' They turn towards the hall, outside which morning coffee is served on the lawn.

'What about the academy?' Alicia asks, linking her arm through Anjali's. 'Maybe they'll be able to help you, give you the right advice or whatever.'

'I don't know. I don't even want to go there. I can't face it. But if I don't, I'll have to do something else, and I don't know what to do. I got three A levels and Mum says maybe I should go to university, but . . .'

Alicia is silent, horrified that Anjali might be beset by problems that make it impossible for her to continue with her studies, problems that might scupper her intention of being a pianist – when two years ago, she'd seemed almost as at home on stage as Alicia is. What's happened to her? Why? And when? What happened to one would-be pianist could easily happen to another. Alicia thinks the unthinkable. What if it happened to her? What will she do if, for some reason, she can't continue playing?

Her train of thought screeches to a halt as she finds herself face to face in the coffee queue with Dan Rubinstein. Blood rushes into her cheeks. 'You'll have to explain,' he says to her at once. 'Why does everyone know you except me?'

'Oh, I won a prize on TV,' Alicia says, crimson. 'Hey, I loved your playing.'

'And I love your accent. It's cute. Where do you come from?' Alicia tells him. 'What about you?'

'Let me get you a coffee, then we can talk.'

Alicia glances round for Anjali, who's vanished, probably trying to muster courage, alone, for her audition. She should look for her. She should look for Mum. But she'd rather talk to Dan than do either. She stays. With their coffee, they make for the shade of the tree in the middle of the lawn and sit cross-legged on the ground, their restless fingers pulling at the green spears of grass.

Dan is the most direct boy Alicia has ever met. She'd never imagined that getting along with anybody could be so easy. Maybe it's because he's American; or maybe it's because they're in tune, on a shared wavelength. There's no pretence in either of them. You take us as you find us, she could have said at once, for both of them. It's a relief, a release, a rush of energy. She feels as if she's not met him, but found him: someone she'd been looking for, without knowing it.

He tells her about his studies – he's at a university in the Midwest that has a massive music department, though he'd grown up in Boston – and soon they're talking about Chopin and Schubert, Lucien and Anjali, and before they know what's happened the break is almost over and Alicia's mother is striding towards them in her linen trousers, saying, 'Ali, *there* you are. I've been looking everywhere for you!' Dan gives Kate a brief, shrewd glance before turning on the charm and introducing himself.

*　　*　　*

Kate hasn't really been looking for Alicia; she's been talking to Lucien in the sunshine on the studio-block steps. She should have tried to find her daughter and the ailing Anjali; but she'd rather talk to Lucien. She'd stayed.

'You are looking extremely well,' he said to her, staring at her figure with approval.

'Thanks. So are you.'

'So, tell me, Kate, how is life?'

'Fine. Busy. Now that Ali has finished school, we're planning next season very carefully with Phyllida.'

'Lovely Phyllie. She is a gem.'

'She thinks you are too,' Kate pointed out, a little sharply.

Lucien regarded her with eyes slightly lowered, as bashful as a naughty schoolboy. 'It was so difficult,' he said. 'She would never have been happy with me. She needs someone who is there. Not travelling all the time. I was not right for her.'

'My husband doesn't travel so much,' Kate remarked, 'but he's never there either.'

Lucien's eyes glittered into hers. Kate blinked. This is crazy, she thought. My daughter's teacher is making eyes at *me*? If it wasn't her imagination, she'd be the envy of all the bright young things who adored the adorable Lucien.

Rebecca has regaled her with stories of professors taking their students to bed; some who will only give their pupils an exam pass at a certain price; tales of abuse of underage girls by teachers whose employers protect them for reasons of their own. This wouldn't be tolerated in any other profession, Rebecca opined. Masterclasses, she said, ought to be called mistressclasses. She's said nothing, though, about teachers taking a liking to their students' mothers.

'I love this place,' Lucien said, gazing at the gardens, the sunlight and the ancient hall across the lawn. 'There is magic in the air.'

'You've been before, obviously?'

'I used to come here as a student. I will show you some special places in the gardens. We have a whole week. Did you know there's supposed to be a ghost? I'm sure I saw it last night. My room is in the courtyard, on the ground floor, and around three in the morning it became extremely cold. I got up and looked out of the window and this grey shape went by. Very strange. It was transparent, but it was there. Kate, do you believe in ghosts?'

'No, Lucien, I *don't*. Not remotely. But please don't tell Ali, she might be afraid . . . I wonder where she is?'

'With her friends. That's good. I worry about Alicia not having friends.'

'She hasn't had much time to have friends.'

'Make sure she does. We all need friends.'

'Mm-hm,' said Kate, holding his comment at arm's length.

'I know it's difficult. When I was a kid, I had hardly any friends until I went to summer schools and met other kids who were musical too. I was so lonely. Now I know it's not necessary! We'll have some duet sessions in the evenings – it helps the students relax and get to know each other. They need to be friends, not enemies, not competitors. Kate, you'll come, won't you?'

'I can't play, Lucien.'

'You don't need to. You just need to be there and listen and look beautiful.'

'Oh Lucien, *honestly*.'

'Yes, Kate, honestly.' He winked at her. 'Sisters.'

Kate flushed; she couldn't help it. She forced herself to make an excuse about needing to phone home; and hurried away through the garden to find her daughter – who is not her sister and has been getting on far too well with the attentive American boy who says his name is Rubinstein.

Adrian, after making sure the windows and back door are locked, says goodbye to the lonely Cassie. She'll howl if left by herself too long, but what's he to do? His father is AWOL, his mother's fussing over his sister in some fancy course at the other end of the country and he's damned if he's going to let his life be wrecked by keeping house for them all. He slams the front door and heads up the hill and out of town.

The others are there already and Josh pats his shoulder in greeting. Over a pint, Adrian tells him something about what's happening at home, in as few words as he can, for the bikers don't talk on the whole – they just bike.

'Time to move out,' Josh says. 'I did that. Know what it's like.'

'Can't, really. Can't afford it till I get a job.'

'Sure you can. There'll be a way. I'll ask around.'

Today they're going to do speed tests. They'll pick two spots, a good distance apart, on the A537 between Buxton and Macclesfield, and they'll go one at a time and see who's the fastest. Adrian is bothered that, riding pillion with Josh, he'll slow him down and be a handicap. Last time, some of the others did wheelies through a busy Peak District car park and Adrian had to stand and watch, feeling half an inch high. He'd loved the sensation, all the same, of being part of something that stuck two fingers up at all those respectable, law-abiding, 'decent' families, who pulled faces and sometimes, when they dared, yelled abuse at them. His family, he told Josh once, rolling a spliff in Macclesfield, was supposed to be 'decent'.

'All right, Ade,' Josh says today. 'Use the bike on your own. You've got to try speed tests some time. I reckon you can do it.'

'Thanks, mate.' Adrian tries to keep cool, but his heart pounds so hard that he half fears the others can see it under his leathers (old ones of Josh's, out of fashion but good enough for starters). He takes a long breath and begins to prepare himself inwardly for his first solo speed test.

Half an hour later, he's alone astride Josh's bike, waiting his turn. The others set off, a safe distance apart – Charlie, their unofficial leader (the gang prides itself on its democracy), is a stickler for safety, rather to Adrian's surprise and vague disappointment. Charlie shoots away down the hill, bending the bike to the curving slopes, tipping over so far that he'll almost scrape the road with the Velcro slider pads on his knee. His bike is a blur of blackness, noise and exhaust. Dave, who's a plumber when he's not biking, goes next, his red bike and helmet streaking along, sending up wafts of dust or smoke, Adrian can't tell which. One by one the others follow. Adrian is last.

He says the nearest thing he'll ever muster to a quick prayer, though of course it's nothing of the kind. He revs his engine, slips the clutch. The bike leaps under him like a racehorse and he's in perfect control as he takes off, concentrating harder than he'd imagined he could. He'd hate to let Josh know, but he's scared witless. And he can't turn back. He must keep going, clinging on and trusting in something, God or the bike, that he'll make it. Before he knows what's happened, though, he sees the group waiting at the finish and they're cheering as he pulls in. When he dismounts his legs are watery under him with the fright and the thrill and the power.

17

'Katie,' Rebecca says, 'be careful.'

'I don't know what you mean.' Kate is sitting on a bench under a beech tree. Rebecca is in her London office. She sounds tense and alarmed.

'He's charming. He's a great musician, I'm sure he's a good teacher. But be careful. I'm not having you go the same way as Phyllida.'

'Becs!'

'Sorry, darling, I have to go, I'm meant to be in a meeting. Call me later.' Rebecca rings off.

Kate stays in the shade, pondering. Why should Rebecca be so worked up about her relationship, such as it is, with Lucien? Guy in his worst moods, and there are plenty, has sometimes called Rebecca names that make Kate extremely angry and are, moreover, nonsense. Anyway, he's a fine one to object to someone else's sexual preferences. Familiar pain tunnels through Kate; she lowers her head, feels it, tries to let it pass.

Rebecca isn't butch. She wears expensive, stylish clothes and makeup. OK, she's divorced and hasn't shown any particular interest in men since she reappeared in Kate's life. But that may be no fault of hers, since men who'll look at women in their late forties, rather than twenty years younger, are in short supply. What's certain is that she doesn't fit any of the stereotypes that Kate associates with terms like 'dyke'.

She remembers the college rumours well enough. Rebecca liked experimentation, they said. She had countless boyfriends (this was the seventies, post-Pill, pre-AIDS) while Kate stuck doggedly to Guy. Rebecca slept with other women too, they said; but since nobody had been under the bed at the time, it couldn't be proved. Kate had dismissed it as malicious gossip. Nearly thirty years later, she still does. Ridiculous. Totally ridiculous. How could her one close friend, the only friend she really has, be a lesbian? It's outside her range. It's not a stitch in any pattern she's yet learned how to knit.

Perhaps she's winding herself up because she has too much time to think. While Alicia practises, Lucien teaches and students flock to choir practice, cello workshops, tango lessons or the Indonesian gamelan, Kate is at liberty to do nothing. She hasn't much to occupy her except watching Alicia, observing the masterclasses, chatting to her new Liverpudlian friend, Mary, enjoying the gardens and, between classes, talking to Lucien.

Perhaps it's the encroachment of nature in every corner, the overwhelming presence of music, or the headlong collision of like-minded souls with just one short week to spark off one another; but the summer-school air feels humid with the promise of sex. To Kate – who hasn't had sex in a very long time – it's profoundly disturbing.

Musicians are often passionate, highly sexed people. She's not a musician. She's a mother, a cool-headed former lawyer, a survivor of tragedy. Sex for its own sake has never been important to her. Except for those early years, especially the honeymoon in Paris, she's never even liked it much. But now her body is doing strange things to her mind. She's breathing in the scents of herbs, fresh-mown grass and ripening wheat as if her life depended on it; she's been enjoying post-concert drinks in the bar; she's been assessing the physical merits of the youngsters in the masterclass. As for Lucien, sometimes she doesn't listen to him at all: she only looks.

She'd mentioned it to Rebecca. Talking was a relief, thinking aloud, wondering whether she was under a spell, or whether

her hormones were playing tricks on her. She's neither an artist nor a sensualist; and she's never been closer to regarding herself as a mixed-up, middle-aged mum.

'Katie, of course you're a sensual person!' Rebecca exclaimed, derisory. 'Of course you're artistic. Look at your wonderful house. Look at your knitting. You could charge a fortune for those jerseys. You love texture, colour, design – there's nothing more sensual than soft fabrics.'

'Yes, but . . .' Kate didn't like to carry on this strand, especially in the light of Guy's opinions, which she was trying to banish from her thoughts. Now and then, when they meet in London, Rebecca looks into her face with some unfathomable *thing* in her gaze, something chemical that induces a direct, physical reaction in Kate over which she has no control and which, if she's honest, she can see is not so different from that induced by Lucien. Other women don't, in her experience, look at her like that. And she certainly doesn't look back, or doesn't mean to. Under her tree, she fights with herself, some idiotic craving for physical affection threatening mutiny of many horrific kinds.

That night, she dreams about Lucien. He's running to meet her by a lake; there he is with his long legs, bright shirt and deep eyes, smiling, greeting. Behind him hovers a grey ghost. She wakes to find herself alone on the thin mattress in her cubicle room. Outside, planets hang low over the wheatfield and the distant dark hills. She tries to go back to sleep – Tuesday will be a big day, with Alicia the first participant in the piano masterclass; and Lucien is planning to round everyone up to play duets later.

Sleep, though, is elusive. Kate's head is still spinning, as she had spent most of the evening after the daily concert drinking too much cider with Mary, who loves singing and has been trying to recruit her into the summer-school chorus. Mary is a nurse and has three children. Already they're discussing the best route from Buxton to Liverpool so that they can get

together again when the week is out. Further along the wooden
trestle table in the bar – a cavernous fourteenth-century room
behind the hall, where golden lamplight shimmers on white-
washed stone walls – Alicia had sat with Anjali and Dan. Alicia
is developing a taste for chardonnay, which, Dan teases her,
she wouldn't be allowed in the States, being too young (she's
too young here as well, but nobody's batted an eyelid). Dan
is doing his best to make Alicia inseparable from him; Kate
supposes she should object. But she's intrigued by the impression that now it's almost as if Dan is Alicia's old friend, while
Anjali is the stranger.

Kate lies awake in her uncomfortable bed and replays the
day, its music and its relationships until the first streaks of
dawn lighten the lilac night. She's beginning to feel that she's
seventeen again herself.

'Stop.'

Alicia, at the piano in the packed studio, stops. Lucien stands
beside her, looking over her shoulder at the first page of the
Chopin B minor Sonata.

'What is Chopin's indication here?' He points.

'Allegro maestoso,' Alicia squeaks.

'Which means?'

'Fast and – magisterial.'

'And you are playing – fast. Allegro, yes. But not maestoso.
More maestoso, Alicia, less allegro. And don't hit the piano,
because it hits back! We want a beautiful tone, not only a loud
one. Start again.'

She starts again.

'Alicia.'

Her hands freeze.

'What is this mark, here?' Lucien indicates a shape in the
score.

'A crescendo.'

'And this?'

'An accent.'

'So what is the direction of this phrase? Try again. Shape the music. This is an opening allegro maestoso, but it also sings. Shape it as if you're a singer. Sing it to me.'

'Pardon?'

'Sing, please.'

Alicia sings the phrase; it comes out as a soft, unhappy chirrup. One of Kate's hands clutches at the other. This isn't like Lucien. Alicia is supposed to be his star pupil.

'Darling. Chopin loved singers. Chopin was in love with a singer when he was young. He went every night to the opera to see her sing and he heard Italian composers, whose influence infuses every part of his music. You know any music by Bellini?'

'I thought a Bellini was a kind of cocktail.' Alicia gets the laugh she wants – for a moment.

'Darling, you must hear Bellini if you want to understand Chopin. And you must hear Mozart's operas. You've seen *The Marriage of Figaro*?'

She shakes her head, mute.

'OK. What about Chopin's great friend, the painter Delacroix? You've seen his paintings?'

'Only a few.' Alicia's eyes are gleaming with tears.

'Because what you do is you sit at home, you practise and you perform. *Fin. Voilà.* OK. Once more, again, please, from the top. Phrase the melody the way you just sang it to me.'

Alicia plays. It sounds better, to Kate's ears, but that doesn't change the fact that her daughter is being humiliated precisely when she is supposed to shine.

'Stop,' says Lucien. Alicia pulls her hands from the piano as if she'd been whipped.

'You're trying to give us a finished performance. I don't want a finished performance. This is work in progress. I want you to adapt. Just try it my way. OK? *Think* about what you're doing. *Apply* the ideas. Remember what I've been telling you and apply it! Don't plough on, exactly like before. The phrasing is vocal all the way through – not just at the beginning. Keep thinking. Keep applying. No?'

'Yes,' Alicia says, half choked.

Kate closes her eyes. Why has Lucien chosen today to put Ali through this? She wonders, too, what's happened to Ali. In the Ravel concerto she'd played in the competition, she'd phrased so beautifully. That was only two years ago. What's gone wrong? Is Lucien right: too many concerts, too little thought?

After an hour and a half, Lucien has deconstructed the first movement of Alicia's Chopin sonata. Alicia is normally a statuesque, glowing seventeen, a seventeen that could pass for twenty-one, were it not for the wide-eyed aspect that betrays her innocence. Now she looks like a little girl of twelve.

'All right,' Lucien says, pressing her shoulder. 'Time for coffee. But I want to say one thing.' He turns – hand still on Alicia's shoulder – and addresses the listeners. 'I've been very hard on Alicia this morning. But only because she's worth it. She has a fantastic talent. If there's no talent, why work so hard, why suffer such pain? Alicia, you've done well, darling.' And Lucien starts the applause himself.

Alicia walks out of the room, head held high, without looking round. Kate leaps up and fights through the crowd milling towards the door, almost pushing Lucien aside in her haste. Her hands itch to hit him for treating her daughter so. She thinks of her dream and smarts with mortification.

'Kate,' Lucien calls after her. She doesn't turn.

In the courtyard, Alicia gives way to hysterics. Anjali and Dan flank her and as Kate hurries over she seems to see reproach in their eyes. Why should Anjali and Dan reproach *her*? This débâcle was Lucien's doing. As she nears them, she's certain she hears Dan say to Anjali, 'And now the mother has to join in . . .' Or is she imagining it?

'Darling!'

Kate holds out her arms to Alicia, who swings round and clings to her like a baby. The two of them, she thinks, holding her tightly, must seem as alike and interlinked as Russian dolls. Never in seventeen years has she seen Alicia as upset as this, not even when the school bullies put glass in her bag. How could Lucien do this to her? Doesn't he know what power he has over these young people? Doesn't he know what power he has generally, over everyone he meets? Even as she thinks this, Kate understands: the problem is that he *does* know.

'Come for a walk, darling,' she says.

'Oh, please, Kate,' Anjali cuts in, 'let her stay with us? We'll look after her.'

'You bet we will,' Dan adds. Kate gives him a hard stare over Alicia's shoulder, but he gazes back, unflinching. His expression holds an echo of her own anger. It strikes her that Dan could possibly be a man – a boy, anyway – of more substance than she'd assumed.

'Ali? What do you want to do?'

'I'll just stay here, Mum. If that's OK with you.'

'Of course, my love. Anything is OK.'

Later, when Anjali and Kate have gone back to the studio, Alicia and Dan bunk off the masterclass and walk into the gardens alone. Climbing the stone stairs, Alicia blows her nose. She can't help remembering that only the other day it had been her comforting Anjali in tears.

'The thing is,' she tells Dan, who seems to sense instinctively that she needs to talk, not be talked to, 'I know he's right! I know I don't know anything. But what can I do? I've got all these concerts, I *have* to learn new pieces, I *have* to be at home practising and there just isn't time. I want to learn about poetry and art and literature, but there's so much to do . . .'

'Your old teacher sounds like a head-case.'

'Oh, God. I *hated* her!' Alicia, letting the words out, finds she's laughing and crying at the same time. 'You wouldn't believe how I hated her. And nobody would listen. They thought she was so great because she taught me to play fast and win prizes.'

'Fast and loud. The hardest thing, my teacher says, is to play slow and soft.'

'I knew it was all wrong, and now I feel so – lost.'

'You won't be lost for long. You're too good.'

'I feel like everything went wrong because everyone thinks they know what's best for me better than I do – and of course they should, but they don't. I'm stuck. I don't know what's going to happen to me.'

'Hush, Al. Let's go and sit somewhere. There's a great spot over here.' Dan reaches for her hand. She lets him take it. Energy courses through his palm, across the intervening millimetre into her own. She curls her fingers around his and feels him squeeze back, natural, necessary.

They walk, hand in hand, under the trees along a small grass track to the edge of the hill. Here there's a landscaped circle, virtually a turret laid open to the elements: it's paved with slabs fanning out from a central round stone, and edged with benching curved against a low wall.

'They call this the Magic Spot,' Dan says. 'You stand here – on the spot in the middle – and you speak, and you get the weirdest sensation. Like you're in a tunnel. Try it.'

Alicia plants herself on the central spot and says, 'Hello, Dan!'

'Anything?'

'No.'

'Say something else.'

'OK – "something else"! No – wait. I can feel something. If I keep on talking – it's like I'm in a tube or a chimney. It's echoing round me!'

'The sound bounces back from the wall. Say something. What do you most want to say on earth?'

'I don't know.'

'Yes, you do. Say it.'

'Anything? Even if it's *horrible?*'

'Yes! Go for it, Al!'

'OK. What I want to say is – Dan, this doesn't mean you . . .' Alicia glances about; the gardens, mercifully, seem deserted. She closes her eyes, takes a deep breath, and falters.

'Just say it!'

'I want to tell everybody to fuck off!' Alicia cries. 'Everybody! Mrs Fucking Butterfingers! Rebecca Fucking Harris! Young Musician of the Fucking Year! Even Lucien Fucking Delamain! And my fucking mother who doesn't do anything except say "Go and practise"! *I can't stand it!*'

'Yay, Ali! You've done it.'

'I WANT TO SCREAM!'

'Go on, then. Scream. Nobody can hear you.'

Alicia turns a full circle on the spot. The place is empty. She opens her mouth and screams blue murder. The sound shoots up and down the invisible column of air that holds her transfixed on the Magic Spot. Dan, sitting on the wall with his feet on the bench, claps and cheers.

Her fury spent, Alicia flops on to the bench, shaky and exhausted. Dan slides down and slings an arm round her shoulders. She leans her head on his chest as if she's been doing it all her life.

'Al, you're great,' he says. 'Damn the piano-playing, I think you're wonderful. I'd still think you were wonderful if you worked in a burger bar.'

'I think you're wonderful too.'

'Feeling better?'

Alicia looks up at Dan and says nothing. Then she does what she wants to do: she reaches out and pulls his head down towards her. His lips feel hungry on her own and, kissing him, she does feel better. Much better.

In the evening Alicia sits in the Great Hall with her mother on one side, Dan on the other, Anjali on the far side of Dan,

Mary on the far side of Mum, and Lucien a little way off on a bench beneath a window. A string quartet is playing Schubert. Alicia feels the music's sombre colours dancing through her mind like dusky moths. She can't concentrate. She hardly knows Dan, yet he seems to know her so well; and somehow she knows him too, although logically she can't. It doesn't make sense. She'd thought she loved Lucien.

She hasn't seen Lucien since this morning. Now he's a short distance away, his face illuminated by the setting sun. There's something catlike about the way he curves his long limbs and casts shafts of dark light out of his eyes. Dan doesn't transfix her the way Lucien does. But Lucien, whom she reveres, had deliberately humiliated her in front of fifty people a few short hours ago. She knows him better than Dan – she knows his restlessness, his hunger for knowledge and adventure, his passion for poetry – yet Dan is part of her and Lucien isn't and she doesn't understand it. She shifts in her chair while the musicians pound through the finale of the 'Death and the Maiden' Quartet. Dan moves as if to take her hand, but Mum is watching, so he stops. Sensible, Alicia agrees silently, beaming the thought towards him. If Mum thinks he's getting too close, there's bound to be trouble.

Since her screaming episode, Alicia has been most horrified by just one of those pent-up emotions: the desire to tell her mother to fuck off. She'd be nowhere without Mum. She owes Mum everything (as Mum has told her often enough). There's nothing Mum wouldn't do for her. How ungrateful is she? What does she expect? What does she want? What on earth is happening to her in this bizarre place?

'You OK, Al?' Dan whispers, while the applause rings out.

'Kind of.'

A whisper is spreading along the row of piano students, a private message from Lucien: they're going to play duets in the studio later tonight.

*   *   *

Adrian and Josh are in the Buxton graveyard, smoking a spliff. Maybe it's a macabre place to hang out, but it's peaceful. Nobody bothers them. Nobody tells them not to smoke. People would think they're up to no good – but since he's graduated from hooded tops to biker leathers, Adrian's noticed that passers-by look at him with less suspicion and more respect. Anyway, hooded tops are stupid, unless you're trying to avoid the CCTV cameras that seem to be everywhere nowadays.

Walking by the forest of gravestones – some from the eighteenth century, some from last week – Josh and Adrian talk bikes, fuel prices, hire-purchase schemes. Adrian explains his own situation: no more school, no uni because he doesn't know what to do, angry parents the cumulative result. All he's got is his Saturday job in Macclesfield. Josh talks a little about his own job, but not much. Computers. Boring stuff, he shrugs, but it pays OK. It's a means to an end.

Adrian knows he can't go on using Josh's Suzuki much longer if he's going to stick with the gang. He needs a bike of his own.

'If that's what you want, there'll be a way to get it. Take any job that'll help you fund the things you want to do,' Josh suggests.

'My dad will kill me. He edits a fucking newspaper.'

'Then he ought to fucking help you,' Josh points out.

'They don't know I exist. Cos of my sister.'

'I like the look of your sister. It's great, what she's done. Because she's done it herself. It's *her* talent, nobody else's.'

'See? Can't get away from her, can I?'

'You've got to move out. There's a house of bedsits two doors down from my place. Interested?'

They're strolling along a track near the edge of the graveyard. Something catches Adrian's eye: a bright splash of colour in a small vase, balanced beside a whitish stone that appears recently scrubbed after long neglect. Green lichen splatters the edges, but the pale marble shines when the evening sun strikes it.

'Victoria Bradley,' Josh reads. 'Relation?'

'Shouldn't think so. Thousands of Bradleys all over Derbyshire.'

Josh reads the dates on the stone and draws in his breath. 'This was a baby,' he points out. 'Three weeks old. Poor buggers, that must be the worst thing. Losing a baby.'

'Yeah. Guess so.' Adrian is surprised – big, tough Josh, who's a computer genius and a top biker, seems to have a soft side.

'I had a friend in the gang. Killed on the A537. He hit a lorry, or it hit him. Would have thought, with him, the lorry would come off worst, but it didn't.'

'Long ago?'

'Couple of years. You've got to be careful on that road, it's one of the worst in the country. I'm not being a wuss. You can't mess with your life. OK?'

'You do,' Adrian points out, thinking of Josh's wheelies in the car park, the most extreme, daring and crazy of any of them.

'That's different,' Josh says. 'You're still a kid.'

Adrian, burned by this put-down, reads the date on the stone. This small Bradley would have been only three years older than him. The wilting flowers in the vase are red, pink and purple anemones. They're familiar. He sees them at home the whole time. 'My mum likes those,' he remarks, as they wander by.

When the caretaker, rattling his keys, throws the pianists out of the studio at eleven o'clock, Lucien waves a wide arm as if to embrace everybody and says, 'OK, we go to the hall.'

The students have been taking turns, side by side with each other or Lucien at the keyboard, one playing the top half, the other the bottom. With four hands playing instead of two, the piano sounds like a full orchestra.

To avoid feeling useless, Kate turns the pages, following the music over the pianists' shoulders. Lucien plays a great deal and she tries not to relish her closeness to him, standing behind his left arm, reaching across at intervals to swing over the page. She's transfixed by his grace at the piano: he reminds her of a cat toying, light and swift, with a ball of wool. She breathes in the scent of his aftershave, watching the way his hair dances above his ear, the twisting mazes of the ear itself, the Adam's apple in his throat. She'd arrived hating him for Ali's humiliation; yet the minute the music began, the tension vanished while nine students, one professor, a doting mother and one or two listeners together steeped themselves in Mozart. Maybe that accounts for Moorside's atmosphere. Here, people share too much: not their lives, but their dreams. Sometimes dreams are more powerful than life.

In the Great Hall, the students grab chairs from the empty rows and carry them on to the platform, grouping close round the piano. It's late, but everyone is wide awake. The huge medieval blocks of stone, the soft lighting and the towering, dark windows have seduced all of them; even Anjali has been taken out of herself and is gazing at her fellow students as if she loves them like siblings.

'Alicia,' Lucien says, 'you haven't played yet. Please, play with me.'

'I'm surprised you want me to,' Alicia says, but it comes out as a laugh, not an accusation. Dan, beside her, gives her a quick glance – they'd promised each other they'd play together – but Lucien's invitation can't be refused.

'I do,' Lucien says simply. 'Schubert. We read the Grand Duo if you like.' Lucien takes the bass position and motions Alicia to the treble.

'OK,' says Alicia, who's never heard of the Grand Duo and wonders why Dan has raised his eyebrows.

Soon she understands. The Grand Duo, as her fingers etch it out, is a symphony on a piano for four hands. She has to employ every sliver of her brain to get the notes right, but it's worth it: the melodies and textures are so rich and beautiful that they turn her knees weak. Lucien's arm brushes hers as they navigate the keyboard. His warmth, close beside her, enters the music like a dancer, his aura blends with hers and she forgets her confusion and anger and loses herself, becoming one with Schubert and Lucien and the instrument. Dan's kisses – there'd been lots – are fresh in her mind; she feels vivid, turned on, wanting more. And wanting, she realises, not only Dan but Lucien as well. A year ago, she'd have been over-whelmed by the idea of playing music with her hero. Now she's a different person. She lets sensuality direct her fingers and help her shape a particularly gorgeous passage, like a singer, just as Lucien had instructed her in her Chopin.

'Beautiful!' Lucien breathes, without stopping. Their little fingers collide. Alicia's innards give a deep, resonant twang.

Kate is transfixed. Her daughter, nearly grown-up, beautiful, gifted and famous, is playing music with the world's loveliest man (she's mysteriously forgiven Lucien everything) in a medieval hall spellbound in ebony and gold. Guy and his mistress are a world away. Adrian can look after himself. The dog will be happy as long as she's fed. Kate, for once, is living for the present. The music, the warm night air, the vaulting roof weave into one engulfing pattern, full of unfathomable, magical symbols. She's overwhelmed, tearful, her longing tougher than she is.

When Lucien and Alicia finish the last movement, nobody wants them to stop, so Lucien turns straight to the next piece. And after that, yet another.

'More!' beg the students. Lucien and Alicia oblige. Schubert wrote a great deal of music for piano duet and most of it is in Lucien's book. Kate wonders whether Ali is tired, but her face is transfigured by the music. She's filled with inner light, even if there are shadows below her eyes.

Her radiance is approaching full bloom. Dan, who's taken over the page turning, misses one because he's watching her, not the notes.

It is one o'clock when Alicia and Lucien finish the book. Lucien closes the back cover; then, reluctantly, the piano.

'We have to stop,' he says. 'The caretaker will have our skins. But more soon, yes?'

Everyone choruses assent; but outside, in the deep night on the lawn, nobody can quite let the evening end.

'Anyone want to go for a walk?' Lucien suggests.

A small group wanders out into the dark grounds: Lucien, Alicia, Kate, Dan, Mary, Anjali. What light there is comes from the moon, slightly egg-shaped yet vast, amber luminous in the harvest sky.

'Let's go up to the Magic Spot,' Dan suggests, positioning himself beside Alicia as they walk.

'What's that?' Kate says, trying to take a place next to Lucien.

'It sounds intriguing,' Mary says, on Kate's other side.

'I know it.' Lucien points. 'Up there, *non?*'

Climbing the stairs, nobody is quite where they want to be, yet everyone is together. Alicia wonders how to describe it to Grandma Didie. She's never experienced this kind of comradeship before, even though it's full of peculiar edges that don't seem as comradely as she'd like.

'Al,' Dan whispers, manoeuvring her aside, 'can't you get rid of your mother for even two minutes?'

'This morning was the longest ever.'

Alicia has been fighting her resentment of her mother for half the day. But whatever had lurked in her mind, half formed for months, maybe years, alarms and shames her now that she's expressed it. Letting it out was a massive relief, but that makes the shame worse.

The Magic Spot is in front of them. Dan strokes her arm

for a second, away from Mum's gaze. Mum seems to have eyes only for Lucien, who's explaining to her, Mary and Anjali how the spot's acoustic illusion works. They take it in turns to test the sensation. Alicia lets nobody know that she's tried it already.

'"To be or not to be, that is the question,"' Kate says, standing on the spot with her eyes closed. 'It's no good, I can't feel anything.'

Mary tries instead.

'"This above all: to thine own self be true,"' she quotes. '"And it must follow, as the night the day, thou canst not then be false to any man."'

Above the faraway hills, the moon has turned blood red.

'I like that. What is it?' Alicia asks.

'*Hamlet*,' says Mary. 'It's Polonius's advice to his son, Laertes. Before he's stabbed behind the arras.'

'You know some Shakespeare to say for us, Alicia?' Lucien asks.

Alicia – not certain whether he's taunting or encouraging her – rises to the occasion. 'Better than that,' she declares. 'I know some Verlaine.'

She moves to the central stone, while the others form an audience of dark outlines on the bench around her. She recites 'En sourdine'. Nothing could be more appropriate, she feels, letting words and air, black trees and red moon blend into a spell she's ready to claim for her own.

> '*Calmes dans le demi-jour*
> *Que les branches hautes font . . .*'

Kate can't ignore the sensual promise in her daughter's voice, reciting French with a bizarrely good accent, magnetising Lucien and Dan to her rapt, moonlit face, her long legs, the golden hair that showers down her back.

A new fear is assailing Kate. Ali is a virgin, of course she is, Kate would know about it if not. But something in her is opening out and there's nothing Kate can do to stop it. Today has been one mad, emotional bungee jump; it's not healthy; maybe they should go home. But she can't, at this moment, march Ali away, pack the suitcases and drive back to Buxton. In any case, she doesn't want to. If they left, they'd go to London, to Rebecca's. Not home.

Alicia finishes her poem; the others applaud. Kate, mind divorced from body, applauds too. Then, led by Lucien, they leave the Magic Spot and amble towards the long, sloping path that finishes at the furthest of the three residential blocks near the back gate.

'Kate,' says Lucien's voice in her ear, his breath hot on her skin. She jumps.

'Lucien,' she says brightly.

'I must talk to Alicia. May I?'

'Anything I can help with?'

'No, Kate, I need to talk to her on her own this time. It's OK with you?' Lucien touches her forearm and Kate melts instantly and says, 'Of course.'

What else can she say? She can't tell Lucien not to speak to his student; she can't lose dignity by pleading harder, trying to persuade him to talk to her instead. But as Lucien puts one arm gently round Alicia and slows so that they fall behind, Kate wrestles with jealousy. She'd have let Lucien seduce her if he wanted to, despite everything. For a few, fleeting minutes she'd thought that he might. She must therefore be exceedingly stupid.

She buries humiliation behind a raised chin, a defiant stride and a bright smile to Mary, who, prompted by a couple of suitable questions, begins to tell her about the difficulty of combating the MRSA superbug in her hospital. 'People walk in to visit or go to outpatients and they bring in all sorts of muck from the street,' Mary says. 'You can't stop them moving around . . .'

Nearby, Dan is saying to Anjali, 'So you'll have to have an

arranged marriage?' and Anjali is saying, 'Well, not exactly, but . . .'

And behind them, Lucien and Alicia are lingering further and further away.

'Don't worry, they'll be busy debriefing about this morning,' Mary says, when Kate glances round. 'As I was saying, the real problem with superbugs . . .'

'You've been learning Verlaine.' Lucien's arm is still round Alicia's shoulders. It feels oddly languid. Dan's – more muscular, because he goes to the gym – is all concentrated energy, heat and passion. Lucien's arm is relaxed, cool, assured. He has all the time in the world and he knows it.

'I've been reading that book you gave me,' Alicia tells him. 'With a dictionary. It's incredible.'

'I'm pleased that you love it,' Lucien tells her. 'Darling, I know I gave you a bad time this morning, but I think you learned something. Will you forgive me?'

Alicia beams up at her mentor, trying – without much success – to read the mix of feelings she sees in his face. Regret. Sweetness. Hunger, of a kind?

'So on Friday you play your Granados, yes? "The Maiden and the Nightingale".'

'It's so beautiful! I love it so much!'

'It's a very sexy piece,' Lucien says. 'The feeling, the atmosphere – this is difficult to capture. You're so innocent, Alicia. You don't even know how beautiful you are, do you?'

Alicia tries to laugh, but Lucien doesn't want her to. 'I mean it, Alicia. You are an astonishingly beautiful girl. You have a glow that I've never seen in anybody else. Men look at you and they love you instantly. You know?'

'No! I don't know!'

Alicia, Lucien's shoulder brushing close to her, sees Dan in the group ahead looking back at them. A bell shrills in her imagination.

'You must know. You must take notice. You can't ignore it, because as you grow up it will grow with you. You must use it for your own advantage, not other people's. You understand?'

'No! I don't.'

'Your mother – forgive me, because she's a wonderful person who cares very much about you – your mother has the same power that you have, but she buries it. She has put everything, her entire soul, into caring for you.'

'She thinks I'm still six.'

'Of course. To her, you'll always be her little girl. But, Alicia, you are a young woman and you mustn't deny your womanhood the way your mother denies hers.'

'Does she?'

'Oh, yes. She doesn't mean to, but she does. It's not good. You are not going to repeat any of this to her.'

'No.' Alicia sees the red moon reflected in Lucien's dark eyes. The others are out of earshot, a cluster of trudging charcoal shapes far ahead. Lucien's feet, which had been crunching along on the track, come to a stop.

'Alicia, you cannot play this Granados if you haven't been in love,' he says. 'It won't work.'

'Oh, Lucien!'

'You laugh. So English.'

Alicia hesitates. She doesn't like to tell him that what he's just said seems – well, laughable. Not that she's seen many caricatures of suave French men trying to seduce young English girls, but she imagines that they'd look like this. Still – and here confusion kicks in – this is Lucien, her hero, her teacher. The person who has brought back her love of music, reconnected her with everything she'd lost through Mrs Butterworth. 'Lucien,' she says, 'is it possible to love more than one person at a time?'

'Darling, of course it is. We're not supposed to. Society doesn't want to let us. But your capacity to love is your own and the most important thing is that you possess that capacity.

If you have it, you will find your own way of expressing it. Sometimes it is so great that you love not only one person, not even only two.'

'But to be – well – *in love* – I mean . . .'

'That too, *chérie*. Our rules say one thing, but our hearts always say another. It's one of the most important things, how to reconcile this conflict. Alicia, have you been in love?'

'I don't know.'

'Alicia, you are so innocent. That means no. Yet you have that capacity. Perhaps the capacity to love many, which must be why you ask me this strange question. You'll know, when it happens, and then you must decide what to do about it.'

'Lucien?'

'Darling?'

'I can still play my Granados on Friday, can't I?' Alicia has just remembered that Lucien had set her 'The Maiden and the Nightingale' in the first place. Although he must realise she's never had a love affair – it's obvious – *he* set her this piece that he describes as sexy, this piece he says she can't play unless she *has* been in love.

Lucien bursts out laughing. 'Of course, *chérie*,' he says. 'Of course you can.'

Kate, walking ahead with Mary and half listening to Dan and Anjali's conversation about self-hypnosis for countering nerves, battles fright, shame and feeling too old beneath her polished exterior in the red moonlight.

18

Emily's birthday falls two days after Kate and Alicia are due home from Moorside. To celebrate, Guy takes her and Ingrid out four days earlier. 'Your official birthday,' he suggests, filling her arms with sunflowers and a bulging plastic bag of parcels.

He loves to buy presents for Emily and the baby. Emily neither has nor desires much, but whatever he brings her seems to be right. They have the same taste. They like tall glass vases and earthenware mugs with daft writing on the side. They prefer light, bright, simple rooms, curtains no heavier than muslin, floors wooden rather than carpeted. Emily says that in Denmark people generally don't have curtains and carpets. She's convinced that they do nothing but collect dust, cause allergies and shut you off from everyone else.

They love the same things beyond the house, too. Walking in the Peaks. Unusual cheeses. Sunsets over lakes. Relaxing with coffee and a good book or intelligent journal. Best of all, lots of sex. Once they'd conquered their guilt in bed, they'd begun to come together and now they've turned it into a fine art. Emily, gasping and contracting, laughing and crying against him, sometimes whispers that she can't tell which of them is which.

Today he embraces her the moment he's inside the flat, then hoists Ingrid into the air where she shrieks with excitement. Most of the presents are for Ingrid: plastic ducks for her bath, a mobile of dolphins to hang over the cot, a cute pink hat to protect her delicate head for the rest of the summer. Finally

Guy says, 'I hope you like this,' and pushes a parcel wrapped with silver paper and pink, curled ribbon into Emily's hands. 'I can change it for you if not.'

Emily lifts out a creamy-white wrap made of fine, knitted silk. She's allergic to wool, she'd explained once, when he'd tried to buy her a jersey. It makes her skin turn red and lumpy. Silk, though, is perfect. Guy folds the soft garment round her shoulders and kisses her. Associating wool with his wife, he's glad Emily can't wear it.

He dreams of spiriting Emily to London, dressing her in grey satin and pearls and taking her to the Savoy or Claridges to shower her with the vintage champagne she deserves. Instead they head for Pizza Express on the local high street. It's the only restaurant that seems to welcome the baby in her buggy, though Ingrid is a good sleeper – no child could be less intrusive. Emily chooses a Fiorentina, Guy an American Hot, and they share a salad and a bottle of house wine. When they've finished, they go back to the flat, settle Ingrid in her cot and retreat to make love.

At the end, half asleep, Emily sighs. 'I wish you could stay tonight. Can't you? With them away?'

'I have to walk the dog.'

'Oh, God. The dog.'

'She's a great dog. You'd love her.'

'Sometimes I think I'm more jealous of her than of Kate.'

'Because I have to walk her?'

'No. Because I think you love her more than Kate.'

Guy holds her while she dozes, her hair drifting across his shoulder. He has never known such raw love, love that lifts his heart clean out of his body as a butcher would lift the heart of a slaughtered creature. He wonders if she knows how he feels, if she feels the same and, if so, how they can stand it much longer. Pain flickers in his chest and rebounds in his left elbow.

★　★　★

At Moorside, the summer school steams into its final day. The temperature is up, a layer of clingy cloud veils the sky and Alicia complains to her mother that the piano keys are laced with moisture. That evening she'll be a star turn in the student concert, performing her Granados. Lucien had been gentler with her in class that morning, going out of his way to praise her, and Anjali, who had played before her and acquitted herself excellently, had hugged her afterwards. Dan sat listening, a half-smile on his face as Lucien said, 'Come on, Alicia, don't be so innocent.'

Dad phones at lunchtime, while Anjali is telling Dan how wonderful Alicia had looked in a sari. Mum and Mary are sitting nearby, trying to pretend they aren't chaperones. Alicia hasn't stopped to think about why Dad calls her, but doesn't always speak to Mum as well. She senses dislocation under the surface, a shark within a sunlit sea, but she doesn't want to put herself in danger by venturing closer to it. She has too much to do.

'Play beautifully, darling,' Dad says in his office.

'I'll do my best,' she tells him. 'Give Cassie a hug.'

Alicia wanders on to the platform in the empty hall for her practice session. The hall glows, rafters rearing towards the sky, wood, stone and glass cradling her in a sound-enhancing cocoon as she begins to play. Caressing Granados's melody, hearing it sing, Alicia can't quite believe that this week – weird, painful, inspiring – is about to end. She hates the idea of saying goodbye to Lucien and her friends, Dan most of all. Yet she's been aware of certain uncomfortable elements, a rustle of cynicism when she stepped forward to play in the masterclass that morning (it had evaporated by the end) and the odd looks that some of the listeners cast at her and her mother, especially when Mum turns promotional and tells people, 'She's just had her seventeenth birthday.' What has she done wrong? Alicia pushes the thought aside. The important thing is to play well today. That's all that matters.

★   ★   ★

'Something's not right.'

Kate is on her favourite bench, looking down at the hall and the herb garden from the beech trees close to the Magic Spot. She's calling Rebecca. Again. Trying to articulate the sensations that have been crowding her all week.

'With Ali?' Rebecca prompts. 'With Lucien?'

'It's the way people view Ali. They're so cynical. It wasn't just that Lucien took her Chopin apart. It's how they look at her and talk about her. She's been having so much fun that I don't think she's noticed, but I'm worried.'

'Darling, people are always cynical about prodigies. Either they adore them or they shred them.'

'But it's like – they view her as a downmarket bimbo. It's horrible. And there've been comments. Not to my face, but Mary's told me about it. People think I'm a Piano Mum. One of those ghastly, pushy mothers who try to live through their child. It's the stupidest thing I ever heard! It's not like Ali is talented because I made her work when she didn't want to. Ali has an amazing gift. I'd much rather she didn't. All I ever wanted was a normal family.'

'Katie, calm down. Stop worrying. It's up to Ali to prove herself in the concert today. And she will. I know her. I know she can do it. And so do you.'

'She's wonderful.'

'So are you, Katie. And don't you forget it.'

'Rebecca?'

'Everything's going to be fine, you'll see. Love you. Gotta run.'

The line goes dead before Kate can give even the most unthinking reply to her friend's farewell message. 'Love you'? What do you mean, 'love you'?

Alicia looks up as if returning from time travel. Someone is leaning on the end of the piano, smiling. It takes her a moment to realise it's Dan.

'Hi, gorgeous,' he says. 'Gonna be long?'

'Does someone else need the piano?'

'No, but I need you. Come for a walk. It'll do you more good than sitting here slogging. You're on in a few hours.'

'You sound like my dad. He also thinks it's better to go for a good walk than practise too much.'

'What do you say?'

Alicia jumps up.

'You live in good walking country, don't you?' Dan says, while they cross the lawn towards the herb garden.

'It's wonderful, where we live. I wish you could come and visit. You'd love it. There are wonderful old stately homes and little villages and pubs. The moors are so beautiful that I could live up there and never be bored because the light changes all the time.'

Dan laughs. 'I grew up in Boston, which has a bit of history to it, but Indiana's serious Midwest. Not many historic palaces! What I love about the States is that we're a country of immigrants. Most people originated somewhere else, a few generations back, but everyone pulled together. They all wanted to be American. Did you know we're the only country in the world that has the pursuit of happiness written into our constitution as a right?'

'The pursuit of happiness?' Alicia says, thinking. It has never occurred to her that this could be one of life's aims. 'I like that.'

'*You* should come and visit. You've never been to the States.'

'I'd love to. I'd love to so much.'

'So come. When can you come?'

'I don't know. I've got concerts.'

'You have to have a holiday some time.'

Alicia rattles off her schedule for the year ahead – music-club recitals, festival recitals, concertos with orchestras both local and national, plans for another CD – and watches Dan's face as she speaks.

'Al, you're seventeen. This is crazy,' he says, when she's finished.

'But what can I do? I can't get out of it. I can't just let everyone down and say, "Sorry, I'm off to America for two weeks."'

'I wasn't thinking of two weeks. I was thinking of two months. Or two years.'

'Two *years*?'

'You need time. You need to study properly. There are worse places you could go than Indiana. And you'd love my teacher, Professor Feinstein. He's a kind of guru. He's eighty, but he's got more energy than most guys of twenty-one.'

'Eugene Feinstein?' Alicia asks. 'I've heard of him.'

'You should meet him. Play to him, get some advice. He's one of the last Golden Age teachers. He got out of Poland as a kid in the war, made it to Paris, studied with a pupil of Busoni's, got out of Paris just before the occupation and wound up in Los Angeles. He worked in Hollywood as a youngster, then started to concentrate on chamber music and teaching, and now he lives for his teaching. He's a hoot, too.'

'I can't even think about going to study in America. Mum'd kill me.'

'That,' says Dan, 'is exactly what I mean.'

They walk up the steps, arms brushing together. At the Magic Spot they sit on the wall side by side and gaze out at the wide, green and grey view.

Alicia takes a breath and moistens her lips. Then she says: 'To me, this view is in G flat.'

'What?'

'I've never told anyone about this before. But it's something I've always felt. I see different keys and individual notes in different colours. I always feel this kind of green is G flat major. C is scarlet, A is sky blue, E is yellow. Do you think I'm crazy?'

'But that's amazing!' Dan, Alicia sees, is not distressed but delighted. 'You've got synaesthesia.'

'I've got *what*?' Alicia had thought synaesthesia was a mental illness that made you hear voices.

'No, no,' Dan says, 'that's schizophrenia. Synaesthesia is exactly what you described. You experience impressions of one sense in another. Loads of composers had it. Rimsky-Korsakov, Scriabin and Messiaen. Especially Messiaen. When he wrote about his music, he often described it in terms of colours.'

'Seriously? There's nothing wrong with me?'

'Of course not! It's a wonderful gift. It adds all kinds of sensitivities to you that the rest of us don't have.'

'That's why I make such a fuss about my concert dresses,' Alicia confides. 'If I'm playing a concerto, I won't feel comfortable if I'm wearing the wrong colour for the key. Mum thinks I'm being stupid, but I'm not.'

'Why don't you tell her?'

'Because . . .' Alicia pauses. She hasn't thought about how to articulate this. 'I think,' she says, 'that if I tell her, she'd tell Phyllida – my agent – and Rebecca and there'd be all kinds of fuss. And I don't want more fuss than there is already.'

'You see?' Dan holds out his hands to her. 'You've got to get away.'

Alicia plays last in the concert. The Granados piece, she imagines, is about a girl standing by her window, longing for her lover and listening to the song of a nightingale in the woods. For Alicia, the music is a deep shade of lilac, the colour of half-hidden floral bushes in a midsummer night. She doesn't have a dress that colour, so she wears blue, as she often does – it suits her and doesn't clash with foreign keys as red, pink or green might. Her mind is full of her talk with Dan. It's all right, then, to see her colours? To relish their shifting, melding beauties and let them seep into her playing?

The humidity makes the keys slippery and she can feel her dress soaking with sweat; but she's in perfect control of the piano. She feels the chords ease from one colour to another as the harmonies change; she highlights them with a subtle spot of pedal. She softens the tone as the melody slips from pink to purple and deepens to indigo. She gives her colours their head – and senses, despite her absorption, the stilling of the audience. Everyone thinks she's the Poor Little Prodigy with the Terrible Mother. It's up to her to show them that she's not; that she's a musician with something to say that's worth hearing. And show them she will.

When the applause thunders out, she stands up and sees hands clapping everywhere, flickering like a flock of birds taking wing from Grandma Didie's garden, and the tension inside her flies away with them. Dan's eyes beam out of the crowd as if from her own mind, an idea that makes no sense. Anjali waves and smiles, happy now that she no longer has to worry about her own playing in the masterclass. Lucien's in the front row, cheering. And Mum—

Mum isn't there. At the end of the hall a door opens and closes – there's a swish of linen – and Alicia understands that her mother has fled. What on earth—

A minute later she's in the green-room, being mobbed. Dan lifts her clean off her feet and she hugs him, loving the soapy, suedey scent of his neck. It's so easy to love Dan. It's as if she's loved him all her life. Anjali too – her oldest, dearest friend, cheerful though inwardly preparing to give up her dream. And everyone else, crammed into the oven-like space, pressing her hand, kissing her cheek, patting her back, stroking her hair, treating her like a prize cat in a show, but approving of her in a way that they haven't until now. She wipes moisture from her forehead. Where is her mother?

★　★　★

'I don't know,' says Lucien, the last person in the room. Dan and Anjali have left her to get changed, saying they'll see her in the bar. Alicia lingers in her blue concert dress, looking up at Lucien.

'Did you see her? Did you talk to her?'

'No. *Chérie*, could you bear to come back to the piano with me for just a moment? I want to show you something. You did so well. Something changed inside you, no?'

'How amazing that you noticed!'

'Not so amazing. Because, since this morning, something is different. This morning you sounded like a talented kid. Tonight you sound like an artist. What happened?'

Alicia reflects. If Dan says it's OK, then it's OK. 'Apparently,' she begins, 'I've got this thing called synaesthesia, where . . .'

Ten minutes later she's still talking. About how she never believed it, she never trusted it, she was scared to let anybody know – until now. When it was for her, not against her, the whole time.

Lucien sits at the piano, his wide smile widening. 'Something is freed in you,' he says. 'Wonderful. Now, listen. You know this melody . . .'

He begins to play Alicia's piece. Alicia finds she's holding her breath. A disturbing depth, sinister and dangerous, shines out of the music in Lucien's hands, something she hadn't put in because she never knew it was there.

'You play it beautifully, Alicia. As a young artist, you play it like a beautiful dream. But what's behind the dream? Where does the dream lead? You are a wonderful girl, but you are too innocent. You play it singing. My professor at the Conservatoire showed me this. I, too, was playing it – singing. Then he played it – weeping.'

'Lucien,' Alicia says, stepping nearer to him, 'I don't *want* to be innocent.'

★　★　★

Kate, gulping down fresh air after escaping the hall's oppressive heat, flops on to a bench and fans herself with her scrunched-up concert programme. It is a mystery, the way revelations come to you when you are clearing your mind, concentrating on listening, quieting the constant brain-chatter, but there it is, staring at her bright and clear: if Ali hadn't made that first CD, people would now take her seriously. It's not her playing that lets her down; it's the CD's presentation. And whose idea was that? Not hers. Certainly not Ali's. It's not as if she hasn't known this all along. But now she feels she understands it for the first time – and its implications.

Why did Rebecca want to sign Ali? Is she so devoted to Eden Classics that she will manufacture the rekindling of a close friendship, cultivate a young talent and then turn it in the wrong direction solely to make the company a bit of money? Where does 'love you' fit into that? What does 'love you' mean, anyway? Most troubling of all, why had she been so desperate for Rebecca to be right? She'd listened to her, not Ali, not even the advisory scheme director, all the time. She'd been too dazzled by Rebecca to hear her own daughter's anxieties. Questions pound upon her. She'd have done anything to please Rebecca. Why? The potential answers that present themselves are so frightening that only two solutions are possible: fight or flight. Maybe both.

She has several options. She could pussyfoot about, waiting for the right moment, once they're home and the dust had settled. She could accost Rebecca face to face in London tomorrow and tear up Ali's contract under her nose. Or she can phone her now and get it over and done with.

She presses her lips together, breathes deeply, then dials 'BECS MOBL'.

'I've been thinking,' she says, calm and collected, when Rebecca answers with a happy 'Helloo!'

'Is everything OK?'

'Yes,' Kate says, 'and no. Ali has just played in the concert. She was wonderful. She's won everyone over.'

'As we knew she would.'

'I've realised what the problem is. Or was. The problem is not Ali. It's not me. It's Ali's CDs. The downmarket give-this-to-Granny-for-Christmas image. I never believed that before, because I didn't *want* to. I trusted you. I wanted you to be right. I was wrong. You were never interested in what was good for Ali, only in how much money Eden could squeeze out of her. Rebecca, I'm severing our contract. Ali won't be making any more recordings for you. When I get home, I am going to phone Deutsche Grammophon and EMI and Warner's and I am going to fight and fight until I find someone who will take my daughter as seriously as she deserves. You've done her a disservice. I think our friendship is over.'

She doesn't wait for Rebecca's reply, but presses the red button with one wobbling thumb. Then she puts her head on her knees and tries to get a grip. Beside her, the phone begins to ring, tootling Bach. She turns it off.

When Alicia still has not appeared in the bar after forty-five minutes, Dan tells Anjali he's going to look for her. Kate, wandering in, pale and tired, is alone. He tries Alicia's mobile, but it's off. He doesn't want Kate to worry, so he motions her towards the glass of wine waiting for her at their table with Anjali and Mary, then slips out.

In the courtyard, he notices a light in one of the staff bedroom windows on the ground floor. Several times he's seen Lucien heading towards the big oak door that fronts this staircase. It's Friday night, the last night, the party night. Nobody in Moorside is ever in their room this early on Friday night. The curtains are not fully closed. Acting on some unhappy intuition, Dan walks quietly across the grass and peers in. The sight that meets him is not what he'd wanted to find.

Furious, hurt, he retreats, thinking quickly. He can interrupt this himself. But he doesn't want Alicia to know that he's witnessed it, let alone for her to see how upset he is. If he doesn't interrupt, though, what will happen to her is potentially a lot worse. He dashes over the lawn, back to the bar.

'Kate,' he says, 'come quick.'

Lucien hasn't locked the door; he must have been in too much of a hurry. Alicia is on the bed, her concert dress ruffling round her hips, its shoulder straps slithering towards her elbows as Lucien's hands caress her hair and her thighs while his lips and the tip of his tongue travel across her face, her arms and her neck.

Kate doesn't recognise the sound that comes out of her mouth or the strength that annexes her hands. There's a shout as Lucien collides with the open door, a cry of protest from Alicia, a flurry of blue material and soft white flesh trying to put itself back together, and a yell that emerges unbidden as if from a creature trying to save its young.

Later, calming down over a brandy, Kate will cast her mind back to a day when she had stumbled across a ewe on the moor trying to protect a lamb that was being attacked by a hawk – remembering the fearsome, unsheeplike noises that the animal emitted against the swooping predator, incandescent with the rage of mother love.

Lucien, one hand pressed to his face, does all he can do: he fastens his trousers and runs for his life.

'Ali!' Kate reaches out her arms to her daughter. 'Oh, my darling, are you all right? What's he done to you?'

Alicia is sitting up, her flushed cheeks damp with tears. Kate can't help casting her gaze down the girl's exposed legs in case there's any streak of blood on the inner thigh.

'Mum,' Alicia sobs, 'why don't you just get the hell out of my business?'

Kate can't believe her ears.

'Your business? Lucien tries to rape you and it's *your business*?'

'He wasn't raping me. He was making love to me.'

'A man like that doesn't make love to a seventeen-year-old student.'

'Mum, I *wanted him to*,' Alicia shrieks. 'How am I supposed to understand music if I've never loved anyone?'

'You stupid child!' Kate screams back. 'He's filled your head with that crap just so that he can jump on you. Can't you see that?'

'Just because it wasn't you! Just because you're jealous! He was flirting with you and flattering you to get closer to me!'

'Alicia, how dare you talk to me like that?'

'You're jealous! You want to live my life because you've got none of your own!'

Kate lifts a hand and slaps her daughter across one cheek, just hard enough to silence her. Alicia stops, stricken.

'Supposing you'd got pregnant?' Kate says. She controls the desire to slap her again, a great deal harder. 'Did you ever stop to think about that?'

'I wouldn't have,' Alicia mumbles. 'It's the wrong part of my cycle.'

Kate hadn't guessed that Alicia knew about fertile times. It's a sobering thought. 'How far did he go?' she demands.

'I'm *intact*, if you must know.' Alicia gets to her feet and pulls her skirt over her knees. As she rises to her full height, they're nearly eye to eye. 'Mum, I think you should say sorry.'

Kate says nothing. Alicia, staring at her with utter contempt, gathers herself and marches, tall, blue and gold, out of Lucien's room.

The pain is predictable, but excessive. Across the courtyard the hall, floodlit, looms out of a gathering night mist.

Kate moans aloud. She shouldn't be surprised. To be half in love with Lucien, to imagine he'd been attracted to her, had been pure self-delusion. Of course he'd been flattering her to get to Ali – simple and, with hindsight, so obvious. But she'd fallen into the trap, because in this summer-seduced atmosphere one kept feeling that anything could happen and probably would.

A silhouette is moving towards her through the floodlights. It's Dan. He looks at her white face and her tears and says, 'Is Ali OK?'

'You haven't seen her?'

'No. I saw Lucien. He's gone to the kitchen to ask for a beefsteak to put on his black eye.'

Kate can't help laughing. Dan smiles, but she can see genuine sorrow in his eyes.

'Can I tell you something very personal, Kate?' he says. 'I love Alicia. I know we only just met, but I really love her.'

'Oh, Dan. I'm so sorry. I wish this hadn't happened.'

'So do I. I thought – we were – I thought she cared for me.'

'She's so young. She's very inexperienced. I don't believe that what happened this evening has anything to do with her feelings for you. I think she does care for you. Maybe she doesn't know how much.'

'It's Lucien's fault. Of course it is. She doesn't know any better. But . . .'

Dan and Kate stand in silence outside Moorside Hall, thinking about Alicia. The medieval stones, Kate feels certain, have seen this many times before, and will see it all again.

The next morning, Kate taps on Alicia's door before seven.

'Ali, come on. Let's get going.'

Alicia emerges, weary and sleepless. 'Ten minutes, Mum.'

They slope away with their suitcases across the hushed and

hung-over complex before anybody is about: not Dan, not Anjali, certainly not Lucien.

The drive home is not accompanied by Louis Armstrong, sunshine or singing. Kate drives up the fast lane, concentrating hard so that she doesn't have to talk. Alicia is fuming, grudging, miserable. A week ago she had a mentor and a recording contract. Now her playing may have broken through a spiritual barrier, but she's been forbidden to see Lucien again and the contract will be torn up as soon as they're home. At eight thirty, Kate's mobile phone begins to pipe its Bach tune – ceaseless and infuriating. Kate doesn't answer and neither does Alicia.

Near Malvern, Alicia fumbles for her own phone and begins to press buttons with her thumbs.

'What are you doing?'

'Texting Dan. We didn't say goodbye.'

Kate says nothing. A few days ago, if she'd caught Alicia *in flagrante* with Dan, she'd have been furious. Now she feels she'd give anything for that to have happened instead. After yesterday, she wants Dan's forgiveness for Alicia almost as badly as Alicia does.

Fifteen tense minutes pass before a reply bleeps in. From the corner of one eye, Kate sees something approximating happiness illuminate Alicia's tired face as she reads.

They turn into their driveway at two o'clock in the afternoon. Alicia sprints into the house; Cassie greets her with noisy delight.

'Dad!' she shouts, hugging her dog. 'We're back! Dad?'

There's no reply. Dad, as usual, isn't there.

'Adrian?' says Alicia, softly.

Adrian's bed is made, the desk is empty and the ghetto-blaster and TV have gone.

In the kitchen, Kate, her suitcase by her feet, is standing

with one hand on the back of a chair and the other holding a note on a torn envelope.

MOVED TO MACCLESFIELD. WILL RING. ADRIAN.

'Ali,' Kate says, without looking up, 'why don't you go and unpack and do some practising?'

19

FROM: Dan Rubinstein
TO: Alicia Bradley
DATE: 31 August 2003
SUBJECT: Miss you

Dearest Al,

Hi from Boston. I'm home with the folks for a week or two now. I got your card – it's cute. Thanks.

I KNOW what happened wasn't your fault. I just hope you're OK, because you matter to me so much that writing this doesn't say the half of it. You've got to take good care of yourself because it's a very, very long way from Bloomington or Boston to Buxton, and I can't cycle over and check up on you. Forgive you? What's to forgive? I want you in my life for keeps, even if you are 4000 miles away. Do you mind?

Not great to think of you with no teacher, no school, no recording deal and all those concerts. Here's an idea. I think the problem is that you're stuck at a level of perception that you need to break through – and, goodness knows, you deserve to. The Leeds International Piano Competition's accepting applications for next year. You're probably sick of competitions, but it's a good one and I'm planning to do it myself, if they'll have me. Why don't you go in for it too? If you win a prize, you'll be taken as seriously as you should be, and if you don't, then at least you and I will have had a chance to be in the same place at the same time. Good plan?

Think over what I said about Bloomington? I'm posting you some of the official info. Told Prof Feinstein about you and now he's dying to meet you. And . . . drumroll . . . he's going to be on the jury in Leeds! So come to Leeds, whatever happens, even if you only come to play to him. Seriously, Al, I think it might be a good idea. Go to one of those teachers who specialises in preparing students for competitions and then GO FOR IT.

Write soon. You're wonderful. Miss you.

Much love,

Dxxx

FROM: Rebecca Harris
TO: Kate Bradley
DATE: 5 September 2003
SUBJECT: (no subject)

Dearest Katie,

I've been ringing constantly, but you never answer. I'm devastated. I wish you'd tell me what happened, because I think I'm entitled to a little more explanation.

I've done everything I can to help you and Ali, from the beginning. I feel hurt that you'd suppose, even for a moment, that I'd set out to do anything else. Of course Eden has done well from Ali's success, but so, I think, have you.

Please talk to me. Let's try again, sort out the problems and put them right. We can't do this if you won't talk.

I miss your friendship. As it happens, I always have. I beg you, Kate, call me. There's so much good, creative energy between us. Why throw it away?

Yours ever,

Rebecca

FROM: Anjali Sharma
TO: Alicia Bradley
DATE: 30 October 2003
SUBJECT: Giving up piano dream

Hi Ali,

I've done it. I've applied to uni. It seems like the best thing and unbelievably my dad thinks so too. I've applied to Manchester, York, Birmingham, East Anglia, Warwick and Liverpool – I hope I get Manchester so I can be nearer to Buxton! I'll have a year out because I'd have been at the Academy by now. But that's fine. It gives me a chance to get my head together.

It feels odd – all I ever thought of doing was performing. But I have to face it: I don't have your kind of talent. I've been having some counselling and I can see now that it was my father who decided I should be a pianist. If he hadn't pushed me so hard, I might never have tried. It's not like I'm giving up music – maybe I can do something else with it. Goodness knows what. But uni should be fun and it'll be nice to meet people who do other things besides playing musical instruments.

So you're entering the Leeds? Good woman. Go for it! Have you started driving lessons yet? I'm having my first one tomorrow – I didn't get round to it last year. Wish me luck!

Love,

Anji

PS – Say hi to your brother from me. He was in Birmingham last week, I'm not sure why, and we met for a drink. Amazed he remembered me, but it was nice to see him.

FROM: Alicia Bradley
TO: Anjali Sharma
DATE: 31 October 2003
SUBJECT: Driving

Hi Anji,

How did you get on??????!?!?!?

I have GOT to learn to drive. Mum doesn't want me to (why are we not surprised?) but the idea of driving to my own concerts is bliss because every time she takes me there's so much fuss. She has to treble-check everything in the cases before we set out and there are always problems about who's going to walk the dog.

It's completely freezing here.

My new teacher, Ian, who's head of piano at the Manchester Music School, is fantastic. He's letting me learn the Rachmaninov Third Piano Concerto. Might do it for Leeds. Nobody can say I'm a bimbo if I turn up with *that* and play it well. Did you know I'm doing the Tchaikovsky Concerto at Symphony Hall, Birmingham, in a couple of weeks? Aak! I haven't been there since the final of the BBC competition. There was a cancellation, another pianist who's with Phyllida's company, and Phyllida persuaded them to have me replace him. I hope you can come – let me know and I'll get you a complimentary ticket. Mum says the hall feels like a conference centre, but I remember liking it because the acoustic is so good. You can play as softly as you like and still be heard. Ian loves soft playing with lots of colour – so did the Unmentionable Lucien, of course. I miss him, but Mum wants to shop him to every newspaper in the country.

Apropos de Lucien . . . I don't know what to do about Mum and the papers. She's obsessed. Apparently I'm not the first student Lucien's jumped on. Phyllida mentioned that he'd done it before, a while ago, and Mum yelled at her, wanting to know why she hadn't told us earlier. Poor Phyllida was very upset. Lucien must have been her boyfriend at the time, so I guess she couldn't quite cope with it. Dad says that of course none of the newspapers will run anything about it, because they could be sued for libel. Mum says why would they be, if it's true? But I'd have to testify against him in court and I won't do that. So Dad tells Mum not to be stupid and then they row about it. It's crazy – it's been months now and she's still hopping mad! Now she's threatening to take my management away from Phyllida. And she and Dad are at each other's throats the whole time. It's HORRIBLE. I'm practising extra hours because while I play I can't hear anything but the piano.

I guess you know all about Adrian moving out and working full time in that motorbike shop!! He's learning everything there is to learn about motorbikes. Dad is livid because he wanted Adrian to go to uni. I think he's ashamed to be the editor of the biggest newspaper in the north and find that his son's not interested in studying Greek literature or whatever.

I'm pleased for Adrian, because he's got his life together. He's turning into a real biker. He wears leathers and talks about all kinds of technical things that I don't understand. Did he show you his new bike? It's wonderful, really fast – and he wanted to take me out on the back of it, but Mum went ballistic and wouldn't let me go. I don't know how I'll ever leave home, because of the piano. I couldn't move my Steinway into a Macclesfield bedsit – it would drive everyone bananas.

I miss you, Anji! I miss Lucien, despite everything. And I miss Dan . . . He's coming over in summer before Leeds, but it's ages away – it'll be ten months since I last saw him. I wonder whether we'll get along. I still don't understand how I really feel about him and Lucien. It's confusing.

So, basically, all the news I have is that I practise, give concerts and try to stay on the right side of Mum and Dad, and I haven't got anyone to talk to but the dog, who's going deaf.

At least I've got my own computer now. Thank God for email!!!

Lots of love,

Axxxx

TO: Phyllida Brown
FROM: Alicia Bradley
DATE: 4 January 2004
SUBJECT: Leeds

Dearest Phyllida,

I hope you had a wonderful Christmas. I thought I should let you know that I've been accepted for Leeds. I'd like to do Rachmaninov No. 3 if I get to the final, so I'm working hard on that at the moment, but the Tchaikovsky, Chopin and Ravel are still in good shape so if any last-minute dates come in for those, that's fine with me. Sorry you couldn't make it to Birmingham – hope you saw the reviews!!!☺

Where were you for Christmas? Did you go to your mum's? Ours was awful – Mum and I were down in Harrow with the Horribles, sorry, Uncle Anthony and Auntie Fiona and their kids who think I'm off my head. Dad didn't come. He said he had to work.

See you soon, lots of love,

Axxxx

TO: Alicia Bradley
FROM: Phyllida Brown/MCAA
DATE: 4 January 2004
SUBJECT: Out of Office Autoreply: Re:Leeds

Phyllida Brown is on leave until further notice. Please forward any urgent message to Alison Harvey.

TO: Dan Rubinstein
FROM: Alicia Bradley
DATE: 21 January 2004
SUBJECT: Miss you

Hi Dan,

Isn't it amazing that we can write to each other and the message goes 4000 miles right away?!?

The Rachmaninov is going fine, thanks. I love it to pieces. I'll wear black to play it – red would suit it too, but I think black will look more serious. Assuming I get to play it at all, that is. There's such a lot of repertoire to learn for Leeds. I'm working about nine hours a day and seeing Ian twice a week. It's crazy and tiring, and sometimes at night my head is so full of notes and colours that I can't sleep. Anyway, you know all about it because you're doing it too. We could work like this all year and then be thrown out after the first round . . . but I'm trying not to think about that. Driving lessons are fun – they get me out of the house and if I pass my test, I'll be able to jump in the car and just GO.

I'm worried about Mum. I think she's depressed. And Rebecca

won't leave her alone. Adrian came over yesterday on his bike
(I'm still not allowed on the back) and he tackled her outright. Of
course she told him to shut up. But he's right. She doesn't have
any life of her own. She hardly talks to Dad. She doesn't do
anything except manage me, especially now that Rebecca's in the
doghouse and Phyllida's in hospital. It's awful about Phyllida. She's
had a kind of breakdown. I miss her so much. Nobody knows
how long she'll be off.

Mum says that now my career's better established, it's easy for
her to manage me herself. She used to be a lawyer, so she knows
about contracts and she's very organised. The only trouble is that
she's raised my fee and I feel embarrassed. Not that it puts people
off, so I guess it's OK.

It's not like I get the money – she's investing it for me, and
paying off the piano (a.k.a. the mortgage). She gives me an
allowance, which Adrian keeps telling me is too small, since I'm
the one doing the work. I don't like to complain, though. I spend
most of it on concert dresses, music, books and getting my hair
done at a really good salon when I go to London. I hope she'll let
me put it towards buying a car when I pass my test.

Now that I'm with Ian I can see that he's a much better
teacher than Lucien. Lucien was good at giving me reading and
listening lists, poems, paintings, etc., but for preparing for Leeds,
Ian's the right guy. I wish I'd gone to him years ago. He's good on
poetry and painting too, as it happens.

Dan, I MISS YOU. I think a lot about last summer. Do you, too?
Here's what I feel now:
1. I'm very, very sorry about what happened on the last night at
Moorside.
2. I wasn't in love with Lucien at all. Even when I thought I was.
3. I wonder if love is maybe not what we think. I imagined it was
about being starry-eyed, feeling fluttery when you're near
someone. But now I think it's more in the mind than in the body.
It's like being in tune. It's like singing in the same key, feeling
things in the same colour (I know you understand this!), not
having to guess or doubt or fight. Feeling like you've known

someone all your life. You can relax, be yourself and know that they appreciate you exactly as you are, at your best.

That's what I feel about you. I feel like you're part of me and I'm not scared to tell you that. I don't want to hide who I am or how I feel. I used to watch girls at school playing stupid games with the blokes they liked and I don't want to do that. Perhaps I show too much – but that's tough. That's me. That's how I am. Why should I be ashamed? It's only shameful if you direct it to the wrong person. Perhaps that's what happened with Lucien.

Tell me it's not only me? Tell me you feel the same?

Lots of love from a very wintry Buxton.

A xxxxxxx oooooooo xxxxxxxxx

FROM: Dan Rubinstein
TO: Alicia Bradley
DATE: 21 January 2004
SUBJECT: YES

YESYESYESYESYESYESYESYESYESYESYESYESYESYESYESYESYES.

I feel exactly the same.

Love you. Am with you every moment.

D xxxxxxxxxxxxxxxx oooooooooooo xxxxxxxxxxxxx

'Let's go to the lounge,' Phyllida suggests. 'I need a change of scene.'

Alicia is in Phyllida's room in the hospital, which, she thinks, feels more like a prison than a place where people are supposed to be healed. It's a large, red-brick building hidden behind a wall on a busy road in south London; the soundproofing is so good that you can't hear the lorries going by, or any noise from patients in surrounding rooms. The atmosphere is heavy with accumulated misery. If so many suffering people are thrown in together, Alicia muses, how is anybody ever supposed to get better?

Phyllida blows her nose.

'I go home from time to time. But I have panic attacks when I walk into my own flat. God, I feel so stupid.'

'Phyl, you mustn't! You're fantastic.'

'You're a sweetiepie, Ali. Just make sure this never happens to you, yeah?'

'Phyl—'

'Let's get you a cup of tea. I can't believe you came all this way just to see me.'

'Of course I did!' Alicia protests, following Phyllida, whose walk no longer bounces. As she wanders down the green and pink corridor towards the patients' lounge, Phyllida seems to be moving in a dream, almost under water. It must be the pills.

'When are you going back to work?' Alicia asks, when they've helped themselves to tea from an urn and settled down on a relatively secluded pink sofa.

'No idea. I can't face the office. And the idea of getting my head round the paperwork . . . it's just . . .'

'You must take as much time as you need,' Alicia encourages. 'You've got to get better. That's the only thing that's important.'

'I'm so ashamed of myself.' Phyllida sits with one hand over her eyes. Alicia can hardly recognise the elegant, sharp-nosed, besuited executive she first met in a Kensington restaurant. In jeans and soft purple jersey, without glasses, without makeup, her hair growing longer, Phyllida's lines have crumbled to dust.

'You mustn't be. It could happen to anyone,' Alicia says. She wants to ask if it's about Lucien. But she dares not say his name, in case it is.

'When you fall in love, Ali,' Phyllida says, without being asked, 'make sure it's with someone who loves you too.'

'But surely . . .' Alicia bites her lip. She wants to be tactful, but she also wants to find out what happened, and why. 'If you know he doesn't feel the same,' she begins cautiously, 'and you know he's cheating on his girlfriend and jumping on his students – doesn't it stop you loving him? It would stop me.'

'That's the bloody awful thing. It should, but it doesn't. After we had our – our – OK, call it an affair if you like, I suppose that's what it was, I honestly thought I could turn him into a friend. And then I thought that if I did everything for him and built up a fabulous career for him, he wouldn't be able to do without me. Instead, what happens if you behave like that is that he takes you for granted, he uses you, he tramples you underfoot. It's almost as if I've been begging him to walk on me. I'd lay down my life for him – so that's what he wants me to do. He doesn't feel anything for me except power.'

'Lucien likes power,' Alicia remarks.

'It's so demoralising. I feel so awful. I feel old. Fat.'

'You're not fat!'

'I feel fat because I feel so unattractive. I'm hopeless. I'm past my sell-by date. I don't even feel I can be any good at my job because when I'm with Lucien I start feeling like a stupid, insecure kid.'

'Phyl, I think you're *wonderful*,' says Alicia, her lip wobbling. She's never seen anybody in such a ferment of honest, devastated emotion and she wants to howl in sympathy – though that wouldn't help Phyllida in the slightest.

'You're a darling. I hate to think of him using you.'

'I can forgive him for Moorside, but if he's done this to you, I never want to see him again.'

'It's not him, really. It's me.'

'I think it's him. Not you.'

Phyllida wanders over to the window and watches the clouds chasing each other across the sky. Alicia isn't used to seeing her without her glasses. Her turquoise eyes are clear, deep and full of sorrow.

'You know, we deny these things,' Phyllida says, without

looking at Alicia. 'In the nineteenth century, a lot of opera and ballet stories were about girls going mad when they're betrayed by their lovers. Today, no matter how awful we feel, we're meant to *get over it*. Well, supposing I don't *want* to get over it? Supposing, despite everything, Lucien is still the most beautiful thing that ever happened to me? But it's not romantic today. It's pathetic. Look at this poor old bat who can't get her life together because she's hung up on a man who doesn't love her and she's wasted her youth trying to win him and suddenly found she's past forty and it's too bloody late?'

'Oh, Phyl! None of that's true!' Alicia protests, trying to imagine how it must feel to be forty. 'You're beautiful, you've done everything to make Lucien who he is today – and if he doesn't love you, he's an idiot! He doesn't deserve you. Tell me what happened. Why did you come here?'

'It didn't exactly happen overnight, but I lost all my confidence. I started having panic attacks, especially on my own at home, and then at Christmas . . . I sort of lost it. All these images of happy families and smiling children and Christmas carols and presents and people 'being together' – and there's my mum on her own, she can't get around because of her bad knee and her operation had been cancelled again. My dad's out in Australia with his new wife, playing happy families with them instead of us, and there are all my friends with their kids – and then there's me . . .'

'Phyl, Christmas is terrible,' Alicia confirms. 'I heard that more people—' She's about to mention that more people attempt suicide at Christmas than at any other time of year but stops herself. She wonders whether Phyllida had made such an attempt. Something must have happened to land her in hospital.

'It's a vicious circle,' Phyllida explains. 'You get yourself into a state over something, and then you get into a state over the state you're in . . . and you just spiral down. I'm taking these antidepressants, I have other pills to help me sleep, I have psychotherapy, I'm supposed to do lots of exercise and stop drinking and smoking. But I feel so *stupid* for having let this happen. I don't know if I'll go back to work. I'm not sure I can face being a manager any more. I can't even manage myself.'

'Listen,' Alicia says, 'you're going to get better. You are. Take the time you need. And when you're back at the office, I want to be back with you, because you're the only person who understood me. I hate Mum doing my management. You see, *I* need you, Phyl. You might have wanted Lucien to need you, but I really do.'

'Darling,' says Phyllida, 'you're an angel. You just take good care of yourself. OK?'

Back at Euston, Alicia has more than half an hour before her train, so she goes into an Internet café on the concourse and writes to Dan: 'We're so lucky to have found each other. I can't believe the things that happen to people because – they say – of love. To look at Phyllida, you'd think that falling in love is the worst thing that could happen to anyone.'

When she's finished, she sits over her coffee and thinks herself into her Rachmaninov concerto. The piano comes in at the start, in a simple tune that rises and falls, the hands playing in unison. Then, from this strand of sound, there unfolds a stream of emotion, counterpoint and figuration, unravelling under her fingers as if the opening melody were a plain box concealing every colour of the prism. You lift the lid and watch the ideas ripple towards the sky, bursting out beyond the confines of the human heart. Alicia remembers reading the Greek myth of Pandora's box: the girl, ordered not to look inside it, does so from curiosity and out fly all the most terrible things in the world. Death, disease, famine, hate, jealousy and evil take wing; Pandora can't put them back. At last, from the bottom of the box, a beautiful white bird emerges. Its name is Hope.

Does love live with hope or with horror? Must they all hide together, under that lid, deep inside the music?

'The train at platform six is the 17.05 to Manchester Piccadilly . . .' comes the announcement. Alicia pulls on her raincoat and wanders towards the train, camouflaged: just another young girl among the crowds, going home.

Kate, in her study, tries to work while waiting for Alicia to come back. The battle that morning had left her weak and drained once Alicia had marched out, vanishing down the road towards the bus stop. No argument had budged her from her purpose. Nothing on earth would stop her going to London, alone, to see Phyllida.

Kate had tried everything. You have to practise, it's your lesson tomorrow. You can't possibly find your way to Roehampton on your own. The weather is dreadful, the trains will probably be disrupted. Then, finally, I'll come with you (that had been the worst one). Ali's willpower reminded her fiercely of the day she'd tried to save her dog from the river. Cassie, who has cataracts and arthritis, would no longer dream of going for a swim; but Ali hasn't changed. When her mind is made up, nothing will hold her back.

Alicia has decided, similarly, that she must learn to drive. They've found a local teacher and she is applying herself with the same determination she lavishes on her Rachmaninov concerto. The idea of Ali out alone in a car makes Kate feel faint with terror, but as nothing will stop her, it seems better to help her than to try, Canute-like, to hold back the tide. Her test is in May and the indications are that she'll pass. Sooner or later they'll have to buy another car.

Kate spends half an hour searching on the Internet for good second-hand car outlets in Derbyshire. She'll need to find around five thousand pounds if Alicia is to have a reliable tin box to get her safely from A to B. On Guy's salary, it ought to be possible.

These days, Kate has few qualms about invading Guy's study. She strides across the mess of paper, books and old newspapers that furnishes the floor and tackles the filing cabinet where he keeps the bank statements.

She runs a quick, practised eye down the columns of figures. Then she does it again, double-checking. And a third time. The pattern is not difficult to spot. A direct debit to an account entitled Music Fund swallows around a third of Guy's salary per month. Where does Music Fund go?

Cross-referencing is equally easy. Another file contains Music Fund statements. Copies, it seems, are being sent to an address in Victoria Park, Manchester. Music Fund has nothing to do with Alicia. It's the money he gives Emily to support her child. The name, she understands, must have been coined specifically to dupe her.

Kate tells herself she shouldn't be surprised, but her stomach heaves. She closes her eyes and breathes, waiting for the attack to pass. Sometimes she keeps the thought of Guy's other life at bay for so long that she almost forgets it exists. Moments like this make her realise the extent to which she's capable, even now, of kidding herself.

Since the Lucien incident, Kate has snapped shut like an oyster. If barnacles were to grow on her shell, she wouldn't care. Nobody but her children will have a place inside her sealed heart. This began as a conscious decision, following Moorside, but it has moved from thought to feeling, from deliberation to reality. Guy is an irrelevance: nothing more than a facilitator for Alicia, someone to share the bills and present a united front when required. He dares not go against her conditions.

Alicia, in blissful innocence, throws herself into her music, her driving lessons and her determination to love with all her soul those whom she loves – Phyllida, Anjali and Dan, who phones frequently, sometimes for two hours at a time. Ali has a normal family behind her, a solid base for her music. That solidity, or the illusion of it, is the string that flies her like a kite. And so Kate closes herself to all else.

Despite everything, she misses Rebecca. She misses her warm eyes, her caring voice, her athleticism, poise and the soft scent of Yves Saint Laurent. Mary, her auburn-haired friend from Moorside, is no substitute. With her normal kids, her husband who spends weekends on DIY and gardening, her sensible job in the hospital, helping people who need help, well-meaning Mary tends to make Kate feel worse than ever when they meet for lunch half-way between Buxton and Liverpool. Anyway, she doesn't have much time for friendship, now that Ali's career is her sole responsibility.

Kate launches a new document and begins to type a letter to the director of the Proms.

Guy sits in the surgery in Manchester, shaking his head. 'I can't.'

'Mr Bradley, I know you're a busy man,' says Dr Simons, 'but if you don't slow down and reduce your stress levels, you might become very sick indeed. There isn't a kind way to tell you this. You've got the symptoms of heart disease and you're not yet fifty.'

'I can stop drinking. I can watch my diet. But work . . .'

'How are things at home?'

Dr Simons, Guy thinks, can see straight through him. 'Stressful,' he says.

When he goes back to the waiting room, Emily is there to take him home – her home. Because of a bout of pain that had left them both dreading the outcome of this consultation, she wouldn't let him drive. Guy pauses in the doorway, looking at the image ahead: Ingrid on Emily's lap, being read a baby book full of pop-up pictures. He crouches, holds out his arms to his daughter and watches her face – the image of her mother's – crease into a squeal of joy as she slides off Emily's knee and bounces towards him on small, heavy feet that remind him of Alicia at nearly two. Pain twinges in his arm.

'Did he refer you?' Emily demands, taking his hand.

'Yes. I have to wait for an appointment.'

'How long?'

'Not long,' says Guy, who has no idea how long 'not long' may be. Emily pulls a face and looks away. Her hand in his feels clammier than it had a moment ago.

In the car, Emily does something unusual: she talks about Alicia.

'I don't see how you've managed to keep everything from her,' she tells Guy, who's in the back with Ingrid. 'She's a bright girl. Can't she guess?'

'She's wrapped up in her music, and Kate keeps it that way.'

'The longer she doesn't know, the worse it's going to be when she finds out.'

'Christ. I know that. You know that. But try telling Kate. She's got me over a barrel and there's fuck-all I can do about it.'

'Forgive me, darling, because I know that – in a funny way – it's not really my business.' Emily pulls up at a red light and gazes at Guy over her shoulder. 'But I have to say, it doesn't make sense. What does Kate think she's going to gain from behaving like this?'

'Power,' Guy suggests, staring out at the bleak, late-afternoon twilight. 'Power to control me, I guess. Power to stop me being happier than she is. But it's more than that. She has this ingrained idea about families. That a 'normal family' is the only way to be. That if Ali doesn't have a normal family behind her, it's going to ruin her career. This kind of twaddle, I'm afraid.'

'That *is* 'twaddle' and you know it. Kate's an educated, intelligent woman. She doesn't need to think like that. There must be something deep-rooted in her that's making her behave in such a twisted way.'

'Perhaps.'

'Do you know what?'

'No. Do you?'

Emily gives a soft laugh, though her face reflected in the rear-view mirror seems sad.

'There are plenty of possible reasons,' Guy thinks aloud. 'The premature baby we lost. That's when everything began to go wrong. Or that cold, proper, pressurised background of hers. It's one of those families that just doesn't allow emotion – though Kate's had plenty of emotions in her time. But why these things add up to one kind of behaviour in one person and something different in another isn't my area of expertise.'

'Nor mine. I guess Kate's had a hard time and it's catching up with her. Maybe it's as simple as that.'

'Sweetie, don't do that,' Guy says softly to his daughter, who's finding it fun to pull off her shoe and sock, throw them on the car floor, then wait for him to retrieve them and tell her not to do it again. She grins at him and, while he straightens up, she pulls off her other shoe and sock.

20

Mum is too scared to take Alicia out to practise driving, so Adrian comes over from Macclesfield and takes her instead. He'd passed his driving test first go, though Alicia doesn't know why he'd bothered since he refuses to take the one for his motorbike, the vehicle he actually owns. Crazy brother, thinks Alicia, beside him in their mother's car, bowling across the moor and handling the wheel with the smoothness and panache she tries to give her piano-playing.

'Good girl,' Adrian says. 'Don't look at the lambs. Watch the road. Here comes the left turn. Mirror, signal, manoeuvre. That's it.'

Alicia swings the car down towards the valley and smiles sideways at Adrian.

'Staying for supper?' she asks him, pressing her foot down.

'If Mum's in a good mood.'

'How's Macclesfield?'

'Cool. It's great being near Josh.'

'I wish I could live with my friends.' Alicia sighs.

'Which friends, Al?'

'The ones nobody knows I have because I never see them.'

'The Indian girl? She's fit. I like her.'

'Anjali. She's going to stop doing concerts. She kind of can't deal with it. At Moorside she had to be sick before she played in the auditions. Did you know there are musicians who are sick with nerves every time they go on a stage?'

'Not you?'

'No. I love it. I wonder if there's something wrong with me.'

'Cripes, Ali, just enjoy it. You don't want to throw up.'

'It's like driving. I love it and I can't wait to pass my test. But Anjali says she's too scared to learn. She stopped her lessons.'

'Anjali's dad is a control freak.'

'And Mum isn't?'

'She is, and how! But it's worse if it's a dad.'

'At least I'm not scared of Mum. Anjali's scared of her father.'

'There we are, then. How's the Boy In Bloomington?'

'Blooming far away! But he's coming over. He's coming to stay.'

'Mum's letting him stay in the house? That'll be interesting.'

'Dan says he was lucky I got into trouble with Lucien last summer because it makes *him* look like an angel. Mum likes him because he's not Lucien!'

'Mum was in love with Lucien herself. She just couldn't admit it.'

'Everyone was in love with Lucien,' Alicia muses. 'But – *why*? I know he seemed wonderful. I thought so too, but when you see who he really is, how he really behaves – why do we all fall for it? And why does he do it? I don't understand.'

'That's what every guy wants – to have every woman on earth wanting to go to bed with him. Most of us can't have that. When someone can, because he's rich or famous or good-looking, then he does. That's all.'

'I don't think Dan wants that. I think he loves me.'

'So what's he like? All I know is you met this bloke who lives four thousand miles away and you're determined to wait for him.'

'He's . . . he's lovely. He's twenty-one. He's funny. He reads a lot and he's clued up on politics and languages and movies, much more than I am. He comes from Boston, his dad's a doctor, a psychosomething, his mum's a cellist and he's got a little sister who's six years younger. He likes dogs and walking.

He's a fantastic pianist, but he's not so ambitious. He says he'd like to be a top professor and have masses of good pupils.'

'How would it be, two pianists living together? Noisy? Competitive?'

'Bliss. Someone who understands from the inside what you're going through every day.'

'Ali . . . You haven't seen Dan since August. You've known him for one week, plus lots of emails and phone calls. But you don't really know each other. And you're so young. Are you sure you're not just seeing in him what you want to see?'

Alicia is silent for a long time. The speedometer rises from forty-five m.p.h. to fifty-five.

'Steady on the bends,' Adrian says.

'I believe in him,' Alicia says at last. 'I believe in us. If I don't, who will?'

Later, Adrian sits at the kitchen table and glares.

'Adrian, why don't you take off your jacket?' Kate says, fussing over the sink where she's preparing a chicken in a roasting pan. 'It's warm today.'

'Not in here, it isn't.'

'I've got a few things to do upstairs,' Alicia says. 'Will you excuse me, please?'

'Don't be long, Ali. It's not often we have your brother and your father home at the same time.'

'Are you surprised?' Adrian mutters.

Alicia flees. Her laptop computer offers her escape via cyberspace. She dives for relief into her email, where a long message from Bloomington is waiting. She reads it three times.

Her emotional life centres on her email. She's devised a password that she's sure her mother will never guess, but deletes messages once she's read them, just to make certain. She's taught herself how to touch-type via an Internet program and when she expresses her thoughts on the computer keyboard instead of her black-and-white musical one, she's thankful for the piano exercises that have honed her fingers' responsiveness. She can type almost as fast as she can play.

At seven o'clock the front door opens and closes. Cassie gives a half-hearted bark, then drags herself to the entrance hall to welcome Guy, who has arrived from his hospital appointment.

'Dad!' yells Alicia, and careers down the stairs.

'Hello, Ali.' Guy hugs her. He looks exhausted. 'Come and sit down. I need to talk to all of you.'

Alicia follows him into the kitchen where Mum, reproachful, turns round from the oven and Adrian waits, drumming his fingers on his leather-clad knee. Guy pats his shoulder as he goes past and sits down.

'Apparently I've got angina,' he says, 'so I have to change my diet, my lifestyle, basically everything.'

'That's ridiculous,' Mum protests. 'You're too young. Why don't you ask for a second opinion?'

'This *is* the second opinion, Kate.'

Alicia hasn't heard Dad call Mum 'Katie' for a long time. Mum is no longer a convincing Katie. Kate, yes: her manner clipped, professional and sharp-edged – not a blowsy, relaxed Katie, happy to laugh and chat.

'They've given me some pills and a diet plan,' Dad says. 'As low fat as humanly possible. And I'm supposed to join a gym and reduce the stress in my life.'

'I see,' Mum says.

'In this house,' Adrian butts in, 'that's going to be easy, isn't it?'

'Adrian, watch your mouth!' Mum snaps. 'Don't talk to your father like that.'

'It's true. Living here's enough to give anyone effing angina.' Adrian shoves back his chair and strides to the window. He towers over the rest of them.

'How dare you?' Kate says.

'I'll say what I like, because it's true. You're bloody hypocrites!'

'Adrian,' Alicia pleads.

'Not you, Al. You keep living in your own little world. It'll help you stay sane.'

'Alicia, go to your room. Now.'

'Mum!'

'Let her stay, Mum. She needs to hear this as much as you do.' Adrian swings round. His face has turned scarlet. 'Because if you don't stop pretending, if you don't stop making such an effing charade out of your perfect family and your perfect talented daughter and you don't stop taking over Ali's life, then you're going to wreck everything for her and Dad and yourself! The atmosphere in this house isn't fit for anything to live in that isn't born with a suit of armour. I'm not coming here again.'

In a rush of helmet, leather and keys, Adrian's hulking presence tears itself up by the roots, bulldozes across the hall and is gone. There's the thunder of powerful engine; Alicia, running after him, reaches the front steps in time to receive a blast of motorbike exhaust in her face. Half dazed, she trails back to the kitchen, where Dad is sitting at the table with his chin in his hands.

'Ali,' Mum says, 'go and practise, there's a good girl.'

FROM: Alicia Bradley
TO: Dan Rubinstein
DATE: 5 May 2004
SUBJECT: HELP!

Dan, please help me. I'm going out of my mind. I think Mum is going out of her mind too. Dad's got angina. My brother blames Mum and says he's never coming back. I don't know what to do. Mum doesn't do anything except tell me to go and practise. Please help me, because I'm stuck.

Axxx

FROM: Dan Rubinstein
TO: Alicia Bradley
DATE: 5 May 2004
SUBJECT: Re: HELP!

Hang in there, Al. I'm coming over soon. I'll change my ticket.

Just hold on for now, OK? Keep practising. That's the most important thing you can do, because that's your get-out route. And be nice to your dad. Sounds like he needs you.

Do you know anywhere other than your house where I could practise? I want to be with you, but I don't want to get in your way.

Good luck for your driving test! Will be holding thumbs for you.

I'll let you know as soon as I've booked the flight.

Dxxx

FROM: Alicia Bradley
TO: Rebecca Harris
DATE: 10 May 2004
SUBJECT: An idea

Dear Rebecca,
Mum doesn't know I'm writing to you, but I've got an idea I want to run by you.

I'd love to make another CD. I wouldn't want to do another super-popular compilation, but how about French music? Debussy and Ravel, with a cover that looks classy? I'd love to work with you again, and if I do well at Leeds, that would help sales, wouldn't it?

Please let me know what you think. Maybe we could get together to talk about it. I've just passed my driving test so I can drive myself to London any time. Theoretically.

I hope you and James and Oscar are all well. I hope we can meet again soon. I miss you.

I'm going to delete this message from my outbox because I

don't want Mum to see it, and will do the same with whatever
you write back.
   Love,
   Alicia

FROM: Rebecca Harris
TO: Alicia Bradley
DATE: 10 May 2004
SUBJECT: Re: An idea

Dear Alicia,

   It's good to hear from you. Very pleased to know that you'll be
doing Leeds. You must be working extremely hard.
Congratulations on passing your driving test.

   As you know, I've been deeply distressed by the change in your
mother. I can see why she's not happy with the perceived
outcome of the first CD, but I can't understand why she won't
talk to me about it. It's quite extraordinary.

   I'd be delighted to meet you and discuss the possibility of a
new recording. If you can persuade your mother to be a little
more forgiving than she has found possible so far, that would be
wonderful too. But I'd like to see you, no matter what. Please
call me and we'll make plans. Don't forget to delete this
message.

   Yours ever,
   Rebecca.

FROM: Adrian Bradley
TO: Anjali Sharma
DATE: 20 June 2004
SUBJECT: Visit

Hello Anjali,
Ali tells me you're coming to visit. I'd like to see you too, but I
don't go to Buxton any more. Any chance you might come to

Macclesfield? I could take you out on the bike after work. Glad
you got into uni. Hope you're well.
Adrian

Dan is flying to Heathrow on 25 June. He's managed to get a
cheap flight earlier than he'd originally planned, but it arrives
in London rather than Manchester. Alicia decides she will drive
down to meet him in the second-hand Renault that is now 'hers'.

'You're not seriously going to drive to Heathrow on your
own?' Mum exclaims.

'I've got a driving licence. We've got a car. I've got a boyfriend
in America. So I am going to use my driving licence and our
car to go to the airport and fetch my boyfriend.'

'I'll come with you.'

'Mum, no, you won't.'

'But, Ali—'

'It's much easier to drive without you breathing down my
neck worrying that I'm going to do something wrong.'

'Supposing we ask Uncle Anthony if he—'

'No, Mum. *I*'m going.'

After ten minutes of this, Alicia is almost in tears with
frustration; Kate is white, with red patches across her cheeks.
The phone saves them. Kate answers, efficient and profes-
sional as she speaks to the manager of the Manchester
Philharmonic about Alicia's imminent concerto at the
Bridgewater Hall.

Kate had been keen to arrange a 'run-through' of Rachmaninov's Third Concerto for Alicia before the competition.
Playing it will be her biggest challenge to date; tackling it for
the first time in a televised international competition final
wouldn't be ideal. The Manchester Philharmonic is what Kate
terms a 'windfall'. She'd phoned the manager on the off-
chance that they'd have space for Alicia to do something –
anything – only to find that a pianist had pulled out of a

concerto date at the Bridgewater Proms on 3 July and they
needed a replacement. 'That's Alicia's eighteenth birthday,'
Kate pointed out.

The manager had been hesitant at first, having heard negative comments about Alicia's populist recordings. Kate grabbed
the initiative. She insisted that he see her in person, the next
day. She went to Manchester armed with reams of material:
recordings of recent recitals, Lucien's reference (written before
the trouble), a file of good reviews and a heap of invective
directed jointly at Deirdre Butterworth and Rebecca Harris.
First the manager sat and listened; then he paced about his
office while Kate talked; eventually he suggested Kate put on
the CD of Alicia performing the Rachmaninov G minor
Prelude in last summer's Buxton Festival. While it played, he
grew very still. He wanted to hear the next piece, and the one
after that. At last, he said, 'I see,' pulled a calendar out of his
top drawer, and wrote Alicia's name in one of its squares in
blue biro.

That's what's so annoying, Kate reflected, driving home afterwards. All that needs to happen is that the right people must
hear what Ali can do. When they hear it, it's total surrender. But
they have to be bludgeoned into putting on a CD and actually
listening to it. You can send a CD to anybody, but you can't
make them play it unless you stand over them with a whip.

The upshot is that Alicia is to play at the Bridgewater Hall
on her birthday. But what pleases her most is that Dan
Rubinstein will be there to hear her.

'If you don't let me drive down to meet Dan,' Alicia tells
her mother eventually, 'then I'll cancel the Bridgewater. I just
won't show up. The rehearsal will start and I won't be there.'

'You will do no such thing. How dare you even think of it?
Do you want to ruin your career?'

'Stuff my career,' Alicia virtually spits. 'I'm going to Heathrow
and that's the end of it.'

*   *   *

Alicia sets off from Buxton well before rush-hour on the M1. These days, she always wakes early unless she's had a concert the night before. The prospect of Dan's arrival has changed the world's colours for her. She sometimes stands at her bedroom window and watches the sky lightening from indigo to lilac to bluebell; pale, crystalline sunlight reaches her through the fronds of midsummer leaves. She imagines Dan beside her, imagines what it would be like to wake up with him in a bed somewhat larger than her own. She scarcely remembers Lucien.

That in itself is odd, she muses, making her way over the hills to Ashbourne, then Derby, then the M1 south. How can your mind be full of one person for so long, then suddenly not be? Might the same thing happen again? After longing for Dan for months, almost a year since Moorside, might she wake one day to find that she no longer does? Maybe Adrian was right.

Not that he can talk. 'When are you next seeing your friend?' he kept asking, when she phoned him.

'Dan?'

'No. The girl. The Indian girl.'

'Anjali.'

'Yeah. Anjali.'

'She's coming to the Rachmaninov.'

'Cool.'

It isn't like Adrian to be unduly diffident, or absent-minded about names. Alicia sees the motorway spreading ahead of her and, jubilant, presses her foot on the accelerator.

The traffic builds as she circles London anticlockwise – the M25 at this hour is no fun – and by the time she turns on to the M4 and sees the planes lining up low in the sky, ready to land, she's certain Dan's must be among them and she'll be late. She doesn't become nervous for her concerts, but she's nervous now. Nervous about the traffic, nervous that she won't recognise Dan, nervous that they won't know what to say to one another. Nervous that she'll find she doesn't love him after

all. Or vice versa. And he's here for months, until the competition is over. What if they don't get along? What if the family
feuding sends him scuttling home?

Negotiating the concrete slopes in the car park, Alicia feels
her foot shaking on the clutch and wonders whether she should
leave now and go back to Buxton alone. The construct she's
built around Dan is imaginary. He's a boy. Just a boy – like
all the others she's sent packing on his behalf since last summer.
And there have been a few, even a conductor who tried to kiss
her in the lift at St David's Hall, Cardiff. Maybe she's missed
opportunities. Maybe she's put her eggs into a basket woven
of nothing but dream fibre. Maybe she's too young. Mum and
Dad met when they were eighteen and nineteen and married
when Mum was twenty-three. Maybe that's why they don't
get along any more.

She parks on the roof. When she climbs out of the car, her
legs feel weak. She follows the arrows to the terminal building,
joining the anonymous world with its suitcases, trolleys and
holiday garb trundling towards the escalators. And when she
spots the sliding doors through which weary travellers emerge,
gazing round for their family, friends or taxi drivers, she scours
the crowds for any indication of Chicago, where Dan boarded
his connecting plane after flying from Indianapolis. She finds
a spot to wait against a railing: she needs to prop herself up.
Her head is spinning. Performing a concerto is a piece of cake
compared to this.

The minutes drag; arrivals emerge from Calcutta, Thailand,
Rio, Johannesburg. Just as she's beginning to feel that the plane
is imaginary and Dan a mirage, her mobile beeps with a text:
'Landed ok, cases coming thru, c u any mo xxx.' The woman
standing beside her glances at her. 'All right, love?' she asks.

'Fine, thanks. Excited.' Alicia beams back and notices that
the smile makes the strange woman look a second time, as
people always do. She can't stop radiating just because people
tell her she's radiant.

The sliding doors disgorge a group of Americans. The men are nearly seven foot tall; the women, large all round, stride along in elasticated jeans, T-shirts and sneakers; their aspect is positive and their voices loud; they radiate, too, with sheer confidence.

Then, not far behind them, Alicia spots a curly-haired youth, dark and strong, pushing a laden trolley, a leather music case slung over one shoulder, and it doesn't seem to be her who calls out his name, ducks under the railing and cuts across the stream of incoming travellers. She flings her arms round his neck and feels the warmth of his flight-tired body as he grabs her and kisses her full on the lips. He tastes the same, he smells the same and it's as if they had last seen one another only hours ago, not ten months. They say nothing for several minutes because they're too busy kissing.

'God, Al. Let me look at you!' He stands back, while people push by, tut-tutting because they're blocking the exit, but soon translating frowns into helpless smiles at the look of absolute love on the two young faces. 'You look *fan*-tastic,' Dan says. 'What's happened to you?'

'How do you mean?'

'Last summer you looked like a teenager. Now you look like a woman.'

'I'm nearly a year older.'

'Jeez. A year. There's such a lot you've got to tell me. Come on, let's get out of here.'

'Dan, I hope it's OK with you – I need to go into London to see someone. Mum doesn't know about it, so it's kind of got to be today. I'm really sorry to drag you around. Do you mind?'

'Al, I'll go anywhere on earth with you, you know I will. You'll have to forgive me if I fall asleep, though! Who've you got to see?'

'The woman who runs my recordings, or used to. I'd love to know what you think of her.

*   *   *

On the outskirts of London Alicia has to stop the car, phone Rebecca and ask how to pay the congestion charge. 'Sorry, I've never driven into London before.'

'Ali,' says Rebecca's voice, 'don't worry. Get yourself here and we'll organise it for you. OK?'

'I need to know how to do it myself,' Alicia remarks to Dan, after thanking Rebecca and ringing off.

'I bet people always do things for you,' Dan teases, patting her knee.

Alicia laughs. 'Are you good at maps? We need to get to Kensington High Street.'

Dan, whose eyes are shadowed from plane travel and jet-lag but who still can't stop smiling, takes charge of the map and tells Alicia to head due east. While they crawl along the A4, he tells her his news. He passed his exams with top marks. He's just turned twenty-two, but he hadn't wanted to celebrate because she hadn't been there to celebrate with him. They could save that for later. His parents are dying to meet her. His little sister, who's doing violin quite seriously, is dying to meet her too. Professor Feinstein is impressed that she's going to play Rachmaninov Three at the competition.

'If I get through,' Alicia says.

'You will.'

'I hope you'll be able to stand our house. Mum's putting you in Adrian's old room.'

There's a brief, awkward moment while both of them consider sleeping arrangements.

'Fine,' Dan says. 'Look, we'll play it by ear: if it's difficult, with your parents, I'll go to a bed-and-breakfast or find something to rent until the competition.'

'Seriously?'

'Of course. The important thing is to be here. Whatever it takes.'

*   *   *

Off Kensington High Street, they find a parking meter and fill it with coins ('I knew London was expensive, but this is nuts!' Dan remarks). They stroll past what is, to Alicia, a dazzling array of shops, then down a side-street towards a converted nineteenth-century terrace that declares itself the home of Eden Classics.

Rebecca comes to meet them in the sleek, chrome-laced front hall. She's aged since they last met: her hair is greying at the temples and her face is lined with more frowns but, Alicia thinks, fewer smiles. She's wearing a dark silk top that shows off her sinewy, well-exercised arms, and light trousers that accentuate her long legs. Rebecca, Alicia reflects, looks elegant and beautiful, but oddly unfeminine. With her muscular, slender figure, she could almost have been a male ex-athlete.

'You must be Dan. Nice to meet you.' Rebecca turns her firm handshake on Dan, who greets her with polite words and perceptive eyes. Alicia scarcely hears what he says: she's too busy drinking in the fact that she is looking at his face, not just imagining it.

In her office, Rebecca gives them coffee, which is welcome indeed.

'Now, Ali, you're keen to do another disc. What's brought this on?'

'Becs,' says Alicia, who has never called Rebecca 'Becs' before, 'you know how my mum is.'

'The same?'

'Worse. The more I try to do things myself, the more wobblies she throws. You wouldn't believe the fight I had just to drive down to pick Dan up. You see, all I've got of my own is my piano-playing. If I can make another CD, by myself, rather than involving her – if you see what I mean – and if it sells well, that will give me something to start me off.'

'Are you saying that you want to move out?'

'I don't know how I can, but . . .'

'Ali, you know I can't promise anything yet, but I'm more

than happy to consider it, if we can get the whole package right.'

'There are a few things I'd want,' Alicia says, her tone staying firm, though she doesn't feel so firm inside. 'I'd want the final say on the cover. I'd want to play pieces *I* choose, though I accept that you'd want them to be well known. I'd want it to be a serious, upmarket CD, and there should be proper coverage in the music magazines.'

Rebecca sits back in her chair and stares at Alicia with her head to one side. Alicia pauses, wondering whether she's gone too far.

'Good for you, Ali,' Rebecca says. 'Debussy and Ravel, you said?'

'Yes, I'd love to do that. Nothing too obscure, I promise. Maybe *Images* and *Gaspard de la nuit.*'

'I like that. If you're serious, I can pitch the idea at our next planning meeting and we'll take it from there. What would you tell your mother?'

'I'll think of something.' Alicia breathes again. There are ways. There have to be ways. It's up to her to find them. 'I don't know what's got into Mum,' she says. 'It's always been difficult, but . . .'

'I know that she'd lay down her life for you. And she's a woman of integrity. That can mean, though, that she's almost too consistent for her own good. It's understandable, of course, if you think of what happened to her before.'

'Before what?'

Rebecca stares at her. Alicia stares back. Beside Alicia, Dan shifts in his chair.

'You don't know?' says Rebecca.

'Know what?'

'Oh, God.'

'What is it, Becs?'

'About Victoria.'

'Who's Victoria?'

'Oh, God,' Rebecca says again.

Alicia feels the blood draining away from her head. 'Whatever it is, please tell me,' she says. 'I think I need to know.'

'So she's never . . . Don't worry, Ali, it's nothing that affects you directly. It's all a long time ago. Are you OK?'

'Yes.' Alicia, pale, sits forward and waits. Dan reaches for her hand.

'Before Adrian, your parents had another baby. She was born very prematurely and she died when she was a few weeks old. Her name was Victoria. It was extremely hard for your mother to get over it, and if she's a little over-protective of you, you only have to remember this to realise why.'

Alicia stays silent. She stares at her hands, folded in her lap, one of them encircled by Dan's.

'Oh, my God,' she says eventually. 'Poor Mum. Why on earth didn't she tell us?'

'I expect she didn't want to upset you.'

'Was that when they were still in London?'

'Yes. It's partly why they moved to Derbyshire.'

Alicia's eyes fill with tears.

'It's so weird,' she says to Dan later, walking back to the high street. 'It happened before I was born, but it seems to have affected everything about the way she treats me.'

'Has it, though?' Dan says. 'Isn't it maybe what she was always like, potentially – except that it's been accentuated through losing the baby?'

'I don't know what to think.'

'Nor do I. I've only seen her at Moorside and I guess she was right to be keeping an eye on you then!'

'Dan . . .' Alicia unlocks the car. 'What *did* you make of my mum at Moorside?'

Dan is quiet for a minute. Then he says, 'I thought she was basically a very good person. Complicated. But good. Caring. Solid.'

'I think some people hate her.'

'Maybe that's why she likes me. Because she can see I respect her. People always think that music mums are pushy for the heck of it, but there's got to be a reason you've done so well. You can't succeed at anything unless you've got some kind of support pushing you along.'

'She certainly does that,' Alicia growls.

'But would you have done all you have without that? Think about it.'

Alicia thinks. 'I don't know,' she admits.

'So, Al. Let's go home.'

21

FROM: Dan Rubinstein
TO: Judy Rubinstein
DATE: 1 July 2004
SUBJECT: Hi from Derbyshire

Hi Mom,

I'm going to delete this message the moment I've sent it because I'm using Ali's computer and I don't like the thought of her reading it.

You wouldn't believe this place. It's a weird set-up. I'm trying to stay sane – more important, I'm trying to keep Ali sane. I knew she was over-protected and prodigy-mothered, but I hadn't realised how much.

Ali turns eighteen the day after tomorrow. Her mom, Kate, does all her career management now because the agent she was with is on long-term sick leave. Kate books her masses of concerts and Ali spends all her time working for them, because although she's the biggest talent I've ever seen, she has a conscience and she's afraid of not doing her best. She's also preparing for Leeds.

It's not that I don't like Kate, because I do. She looks very much like Ali; she has a lovely smile, when she remembers to use it; and she'd do anything for that girl, and I mean *anything*. At first I was amazed she let me stay in the house, but I think she knows I really care for Ali. It's something we share and we respect one another for that. She knows Ali could have gotten involved with somebody far worse.

Ali's dad, Guy, is great. Warm, caring, extremely bright and he has a fantastic ear for music. He works round the clock and stays in Manchester several nights a week. He's supposed to take care of his heart, but I don't think he does. Ali worries; he always tells her not to. She says she hardly ever sees him. I guess Dad, if he psychoanalysed her, would say it's no wonder she's fallen for someone who lives 4000 miles away – she's used to never seeing the man in her life.

Her brother left home after a massive row with the parents. Ali sometimes sees Adrian on his own. I haven't met him yet, but on Thursday we're going for a curry with him in Macclesfield, and Ali's friend Anjali is coming too. Ali's been hinting that Anjali is sort of involved with Adrian, but I don't know how much, since she's from a strict Asian family and is meant to have an arranged marriage. Very complicated.

What bugs me is that these people never *talk* to each other. I know we joke about how English people drink tea and discuss the weather. Well, I come down in the morning and Kate says: 'Good morning, Dan, did you sleep well? It's going to be a beautiful day, I hope you and Ali will find time for a walk. Would you like some tea?' I'm not kidding.

The house is spotless. Everything is lined up straight and tidy and it smells of beeswax and pot-pourri. Every last inch is clean and tasteful. It feels like a showhouse for a real-estate firm, not a home. Ali's allowed to have mess in her room, but she has to keep the piano room tidy – she's in there practising most of the time. Kate isn't a bad cook, but she scrubs down the kitchen as she goes along. She'll chop an onion and while it's frying she'll clean the chopping board and rub down the work surface; then she'll slice some mushrooms and do the same thing all over again. And at the end of each day she takes everything, and I mean *everything*, off her desk. Apparently Guy's study is a disaster zone – at least that sounds human. Except for Ali playing the piano, there's a silence here that works its way into every corner of your brain. It's like a negative energy. A black hole. An absence of livingness.

Ali's incredible. I know you say I'm besotted and I'll come to my senses, but I swear to you, Mom, I'd rather die than come to my senses over her. I've never met such a good person. It's like she's from another era, another century, maybe another universe. She's pure gold and I'm almost scared to touch her in case I'd contaminate her with the outside world. I don't understand how her parents can live as they do and have a daughter like her. I don't see how they can have a daughter like her at all.

She's never had a boyfriend before – she said she 'nearly went out with someone at school once, but didn't'. She doesn't go to parties. Seems her brother took her to one and she was so sick afterwards that Kate hasn't allowed her to go to any more (not that she was meant to go to that one either; Adrian smuggled her out of the house! Can you believe it?!?). She never listens to pop music – she's not snobby, she's doesn't dislike it, she just isn't bothered about it. She doesn't even bother much with TV. She does her own thing and as she sees it, that's her business and no skin off anyone's nose. Anything else bounces off her. She must be incredibly strong and, inside, secure about who she is. I hope that's true – for her sake.

She loves movies and there's a video-rental place down the hill, so I've been showing her my favourites. Buxton doesn't have a cinema and although Ali could drive to Macclesfield or Stockport, she's got no one to go with. Sometimes she meets Anjali in Macclesfield, or Derby, which is about half-way between here and Birmingham, but they always eat Indian food rather than see a movie, so that they have a chance to talk.

Anyway, she practises such long hours that she doesn't want to sit still afterwards. When we go out, we go jogging together, or drive into the countryside and walk. The air is incredible, so fresh and clean. I always thought the UK was a polluted, over-crowded, grey island, but Derbyshire is unbelievably beautiful, although it's bleak and quite cold even now. The villages are cute and the hills are full of fluffy sheep. Everything seems tiny compared to home. It's like walking into a storybook. I keep expecting witches and hobgoblins to jump out and start doing little dances in the road.

People are friendlier here than in London. The day I arrived, Ali and I bumped into her first piano teacher from when she was three years old, and this lady said at once that I could go and practise at her house. Amazing – catch anyone saying that in London. Ali ought to move to London, but she says she'd miss the countryside. Now I can see why. At least she has that to keep her on an even keel, and her dog, Cassie – though the dog is ancient. She's like Ali's alter-ego – a sort of 'familiar'. I hope Ali will be able to handle it when Cassie goes to the great hunting-ground in the sky.

Of course Ali's naïve and not very well educated – she left school early – and in some ways she's young for her age. But she works so hard that she never stops to wonder why she's doing it, why she never has any fun, why she never goes out or meets other kids. It's not healthy for an eighteen-year-old girl. And yet she's perfect. She's a natural, loving, passionate, instinctive, strong-minded young woman – as well as an over-protected little girl and an extraordinary musician. I only hope I'll know her in ten years' time, and twenty, and thirty, so that I can watch her real-ising everything within her to the full, and help her. She's wonderful. All I can do, for now, is be there for her. I want to take care of her. I want to get her away from here.

Take good care, Mom. Give my love to Dad and Steph and write soon.

Love,

D x

Alicia believes that time doesn't exist, not in its expected form. It's infinitely malleable. Days shoot past when you have too much work, a deadline for a lesson, an impending international competition. When you're waiting for something, or someone, minutes drag like months. As for distance – if you love someone, distance becomes even less distinct than time.

It should be incredible that she and Dan get along so well. Technically, they have little in common except music. Dan grew up in a family that never fights, or so he says, in a country she's never visited, and he's Jewish, a race, religion or both of which Alicia knows nothing. But through their music, they share everything that's most important to them. They exist in harmony. They feel music the same way: when they listen to a recording or to each other playing, the expression on Dan's face mirrors exactly the emotion inside Alicia. Even their favourite composers are the same: Rachmaninov, Chopin, Debussy, Ravel and Beethoven.

They both like to get up early to go running. Mum's face, when she sees them heading out for a jog in the rain on Dan's first morning, jet-lag or no, is a sight to remember. Dan loves dogs, and Cassie is trying valiantly to adore him, though Alicia suspects she's jealous. And although Dan is cleverer than she is – he's feeding her countless books and films – being with him isn't like being with another person. It's so easy. As if someone's watching over them.

Backstage in Manchester, preparing for her Rachmaninov concerto, Alicia can't work out whether time goes too fast or too slowly. Before her first few concertos at major halls, she lay on the sofa in her dressing room, trying to imagine she was anywhere else but there; yet also she couldn't wait to go on stage and begin. The longer she has to hang around, the more drained she feels.

Today she lies on the floor instead, knees up and spine flat, head resting on a pile of programmes. Ian has told her that this position helps to straighten the back and let the tension sink out of the body into the ground. Mum, Dad, Dan, Adrian and Anjali all want to stay with her, but she won't let them. She delivers her best Greta Garbo impression: 'I want to be alo-o-ne!' That makes them laugh, which is important. They mustn't feel offended if she sends them away.

There's more tension than usual in her at the moment.

Whenever she closes her eyes, she starts thinking about Mum losing her first baby.

It's obvious that Mum didn't want her to know, so Alicia has kept quiet. She's told Adrian, whose expression showed little emotion, although he revealed that he'd unwittingly come across the grave, which bore signs of recent attention and a jar of faded anemones. She's talked to Dan at greater length; but, being an open, non-secretive American, he doesn't see why she won't talk to her mother. Alicia can't explain. The last thing she wants is to upset Mum – who is easily upset these days.

She wonders what her sister would have been like. She'd have been twenty-three now. Maybe she'd have been musical. She might have played an instrument, the violin or the cello. They could have been the Bradley Sisters Duo. She could have had a real friend – the sister she'd wanted so much – instead of feeling so alone. She and Adrian are close now, but they'd had to grow up first.

It's difficult to see how lonely you are if you're used to it. When you find you're not alone any more, that's when it hits you.

The first morning at six, before they went jogging, Dan slunk into her room and her bed. They lay still and held each other. Now every morning, before anyone else wakes up, he comes in and they have time in bed to be themselves together. They touch each other, but no more, because Dan says he doesn't want to rush her. Alicia doesn't think it would be rushing, given their year apart; it's not as if she doesn't want to make love with him. But if he prefers to wait, she'll wait. She closes her eyes: heaven. To love him and to be free to express that love is all she wants. Not the competition prize, not having her picture in the paper, not being asked for autographs. Stuff that. Being in love, being with the person you love, that's what life is for.

Her new-found love doesn't stop her going through the

routines required of her. Dan has remarked on how 'professional' she is, and it's true that aspects of performing have grown easier through habit. She knows that, on the morning of a concert, she must try everything through on the venue's piano and, if it's a concerto, rehearse with the orchestra as much as the conductor permits; after that, it's best to let well alone. If she works all afternoon, she'll end up exhausted and confused. She sleeps from about two o'clock for as long as possible; and however tempting it is to test the most difficult passages, she forces herself not to. If she doesn't know it by then, she never will. Warming up before the concert, she'll play anything except the piece she's about to perform.

The Tannoy alerts her with a call: 'Five minutes, please, Miss Bradley.' Alicia picks herself up and gives her hair a final shot of spray. Looking at herself in the dressing-room mirror under the rectangle of bare lightbulbs, she can hardly believe that this glamorous blonde woman is herself.

Dan has given her a wrap for her birthday – blue silk that he says is the colour of her eyes. It's not as warm as the woollen shawls Mum knits her, but it looks better and Alicia adores it. From now on, she will use nothing else. Tonight it's the last thing she puts down before striding on to the platform.

Leaving the stage with her arms full of bouquets as the applause subsides, Alicia knows she hasn't played her best. Her stomach is knotted with anxiety. The Bridgewater Hall is an important venue and she'd wanted it to go better. Her concentration isn't brilliant at the moment and she'd had some small memory lapses. Not many of the audience would notice – but a crucial few would.

Well-wishers surround her backstage, hugging and kissing her – she's convinced she doesn't deserve it. She puts on a stage smile, greets people, thanks them, trying to make them feel important. Inside, she's feeling slightly sick and faint, wanting to cry. Those months of work – and that was *it*?

Even Anjali, who knows this feeling better than anybody, scarcely notices her subterfuge – but that could be because Adrian has muscled through the crowd to monopolise her. Anjali looks stunning, slender and huge-eyed amid the throng. Perhaps, Alicia reflects, she's too delicate for a life as destabilised as a musician's. Her brother, tall and hunky and biker-rough at the edges, slides a protective arm round Anjali's waist. He glares sideways at Mum, but because it's Alicia's birthday, he's promised a cease-fire for the evening.

It's Mum who has to make a *thing* of the memory lapses.

'Ali, what happened?' she demands, as soon as Alicia has bundled everyone else out of the dressing room so that she can change.

'I slipped a bit.'

'You certainly did. Why?'

'Dunno. It happens.'

'Not to you it doesn't. What were you thinking about? Was it Dan? Because if it was, Ali, if he's distracting you from your work, we'll have to send him to stay somewhere else.'

'Mum, I'd be much more distracted if I was going somewhere else to see him every day.'

'It's not good. It's ruining your concentration.'

'"It",' Alicia tells her, 'is the best thing that ever happened to me.'

'Not if you give a bad performance because of it.'

Alicia feels stuck. Dan hasn't been distracting her – anything but. He listens to her play and advises her. She does the same for him. They inspire each other, spur one another on. What's been distracting her is the thought of the unknown sister she'd lost; and the fact that Mum has never once mentioned her in all Alicia's eighteen years. If she's distracted, it's not Dan's fault. It's Mum's.

Anyway, she hadn't played that badly. It could have been a lot worse. She'd had to take six curtain calls.

'Mum, it's my birthday,' she declares. 'Can we save the recriminations for tomorrow, please? I'd like to be able to celebrate with my friends.'

'In other words, Dan.'

'Tonight was nothing to do with Dan!'

'Ali, don't shout at me.' Mum's eyes are wild with fury.

Dan must have been listening outside the door, because he comes striding in on cue and exclaims, 'Come along, ladies, break it up. Miss Bradley, your carriage awaits!'

They leave the hall by the artists' entrance at the back after the orchestra has started the second half. Didie and George hug Alicia, but then go home – Didie isn't in the best of health. Alicia doesn't know what's wrong: all they tell her is that Grandma is 'feeling frail', a term that could mean anything and fills her with fright. Nobody will say more, so she has, somehow, to live with the uncertainty.

Dad has decided to treat everyone to dinner at a busy, brand-new restaurant that offers a menu of English, Italian and Thai food rolled together into unpredictable delights. The party sits at a round table: Mum and Dad, Adrian and Anjali, Alicia and Dan, Ian and his wife Carole. Dad orders champagne.

'Daniel, why don't you make a toast for Ali's birthday?' he says gallantly. Thank God, Dad likes Dan. He won't hear a word against him. Alicia thinks she may have to leave it to him to make sure Mum doesn't throw Dan out.

Dan jumps up, tapping his glass. 'Ladies and gentlemen, I'll be brief,' he says, without a moment's hesitation. 'Here's wishing a very happy birthday to our wonderful Alicia! Al, you're a star. Tonight's your night. All together now!' He conducts 'Happy Birthday' and Alicia, embarrassed as the whole restaurant joins in, sits and radiates as best she can.

This should be the happiest day of her life: turning eighteen, having just played Rachmaninov's Third Concerto for the first time, surrounded by the people she loves most. But even now, she can't enjoy it as much as she wants to, because she knows she hasn't played well enough. While she kisses Dan and thanks everyone for their moral support, in the back of her mind she's wondering whether any of the critics noticed her duff up that bit in the last movement.

The restaurant door swings open and a youngish woman walks in. She looks familiar; Alicia can't place her at first, but it turns out she's one of Dad's journalists. She vaguely remembers that she'd come to dinner years ago, when Alicia was too young to join in. Alicia notices her eyes: huge and light, almost silver.

She's come to meet a friend, but spots them, as they are relatively hard to miss. Dad leaves the table and goes to talk to her; it looks like quite a deep discussion for a chance encounter, but oddly he doesn't invite her to join them. She leaves immediately; her friend, it seems, isn't there. Mum stares after her. Alicia thinks that Mum has started to dislike younger women, though the journalist had seemed so calm and self-possessed that Mum could have learned something from her.

In the car going home, Alicia leans on Dan's shoulder and pretends to be asleep. Between Kate and Guy hangs a silence the thickness of velvet curtains. Dan stares out of the window. The moor is bleak and empty, other-worldly under the glow of a full moon. He holds the not-asleep Alicia against him – he knows what she's up to, even though her parents don't – as if to protect her brightness from the encroaching night.

The silence goes into the house with them. It's one a.m.; they hadn't left Manchester until after eleven thirty. Adrian and Anjali, who'd lightened the atmosphere at dinner, had last been seen talking to one another across Adrian's motorbike – Alicia hoped he wasn't going to take her friend back to Birmingham on it – and Ian and Carole had embraced Alicia, then headed home to relieve their babysitter. Alicia knows that Ian will have heard every error in her performance; her next lesson will involve a detailed post-mortem.

'Something to drink?' says Kate, in the kitchen.

'Thanks, Mum, but I'm going to turn in.'

'Not even chocolate?' Chocolate is Alicia's usual wind-down drink after a concert.

'Thanks, Mum, no. It's too hot.'

'Dan?'

'I'm going to get some sleep too, thanks, Kate. Goodnight, and thank you for everything.'

They hurry upstairs before anybody can say more.

On the second floor landing outside their separate rooms, they stop and kiss for a long time.

'Goodnight, darling,' Dan says. 'You were wonderful. You played so beautifully. I'm proud of you.'

'Night,' says Alicia.

Now that she can throw aside her protective mask, a tide washes towards her: anxiety, terror, panic. Yes, she is distracted – haunted by her mother's silence and the image of a small girl who had never lived. In her bedroom, she pulls off her post-concert summer dress, plus her underwear, and tosses them on to a chair in the corner. She's too keyed up and too hot to sleep. She takes a book from her bedside table and tries to read, but she can't concentrate and she's sweating terribly. Nothing helps the pent-up howl in the pit of her stomach.

She puts down the book and lies flat, naked, on her bed, with her curtains open, letting in the moonlight. Eighteen, distracted and desperate. She turns on to her front, holds the pillow over the back of her head and screams into the mattress. It's a valuable release and she's certain nobody can hear her. She screams several times, then lets herself cry, sandwiched between mattress and pillow to muffle the sound. She wonders whether her mother had cried a great deal after her baby died. She doesn't know where the pain inside her has come from.

Because of the pillow, she doesn't hear Dan's tap at the door or his voice calling her. She doesn't know he's there until her bed depresses under his weight.

'I'm not decent,' she manages to sob into the mattress.

'You're extremely decent.' Dan is stroking her bare back with the tenderest touch she's ever felt. 'What's going on?'

'Oh, everything. Mum. Rachmaninov. Dad. Leeds.' Alicia turns her gaze, though not the rest of her, towards him. She sees his eyes, black in the silver moonlight, caressing her face.

'Is your mum right? Am I distracting you? Al, this is it, you know – Leeds is your big chance. You've got to give it everything.'

'Don't you start. You sound like Mum.'

'Something's not right. Is it me? Because if it is . . .'

'No!' Alicia wails. 'It's not you. It's all kinds of things. Mum, mainly, and what – what Rebecca told us in London. I was so upset. It's got under my skin.'

'That happened a long time ago. You must try to put it aside. Yeah?'

'Dan, what if I screw everything up? What am I going to do? You know what happened to Anji last year. If that's going to happen to me . . .'

'It won't. I promise.'

'But what if it *does*?'

'Ssh,' says Dan. 'You're going to be fine.' He runs his hand up and down the full length of her spine, comforting and calming her by the second. She's forgotten to be shy about wearing nothing. 'My God,' he whispers. 'You're lovely. You're so beautiful.'

'Dan,' she breathes, closing her eyes.

'Do you want me to go?'

'*No.*' She turns over at last, lifts an arm towards him. He swings his legs on to the bed and gathers her to him, his lips in her hair and under her ear. The kiss on her neck is like tiger balm. Now, finally, she thanks heaven, and her mother, for having stopped Lucien. She reaches for his belt and undoes the buckle, and the button and zip below, because they both know they can't wait for each other for one more second. And when he comes into her, he's so gentle that the taking of her is not his possession but her gift. The tenderness shocks her, submerges her. Tears spring to her eyes while she moves with him, in consonance. Such unimaginable beauty, then, does exist; it's not confined to music. It's real.

Later, they lie still, getting their breath, half dozing, holding each other. Outside, the full moon hangs over the hills – not blood red this time, but a rich, deep gold.

'You know?' Alicia says.

'What, love?'

'I wish we'd done this yesterday.'

'I wish we'd been doing it all year.' Dan flops on to his back and gives her the naughtiest grin she's ever seen. She giggles, trying to stay quiet. 'Why yesterday?' he asks, stroking her damp hair away from her forehead.

'Because I think I know what to do with the Rachmaninov now.'

'Oh, Ali,' Dan mumbles into her shoulder, eyes closed. 'I love you. This is the real thing. I'll never let you go.'

'I love you too, Dan. Much more than any piano concerto.'

Alicia folds herself round him and, in the soft light of the setting moon, they sleep together at last.

22

Now that it's late July, Kate thinks it's time Alicia pulled herself together. With less than six weeks to go until the competition, she's decided to learn to cook. It's the latest in a stream of activities that are not how a young pianist aspiring to Leeds should spend her time. All because of Dan, naturally. Kate watches Alicia perusing the latest Nigella Lawson recipe book, stripping skins off tomatoes, hunting hopelessly in the supermarket for watermelon, and despairs.

They both practise, of course. Dan is off to Glenda's house by nine o'clock most mornings – though it's been getting later recently – and after he's gone Alicia closets herself in the piano room and works all day, barely stopping even for lunch, unless she goes to Ian for a lesson. But when Dan returns, she starts behaving as if they're a newly married couple. Waiting on him. Touching him constantly. Making fancy dinners ('Mum, do they sell red mullet in Marks & Spencer?'). The sight puts Kate off Alicia's beautifully prepared offerings.

Ian, Kate thinks, is wonderful. She's kicking herself for not having taken his advice, for not sending Alicia to his music school, for not seeing sooner through Mrs Butterworth's dragonish smokescreen. Ian draws Alicia out, lets her be herself, helps her understand and solve her musical problems. He encourages rather than condemns, praises before dissecting, offers new thought processes leading to solutions she hadn't expected. Afterwards she's invigorated and inspired, not drained and tearful.

How could she have been so wrong about Mrs Butterworth?

It's not as if people – including Ali – hadn't tried to tell her. Was it that she knew Mrs Butterworth had lost a daughter? Did that give her some kind of idiotic, misplaced, kindred feeling for her?

No use crying over spilt milk, Kate thinks, knitting. Alicia is doing well with Ian. The immediate problem is how to keep the girl's mind on her work. Kate can hear, from office, kitchen and garden, that Alicia, practising, is repeating things automatically. She's not listening to herself with her usual acuity. She's drilling her muscles; but her imagination is in the stratospheres. She's in love.

Kate saw Dan's withering gaze when she encouraged Alicia not to go out for a day with him and Adrian and Anjali – and she can't deny that her daughter is old enough to drive to Macclesfield for a curry with her friend, brother and boyfriend. Still, a whole day at Chatsworth is too much, and finally Dan let Kate win – 'Actually, Al, your mother's got a point.' An unspoken bargain has materialised between Kate and Dan. He lets her win some battles on condition that, now and then, she concedes him a victory too.

Kate is under no illusions about what's going on upstairs. She hears footsteps at night, the loo flushing at odd hours, an occasional muffled laugh, the creak of a bedspring. Alicia is eighteen; Kate has no right to order her not to sleep with her boyfriend. If she has to have a boyfriend, thank God he's caring, intelligent, understanding and devoted to her. But the devil is in the detail, and the detail is in the timing. With six weeks until Leeds, Alicia is sleeping too little and daydreaming too much.

She takes Dan aside one morning while Alicia is in the shower, and explains rationally and reasonably, Alicia-lover to Alicia-lover.

Dan hears her out. 'I thought you might feel that way,' he admits, 'and I asked Glenda whether, if the need arose, I could rent a room from her for a few weeks. But I think it's a pity for Ali, because we'll have very little time together after Leeds – I have to go back to Indiana. I hear what you're saying, Kate, and I understand, but I'd ask you to think about it a little more, for that reason.'

'I've been watching Ali,' Kate says, 'and I've thought about it a great deal. I think you should give Glenda a call, then pack your things. I like having you here, Dan, but we can't take risks with the Leeds.'

'You know, of course, that it won't make much difference?'

'I think it will, Dan. Because at least Ali will get enough sleep if you're not here. She won't be staying at Glenda's with you.'

When Alicia bounds down, ready to begin her day's work, she finds Dan in the hall with his suitcases. 'What?'

'Your mom.'

Kate braces herself for the onslaught. It's bad: tears, shouts, accusations. Dan tries to calm Alicia, but she weeps as hysterically as if he'd announced he was going back to America, not just moving three streets away. Finally, screaming, 'You're not a mother, you're a *Kamp Kommandant*! Wait till I tell Dad,' Alicia grabs Dan's second suitcase and flies out of the front door. Dan apologises softly to Kate from the front steps, then hurries after her. They leap into Alicia's car and drive away.

Kate waits – picturing them crossing the moor, then crossing the country, putting the car on a boat and sailing to Norway or France or the Hook of Holland. But later there's the crunch of wheels on driveway and Alicia is back, alone, her face tear-streaked. Glenda had comforted them both with tea, and Dan gave her a deposit for the room.

'Wasn't that a little extreme?' Guy says, when he comes home at ten that evening to find Alicia and Kate sitting in silence in the kitchen, without Dan.

'Ali has got to get her focus back,' Kate says.

'Oh, Kate,' Guy says. '*Why?*'

*   *   *

Alicia picks up Dan at half past five the next day, once they've both put in enough hours at their pianos. They drive to Mam Tor and climb to the top.

'This is my favourite place in the world,' Alicia tells him. She watches as he absorbs for the first time the view she knows so well, drinking in the ancient hillscape and the spreading sky.

'I can picture you here as a little girl, in your wellington boots. And maybe a pink coat.'

'Yeah. I had a pink coat once.' Alicia leans her head on his shoulder.

'What are we going to do?' he says.

'I've got an idea. Somewhere we can go. I know all the back routes and the special spots that nobody else knows.' Dan's banishment means that now they have nowhere to make love, for Glenda's house is full of children and pupils and laundry, and Alicia has been issued with a curfew.

'It's left me even more sure than I was,' Dan tells her, while they walk back down the steps to the car. 'We gotta get you out of here. You have to have your own life – preferably with me – somewhere where people talk to each other.'

Alicia swerves off the main road on to a smaller one that skirts the hills with twists and deceptive turns; then a road that is smaller still, transforming itself into a muddy track beside a brook edged with long grass. They pass a group of stone cottages, a barking dog and a field in which some hot but contented sheep are grazing. She turns along another track and a bumpy minute later they reach its end. Here the brook widens into a natural pool beneath a hill; a clump of trees stands close and protective round it.

Alicia switches off the engine. Dan waits.

'What I don't understand is why you take Mum's part in this,' she says finally.

'What can I do, Al? It's her house. I'm a total stranger.'

'That's not the point. She's chucked you out because she doesn't want me to sleep with you.'

'She never tried to stop us before.'

'Because she knew this was the only way.'

'Also, she's right. Leeds is important and you've got to get enough rest.'

'Not to the extent of being in bloody jail. And that's not the reason anyway.'

'What is the reason, then?'

'Don't you see, Dan? She's jealous.'

'What? Of us?'

'Well, of me. Having a gorgeous young lover. Maybe she even fancies you.'

'Ali!'

'I know Mum. I know her too well.'

Dan can't argue with that. Instead, he opens the car door and winks at Alicia.

In a clump of ferns, they throw on the ground the rug Alicia keeps in the boot (Adrian's advice is always to carry a rug, a torch, water and chocolate). Then they throw themselves after it. The landscape around them is deserted: they have no witnesses but a few coots on the water, some fat, late-summer bees and a buzzard gliding far overhead.

'I've always wanted to do this outdoors.' Alicia is kneeling upright on top, stretching out both arms to the sides and soaking up the dappled sunlight.

Her bare skin looks milky, translucent, as though she's never sunbathed in her life. Probably, Dan reflects, she hasn't. 'You only just learned how to do this at all,' he teases her.

'That doesn't mean I didn't want to!'

'Al, come with me to Bloomington.'

'*Dan.* How can I?'

'You talk to Feinstein. You apply. You send in a form and you do an audition so they can make sure you're sane. Then you look for a sponsor or a scholarship – or you get some prize money from the competition you *are* about to win – and, next thing you know, you're on the first plane west.'

'You think Mum will let me go? Do you know how many concerts she's got lined up for me next season?'

'She's nuts. If you win Leeds, you'll have so many concerts you won't know what's hit you. I hope she's left room for those.'

'Oh, God. It's going to be a mess.'

'No, it isn't. It's going to be wonderful.'

'I feel so lost. I don't know what to do.'

'May I make a suggestion?' Dan puts his hands on her waist and turns her over and down.

Walking into the house much later, Alicia confronts her mother's accusing gaze. She stops dead in the hallway. Dan's words about the way people in this house don't talk to each other ring in her mind. Strengthened by love, she no longer feels afraid.

'You've got something in your hair,' Mum says. 'It looks like a bit of fern.'

Alicia takes a deep breath and aims. 'Mum,' she says, 'if you think Dan is the distraction, you're wrong. It's something else.'

'What do you mean?'

'See if you can guess what I've learned.' Alicia makes sure that her tight lips rival her mother's.

'Alicia, what are you talking about?'

'I'm talking about Victoria.'

Mum's colour drains. She's struck silent.

'I need to know things, Mum.'

An avalanche is taking place behind Mum's inscrutable expression. 'Ali,' she says, 'let's sit down a minute.'

They go to the kitchen. Alicia sits at the table. Mum stands behind her so that Alicia can't see her face while she talks.

Alicia listens. She accepts that Mum is leaving nothing out: the difficulty of conceiving, the hated job, the hospital, the flat, the brief little life and its snuffed-out ending, the months of depression afterwards.

'And then,' she finishes, 'your father got a job at the *Manchester Chronicle*, so we moved here and I moved her grave with us.'

'Oh, Mum,' Alicia says, no longer angry but tearful, 'why didn't you tell me?'

'It's a long time ago, love. It's best put behind us.'

'I wish I'd known. All I've been able to think of these past weeks is that I might have had a sister, I mightn't have been so lonely. I've been maybe a substitute for her and no wonder you won't let me out, no wonder you worried whenever I had so much as a cold. It helps me understand. I wish you'd said something years ago.'

'Darling, I did what felt like the right thing at the time. And if I'd had my way, you certainly wouldn't have found out now. When did Dad tell you?'

'He didn't. It was Rebecca.'

'*Rebecca?*'

Alicia explains; as she speaks, a peculiar light of understanding dawns in Mum's eyes. 'Mum?'

'Nothing. Nothing at all . . . Ali, do you think you can get through it now? Do you think you can stop feeling unsettled and get your mind back on to your work now we've had this talk?'

'I'll try,' Alicia promises.

Kate drags herself into her office. The summer evening is fading into night. She sits for a while without turning on the lamp. Finally she reaches for the phone.

'Rebecca? It's Kate . . . Yes, *that* Kate.'

She doesn't stop to think about what Ali is doing while she's gone. She hits the M1 at Derby and makes for the fast lane. Thanks to summer holidays, the London-bound carriageway isn't as clogged as it might have been. Kate has hardly slept. Probably Ali hasn't either, but Kate hadn't waited for her to wake up before she left. Guy has no idea what's happened as he's stayed in Manchester and hasn't called her. Nor is she about to call him at Emily's.

Her mind buzzes like a swarm of wasps while she walks up Kensington High Street. It seems like someone else's hand that presses the bell at the Eden Classics office; another woman, not Kate Bradley, who announces herself to the receptionist and waits, legs crossed, on the leather sofa; and herself merely acting herself when Rebecca appears on the stairs and says, acting too, 'Kate. Do come up.'

Kate thinks, following her, that Rebecca hasn't changed; but in her office, seeing her in the sharper light from the window, she realises that's not true. Rebecca's eyes have grown intent and troubled; she's also thinner. To judge from the ropes that have taken up residence in her arms, she must have been going to the gym even more than usual.

'Ellie will bring coffee,' Rebecca remarks, settling businesslike at her desk. Kate, opposite, sits up straight, puts both feet flat on the floor and stares between Rebecca's eyes.

'So, Kate.' Rebecca moistens her lips. 'I hear nothing from you for nearly a year. Now suddenly you need to see me within twenty-four hours. What's going on? Is this about Ali's new recording?'

'Ali isn't going to make a new recording,' Kate announces, 'but that's not the point. She's a naïve girl. She always thinks the best of people.'

'How nice that *somebody* does.'

'Rebecca, why the fuck did you tell Ali about Victoria? How dare you?'

'Calm down, Kate. Please. It was a mistake.'

'Mistake, my foot. You knew I'd never told them because you asked me, at Chatsworth, the day I made the mistake of telling *you*.'

'But you didn't say they didn't know. You only said, 'We never talk about it.' And I would have thought that since they're grown-up—'

'Oh, you would, would you? Do you have any idea what's been happening since Ali found out? She's not herself. She's distracted. She's having memory lapses. You read the reviews of the Rachmaninov the other week. Don't tell me you didn't.'

'Isn't she preoccupied with the lovely Dan?'

'She says something else is bothering her. The idea that she might have had a sister. Wondering why I never told her. It's affecting her seriously, Rebecca, and don't you tell me you didn't know exactly what you were doing. You can't have Ali, so you've sabotaged her.'

'Kate, hold on.'

'Don't tell me to hold on! You've got the opposite of the Midas touch, Rebecca. You turn everything that's good and beautiful into cheap, third-rate trash, including my daughter.'

'I didn't invite you here so I could listen to this.' Rebecca stands up and makes her way to the door.

'I haven't finished.' Kate seizes Rebecca's wrist, pulling her hand away from the knob.

Rebecca is shocked out of the remnants of her cool. 'I don't have to listen to your crap! You've ruined your family with your lies and your stiff upper lip and your pretending. No wonder your son won't talk to you. No wonder Ali's having problems. It's incredible that any of you manage to stay out of Phyllida's clinic. I'll ask her to put the lot of you on the waiting list.'

Kate hears a noise like a whiplash: her hand against Rebecca's face. Rebecca recoils, clutching her cheek, which bears a red blotch. Silent, she retreats to her chair and puts her head down on the desk.

Kate picks up her handbag.

'Katie. Please don't go.'

Kate stares, contemptuous, at the curve of Rebecca's back.

'You don't understand,' Rebecca says. 'Please don't go.'

'I understand perfectly. Goodbye.'

'No. Listen. You've *no idea*. And if I don't tell you now, I never will. I don't know if I have the courage, but it can't make things worse.' She looks up. Kate is so startled by her expression, not to mention her words, that she stops dead.

She feels peculiarly detached. What a mad, operatic situation – on what is otherwise a plain, sunny summer day off Kensington High Street, with the area's workers, shoppers and tourists going about their business untroubled. Everything is normal around her. Nice and normal.

'I don't know what you're blabbing on about,' she says, staying detached, 'but if you've got to tell me something, then do it, because I'm not coming back.'

'Katie, don't you know?' Rebecca says, her hands cupped over her face. 'Have you no notion of how I feel about you?'

'What?' Despite herself Kate sits down.

'Christ, Kate. Am I such a good actress? I don't think so. I've tried to hide it for a long time. But it's no good.'

'Rebecca, are you saying what I think you're saying?' Rebecca takes down her hands. Kate sees in her eyes a type of anguish that she's only seen once before: on her own face in the mirror after she'd discovered Emily Andersen's emails. 'Becs. No.'

'I think, though I didn't know it at the time, that it was from the first day at college.'

'Don't be silly.'

'No. I swear. I knew there was nothing I could do about it. I saw you and your strait-laced, conservative, churchy, terribly-terribly family. The way you were set on marrying Guy from the start. I knew it was impossible. But we were talking in your room the first day, and you were telling me about your viola and how much you'd loved playing in your youth orchestra, and I suddenly saw something. It wasn't just the physical you, it was something in your soul.

'Insane gibberish.'

'I'll only say this once, Katie. I love you. I only want what's best for you. I thought that if I could help make Ali a success then the money would mean you could get away from Guy and then maybe you'd understand. It wasn't that I expected you to change . . .'

Kate walks over to the window and presses her forehead against it. This can't be real, she reflects. Things like this don't happen to me. I'm Katie Davis from Harrow. I'm Kate Bradley from Buxton. Other women do not fall in love with me. Other women do not destroy my daughter by accident or design in an attempt to get closer to me. She wonders frantically whether to call a doctor, who'd bring a tranquilliser – maybe two tranquillisers; alternatively, the police.

'Becs,' she says, 'what do you expect of me?'

'Nothing, I've never expected anything.'

'In an ideal world, what would you want of me?'

'An ideal world . . . Oh, Kate, it's not an ideal world. End of story. Satisfied?'

'You haven't felt this way since college. It's not possible.'

'I managed to forget about you. I kidded myself into getting married and having the boys. I can't tell you what a relief it was when I threw *him* out. It took me years, decades, to be comfortable with who I really am. There've been others. Plenty of others. Meeting you again, it was different – but also, it was the same. Katie, if I'd had a choice, I promise I'd have chosen otherwise. Just because you haven't experienced something, just because you close yourself to anything beyond what you think is *normal*, that doesn't mean it can't happen to other people.'

Kate holds on to the window-frame with one hand, watching the scene outside. By the end of the road, on the high street, a double-decker bus has half pulled in to a stop, blocking the traffic behind it. A stream of passengers waits at its door: black, white, Middle Eastern, Oriental, some wearing jeans and skimpy T-shirts, others swathed in *hijab* headscarves. You see everything and everyone in London. Around the obtruding bus, drivers are hooting.

'What are you thinking?' Rebecca asks.

Kate watches the bus close its doors and move on. Millions of people, billions in the world, each one living a drama unlike any other. Each a unique mix of world events and intimate psychology, the product of generation upon generation that has struggled or oppressed, survived or squandered, created or destroyed, no two exactly the same. I will soon be fifty, Kate thinks; the world is a different place from the world where my parents grew up. Why should it matter to anyone if my son won't speak to me, my daughter is a musical genius, my husband has a second family, and now my oldest friend tells me she's a lesbian and is in love with me? Why should that be any more extraordinary than the story of any one of those people boarding the number-ten bus on Kensington High Street on a summer afternoon?

'Katie,' Rebecca says, emboldened by Kate's silence and the way she's leaning against the window, 'have you ever stopped to think about who you are? Not who your parents want you to be. Not who you think you have to be for your husband and children. But who you are. Yourself in essence.'

'I've never had time,' Kate says, without turning. 'And, frankly, I've never seen the point.'

23

As Bradley and Rubinstein, alphabetically distant, Alicia and Dan have been housed at opposite ends of the university hall of residence in Headingley. After unpacking, they meet downstairs and set off to explore Leeds.

'It's so cute. I can't get over it,' Dan remarks, looking around as Alicia drives.

'Cute? *Leeds?*' Alicia exclaims.

'Compared to where I come from. It's like being in a box of those things my dad used to collect – Dinky Toys. He had an uncle in London who used to send them over for birthdays and Christmas.'

'You were Jewish and you had Christmas?'

'Sure. Why not?'

'I don't know, I just didn't think you would.'

They chatter their way round the town centre trying to avoid discussing the matters that preoccupy them: pianos, repertoire and the other competitors. Nobody would have guessed they were musicians – but for the way Alicia taps her fingers, as if still practising. For the moment, they've escaped Kate.

After the initial euphoria, though, the intensity of what they must now do begins to dawn on them. Until they are knocked out of the competition, they will work all day every day, occasionally meeting their rivals at breakfast in the student canteen, where the young pianists discuss aching shoulders, repetitive strain injury, likely factions in the jury and fearsome tales from other contests. There'll be no relief from the stress.

Kate is staying at a bed-and-breakfast nearby and drives

over to meet Alicia before the day begins. She fields the attentions of the press officer; Alicia is one of only three British candidates and, with her well-known name, she's number-one target for interested journalists – especially since she's insisted on roping her 'partner', as she now calls Dan, into everything she does. It makes a wonderful story: a British prodigy and her American boyfriend pitted against one another in the country's premier piano competition. Such attention could be detrimental to Ali's concentration.

Leeds's more genteel suburbs are ablaze with enthusiasm for the event, a fixture decades old. Volunteers flock in to drive the contestants around, feed them, let them practise in their houses: Adopt-a-Pianist, Dan jokes. They're like exotic animals, he remarks, lent for temporary pampering. 'Afterwards,' he adds, 'we'll be released back into the wild.'

For daily practising, Alicia has been placed in the care of a retired couple, Leslie and Marina, who have both her CDs and are overjoyed to see her. Dan is down the road with a psychotherapist who owns a Bechstein grand; when she learns that Dan's father is also a psychotherapist, Dan is magically transformed into a member of the family. Glenda, meanwhile, phones him every day to see how he's getting on. Kate has been wondering, troublingly, whether she has ever been truly close to anyone except Rebecca, who fills her thoughts now. She's astounded at the way Dan can make friends so quickly, the way Alicia basks in his warmth, the way he seems so relaxed, practising as hard as anyone else but showing no sign of nerves, let alone competition with Alicia.

'She will,' he tells the journalist from the *Independent*, when she asks who he and Alicia think will win.

'Doesn't it put strain between you?'

'No, it's something we can experience together, something we can share,' Alicia declares. 'We share our dreams.'

'And if he gets through and you don't?'

'That won't happen,' Dan insists. 'Have you heard her play? She's incredible. She lights up the hall.'

Three days later the headline reads LIGHTING UP LEEDS: MUSIC'S NEW GOLDEN COUPLE.

Kate drifts on a lake of helplessness. She has never felt so spare. She takes Alicia and Dan out to dinner on the first evening, but the next day Leslie and Marina invite them for a meal, so she's redundant. The press officer quietly suggests that it might be best if she did not sit in on the interview for the *Independent*. When Alicia walks through the university campus on her own or with Dan, people bound up to her – other competitors, local fans, even one or two of the jurors. When Kate is with her, they don't. Kate can't even serve as chauffeur, since Alicia had insisted on bringing her own car, which, Kate senses, has come to symbolise freedom for her. Sometimes she wishes they'd never bought it.

To pass the time, she goes to listen to the other pianists in the first round, performing one after another in the university's Great Hall. It's not human, she reflects, watching a Russian girl strut to the piano at nine a.m. and play Chopin's Barcarolle. This music wasn't designed to be performed and appreciated in a draughty Victorian cavern at an unearthly hour, with a smattering of audience and a row of beady-eyed jurors listening for every fault. Surely this has nothing to do with music, its meaning, its communication? Whatever the critics thought about Ali's CDs, those discs existed to bring pleasure and insight to their listeners. They weren't part of any stressful, artificial Olympiad. But this is the nature of piano competitions, here and everywhere.

The pianists are good. Very good. Every one is a fully fledged musician, finely trained, determined and driven by vocation. But after the first round, just thirty-three will be left. Fifty-six will have to go home. By the concerto final, only six will remain.

Kate tries to concentrate, but it's not easy. Before long the pianists begin to merge in her mind. The perpetual onslaught of the piano sets up a ringing inside her ears. She starts to take longer coffee breaks – perhaps it doesn't matter if she doesn't hear every last performer. Sipping coffee in the competition tea room, she tries to shake off the strain. She wonders how the jury must feel if that's how she reacts, simply as someone's mother. And how frightening to think that at almost every piano competition in every corner of the globe young musicians are facing this same situation again and again, fighting simply for the chance to be heard, while the outside world shows ever fewer signs of caring twopence for their hard-won art.

The competition's octogenarian founder, Fanny Waterman, is chairman of the jury, a fierce, intently focused figure; beside her sits Dan's professor, Eugene Feinstein from Bloomington. Feinstein, his face remarkably youthful despite his age, has bright blue eyes and a ready smile. Now and then, when they encounter a moment of boredom or depression, he leans across to his fellow jurors and makes them laugh.

Guy phones Alicia every evening, but he's not coming to the competition. He doesn't have time. Alicia's face had shown pain as clear as Buxton water when she discovered he wouldn't be there. Of course, Kate thinks bitterly, if she gets to the final, he'll come to that. When it's important enough.

Alicia is to take her turn shortly before dinner on the third day. Kate feels someone sit down next to her after the tea break. She turns: it's Anjali.

'Darling!' she exclaims. Anjali hugs her. She's looking thinner than ever, Kate notices, and her eyes are bright, though not with happiness.

'I haven't missed her, have I?' Anjali asks. 'The bus was late.'

'No, she's on third.'

Dan clatters across the chairs to join them. 'How're you doing?' he asks Anjali, hugging her.

'OK. Good to see you.'

Kate sees Dan glance at Anjali with the shrewd look that she, for one, has learned to respect. Dan sees things as they are; you ignore that gaze at your peril.

'I can't tell you how glad I am not to be doing this,' Anjali whispers.

'I wish I weren't,' Dan grunts good-naturedly. 'Anji, how's your dad?'

Kate has become used to seeing pain on Alicia's face at the mention of her father, but that pain is only a fraction of what she sees on Anjali's now. All Anjali says, though, is, 'Oh, I'll tell you later.'

Alicia sails across the platform as naturally as a dolphin amid phosphorescent waves. Thanks to her substantial performing experience, she looks more at home on stage than off it, unlike some of the others. She launches straight into Beethoven's Sonata Op.90. Kate relaxes. Alicia's playing at her best, bringing the mood, the tension and the layers of melodic lines into vivid relief, the tone rich and the phrasing, in Kate's opinion, perfect. Kate notices Fanny Waterman sitting forward, her laser-beam gaze on Alicia's every move. Eugene Feinstein folds his arms behind his head, a broad smile on his face.

Kate smiles too. What audience there is has come to be supportive; Ali's host couple, Leslie and Marina, are watching her as if she's the Angel Gabriel. She senses Dan sending energy to Ali, experiencing every note with her, and she feels a rush of gratitude towards him. Everyone there, apart from the jury, is on Ali's side. At least Mrs Butterworth has not staged an invasion, something Kate had dreaded. She is rumoured to hate Leeds with a passion – the result, according to Ian, of never having been invited to sit on its jury.

Kate had also half dreaded – irrationally – that Rebecca would turn up, because she can't cope with the thought of what might happen if she did. Rebecca's image flickers in her mind when she wakes up in the morning and when she attempts

to sleep at night. She tries to concentrate on Ali playing
Chopin's A flat major Étude. A simple, tender melody sails
over an inner waterfall of sound, a countermelody flickering
like a broken reflection in the tenor register beneath the surface.
She remembers Ali listening, entranced, as Guy played Chopin
all those years ago; she'd called the composer Mr Shopping.
Little Ali with her golden hair, her dog, her instinct for love.

Alicia walks off stage. The next contestant walks on. Kate,
Anjali and Dan slink out of the hall.

'Thank God that's over,' says Alicia, when they find each
other. 'Anyone want to go and eat?'

On the way out, they bump into two Russian contestants with
whom Dan has struck up a friendship, and invite them to
come out for curry. Anjali knows the best Indian restaurants
in Leeds, so she goes with Kate to direct her; Alicia drives
behind them, with a carload of pianists.

The restaurant's red walls are decorated with paintings, for
sale, by a local artist. Dan and the Russian girl, Natasha, enthuse
about them. Alicia stares at Natasha – tiny and fair, with a
charming Russian accent. Natasha clearly likes the look of
Dan, which in turn doesn't much please the Russian boy,
Sergei. Who'd be their age again, thinks Kate.

Not that things change that much, deep down. She may be
forty-eight, but since her encounter with Rebecca in London,
the heart that she'd thought sclerotic has been showing her
that it's still capable of the flaying emotion, comprised of pain,
wonder and confusion, that seems so terrifying when you're
young, despite its beauty. The only difference, being older, is
that you should know what to expect next, more or less. She
is on such new emotional territory, though, that ideas about
the next step elude her. She doesn't believe in half of the
shadows her mind is casting across her. It's not possible to
feel such things for a former friend, another woman. Not for
her. So she reminds herself countless times each day; but again

and again, her dreams tell her different stories, leaving her frightened, mystified and wakeful.

Sergei is saying that he isn't Russian at all. 'I'm a Tatar,' he declares, 'like Rudolf Nureyev.'

'So your ancestors have probably killed mine,' Natasha points out, fending off his attentions. 'I am ethnic Russian,' she explains to the others. 'Is not as common as people think.'

'Come on, your people oppressed mine for centuries!' Sergei protests. 'We Tatars endured so much abuse, we were the poor servants, the bloody foreigners, the outsiders.'

'I thought the Tatars were warriors.' Alicia beams at him. Sergei is extremely good-looking: his eyes are as black as night. 'Didn't they have a reputation for marauding?'

'That's us. Marauding Tatars! Yes, we were horsemen and warriors.'

'And Muslims.' Natasha wears a large jewelled cross round her neck.

'Muslim Schmuslim.' Sergei winks at Dan, who's been having fun teaching him a little rudimentary Yiddish. 'I don't believe in any religion crap. Look what religion's done to our world.'

'I am devout Orthodox Christian.' Natasha has a limited sense of humour.

'Hey,' Dan interrupts, 'you guys think you oppressed each other? What about what all you lot did to my ancestors in the Ukrainian *shtetls*? When you weren't busy killing each other, you were raping and murdering my great-great-grandparents.'

'And what about the British Empire, oppressing everyone else?' Sergei takes over. 'You, ladies,' to Kate and Alicia, 'are from a background that made a big, big mess out of America and the Middle East and India! So anyone here who wasn't oppressed by you –' pointing at Natasha '– was oppressed by *you*!' indicating them.

'Even we're not that English,' Kate interjects. 'My grandparents had blood that was Celtic, French and Scandinavian.

If you go far enough back, there's no such thing as "English". We're a great big mix of the different cultures that have settled here over the centuries.'

'Just think where we all come from,' Anjali says, declining Natasha's offer of a poppadom. 'Look at this table. We're a British Indian, a Tatar, an ethnic Russian, an American Jew and two English-ish women, sitting in an Indian restaurant run by Pakistanis in Yorkshire, arguing about who oppressed whom the most! Do you realise this is probably the only time in history when tonight would have been possible?'

'And we're all united by one thing,' Sergei adds. 'We're only here because we love music.'

'If you think about it,' Alicia says, 'music is one of the greatest forces for good in the world. It brings people together, like us, when we'd have nothing in common otherwise. And I remember Dad talking about a journalist who'd been to Sarajevo to watch a music-therapy project for children traumatised in the war – she said music helped them in a way that nothing else could. Music does so many positive things, but it gets bad publicity because there's this daft idea that it isn't "cool". What's "cool" anyway? It's so stupid. It doesn't mean anything. It just comes from people who started out as bullies in the school playground. People who didn't like anyone who was a little different.'

'Is it true that someone at your school put glass in your handbag, Ali?' Sergei asks.

'Yes. I've still got a bit of a scar. Look.' Alicia holds her hand out towards him and points.

He draws in his breath. 'This is crazy. In Russia we have special music schools. People love music and respect musicians. It's a great tradition, a big talent and a lot of work.'

'Oh, people love and respect music and musicians here too,' Alicia says, 'but only as long as you're not too good at it.'

The food arrives, a selection of steaming wonders: chicken in a sauce rich with coconut and almonds, lamb amid onions and tomatoes, a tandoori dish, trays of golden pilau rice, spiced spinach and potato, a vegetable biryani for Anjali, who doesn't eat meat, and several broad, bumpy naan breads. The pianists fall upon the feast in delight. Kate and Anjali smile at each other.

'What's going on with your dad?' Kate asks her.

'It's bad.' Anjali stares into her plate as if she isn't seeing it. 'It's very bad. Has Adrian said anything to you?'

'Adrian doesn't talk to me.'

'Silly boy,' Anjali sighs. 'Well, my dad doesn't want me to talk to Adrian. He doesn't want me to go out with English boys. What am I supposed to do? I live in Britain. I grew up in Britain. We left India when I was two years old and I went to a British primary school and a British boarding-school, and this is my country. Now he wants me not to be part of it, not to behave like other girls. I asked him, "Daddy, if you want me only to be Indian, why didn't we stay in India? Why do we live in Birmingham? And why do you want me to be a pianist, to have a career playing Western music, if I can't have a Western life too?" But he's so angry. I'm afraid every time I go out anywhere. I'm afraid whenever my mobile-phone bill arrives that he'll grab it and see how many times I've called Adrian.'

'You have to move out, Anji,' Alicia says.

'At least I'm going to uni next month but he expects me to go home every weekend. Because it's only Manchester, you see, he thinks that nothing will change. He'll still be in charge of me.'

'And your mom?' Dan asks.

'There's nothing she can do. She's under his thumb. If things are bad she'll hug me and comfort me, as long as he doesn't tell her not to. If he does, she'll listen to him.'

There's a moment of shocked, depressed silence.

'But he was always so kind to me,' Alicia says. 'He was so friendly when we came to visit. I thought you were the perfect family. I was envious that your father was so much with you and so interested in what you did.'

'Yes, and he loved it when I was best friends with the Young Musician of the Year. Now I'm friendly with her brother, he doesn't like it so much.'

'So he has this idea of what your life should be, and all of a sudden you're not complying with it any more,' says Dan.

'Exactly. And he can't talk about it with me. All he can do is be angry.'

'Children never *do* do what parents think they should,' Kate points out.

'Not even me?' Alicia ripostes. Kate winces at the sarcastic edge in her voice.

Just then the waiter comes over, carrying two bottles of red wine. 'Excuse me, madam,' he says to Alicia, 'the two gentlemen at the table in the window have asked me to bring these to you and your friends.'

Dan jumps to his feet and goes over to the two men: they turn out to be retired locals who adore the competition and attend every round. They've been listening since the start, and correctly identify all four pianists, remembering exactly which pieces each has played. There's much pouring of wine, glass-raising and toasting and, in the general geniality, the moments of darkness slide away, at least temporarily forgotten.

Three days later the pianists accepted for the second round are announced. Alicia, Dan and Sergei are through. Natasha is not, although she'd reached the semi-finals at a Russian competition, one of the biggest in the world, where Sergei had been eliminated in round one.

'Her teacher is like the Mafia there.' He shrugs when Alicia expresses astonishment. 'Of course she got through and I didn't. In Russia it's impossible to get anywhere in a competition unless you have the right teacher.'

'Seriously?'

'Of course. Didn't you *know*?' Sergei gives Alicia a withering look.

'I don't really know anything,' she says, making herself smile. 'I just play the piano.'

'You'd better learn something, my girl. It's a tough, nasty world.' Sergei shakes his head. Alicia watches him walk away and bites her lip.

'Do you think that sort of thing goes on here?' she asks Dan, squeezing into her hall-of-residence bed with him that night.

'I bet there are people who think I got through because Feinstein is on the jury.'

'Oh, Dan, you didn't, did you?'

'What do you think? You heard me.'

'I thought you played *wonderfully*.'

'Not that you're biased.' Dan presses his nose to her neck. 'Tomorrow I'm going to introduce you to him properly. Now so many people are going home, it'll be a little easier to catch him with some time.'

'Dan? I played OK, didn't I?'

'You played like an angel.'

'I didn't have any of the problems I thought I'd have. And you know why? I think being away helps. Not being stuck at home in that – that *house*.'

'Being able to spend the nights with me?'

'I like that too.'

'Come on, love, it's nearly two o'clock. We'd better get some sleep.'

Alicia turns off the light. 'Trouble is, Dan, right now I prefer being awake to being asleep.'

Kate, lying under a thin green sheet in the bed-and-breakfast, is having the opposite problem. She longs to sleep, but can't. When she dozes, she dreams: she, not Alicia, is on the platform, playing in the competition, and the jury consists of her parents, her children, Guy, Lucien, Rebecca and Victoria. She hasn't learned the music they expect her to play, and she knows she will lose her way and make mistake after mistake.

She'd felt like a spare part at dinner and hasn't felt much better since. Everyone else is looking after Alicia: her boyfriend, Leslie and Marina, the new friends with whom, despite the competitive situation, she's enjoying a social scene she's rarely encountered before. Kate has work to do – organisation for the season ahead – and Cassie has to go to the vet for a check-up on her arthritis. Alicia doesn't need her. Perhaps she should go home.

She's trying harder than ever not to think about Rebecca. Let that particular cat out of its bag and it will grow into a tiger; nobody will ever be safe again. Perhaps I'm going crazy, Kate thinks, falling asleep at last.

'Gene,' says Dan, standing in a splash of sunshine outside the hall, 'this is Alicia.'

Eugene Feinstein smiles down at her – he is extremely tall. She has never seen such an intent face or such bright, *seeing* eyes. It's as if he's trying to assess the complete span of her mind in a single glance. 'How nice to meet you,' he says. 'Dan has been telling me about you. I understand you may want to come to Bloomington.'

'Well, yes, if my mum'll let me,' Alicia says. She can't be less than frank with this man. If she tries, his gaze will x-ray through her.

'I hope you'll consider it,' he says. 'After hearing you play the other day, I can tell you that I would be only too happy to have you in my class.'

The class, he explains, is more than a lesson for each student. It's a community under his guidance. Everybody listens to every lesson; and beyond the studio they become close friends, encouraging each other without any sense of competition. If she were to go there, she'd be a 'freshman' while Dan, who's just graduated, is to start a masters' programme that will begin to qualify him to teach. But for Eugene, learning about music is learning about music: they work as a group, almost a team, benefiting from one another no matter their official placement.

'It sounds like *paradise*,' Alicia says.

Eugene Feinstein laughs. 'Well, maybe not,' he remarks, 'but I think, Alicia, that you'd like being with us in our little world; and you would get along easily with the others. We're all like-minded musicians. Your Beethoven told me everything I needed to know: you understand what it means to be in a state of grace – even if you don't realise that you understand.'

'How do you mean?' Alicia says, bemused, eyes shining.

'Come and join us, and you'll see. There'll be a place for you, if you want it. Good luck with round two.' He stoops and kisses her on both cheeks.

'Thank you, Professor Feinstein,' Alicia breathes, watching the lanky figure of Dan's teacher striding away.

'You see?' Dan says. 'He's a guru.'

'He's got an aura, hasn't he?'

'Exactly. And what we do in class is absorb it. It almost doesn't matter what he says. We learn from him just because he's him. He can spend two hours talking about the first line of a piece from every angle. Spirit, technique, sound, philosophy, history, literature. You name it, he does it.'

Alicia wonders how on earth she will get the words 'Mum, I want to study in the States,' past her lips. But she soon finds she doesn't have to – not yet. She waits for Mum. When she doesn't arrive, Alicia calls her mobile.

Kate has checked out of her bed-and-breakfast and gone home to Buxton. She says she'll come back for the semi-finals if Alicia gets through. Alicia is so startled that she almost cries. Five minutes later, though, she feels liberated; she wants to run headlong across the campus, throw herself into the air and fly, the way she used to dream of flying with Cassie towards the horizon.

'I've found a room with two pianos,' Dan tells her. 'Let's go and bash through some Rachmaninov.'

24

Alicia can't sleep. Her head is being assaulted by a muddle of music and new impressions that feels bigger than she is.

She's through to the semi-final. Dan isn't. Although he insists he's not disappointed, she's sure he must be. She declares that his elimination isn't fair; he insists she mustn't think about it, but simply concentrate on her own performance. At least, since he had been in the second round, he's allowed to stay and listen to the rest of the competition. But meanwhile pictures of the pair of them are everywhere. The newspapers love them, especially since Alicia is the only British pianist left in the contest, and a northerner to boot: a local heroine. Even Dad has swallowed his pride and run a story about them. They'd arrived virtually anonymous; now the whole of Leeds recognises them. The roller-coaster feels extreme even to Alicia.

When she does sleep, she dreams. About losing Dan in the current of a fast-flowing river. About Dad – that she's looking for him, can't find him and never will. About Mum – which is the worst because she's always doing something she would never do, such as trying to put a plastic carrier-bag over Cassie's head. She dreams about Cassie, dreading that she'll die soon. And she worries about Grandma Didie, whose health is deteriorating for reasons nobody will tell her outright, though Alicia has heard the word 'cancer' whispered when Mum, on the phone, thought she wasn't listening. Alicia can't imagine a life without Grandma or Cassie, but there will be one, and she can do nothing to change that. She can scarcely bear her burgeoning consciousness of life's fragility.

She worries about Adrian and Anjali, because they're going out together behind Anjali's parents' back. And more often than not, they go out on the motorbike. Alicia knows that Adrian doesn't have a licence. Everyone must assume that he does – how else could he work in the shop, advise the customers and hang out with Josh and his gang? With no licence, Dan has pointed out, he probably has no insurance either. Alicia once told Adrian he's crazy, but he shot back that if she dares not get on the back of the bike for even a short ride, she shouldn't order him about. She told him that no way would she get on the back of a motorbike with someone who has no licence and no insurance, even if he is her brother. She'd warned Anjali, too, but to no avail. Adrian, Anjali insisted, rides as if he's been doing it all his life; she has absolute confidence in him.

It's nearly three a.m. Dan is asleep; Alicia watches him. His breathing is quiet now that he's turned on to his side – he only snores on his back. Fragility rips at the palms of her hands; her eyes twinge with unshed tears. It's almost as if the point of the world's existence and of the universe spinning through space is that he can be here and she can watch him, love him, knowing that they belong together. She'd never have believed she could love someone so much.

Mum, phoning her, had asked after Dan. Alicia told her how supportive he is, how uncompetitive, how loving; and that even if she gets nowhere in the competition, her weeks here with him have been the happiest she can remember. She'd expected a piano-focused tirade in response – but instead Mum just sighed and said, 'Enjoy, darling,' her voice full of edgy longing and regret.

Alicia understands. Such a love is something they may never find again. Whether in the end they stay together or not, this is an experience that she must treasure like sacred fire while it lasts. She puts an arm over Dan's chest and closes her eyes. She wonders, falling asleep, why Mum is changing.

On a cream-coloured sofa in Hampstead Garden Suburb, Kate sits next to Rebecca. Table lamps cast bronze glints across their nearly-empty wineglasses. The boys are spending the weekend with their father; the two women are alone at home for the first time. Now and then the blue eyes fix upon the brown, wondering, frightened.

Kate's hands are twisted so tightly together that she's hurting her wrists. She's not sure how she got there, how her resistance ran out, how Rebecca has coaxed her to London, what may happen later, or how she will get through it, or, alternatively, escape, if it does. But there is another choice besides fight or flight: acceptance. Acceptance with, possibly, joy – assuming she can remember how to feel it.

'Have a little more wine.' Rebecca pours. 'I've got news for you,' she adds. 'About Lucien. He's been a very naughty boy.'

'What? More than usual?' The distraction, for Kate, is welcome.

'Oh, yes. He got a girl pregnant. A student.'

'Jesus.'

'She won't terminate. Lucien had to tell his girlfriend and, of course, she left him right away. He's devastated.'

'That's his own fault, *n'est-ce pas*?'

'*Bien sûr*. Katie, I know Guy is a paragon in comparison, but . . .'

'There's something you don't know.' Kate takes a long sip of wine.

'What?'

'I shouldn't tell you this.'

'Oh, Katie. Out with it.'

Kate can't help herself any longer: she reaches out a hand. Rebecca takes it. Their palms press together and Kate senses a strength, a confidence, an honesty that reminds her of her far-off early days with Guy. She begins to tell Rebecca about Emily Andersen.

'My God,' Rebecca says, at the end. 'Why didn't you kick him out?'

'I couldn't let him leave. Not with Ali's career at such a crucial stage.'

'And Ali doesn't know any of this?'

'Of course not.'

'Katie.' Rebecca interlaces her fingers with Kate's. Kate tenses. 'What exactly do you think she's going to do when she finds out? You can't keep it from her for ever.'

'Oh, Becs, I'm afraid I've done everything wrong, but I can't turn the clock back, I can't undo what's done and I can't do anything to put it right.'

'You could do some damage limitation. The way she found out about Victoria was bad – I'm guilty, I know, and I apologise. But you've got to stop it happening again. Once the competition is over, you must sit Ali down and be honest with her about her father. Next, you have to let him go. You'll be better off without him.'

'It's got to the point where I can't stand being in the same room with him, let alone the same bed. But it's been going on so long that I don't know how to change it. And if Ali wins Leeds, there'll never be a right time. Oh, God, how have I let things get so bad?'

'Hush, Katie . . . let me hold you.'

Kate flinches.

'Katie. It's not a big deal. We won't do anything if you'd rather not.'

Kate presses her hands to her face. 'Maybe it's not a big deal for you,' she says, 'but I've never slept with anybody except Guy.'

She looks at Rebecca's sinewy shoulders, her shiny, cropped hair, her open arms. Above all, the warmth in her eyes. The beseeching love that she sees there is real, and its existence casts her, spinning, into an unmapped solar system. Her instinct is to run. This is unfamiliar. Dangerous. Wrong, in a deep moral way.

Or is it? Is genuine love ever wrong? It's so rare. It's so precious; when you find it, how can you push it away? She can move forward, or she can move back. She's forty-eight years old, the mother of two young adults, yet she's trembling at the idea of touching another person for the first time. She begins to move back.

Then she moves forward. Normally, wanting anything so much makes her do the opposite, because it's too much to cope with. But now she understands she no longer has anything to lose. She lets herself go towards Rebecca; and she feels her silk blouse against her cheek and the gentle arms cradling her shoulders, and whatever is going to happen next, she's as terrified as if she's being led to the scaffold. Rebecca moves her mouth upon her own and for the first time the fear inside her begins to drown. Beyond the river is a new degree of hope that has nothing to do with her family, and everything to do with a self that she'd never known was there.

Adrian meets Anjali at Macclesfield station. It's Saturday, and as soon as he'd closed the shop, he'd hotfooted it to find her waiting for him near the ticket office. The blue gleam on her black hair, the sweetness of the light in her eyes when she sees him approaching, they thrill him every time. Adrian has gone out with plenty of girls, especially since he's joined the biking crowd and had a place and a salary of his own, modest though they are. But his little sister's best friend is different from the ones on whom he had, metaphorically speaking, cut his teeth. He'd lusted after pale bare legs, scarcely concealed by microskirts; midriffs gleaming beneath breasts enhanced with padded bras; straightened, lightened hair plastered with shiny stuff that reflects the glare in the clubs where they go to dance. Anjali is from another world.

She's a jewel to him, not just for the street cred he gains for being with an Indian girl, not just for her beauty, deepened by the tragedy that traces its shadow upon her face. He loves going to bed with her, even if he does have to take her home afterwards, but it's more than that: he loves her company. He likes having her beside him, with her sober expression that can unexpectedly blossom into a smile, her small hand resting quietly on his arm. How can she play the piano so well with such tiny hands?

After an hour or two in Adrian's bedsit, they take a shower together, then climb on to the bike and head up to the Cat and Fiddle for the evening. There they meet Josh and Charlie and their girlfriends, who are fascinated by Anjali's stories about the music school where she'd studied and her visits to her grandparents in India, where she'd had to avoid being match-made. Adrian shows off about his sister, who's going to be on TV again – the Leeds semi-finals, in which she'll play tomorrow, will be filmed for broadcast on a BBC digital channel.

The evening had started warm. It is neither still summer nor quite autumn. The sinking sun melts gold over the moor and the scents of distant hay and damp earth are pungent in the air. The warmth vanishes with the sun and clouds start to blow in from the north; but inside the pub the group of youngsters is too absorbed in its conversation and its beer to notice.

Anjali sits with one hand on Adrian's leather shoulder. Their shadows on the wallpaper blend together, streamlined. The beer tastes malty and wheat-laden, refreshing after Adrian's long day minding the shop on his own (his boss is away in the classier part of Ibiza), not to mention the exertion of some fantastic sex. Tomorrow the guys are planning a race all the way across the moor. Adrian, Charlie and Josh talk biking gear and the crazy price of petrol. The girls swap stories about their summer holidays. Adrian sees Josh assessing Anjali. All he'll say will be 'Nice girl, that one,' but from Josh that's praise indeed.

A bell rings for last orders; after a final pint before closing time, they get up to go. The boys load the girls on to the backs of the motorbikes in the car park, where the rain has begun to form great puddles round them. The girls grumble about the wet weather; the boys steel themselves to be strong and capable.

'See you tomorrow,' Adrian shouts, waving to his friends.

'Mind how you go,' Charlie shouts back. Anjali, waving too, fastens the helmet that Adrian's lent her – it's a little too large, but then, as Adrian has joked many times, her head is a little too small.

'Hold tight, Anji.'

'Ready when you are!'

Adrian kicks the engine into gear and they're off on to the A537. It's almost midnight and the wind is rising. Her arms circle his waist, holding on tighter than usual. Adrian screws up his eyes; the road ahead is a blur of black Tarmac, sheep shit and rainwater. It's better travelling after dark, he always thinks, because at least when cars are coming you can see the headlights in good time. It's twilight that's truly deceptive, not the night.

'Slow down a little?' Anjali shouts through the wind, behind him.

'I want to get you home out of this rain!' he shouts back. He negotiates the trickiest bends in the road with his usual expertise; this is said to be the most dangerous road in Britain, but that's only because people do daft things on it, like over-taking in the wrong place. If you don't do daft things, you don't get into trouble.

As they twist and turn, Anjali's warm body presses into his back; the feeling arouses him and he wishes he could stop the bike and fuck her again right there. He's trying to get his head around a fact that bothers him badly: he's in love with this girl. He doesn't know how to tell her, even whether he should tell her. If she knows, if he gives her that power over him, won't she walk on him, use him and dump him? She'll go to uni soon, she'll meet other blokes, maybe more intellectual ones – all the pair of them really have in common is Ali. What will he do? He doesn't want to be without her. Things are hard enough already. Her father won't let him into the house.

'We've got to make a plan to deal with your dad,' he shouts through the helmet.

'I can't hear you,' Anjali shouts back.

'I said we've got to—'

Why it should be then that the animal appears, in the split second when Adrian turns his head the merest fraction to talk to Anjali, nobody can ever know. The sheep is large, pale as a ghost in the night, its face blank and unaware as it trots off the moor into the rainy road. Adrian doesn't even have time to swerve.

Morning streams into Rebecca's bedroom. It's been pouring most of the night, but no longer; now the ripening apples in the garden are brilliant with sun-trapping raindrops. The scent of fresh-ground coffee drifts up to Kate, who lies luxuriating under the duvet after the best night's sleep she's had in years.

'Here we go,' Rebecca says, carrying in a tray of oat biscuits and steaming mugs. 'This is my secret breakfast passion: dunking biscuits.'

'You're spoiling me,' Kate mumbles.

'You deserve spoiling.'

Rebecca is wearing a brown silk dressing-gown embroidered with a Chinese dragon. Kate gazes at the slender curve of her neck and shakes herself slightly. She can't believe she won't wake up a second time and find she's dreamed this entire episode.

'Here's your phone,' Rebecca says. 'It was in the lounge. It's beeping. You've got a message.'

Kate puts the phone aside. She sits up against the pillow, sips her coffee and dunks her biscuit.

'How do you feel?' Rebecca leans over and gives her a slow kiss.

Kate looks at her, smiling helplessly. She can't find the words. Rebecca laughs. The phone shrills out a signal, insistently indicating that Kate has missed four calls. 'It must be Ali,' she says. 'I should let her know I'll be there by lunchtime.'

'When's she playing?'

'Five. She's the last one this afternoon. Let me deal with the phone and then we can have some peace.' She presses a key to access her voicemail.

'Katie?' Rebecca says, watching her face as she listens.

Guy is hunting for his brown shoes in Emily's flat when the phone rings.

'Your shoes are here,' Emily shouts, running to answer it.

'Emily?' comes a strange woman's voice.

'Speaking.'

'Emily, this is Kate.'

'Hello, Kate,' Emily says. Guy, tying his shoe, freezes.

'I need Guy, urgently. It's bad news. Is he with you?'

Ingrid is whimpering and shouting, 'Mama!' in the back room; Guy knows that Kate will be able to hear her. He darts to the phone.

'Guy, sorry to call you at Emily's. Your mobile wasn't on. I found Emily in the phone book.'

'What's the matter? Where are you?'

'I'm in London, at Rebecca's. Listen. It's bad. Adrian's in hospital in Macclesfield. He came off his bike. He hit a sheep in the night. Anjali was with him.'

'Oh, my God.'

'He's unconscious, Guy.'

'I'll go right away. When will you be there?'

'I'm setting out now. I was going to go to Leeds for Ali's semi-final, but I can't.'

'Kate, we shouldn't tell Ali about this until after she's played.'

'Yes.'

'So you should be there.'

'How can I?' Kate's voice cracks. 'I have to go to Adrian. I can't not. Will you go to Leeds instead of me? Can you get away?'

'Tell Ali you've been held up, but that I'll be there. I'll go to the hospital now and when you arrive I'll go to Leeds. OK? Kate, he'll be all right.'

'He'll be all right,' Kate echoes. He can tell she doesn't believe it any more than he does. Dashing to the door, he realises he hadn't asked whether Anjali was injured.

'Darling,' Emily says, 'let me come with you. You mustn't go all that way on your own.' He knows she's silently terrified of the stress that this appalling development will put on his damaged heart. She doesn't want him alone behind the wheel of a car.

'Ingy,' he says.

'We'll bring her. I'm not letting you go on your own.'

'You're an angel. I'll call you from the hospital.'

'*No*, Guy, I'm coming too. I'll wait outside with her, if you prefer. But I'm coming too.'

25

Alicia is lying on the floor backstage, thinking herself into her music. Her recital programme is seventy minutes long, as required. First, Beethoven's 'Waldstein' Sonata, launching her in, cranking up the energy right away; then Chopin, two Ballades, popular but fantastic. Next, the contemporary piece that the competition obliges everyone to play; luckily she likes it. Last, French music: a group of Debussy Preludes and some Messiaen, her new favourite since she'd learned that he'd had synaesthesia. She's been devouring books about him, reading about how he visualised his delicious, scrunchy chords as orange, purple and grey flecked with pink. She wishes she could have met him; it's only twelve years since he died. Dan's been helping her, recommending articles and CDs. One day he'll be a marvellous teacher, like Professor Feinstein. She dreams: a circle of like-minded friends gathered round a wise professor and a piano, while outside the plains of the Midwest spread out to the far horizon.

A text message has told her that Mum is stuck in London with car trouble.

'Al?' Dan appears in the doorway. 'Your dad's here. I just saw him.'

'Cripes,' Alicia says, getting up. 'It takes a lot to get Dad away from his office.'

'It's not every day your daughter plays in the Leeds semi-final.' Dan winks.

'How long have I got?'

'You're on in ten. Break a leg, honey. I'm with you.'

'I know you are.' She kisses him and reaches for her brush.

Her hair hangs loose and straight down her back. She's wearing a plain, purply-blue dress, not too glittery for late afternoon; Dan's silk wrap stays round her shoulders until the last moment. She's cleared her mind of everything but the music. Nothing must put her off her stride today; even if she doesn't make it to the final, this will be her ultimate audition for Eugene Feinstein. She's playing today for him, for Dan, and – for once – her father. Perhaps her music has worked the magic it used to work when she was a small child: it's brought her father to her.

There's a crash of applause as she walks to the piano and bows. The hall is full; a quick sweep of her gaze suggests that every seat is taken. She glimpses a figure remarkably like Phyllida, but can't see Dad or Dan. She doesn't look at the jurors or the TV cameras. She focuses on the keyboard: her element, her home. She lifts her hands, feels the low C major chord starting to depress under her fingertips, hears the first bars in her mind, then leaps, plunging into the sea.

She knows from the first note that nothing can go wrong. She's flying. She's in complete control, showing the music to her audience, telling them the story of Beethoven's power and tenderness, the way he plays with the planets and speaks with the voice of spectral, eternal wisdom. She's fitted her own silent words to the final movement's shining melody: 'Sing out – the ancient story; sing out – the age-old song . . .' Its aural tapestry thrills her ears while her hands dance. She can feel the audience coming to her, giving back their love to refresh hers. She's soaring high as an eagle by the end; she can't wait to get back and play her Chopin. She sails through her two Ballades – No. 3 no longer conjures up riding over the moors, because now she knows that its rocking motion is simply the cradling tenderness of true love. No. 4 frightens her, but with a fear she adores: she imagines it as a great classical tragedy, like Dante's Francesca da Rimini, a crime of passion punished with eternal hellfire.

At the end the audience yells, wanting her to continue, but it's time for a break. She retreats backstage and lies on the floor for a few minutes, resting her arms, her back and, as far as she dares to, her brain, before the second part. She gets through the contemporary piece easily enough. Then she lets her beloved Debussy bathe her in mother-of-pearl and sparkling spiderwebs. And at last, her Messiaen, one of the most difficult pieces from his *Vingt Regards sur l'enfant Jésus* – 'Regard de l'Esprit de joie'. The spirit of joy. Alicia has learned a thing or two about joy recently and she lets rip. The piece is so complicated that it makes Balakirev's 'Islamey' sound like a nursery rhyme. She loves every note of it, has pulled it into herself until she can play it by instinct, not calculation. It's wild, volcanic, roaring with ecstasy, love physical and spiritual in equal measure, uniting her with the immortal soul that pulses through all humanity. Alicia flings the last downward flourish out to her audience and the final note resounds into the ether, deep, true and triumphant.

The sea surges about her, a crashing wave of crazy applause. She walks out of the water, damp, elated, exhausted. The audience is standing, stamping. Eugene Feinstein is smiling out from the middle. Dan is yelling, 'Bravo,' from the side. Leslie and Marina, who've been so good to her, are in the front row, tears in their eyes. Alicia raises her arms, radiating. She's never played better, which means that she's never been happier. Whatever happens next, even if she isn't allowed into the final, she's won her own war.

She walks offstage, her head filled with the ringing piano and the roaring audience. She puts down the flowers Leslie and Marina have sent her and waits for Dan. There's an agonising minute while she is entirely alone, forgotten. Perhaps nobody heard her; perhaps she hadn't played well at all. A second later, a figure in jeans and cotton shirt bursts through the door and she is in Dan's arms.

'You've done it!' He's overflowing with pride. 'You were unbelievable. The Messiaen was a complete knockout. The hall's going nuts and your dad's here, so come out quick as you can, OK?'

'I'll just be half a mo,' Alicia says, relief swamping her. He kisses her nose and hurries out.

She's about to change her clothes when the door opens again and there, to her delight, is Phyllida.

'Ali, you were incredible,' she says. She's filled out a little since Alicia saw her in hospital. Her image is coming back into focus.

'How are you? Are you feeling better?' Alicia hugs her.

'After hearing that, I'm on top of the world. You make it all worth it, Ali. All I want now is to get back to my desk and start fighting for you like there's no tomorrow.'

'I'm so glad you're here. Don't run away, I want you to meet my boyfriend.'

Phyllida lingers, but more and more people are soon crowding into the little backstage area; it's hard for Alicia to get away, and when things begin to calm down and she has done the requisite kissing, handshaking and small-talk, Phyllida tells her that she has to go home – 'Ali, come and see me in London, as soon as possible, OK?' Alicia doesn't want to let her go, but it's a long journey from Leeds to Tulse Hill, so she gives her another kiss and promises to phone to arrange a meeting, mother or no mother. After Phyllida has slipped away and the crowds have left her in peace, Alicia changes quickly into her T-shirt and jeans, then paces out into the hall.

Guy, listening to Ali, wishes that Emily could be beside him; she'd found a seat near the door in case Ingrid began to make a noise. He longs not to have to hide on such a day. Adrian is wired up and plastered over in the Macclesfield hospital; Guy stared aghast at the swathes of bandages round his head, the cage in which his right leg was strapped over the bed, while the doctor explained that he was out of critical danger but severely injured. Guy loathed the idea of leaving; but Kate – at her steeliest – had insisted on staying there herself and sent him away. 'I've failed him,' she declared. 'I'm staying. I won't fail him now.'

'Kate, you haven't failed anybody,' said Guy.

'Don't be ridiculous,' said Kate.

She left him no choice. If he, too, felt he'd failed Adrian, that was apparently not the point. It was the thought of the last time one of their children had been in hospital, fighting for life, that sent him into retreat, back towards the hospital's Victorian staircase, the cool afternoon and the drive over the Pennines to Leeds. He wonders how to break the news to Alicia.

Kate wants to hold Adrian's hand, but she can't: one of his arms is encased in plaster up to the elbow, while the other has been fitted with a clip to monitor something that she doesn't understand. Nor can she stroke his hair: his head, too, is heavily bandaged. She knows what may come next: manslaughter charges, court, possibly prison because he had no licence and no insurance. There's nothing she can do except sit beside him and say his name softly when he begins, at last, to come round.

'Mum,' Adrian manages to say. 'Ali?'

'She doesn't need me,' Kate whispers. 'You do.'

'Crap. Don't.'

'Hush, Adie. Don't try to talk. I'm sorry. I'm so sorry. It's my fault.'

'Not your fault. Mine. Stupid bloody me.'

'It *is* my fault.' Kate can't keep back the tears. 'I was so busy with Ali that I couldn't see how much you needed me.' His eyes close. He may be asleep, or losing consciousness again, but she tells him anyway. 'If I'd been watching, if I'd been looking out for you, this would never have happened. I should never have let you ride a motorbike without a licence. I should never have let you ride one at all. I gave up on you . . .'

'Bollocks.' Adrian is listening. 'Anji,' he says and tries to sob. His shattered bones will barely let him.

Kate can't take him in her arms and rock him like the baby he once was. Instead she rocks herself on her chair, sharing the tears that are all she and her son can share now.

In an aisle seat on the back row, Ingrid had sat on Emily's lap, thumb in mouth, watching the girl on the stage through her big silvery irises. All the way through the second half, even the noisy Messiaen, she'd been riveted, eyes on Alicia. She hadn't made a sound.

'It's incredible,' Emily says, when Guy wends an awkward way towards her across the standing ovation. 'She didn't budge! It's almost as if she could tell Ali is her sister.'

Guy, possessed with a rush of adoration for his two daughters, wonders what Ingrid will look like when she's Alicia's age. Despite her resemblance to Emily, she's not unlike Alicia at two and a half. At three, Alicia's perfect pitch had been discovered. Heavens, she'd been small. 'Do you want to come and meet Ali properly?' he ventures.

Emily crumples slightly. 'Oh, Guy,' she says. 'You know I'd love to. Let me think about it. But I'm desperate for the loo. Look after Ingy while I go?'

Guy takes his smaller daughter's hand, while the nervous Emily makes for the ladies' room; the queue extends into the foyer.

'It's Guy Bradley!' a voice exclaims beside him. He swings round and sees the dean of the university. 'You must be a proud man today,' the dean says, pumping his hand. 'And who's this young lady?' He smiles benevolently at the toddler beside Guy.

'She's the daughter of one of my journalists who's come to

hear Ali. I said I'd keep an eye on her for a minute.' Guy hates
himself, but all this is, of course, perfectly true. 'How's life in the
time of tuition fees?' he asks, to change the subject. He has interviewed the dean several times about the controversial changes
that the government has been making to higher education.

'Hi, Guy! Wasn't she stunning?' comes another voice: Guy
turns and sees Dan, his face full of love and excitement. Guy
introduces him to the dean and, while he does so, Ingrid's
hand slips unnoticed out of his own.

Ingrid is big and curious enough to be fascinated by the piano
and the sounds that come out of it. She's also big enough,
just, to wander away when her father is being distracted by
grown-ups and her mother is queuing for the loo. She's been
amusing herself recently by trotting off expressly against
Mummy's instructions, to see how often she could do it before
Mummy got cross. And she does want to know how the beautiful girl in the purple dress made those wonderful noises.

The hall stretches, vast, before her; her little legs take some
time to carry her along its length. The piano is high up, on a
great platform, glowering over her like a huge, spreading tree.
She looks around for Mummy or Daddy, then finds she can't
see either of them. She's on her own. Ingrid opens her mouth
and starts to wail.

Alicia, coming out into the hall, spots Dan and Dad at the far
end, talking to each other amid a bustling group of people.
She's about to go over, when a distressing noise catches her
attention. She looks down and sees a fair-haired little girl no
more than two and a half or three years old, wearing a purple
cotton jersey. The child is alone and big tears are rolling out
of her strange, silver eyes.

'Hello, sweetheart,' Alicia says, crouching. 'What's the matter?
Where's Mummy?'

'Mama went somewhere,' the little girl says doubtfully.

'She won't have gone far.' Alicia reaches out and takes her hand gently. 'She's probably waiting to go to the toilet. Mummies have to do that sometimes. Shall we go and look for her?'

'What's dat?' says the child.

'What?' Alicia follows her gaze. The little girl, whose tiny hand is warm and sweet in her own, is gazing up at the platform. At the piano. 'It's a very big piano,' she says. 'Did you hear the music?'

'I heared the music.'

'Did you like it?'

The child gives her a smile so wide and bright that Alicia is startled. It reminds her peculiarly of a photo on the piano room mantelpiece of herself at a similar age.

'That was me playing,' she says. 'My name is Alicia. What's your name?'

'Ingrid.' The word isn't clear enough for Alicia to catch it.

'Say it again? Very, *very* loudly?'

'Ingrid!' the child bellows, thrilled to have permission to shout.

'Ingrid? What a pretty name! You're such a poppet, aren't you? While we're waiting for Mummy, do you want to see the piano?'

Ingrid bounces up and down in a way that also seems oddly familiar to Alicia. 'Come on, then,' she says, leading the little girl up on to the platform. There's no sign yet of anybody looking for her. Who could have left such a small child alone at a piano competition? Who would bring such a small child to a piano competition in any case? Perhaps she's related to one of the contestants.

'You sit here—' Alicia sits down at the piano and lifts Ingrid on to her lap. 'Right in the middle. And you press the notes. Like this.'

Ingrid presses. A small note sounds. The Steinway's keys seem huge and heavy beneath her tiny fingers.

* * *

Guy is abruptly aware that Ingrid isn't with him. He'd been trying to avoid the dean, not to mention Dan, becoming conscious that the toddler was more to him than a temporary charge – but he's gone too far. Christ. Maybe Emily's come back and taken her? It's a vain hope, but as he's about to cling to it, he hears some odd, quiet noises coming from the piano. He turns.

Alicia is on the platform, at the piano. Ingrid is on her lap, little hands extended towards the keyboard. And Alicia is helping her to move her fingers and get a sound out of it.

Guy is transfixed. Ingrid looks like Emily and Alicia looks like Kate, yet Alicia and Ingrid look like one another. Ingrid looks like Alicia on the day they discovered her gift. And Alicia's radiance is perhaps not Kate's, after all, because Ingrid has it as well. He hears Emily's voice, calling, but glides on towards the stage, hypnotised by his two daughters.

Alicia, lost in the delight of showing her new little friend how the piano works, glances round and sees her father, white-faced, watching them. Behind him, the silver-eyed journalist is running up the aisle. Those eyes – that's where she's seen them before. She must be Ingrid's mother. Then she looks down at Ingrid. And she sees herself.

'Ali,' Dad calls.

When a train begins to move, it does so with the slightest shudder. A hint, a faint suggestion, then a gathering of pace as the energy feeds in and the speed begins to mount. And now Alicia's world shudders and starts to roll. The air flickers and spins. The hall pirouettes like a revolving door as her mind tries to go through it in one piece.

'No,' Alicia says.

'Dat my daddy,' Ingrid says, looking at Guy.

'Ingy, come here!' Emily calls, running forward.

Alicia gathers Ingrid into her arms and carries her down the stairs. She strides over to Guy, the little girl's warmth against her, soft and innocent. She stands face to face with him, and Ingrid laughs and reaches out her arms as she always does when she sees her father. Guy's gaze meets Alicia's as he takes the child from her. Ingrid settles happily against his shoulder. Alicia's legs buckle. She sits down on the nearest chair, speechless.

'Ali. Listen.'

'Listen to what?'

'I can explain everything,' says Guy.

Alicia glares from him to Emily, who is standing beside him, feet solidly planted. 'Dad, is Ingrid *yours*?'

'She is,' Emily cuts in, calm and firm. 'And mine. Alicia, your father and I are very much in love and have been for several years. We've never meant any harm, but we love each other and we have a daughter.'

'Dad?' Alicia manages to say.

'Yes, Ali. Ingy is your half-sister.'

Alicia glances behind them. Dan is hovering, anxious, wanting to reach her. 'No,' she breathes.

'Ali, darling, I meant to tell you. But—'

'But what, Dad?'

She has fallen out of the sky and is plummeting through cloud towards a mist-shrouded mountain. All the times he worked late. Sandalwood soap. Her mother's obsession with developing her career. Conferences in Denmark. Staying in Manchester because of not driving too much, because of heart trouble.

'So you've been lying to us for years.'

'I never meant to lie.'

'What about Mum?'

'Your mother knows everything.'

Just when you think it can't get worse, it does. They've both been lying. All the time. The recognition slashes across Alicia; the drop through the air brings her crashing into granite. The room lurches. She doesn't know why she's running or where to. She hears Dan calling her, and Dad, but she keeps going, past the concerned Leslie and Marina, past the astounded Fanny Waterman, out into the mindless dregs of the day. Night is falling and the sky, like Messiaen, is streaked with red, green and gold.

Her Renault is in the university car park. She locks herself inside and thumps her forehead with her hands, trying to wake herself up or at least beat out the consciousness that her life for the last few years or longer has been based on deception.

Her mother's transformation from lawyer and housewife into a loathed, over-ambitious music mother. Her father, shut out as Mum stood over her while she practised, instructing, helping, shouting, sometimes making her cry, every waking minute absorbed in what to do next for her gifted daughter. Especially since the one she'd loved best, the first one, had died. Another deception. What more have they kept from her? What further lies have they told her – just because she had to concentrate on practising the piano?

Her music hasn't brought her father to her. It's pushed him away, so much so that he's found another wife, another daughter, to be everything to him that she and Kate cannot be and maybe never were.

Why is she playing the piano in any case?

Alicia starts the engine. She heads west into the sunset, out of Leeds. Her mobile phone begins to ring; she lets it. What could she say to Dan now? Broad brushstrokes of Yorkshire, green and generous, spread round her in the twilight as she accelerates towards the open road. She's just given the best performance of her life – but what for? Why is she there? Why has she put her whole youth into the perfection of this peculiar art? What's the point, if this is the result? Right now, she can't think. A wall has collapsed inside her; it was never cemented.

Rain begins to fall on to the windscreen. She flicks a switch and the wipers swing in front of her. If only she could wipe away this discovery in the same way. If only they'd kept it secret. If only she'd never known.

No. That's wrong. Why can't people be honest? Her family is not the family she'd thought; and as she concentrates on the road through the hills towards Derbyshire, she can see, as clearly as if Dan's psychotherapist father had told her, that her parents' charade has been staged for her benefit, to create the illusion of a life in which her talent came first. As if she would ever put her music before her family! They'd never asked her how she felt. They wanted her to play the piano. None of them wanted her just to be herself.

What about Adrian? What does he know? More than her, presumably, because he'd left. Perhaps he's been hiding the truth too. No wonder he'd resented her. No wonder he cares not a jot for authority, since the authority in his life has always been too busy caring about her instead. And, as clearly as if Dan's father had told her, she understands that she has been living her bizarre life not to please herself, but to get her father's attention. Because it's the only thing that ever has.

She is eighteen years old, about – assuredly so – to be put through to the final of the Leeds International Piano Competition. If she wins, she'll have 'arrived'. The music-business machine will take her and grind her up: concerts, recordings, tours, aeroplanes. Stardom to the rest of the world; prison to her. Supposing they hadn't pushed her? Would she be there now, waiting as she soon will be under the TV lights to play the Rachmaninov Third Piano Concerto with one of the best orchestras in the country? Is that even her dream? Is it not, rather, theirs? A dream that she has to live for them, because they couldn't live it for themselves?

Alicia, watching the wet road, remembers her father holding her up to the window, remembers her little hands – just like Ingrid's – pressing on the glass that shielded her from the skidding raindrops. She'd imagined what it would be like to live inside one: a drop of water could be her whole world. Where

will she go now? What can she do? Will she, too, slide down
the window-pane and vanish into the gathering pools and the
moorland night?

Her phone rings and rings, its screen signalling DAN, but
she doesn't answer. She feels sorry for him, left far behind in
the blissful other world where she'd lived until Ingrid looked
up at her.

Alicia feels something splitting. She would rather not live at
all than live a lie. And what is her life but lies? Why live?

When she reaches the car park of the Cat and Fiddle –
where, mercifully, there's no sign of Adrian's bike among the
others – she has only one thought: she must attach the hosepipe
there to her car exhaust, put the tube through her window,
run the engine and go to sleep. It's the only way to dull the
pain.

The rain soaks into her clothes and her ankles feel damp
and icy under her jeans while she lugs the hosepipe towards
her car. The sheep look on – beastly things. Alicia realises she
hates sheep. She always has. She unravels the hose, holds one
end in both hands and approaches the exhaust pipe with it.

Of course, the two tubes are different widths. They don't
fit together. Alicia has heard that this is a way that people kill
themselves, so she'd assumed there must be some obvious
means of fitting one pipe into the other and keeping them
there while you let their smoke work its chemical magic through
your lungs. In the boot, she has water, chocolate, a torch and
a blanket spattered with dry grass from her open-air adventures with Dan. But she has no tape, nothing with which she
can make a connection and hold it firm.

She tries to force it. She pushes the hosepipe deep into the
exhaust – it finally seems to engage with something – and
carries the other end to her window, which she opens only by
a slit. Inside, she closes the door quietly, then her eyes. She
turns the ignition key.

There's a bang and a horrible noise from somewhere in the

car's bowels. Alicia's stomach lurches with fear. No fumes come in. She switches off and tries again, but it's obvious that all she's managed to do is damage her car. As if things weren't bad enough already, she now finds she's too ignorant to commit suicide.

Stumped, she opens the boot, takes out the chocolate, then gets back in and ponders while she eats. She's losing it. She's lost the plot. She's going out of her mind.

Her phone shrills beside her. She reaches for it. Her hand feels heavy and clumsy.

'Al?' comes Dan's voice. 'Where the hell are you?'

'Darling,' she mumbles. She doesn't know what to say, so she rings off.

She munches the last of her chocolate. There's nothing more she can do. She's out on the moor, alone with nothing but her wrecked car and her wrecked life and a few bloody sheep.

She fetches the blanket and wraps herself in it. It reminds her of Dan and it helps to warm her despite her damp clothes, in which she's starting to shiver. She puts her head down on the steering-wheel and breathes deeply. The chocolate hangs, sweet and sticky, on her teeth. She's never felt so tired in all her eighteen years. She'll rest now, just for a few minutes. Then she'll decide what to do next.

26

Headlight beams wake her up, slamming into her eyes, dazzling her. Hours have passed; the motorbikes have gone; and she recognises, through a blur of unbanished sleep, her father's car. Someone is banging on her window. She opens the door.

'Al!'

Alicia jumps out of the car and Dan grabs her. She breathes his scent – suedey, comforting – and lets him cover her face with kisses. Faintly she can see Dad's dark figure waiting in the drizzle, exhausted and defeated.

'Oh, sweetie. Are you OK?' Dan pleads.

'I guess.' Alicia looks at him, remembering mysteriously how to smile.

'We didn't know where you were. You weren't at home so we drove out to look for you and we nearly went straight past – then your dad thought he'd seen your car. Thank God you're here.'

Dad comes towards them, dragging his feet. Alicia lets go of Dan and Dad gathers her up instead. He's been crying.

'I'm sorry, Dad. I didn't mean to worry you.'

'*Worry?*' Dan echoes. 'All of Buxton and Leeds have been out looking for you.'

Dad, though, seems unable to speak. Alicia notices the distress in Dan's face. 'What's the matter? What's happened? Where's Mum?'

'Sweetheart,' Dad begins, but he's overcome and turns his face away. Dan takes her hand. 'There's no easy way to tell you this,' he says. 'Your mom is in Macclesfield, because your brother's been badly injured and he's in hospital there. His bike crashed on the A537 last night.'

'No!' Alicia gasps. 'He's not dead?'

'He's going to be OK. But, Al – Anjali was with him. Apparently her helmet was too loose. They tried to get her to hospital, but she didn't make it. She died in the ambulance.'

'Oh, Christ. Christ. Christ.' Alicia closes her eyes, taking it in. Then she rounds on her father. 'You knew this earlier?'

'Yes, love. We knew this morning. We didn't want to tell you before you had to play.'

Arctic ice is spreading through Alicia. 'That's why I ran away,' she begins. 'The lies. The pretence. All supposedly to protect me so I can play the bloody piano. *I can't bear it.* I wish I was dead!'

'Hush, Al,' Dan pleads. 'Let's get out of here.'

'No!' screams Alicia. She'd thought she had nothing left inside her to scream with. 'Anji's dead and you didn't tell me! Because of the competition!' She swings round, lashing out towards her father. Guy backs away and Alicia, aghast at herself, pulls up short and covers her face with her hands. Anji. Sweet, serious, pure-hearted Anji.

'Al. We've got to get you out of the rain.'

Dan steers her towards her father's car and fastens her seatbelt for her. 'We'll go in convoy. I'll drive yours,' he says.

'I don't think it'll work,' Alicia mumbles. 'Something's happened to the exhaust pipe.'

Dan gives her one of his shrewd glances, but only says, 'OK. We'll take you home and worry about the car later.'

Dad pulls out of the car park. Drier yet drowning, Alicia pictures Adrian and Anjali in the pub, happy together as they should have been. Anjali. She'll never see her again.

Through her eyelids marches an array of people she's been too close to, then lost. People who'd dominated her life, only to vanish. Mrs Butterworth. Lucien. Maybe even Rebecca. She may encounter any of them again one day, but not Anjali. She's dreaded death for her ageing grandmother and Cassie, but Anjali was nineteen and for her to die was the greatest injustice any cruel god could have devised. Everything moves. Everything changes. You can't prevent time passing and the world around you passing with it. The open air, the sunshine under the hill, where she and Dan had made love. That was their Garden of Eden. Why couldn't time have stopped there?

'You have to try to understand, Ali. I love Emily,' Dad says. 'I love you too, and Adrian. And, in a way, Mum. But things have been going wrong for a long, long time. You must have realised that.'

Alicia, in her dressing-gown, is sipping cocoa in the kitchen. There's nothing like routine for comfort. She's given a concert and so, even if it seems a century ago, she has cocoa. The only time she hasn't had cocoa after a performance was the concerto in Manchester – when she'd had something a lot better. Now it's midnight. She's warming up gradually, the chocolate working on her innards, but she's cried so much that she's almost nauseous.

'Ali, you're in love. You know what it's like,' Dad says.

'Yes.' She glances at Dan beside her.

'So can't we talk about this?'

'That's not the problem, Dad,' she points out, acid. 'I know you're in love. That makes it harder to understand how you've let this drag on. You've been leading a double life. Why?'

'Because of something your mother said when I told her.'

'Which was?'

'Darling, she said that if I left, it might ruin your career, your life. I couldn't do that.'

'And you *believed* her?'

Dan puts out a hand to steady her cup.

'How could I walk out on you? I couldn't do that.'

'It's all because of my piano. If I hadn't been "talented", if everyone hadn't gone around saying I was a "prodigy", none of this would have happened.'

'Ali, don't say that. It's not your fault.'

'I realised, up on the moor, that I'd only been playing as a kid to try to get your attention, Dad. That was all it was at the beginning. And then it took over. I had to be "*talented*".'

'Al,' Dan protests.

'It's true. Who's to say that if I gave up right now, I couldn't find a way to be much happier than I was this afternoon? And there was me thinking that that was the happiest moment of my life!'

'Al, please calm down,' Dan says. 'You're not giving up. No way.'

'Dan, stop it. You're as bad as them.'

The front door opens. Cassie glances up from her basket, which now lives in the kitchen because she can't manage the stairs. She doesn't bark. She's too old to get excited about every arrival at the front door, especially when her family can't pull themselves together enough to make a routine of it. If they can't be bothered, neither can she.

Kate blows in with the wind and runs to Alicia, who gets up to embrace her.

'How's Adrian?' she demands.

'He's going to be all right.' Kate had rung Guy earlier to tell him that Adrian had come round and that the broken bones were all mendable, given time. 'The first thing he asked was how you were getting on.'

'It's a long story, Mum. But I played OK.'

The fire in Mum's eyes has gone out. 'Thanks for looking after her,' she says to Dan. 'Would you like to stay tonight? I think she needs you.'

'"She" does,' Alicia adds.

'Thank you,' Dan says. 'That's kind. Yes, please.'

'Good,' Kate says. 'You're one of the family now.'

At the word 'family', Alicia shivers.

Alicia and Dan curl up in bed together with the curtains open and watch the clouds, above the sparse streetlamps, drifting by in what moonlight is left.

'Anji,' Alicia whispers.

'There's nothing we could have done.'

'But because of Adrian. On his bike.'

'Imagine how he must feel.'

'Sheep do that, you know. There aren't any fences on the moor, so they just go into the road. They're stupid, horrible creatures. They're the most dangerous things in the country-side. Oh, Dan. What do we do now?'

'We live. We make the most of our lives, for her sake, and for your sister who died, and for little Ingy.'

'She's so sweet. I always wanted a sister, but I never thought it could happen like this. It's funny, but part of me is actually thrilled about her.'

'Now this mess is out in the open, you can see Ingy when-ever you like. You'll be her idol, you know? Big sister Ali, at the piano.'

'Don't say that!'

'Al, you did the best performance of your life less than twelve hours ago. You didn't mean it when you said you'd give up?'

'I don't know. I just don't know. Because it's true: I wanted to please Dad, only I didn't realise it. It was Mum who pushed me, not him. But somehow, when I was little, the only thing I could do to get through to Dad was to play the piano. It made him notice me. Otherwise he was always too busy. That was how it began. And then everybody got inter-ested . . .'

'Come on, love. Try and sleep.'

★   ★   ★

Morning brings clarity of a kind, with the rain and wind leaving behind a silvered glint and a suggestion of faraway ice on the breeze. It brings clarity, too, from Leeds – a phone call from the administrator, concerned about Alicia's brother (the news has spread fast) but also telling her that she has been selected to play in the final, the last concerto on the last night, assuming that she wants to go ahead, under the circumstances. Dan fields an anxious call from Eugene Feinstein on his mobile, while Alicia switches hers off and tells Mum that if anyone calls she's practising.

Passing the bedroom door, she sees Dad standing by his cupboard, surveying suits and shirts. 'Are you moving out?' she asks.

He turns and gives her a straight answer. 'Yes, Ali. I'm going to live with Emily and Ingy.'

'Good,' Alicia says. 'I'm glad. Can I come sometimes and see my little sister?'

'It's your home too, darling. Come as often as you want. I'd like you and Emily to be friends.'

'Don't forget to pack your pills.'

Alicia, walking on down the stairs, breathes deeply. It may not be ideal. Her family may not be the perfect nuclear model that means so much to her mother, but honesty is a relief.

In the kitchen, Mum is on the phone, talking in a peculiarly intimate tone; listening the way she never listens; confiding the way she never confides. Alicia hovers. 'Dad's packing,' she says, when Mum hangs up and turns towards her, an odd, soulful expression on her face.

'I know, love.' Mum doesn't say who she'd been talking to.

Alicia sits opposite her, in the place she has sat thousands of times over the years. Mother and daughter gaze into each other's eyes.

'What I can't understand,' Alicia says, 'is why you thought I had to be kept from the truth. Or the truth from me.'

'Sweetheart, we're only human,' Mum says. 'Everyone makes mistakes. I did what seemed like the best thing at the time.'

Alicia has always seen her mother as all-powerful, controlling Mum. Not an ordinary woman, as confused and fallible as she is. She wonders who was on the phone.

She fastens the leash to Cassie's collar and takes her for a breath of fresh air; it hardly amounts to a walk. Gone are the days when they used to run together, pretending to fly. Cassie doesn't bark with joy any more – she's in too much pain, poor thing – and now Alicia runs for exercise, preferably with Dan, and likes the rain less than she used to. She walks past the spot where Matthew Littlemore stopped his bicycle and invited her to a party. Matthew's gone away to London, where he's found a job in a big department store. That's the trouble with small towns. People leave them.

When she comes back, Cassie limping at her side, Dad's car has gone. He, too, has left Buxton. Alicia goes into the front room, where Dan is playing the piano in her absence. She sits on his lap on the piano stool. Dan plays a tune and she picks it up an octave higher. They twiddle, improvising together without speaking.

'You couldn't have stopped it,' he tells her eventually.

'I'd never have wanted to. I wish he'd done this years ago. Poor Mum, living with him that whole time, knowing what was going on! And they did nothing about it because of *me*.'

'Don't be angry, love. Try to make the best of it.'

'I want to give up.'

'No, you don't. You're going on stage the day after tomorrow to win the bloody Leeds.'

'I'm going to phone them and say they've got to choose someone else.'

'They'll have a fit. They can't lose their only British finalist.'

'That's not my problem.'

'Al, wait. Think it through properly.'

'Why?'

'Come on. Let's go for a drive.'

The prominent, ship-like mound of Mam Tor presides over the hills and valleys, as it had when Alicia stood there with her father, pondering her future beyond another competition; as it had centuries before, in an age where there were no cars, no tourists, no National Trust to build flights of stairs and designate areas of Outstanding Natural Beauty. Until the Romantic movement, nobody would have paused to consider the Peak District beautiful, Dan says. Before then it would have been seen as wild and dangerous – chilly, muddy and threatening. Probably full of highwaymen, waiting to rob or murder you. And afterwards came the industrial revolution, the tentacles of its pollution curling round every hill and moor.

'But anyone can see this is beautiful,' Alicia says, lifting her face, the wind in her hair. 'If I have a home, this is it.'

Slivers of cloud like chiffon scarves wind through the valleys below them; the countryside is bronzing as the summer dies. Alicia thinks of Anjali. A tear slides down her nose. She glances round at Dan; his cheek, too, is, glistening with moisture.

'Can you throw it all away, Al?' he asks. 'When you think of the talent Anji had – and it's all gone. You've got the gift to bring beauty and meaning and wonder into people's lives. Can you ignore that?'

'What worries me more,' Alicia says, 'is that I can't do anything else. I've got hardly any qualifications. All I've ever done is play the piano. My future got decided for me when I was about five and now it's too late.'

'Nonsense,' says Dan. 'You're only eighteen. It's up to you. Nothing's too late – not now, and not ever.'

Alicia turns away and blows her nose.

'What are you thinking?'

'Just remembering. Anji. Adrian.'

'What else? Try free association. What's the next thing that comes into your mind?'

'Moorside. The night the moon turned red and we walked through the grounds. And Lucien said to me, "Your capacity to love is your own." He was saying that the way I love is up to me. Not anyone else. If you've got the capacity to feel love, he was saying, you can take it where you want to, where you need to.'

'And that's true of music?'

'I could take all the passion I put into music, and put it into working for a supermarket instead, if I wanted to.'

'*If* you *wanted* to. Exactly.'

'How do you mean?'

'The way you phrase it makes me think you don't want to.'

'I see.'

'What do you want, Al?' Dan asks.

She remembers standing on that spot years before while her father asked her the same question. At least the answer is clearer now. 'I want the freedom to make up my own mind and choose my own future, as a woman in my own right. And I want you. I want us to be together and take life as it comes. Don't take this wrong – I don't want to be pushy, I just want to be open.'

'I'd marry you today if I didn't know that we're way too young and that you've got other things to do first.'

'I do have things to do,' she says, nodding, 'but maybe not what you think.'

'Tell me?'

'I need to take some time out. I want to study and pace things a little more slowly. I'd like to come to Bloomington, if they'll have me, and study with Professor Feinstein. And if I have to cancel concerts, I'll cancel them. I know so little. I want to learn so much. I need to be certain I'm playing not for Mum or Dad, or even for you, but for myself. And I can't do that overnight.'

★   ★   ★

Adrian is flat on his back, his head bandaged, his leg in plaster held away from the hospital bed in something that looks like a cross between a cage and a cradle. Alicia almost cries out in horror, but a second later she's trying to embrace him through the mess. He smells of chemicals and his eyes are full of anguish, but not, she suspects, from his physical pain.

'Anji,' he says.

'Oh, Adie. I can't bear it either.'

'How can you forgive me?'

'It wasn't your fault.'

'No insurance. Nothing. I'll never forgive myself.'

'It was an accident. It could happen to anyone.'

'Can't stand it. Keep thinking I'll wake up and she'll be there . . .' Tears squeeze out of his eyes. His chest shakes. 'Ouch,' he says. 'Ribs. Broken.'

'You must rest and get better. We'll have you out and home soon.'

'I mightn't be home. I'll get sent down for this, Ali. I don't care. Can't live with myself now.'

Alicia strokes the part of his arm that doesn't hurt. She wonders how their parents can live with themselves, for they have a role in this too. 'You're going to be fine,' she insists.

'Prison. Manslaughter. God knows how long. I'm ready.'

'It *wasn't* your fault.'

'I loved her, Ali. I really loved her. She was the greatest girl, the sweetest, the most wonderful. Should have died with her.'

'Hush, Adie.' Alicia puts her head down on the pillow beside him and closes her eyes. They keep still there together, thinking of Anjali. Alicia imagines how she would feel if she had been driving the bike and Dan was killed, and the pain becomes so intense that she wonders how Adrian can breathe. 'You have to get through this,' she whispers to him. 'You have to. She'd have wanted you to.'

'I'll do my time, whatever it takes. She deserves that.'

'And you'll never ride a bike again.'

'You know what the best thing to do is when you come off a bike, Al? Get back on and keep on riding. Or else you never will.'

Alicia says nothing. She takes in his words. They're meant for her.

'Why? How?' she asks eventually.

'I've got a telly here and I want to see you on it tomorrow night, winning that prize. You've got just one chance and it won't come back. If you don't do it, you'll regret it for the rest of your life.'

'You mean, get back on straight away. And keep riding.'

'That's what I mean, lass. The world's your oyster. Go get it.'

It's a clear, sparkling day in the new year when a small group of people and an elderly, arthritic dog cross the teeming threshold of Manchester Airport. Alicia's hair has been trimmed to shoulder length. Behind her, her attendants dart about, helping. Her father loads three bulging suitcases on to a trolley. Her mother, wearing jeans and a leather jacket, runs through the list of things that Alicia must have remembered.

'Laptop.'

'Yes.'

'Rechargers.'

'Yes.'

'Brain,' Adrian teases, leaning on his crutch.

'Ali going 'Merica,' Ingrid pipes, holding Alicia's hand. Adrian smiles at Ingrid and does a Donald Duck impression. He's become very good at Donald Duck and Ingrid squeals with laughter.

Alicia checks in, loads her suitcases on to the belt with Dad's help and asks for a window seat. Her student visa is in place and the university has made a special dispensation to allow her to begin her studies in the year's second semester. Since she won Leeds, any door she touches seems to open. Maybe choosing should have been more difficult. But now, because she knows exactly what she wants, it's easy. As for her concerts, Phyllida has promised to carry out her instructions regarding her 'sabbatical'. Everybody will remember her when – if – she comes back, for no one will forget in a hurry the speech she'd made when she accepted her prize, dedicating it to the memory of her friend.

At the departure gate, everyone comes to a stop. Travellers throng round them, making for Africa, Australia, China, Brazil. Everywhere there are farewells, embraces, tears.

Alicia kisses them each in turn: Dad, Adrian, Ingrid, whom she hugs for ages. 'I wish I could take you with me,' she tells her. 'Will you draw me pictures sometimes?'

'Draw piccies,' Ingrid says. She's too small to understand what's happening, though big enough for Emily to have let her go out for a day with her father and his other family.

'Mum.' Alicia holds out her arms.

Kate steps forward and embraces her daughter. Announcements blare over the Tannoy: 'Last call for the last remaining passengers for Chicago.' Alicia and Kate, golden head to golden head, don't move.

'Call me when you get there,' Kate says. 'I'll be in London.'

'I will. 'Bye, Mum.'

Alicia bends and kisses the top of Cassie's head. She knows she's saying goodbye for ever to her dog. Then she picks up her bag and takes out her passport and boarding card. At the great glass gate, she turns one last time, hair gleaming, face radiant. With a wave, she's gone.

JESSICA DUCHEN

RITES OF SPRING

'Everyone wanted Alicia to play the piano. None of them wanted her just to be herself.'

Forbidden by her parents to become a musician, Kate Bradley is stunned when her small daughter reveals an exceptional talent for the piano. Kate is determined to give Alicia the chance to succeed and it's not long before the fame of the Peak District prodigy begins to spread.

Alicia, though, craves her father's approval: Guy, with a demanding job, is rarely at home, alienated by Kate's obsession with her daughter's burgeoning career. Alicia's tearaway brother is sidelined, and warns his sister that Kate does not mother her but smother her.

As the heap of white lies designed to keep Alicia concentrating on her piano in peace escalates into a mountain of deceit, conflict threatens to overwhelm the entire family – with potentially devastating consequences.

OUT NOW